PRAISE FOR CRYS

TRAITOR'S KNOT

"This exceptional historical novel is a gripping tale of love and jealousy rife with unexpected twists and poignant moments that whisks readers on an unforgettable journey into the past."

— HISTORICAL NOVEL SOCIETY REVIEWS

"A gripping tale of courage, love, and enduring commitment, a story that is well-imagined and executed with grace and mastery."

— READERS' FAVOURITE

"Cryssa Bazos has crafted a complex, entertaining and multi-faceted story in which secrets and intrigue abound and in which the stakes are continually raised."

— ROMANTIC HISTORICAL REVIEW

SEVERED KNOT

"Bleakly impossible choices face the protagonists in the brutal aftermath of civil war. Stark but involving tale of early colonial exploitation strongly centres on an indomitable Scottish hero."

— HISTORICAL NOVEL SOCIETY REVIEWS

"Severed Knot is one of those novels that will be read repeatedly and it will still feel like the first time — a truly unforgettable gem of a historic novel. Ms. Bazos is an author to keep an eye on and one to add to the reading list.

— IND'TALE STARRED REVIEW

"Ms Bazos writes of this heartbreaking period in history with empathy and passion and the result is a novel of depth, breadth and hauntingly beautiful moments."

— ELIZABETH ST. JOHN, AUTHOR OF *BY LOVE DIVIDED*

"Cryssa Bazos's sets the bar in realistic historical fiction. Her ability to precisely set the character conflict with romance, for a powerful and unforgettable, riveting novel."

— GWENDALYN'S BOOKS

"I really enjoyed this tense and romantic thriller and highly recommend it if you want a page-turning read that will leave you enthralled and breathless."

— DEBORAH SWIFT, AUTHOR OF THE GILDED LILY

Rebel's Knot

CRYSSA BAZOS

Published by W.M. Jackson Publishing 2021

ISBN: 978-1-9991067-4-4

Editing and cover design by Jenny Quinlan of Historical Editorial.

In loving memory of Demetra Bazos

REBEL'S KNOT

A NOTE ON IRISH PRONUNCIATION

I WOULD HAVE LIKED to have kept the Irish spelling for the names that appear in this story, but not everyone will be familiar with their pronunciation. For this reason, I've tried to select names, wherever possible, that did not need a pronunciation guide; however, there were some exceptions. I've kept the Irish spelling for traditional mythological figures, and there are a few characters who've insisted on having an Irish spelling.

- Áine is pronounced as "Anya."
- Cúchulainn is pronounced as "Koo-koo-layn." Cúailnge, the battle raid he's associated with, is pronounced "Koolie."
- Diarmuid is pronounced "Deer-mud."
- Fionn or Fionn mac Cumhaill is pronounced as "Finn McCool."
- Ruadhri is pronounced as "Rood-ree."

CHAPTER 1

An Gallbhaile, County Limerick
  January 1652

Áine Callaghan encountered a single magpie on her way to the byre in the early morning. The creature, a large devil, claimed the centre of the pathway, bold as he pleased. He puffed out his white breast, then spread black wings shot with violet, as though to warn her away.

An ill omen.

She looked around to see if she had missed a second magpie, for a second promised joy. Only one. *Sorrow will come this day.*

A sudden chill pierced deep in her bones, and she drew her mantle close about herself. Cold gusts of wind swept across the path, snatching at her loose tendrils of hair. The magpie gave no intention of flying away. Instead, he lowered himself close to the ground, settling on a wet mat of rotting leaves.

Áine glanced around at the strengthening dawn. She did not have the luxury of dawdling. Her mistress expected the cows to be milked, and they would be lowing soon, full of their own distress. She considered skirting around the path to give the harbinger a wide berth but steeled herself instead. She had tasted enough sorrow in her life and never with a warning delivered by a magpie.

"Away with you now," Áine called out to the bird as she continued forward, trying to keep her pace steady and without flinching. She knew well enough that all creatures could detect fear and feast on it.

The magpie gave a shrill cry and lifted into the air before veering towards the manor house.

As Áine approached the byre, she heard a tune coming from inside, a sweet song yet decidedly melancholy. The master's niece, Mairead O'Coneill, was once again playing her fiddle. Most mornings at dawn, before people stirred, the young miss practised her music in the privacy of the byre. She hadn't come down this past week, and Áine found she'd missed it more than she expected.

Instead of rushing into the byre, Áine seated herself on a log behind a drying stack of peat to listen to the song. She never interrupted Mistress O'Coneill for fear that she'd find another place to play, and then this gift of each new morning would be lost to her.

In time with the melody, stories unfolded in Áine's head. Stories of heroes and quests and impossible sacrifices. The notes allowed her to feel the tremors of heartbreak and longing.

Finally, the song ended, but Áine still remained seated on her log until the postern door opened and shut. She waited until the soft crunching of footsteps headed back to the manor.

Now her day could start.

She hurried to the front doors of the byre and lifted the bar. Hinges creaked as the doors swung open and the dawn flooded in. Warmth and the earthy scent of straw and manure enveloped her.

"Rise and shine, my dears," she greeted the small herd before grabbing a tin bucket and her milking stool. "Mab, always the first to be awake, there's a sharp girl. And how's our Clover this day? Did you enjoy the young mistress's fiddle playing? What story do you want to hear this frosty morn?" Before Áine led the first cow out of its stall, she caressed its wide forehead. "The obvious choice is the tale of Cúchulainn and the Great Cattle Raid of Cúailnge; I haven't recited that for some time." She settled herself on her milking stool and canted her head in thought, remembering the story that the fiddle had conjured for her. "Perhaps not. You'll simply have to be satisfied with the great outlaw warrior, Fionn mac Cumhaill, and his hounds."

While she worked, she spun the story to the rapt interest of the herd, and since she wished she *had* seen a pair of magpies, she told the part about how Fionn found his enchanted bride. She even gifted the maid with the same bright red hair as her own. A vain thought, but the cows wouldn't give her away.

Lately, she found herself focusing on Fionn mac Cumhaill and his outlaw warriors, the Fianna, for they reminded her of their own Irish soldiers, the Tóraidhe, who had been fighting against the English invaders to keep them from conquering Munster and the rest of Ireland. These old stories had always been a comfort to her since learning them on her nan's knee. Even with times being so unsettled, she reminded herself that they had been so before, and men who did not lack courage still prevailed.

Áine settled into the rhythm of milking. The disquiet that had burrowed into her with the magpie's visit began to fade. A bird was a bird, and a single one was not an unusual sight. Such a common occurrence could not possibly mean sorrow to everyone who ran across a single magpie. Most of the country would be afflicted.

But are we not . . . ?

The thought trailed. After a decade of strife between the Irish Catholic and the Protestant settlers, the English had landed in force on their shores a couple of years ago, determined to sever any Royalist support that King Charles the Second might have relied on. In the first year, the English overran the port towns, but over time English troops spread across Munster like the plague. At first, they were a distant threat, nothing of concern for a dairymaid so far away from a major town and cradled in the lee of the Galtee Mountains. But recently the carrion birds flocked closer.

An icy shiver traced down her spine.

The cow nudged her with its flank, breaking her maudlin

thoughts. Áine laughed out loud. "Another story, Clover? As you wish—"

At the sound of footsteps, Áine silenced immediately. She looked over her shoulder and found the two housemaids, Roisin and Orla, carrying an empty jug between them.

"She's talking to herself again," Roisin said to the other maid, not bothering to lower her voice. "Touched by the Faerie Folk, I tell you."

Áine averted her face so they wouldn't see the flush of her cheeks.

"Good morning, Áine," Orla called out a bit too brightly. "We're here for the milk."

"Cook must be anxious if she couldn't wait until I brought it down," Áine said, focusing once more on her work.

"Didn't trust you not to spill it. She needs every drop this morn," Roisin said, scuffling the straw with the toe of her shoe. "*I* assured her that you knew your business, but she wouldn't listen." Roisin speaking a word in Áine's defence was as likely as the magpie transforming itself into a mourning dove.

"I'm always careful," Áine said sharply. Roisin blew hot and cold, one day overly affectionate, the next caustic. Today showed signs of being a poor day, she thought wearily.

When Áine had first arrived at the Mulrianes' estate, Roisin had fussed over her, shamelessly attempting to pry into Áine's former life in Cork. But Áine was as wary of warm words freely given as she was alert to the signs of brewing anger. Her cautious nature had stood her well, for it had soon become apparent that Roisin's tongue was a sharp blade wielded against the unsuspecting and naive.

"Since you're eager, could you hand me that spare bucket on the hook?" Áine asked Orla. She passed the half-full bucket for a fresh one.

As Orla strained the milk into the jug, Roisin draped herself over a stall gate and propped her chin on her clasped hands. "Diarmuid has set off on his adventure," she said archly. It annoyed Áine when Roisin called the master's son by his Christian name. "I've never seen such pinched and dour faces from the manor folk since he left. No one believes the long tale of him going off to visit a relation with only a single friend as a travelling companion. Where do you suppose he truly went?"

Áine glanced up, relieved to find that Roisin directed her question to Orla.

"Before he left, there had been much traipsing back and forth between the manor and the byre," Orla said. "Perhaps Áine knows more since she practically lives out here?"

Áine focused on her work. "I'm sure I don't."

Knowing when to hold your silence showed signs of wisdom, her nan had always said. Áine watched and listened, aware of the comings and goings of the manor folk, and she knew very well that the Mulrianes' only son, Diarmuid, had set off with a friend to join the Tóraidhe. But she'd cut off her tongue before telling Roisin so. The girl could hardly be trusted with dangerous information.

Áine had served the family for the last four years, and she was grateful for every day, no matter how dull. Rise with the sun, milk the cows, clean out the stalls, see to their needs. Her life would have been very different had she remained in Cork. The Mulrianes had had no obligation to take her under their protection. She had arrived with nothing more than a prayer that Mistress Mulriane would remember Áine's nan kindly. There had been no time to engage a scribe to petition the Mulrianes for a place in their household, nor could Áine have risked the wrong ears hearing of her plans until she was well and gone.

Mistress Mulriane's kindness was like spring's sun warming the ground. Roisin's thirst for gossip would not find a functioning well with Áine. To gain attention for herself, she'd be sure to spread the news on the next market day, giving no thought as to who might wish the Mulrianes ill. Admitting any knowledge of the Tóraidhe, or worse, admitting to a connection, had been known to draw the English like wasps to honey. Reprisals against Tóraidhe sympathisers and collaborators had been vicious and swift.

Áine would never betray the mistress and the safety of her family, especially not to curry favour with a shrew.

"Mistress will, no doubt, be missing her only son fiercely. Have some respect for her sorrow," Áine said.

Roisin lifted her nose in the air. "Áine knows precious little, at least about anything useful. If we want to know about the toing and froing of the Faerie Folk, we'll be sure to ask Áine Callaghan, Mistress Fae herself."

Áine sighed. This again—Roisin's favourite taunt. "Then why do you bother to ask me anything?"

"Isn't our Áine bold today?" Roisin said with a cold smile.

"Leave it be, Roisin," Orla huffed. "She only minds the cows—she's nothing. Now come help me with this jug."

Áine lowered her head and pretended to adjust the tin bucket at her feet. Orla's words stung more than they should have. It could be worse. It could always be worse. She didn't need to be liked. Safety was far more preferable. She laid a hand on the nervous cow until they both settled.

A sound caught Áine's attention, and she looked up to find Mairead O'Coneill returned, standing at the open doorway with her attention focused on Roisin and Orla. Her disapproving frown made Áine wonder how much of their chatter she had overheard.

"Miss, did you need something?" Áine asked, rising to her feet. Orla whirled around and nudged Roisin with her elbow.

The young miss's expression softened when she turned to Áine. "Nothing from yourself, Áine, thank you. I've come to fetch these two." Facing Roisin, she said, "Cook is wondering what is taking you so long."

Roisin's sly gaze slid to Áine, and she opened her mouth to speak. Áine braced herself to be blamed for their tardiness, but Orla clearly thought better of it and headed Roisin off. "We're coming, miss."

The two maids hurriedly departed the byre with the milk jug, leaving Áine alone with the master's niece. She rarely had cause to speak with her, so she was at a loss as to what was expected.

The young miss smiled. "Instead of hovering outside in the morning, you're welcome to come inside and listen to me play. If you like."

Áine looked up, startled. Mairead gave her an encouraging smile, and Áine answered it shyly. "I'd enjoy that. If you wouldn't mind."

"Not at all," she said with a pleased smile. "It's settled, then. I'll see you at dawn."

ÁINE WENT THROUGH HER MORNING WORK SIX FEET ABOVE THE ground. The master's niece would welcome her in the byre while she played! Mairead O'Coneill trusted Áine Callaghan with her music. She knew how precious this was—Áine wasn't sure she could ever trust anyone with her stories.

But then Roisin scooted into the byre with no other intent than to pester Áine, and the rest of her day deteriorated. Although Áine knew the housemaid was lashing out at her for being caught gossiping and dawdling, it didn't soften the blows. Áine tried to ignore her, but Roisin would not be put off.

"Mistress Fae . . . simpleminded chit . . ." Roisin danced around her as though *she* were touched by madness.

Áine closed her ears and retreated into herself, anything to block out the taunts. Had it not been for the housekeeper rushing out to find where Roisin had gotten to, Áine would have been pushed past her breaking point. Though the housekeeper hauled Roisin back to the manor by the ear, the damage to Áine's day was complete. Her nerves were as brittle as dry twigs, and even the herd remained unsettled.

She desperately needed solitude.

Managing to winnow an hour for herself, she wrapped her mantle firmly around her and headed into the forest. She kept to the main path until it splintered off into a narrow tract that plunged into a gorge with a rushing stream.

She followed the water upstream, careful to mind her footing. The musty scent of decaying leaves mingled with the bracing wind. She breathed deeply, filling her lungs and clearing her mind.

A silvery mist drifted over the shallows. The sound of the stream tumbling over mossy rocks grew louder as she continued, its source a small waterfall at the top of a ridge. Beyond the ridge was the main road and a wooden bridge that spanned the tumbling stream.

Áine picked her way from rock to rock to reach the other side.

She stepped on a loose stone and teetered, sticking her arms out to steady herself. Then she darted to the next flat rock and leapt to the bank. She made her way to a fallen tree trunk and perched on it, staring at the glade she often sought alone.

Here in this enchanted dale, she might forget the world for a space, forget the state of anxiety that gripped everyone. Welcome the solitude on her own terms.

But not today.

Either from Roisin's taunts, the early morning magpie or something else entirely, Áine felt on edge, like the air after a lightning storm. Closing her eyes, she concentrated on the waterfall, but her mind refused to be quieted. With a sigh, she picked at the bark beneath her and watched as the pieces dropped to the ground at her feet.

The glade was worthy of the Faerie Folk and the old stories. Any moment, Fionn mac Cumhaill and his hounds would burst from the trail with his men in his wake. Running ahead in the shallows were the dread host of the Otherworld on their horses, faerie trumpets blaring a warning—*the Wild Hunt is on and no mortal soul is safe.* Only a true hero could defeat them. Áine imagined their steeds galloping in the stream, spraying droplets into the air like glittering stars.

For a moment, Áine was lost to her imagination, and it became so real that she heard the drumming of hooves, like thunder rolling across the hills.

But the sound persisted. This was not her imagination. Horsemen —many, by the sound of it—were coming closer.

Áine scrambled down from the log and backed into the trees, covering her distinctive red hair with her mantle. She peered through the evergreen fronds to watch the wooden bridge, waiting to see if the riders who passed were friend or foe.

Then she saw the foremost horsemen in their red coats and steel-grey helmets.

English.

The rest of the troop swept across the bridge, the sound of a hundred drums under the horses' hooves. And they were heading for the Mulriane estate.

She had to warn her master.

Áine backed away, half sliding down the hill, rock and shale shifting under her feet. When she reached the waterfall, she straightened and dashed down the gorge as fast as she dared.

The main road followed a wide sweep along the bogs to reach the Mulriane estate. If she spared no speed and cut through the forest, she might make it back in time to warn everyone.

Áine slid along the slippery rocks and riverbank, falling and scraping her knees and hands. She reached the pathway out of the gorge, and as she climbed the steep hillside, her chest burned and a stitch bit into her side.

Finally, she reached even ground and flew along the forest path, leaping over fallen logs and avoiding the upthrust of roots. Through the thinning trees, she saw the roofline of the byre and, beyond that, the manor.

"English!" she yelled, hoping someone might be close enough to hear her. "English soldiers!"

She reached the byre, then pulled up short. *Too late.* Enemy troopers barrelled into the courtyard. Áine dove behind the stacked peat. Panting, she took big gulps of air and cautiously peered around the pile.

"Brian Mulriane. Show yourself," the English commander called out in such a loud voice that Áine had no trouble hearing him.

Her master strode into the courtyard carrying a sword, the male servants running behind him. Áine squinted to get a better look, but the horsemen closed in and cut off her view. She detected only snatches of their argument, but her master's rage came across clear.

The English commander barked an order, and several soldiers dismounted. The men fanned out, some heading for the manor and the others coming towards the byre.

Áine gasped—she had to hide.

She darted inside and, without considering options, hurried up the ladder to the loft. Below, the soldiers were swarming the main level. Careful not to make a sound, she hid in a small nook in the corner.

"Seize the cattle—leave nothing behind."

Gates slammed, and men shouted. Someone started clanging metal against metal. The herd grew distressed, crashing into their stalls and bawling fearfully. Áine cringed, helpless to stop the madness.

High-pitched shrieks came from the courtyard. The soldiers were dragging the women from the manor outside. Áine hugged herself to still her uncontrollable shaking.

Then Áine heard what she most dreaded—the sound of someone climbing the ladder. She shrank into a ball and looked around the loft. No weapons—nothing to defend herself.

Helpless.

The old fear seized her. Blood pounded in her ears, and a silent scream built in her throat.

Then below, a woman's shriek pierced the air, followed by the pounding of horses outside the byre. The creak of the ladder halted, then the footsteps descended in a rush.

The woman screamed and pleaded with the soldiers—something about her fiddle. Áine's breath hitched in her throat. It had to be Mairead O'Coneill. The shrieking continued but grew fainter, as though someone was carrying her away.

Why would she direct the soldiers to where she hid her treasure?

And the answer to that question came on the smell of burning wood and the roar of flames.

Fire!

Smoke soon filled the loft. Choking, Áine covered her nose and mouth with her mantle and scrambled towards the ladder. The air grew stifling and heavy—she couldn't breathe. Her eyes stung, and tears blurred her vision.

She gripped the top of the ladder and swung her leg over, groping to find the first rung. Fire ran across the beams, and Áine hurried down the ladder. One rung snapped, and she slid the rest of the way down. Thick plumes of smoke made it impossible to see. A blast of hot air, and there—*the door*. A dark shape suddenly appeared at the entrance—a cow—and it charged back into the byre.

Clover!

Áine screamed at her to get out, but the poor creature was in a panic, running this way and that, crashing into the stall gates. Áine reached the cow and pushed and prodded the animal to urge it towards the entrance, but the cow refused to budge. The flames were snaking closer to them. In desperation, Áine whispered reassuring words in Clover's ear. Her voice must have cut through the cow's panic, for Clover allowed herself to be manoeuvred back to the entrance. A shower of sparks landed on the cow's shoulder, sending her bolting from the byre.

A pair of overhead timbers crashed across the main entrance in a fiery blaze, blocking Áine's escape. Sparks flew from overhead. The smoke was choking the breath from her, and she swayed on her feet. Remembering the postern door, she retreated deeper into the burning byre and made her way around the flames to reach the side entrance.

Áine gained the door and tried to push it open—it wouldn't budge. Sobbing, she pushed her shoulder to the door and heaved. It moved a fraction. She pushed harder. Her lungs burned; her breath came in desperate gasps. She threw all her strength against the door and managed to open it a little more, enough to squeeze herself through.

She stumbled towards the forest. Her limbs grew weak, and her head spun. She had just passed the stack of drying peat before the blackness enveloped her.

ÁINE AWOKE TO THE SENSATION OF HER LUNGS BURNING. ACRID smoke filled her nose and the back of her throat. She strained to prop herself up while her head swam. Deep breaths felt like sharp glass, and she started coughing and retching until she fell back weakly.

A magpie chittered from somewhere. The sound cut through Áine's disorientation. Then it occurred to her—she heard nothing else. No horses, not the barking of English voices. No women screaming in fear.

Áine struggled upright and pushed the mantle off her head. She found herself behind the stack of drying peat and peered over it. The byre was a smouldering mess with the last of the fire glowing beneath ruined timbers. Áine weaved towards the charred wreckage. All the cows were gone—no sign of them. A confusion of criss-crossing tracks churned up the ground, leading back to the court-yard. The herd would be a valuable prize for the English marauders and leave the family without food for the rest of the winter.

Where was everyone?

Áine squinted into the distance. The manor was silent—everyone must surely be inside, in shock and in grief. She started for the court-yard and saw in the centre what looked to be a pile of clothes thrown in the mud. But as she hobbled closer, the truth assaulted her.

Master and Mistress Mulriane were lying in a pool of blood.

Áine's knees buckled, but she forced herself to remain on her feet. *Don't run away.* She continued walking until she reached them. The master's eyes were wide and staring, his face contorted in pain. His wife was curled up beside him, her eyes shut. Both dead. A wave of sorrow choked her. Áine prayed that they'd had a swift and merciful end.

She bent over the master, brushed her fingers across his forehead and quickly drew away. Steeling herself, she reached down and closed his eyes. She owed him that much at least.

Why had they been left here, unblessed and unburied, a feast for carrion? Where were their daughters . . . the other servants?

Áine scanned the courtyard. She headed towards the silent manor, then saw them—a pair of severed heads, each staked on a pole.

She recoiled and screamed. Her body started shaking at the grue-some sight. The urge to run was overwhelming. She didn't need to get closer to learn who they were, for even from this distance, she knew. Diarmuid Mulriane and his hapless friend. Both had left home a fortnight ago to join the Tóraidhe.

The English had made a warning of them.

CHAPTER 2

NIALL O'CONEILL RODE along the forest trail and kept an eye on his wolfhound, Fionn, who loped ahead of him—the hound's hearing was keener than his. With one hand resting on his sword's hilt and the other gripping the horse's reins, Niall scanned the tangled woodland for any sign of an ambush. Crowding trees and darkly shadowed hollows could hide an entire troop of English soldiers. The invaders would consider the capture of any Irish soldier a prize.

It had been three days since Niall left Ross Castle, carrying dispatches for his commander, Colonel O'Dwyer, from the leader of the Kerry forces, Viscount Muskerry. No good news to be had— Niall did not relish telling O'Dwyer that the promised ships from Lorraine still hadn't reached Irish shores. Twenty ships to carry desperately needed supplies of ammunition, weapons and grain—the lifeblood of the Irish brigades and needed to drive away the English invaders. Twenty ships still not come. Without relief, they couldn't go on. Niall dreaded to think of what that meant for them. *Saints preserve us all.*

From the time that Niall had crossed back into County Cork, the knot in his stomach had grown to the size of his fist. He had travelled this route countless times during the past two years, from their constantly shifting camp in the Glengarra Woods to Muskerry's stronghold at Ross Castle. The last time he passed this way was no more than a month ago. Then, the only animal tracks he'd found belonged to a pair of foxes and a small herd of deer. But now the road was freshly churned and deeply rutted, branches snapped and broken—clear signs that a troop of horse had passed this way. There were no Irish brigades in the area, and able mounts were scarce. Besides, they weren't foolish enough to ride openly and in strength. Their strategy had always been to strike and hide, disappear into the bogs or woods.

No, these tracks could only have been made by the English. Niall grew more uneasy. The closest English garrison was at Cahir—a day's hard ride and a mountain range away.

He gave a low whistle for Fionn and slowed his horse. The wolfhound returned to his side. Niall dismounted, then dropped to a crouch to examine the chewed-up ground. He passed his hand over the tracks and tested the hardened ridges. Beside him, Fionn sniffed at the tracks. A hard frost had set over a fortnight ago, following a month of solid rain. "Couple of weeks, that's what I think," Niall said to the wolfhound, who lifted his head and seemed to agree. He scratched behind Fionn's ears, then rose to his feet.

A troop of at least fifty, by the look of it. Niall raked his fingers through his dark hair. *By Jesus.* "What is the devil up to now?"

By rights, after the English captured plague-infested Limerick a few months ago after a long and brutal siege, then lost their commander-in-chief to the same illness, they should have been demoralised—should have hunkered down into winter quarters with very little to say until spring. And yet these invaders had become more brazen, ranging farther from their occupied territory with each passing week.

Niall rose and sniffed the crisp air—no hint of cook fires. He frowned, gauging the patterns frozen in the mud—the tracks headed in the same direction as he was travelling. "Keep a sharp ear, my lad. The bastards may yet be around."

He mounted his horse, and they set out again with a cautious yet brisk pace. His unease deepened as he considered the stretch of road he was on. Bogland spread on either side of the road, offering no escape route except by slipping into the bog. He didn't want to leave his horse behind. The animal was worth more than gold these days.

The road ahead curled in an arc and became hidden by trees. As Niall approached the bend, Fionn shot past him, then halted. He caught sight of the wolfhound in the middle of the road with his hackles rising. A low growl rumbled deep in his chest.

Niall drew his sword and continued to advance slowly. The horse pranced and worried at his bit. The wind shifted, carrying the rotted stench of something dead.

Dangling from a tree bough a short distance off the road, the remains of a man swayed at the end of a noose. Niall did not flinch or turn away. The limbs extended out as though grasping for empty air; carrion had pecked away much of the face.

The terrain leading up to the tree told its own story. A clear swath of hoofprints swept away from the main road and trampled the ground around and beneath the tree. Niall imagined the man bolting for the bog but being captured before he could reach safety. He saw signs of where they'd dragged him to the tree.

Numbness smothered Niall. He should be outraged, hurtling curses strong enough to follow the English invaders to their graves. Instead, a bone-crushing weariness washed over him. Yet another nameless soul.

Grimly, he urged his horse into the woods until he was alongside the corpse. The dead man appeared to be a peasant, judging by the plain cloth of his tunic and trews. If he had worn brogues, those had been stripped from his feet. In that moment when the rope had been thrown over the bough and the noose bit into the man's throat, had he felt a small measure of relief that it was finally over? No more running and hiding.

If it were him, would he have fought to the end? Six months ago, he would've torn the throat of anyone who suggested otherwise. Now? He wasn't so certain.

Niall exchanged his sword for a sharp dagger and sawed through the rope. Averting his face, he held his breath to avoid gagging on the overpowering stench of rotting flesh.

Carefully, he lowered him to the ground. "Stay, Fionn," he called out to the wolfhound when he edged closer to investigate. "Give the poor soul a bit of space."

After tethering his horse upwind, Niall dragged the corpse to the edge of the bog and covered him with evergreen boughs. This was the best he could do since the ground was hard. When the weather softened, the bog would provide its own burial.

Niall strode back to his horse. He adjusted the girth in short, sharp movements. He gripped the saddle's pommel to hoist himself up, but before he mounted his horse, his gaze lit on the cut rope still hanging from the tree. Niall touched his forehead against the arch of his horse's neck and closed his eyes. After a moment, Fionn nudged his hip, and Niall released his breath slowly.

"Time to leave, old man," he told the wolfhound gruffly. The urge to quit this place left a sharp taste in his mouth.

Niall now set a brisk trot and continued to follow the tracks, his unease growing with each mile. He hoped to see evidence of the English veering south towards Cork. Instead, the tracks continued resolutely east—towards the Tóraidhe camp at Glengarra.

Later that morning, he reached a crossroads, one branch continuing east while another route veered north towards An Gallbhaile. In that direction lay the home of his Mulriane kin and his sister, Mairead, who was sheltering with their uncle during the war.

Niall eased his horse to a halt. When was the last time he had seen his sister—his only sister? A sudden wave of homesickness swept through him. To once more see his family. To gather around a peat fire with the company of kin and a hot meal filling his belly.

The last two years had ground him down. Two years of fighting an English army, shipped across by their Parliament to crush Ireland's two unpardonable sins: Catholics and Royalist supporters of a king without a crown, the exiled Charles Stuart. Endless skirmishes, defined by strike-and-hide tactics, were a grinding and wearying game that wore the Irish brigades down as much as they did the enemy.

Where was the drive that had spurred Niall to leave his father's home in Galway, sword in hand and a burning in his belly? When was the last victory he'd celebrated? Weariness banked his fire, and that pained him more than his empty stomach rubbing against his spine.

Fionn returned to his side, as stately as a wise king of Éire.

"And what have we accomplished these past two years, old man?" Niall asked him. Fionn canted his head. "Right, then, you're not old. 'Tis only me who feels it."

A border of twisted blackthorn lined the northern track. The wind sent a spray of dead leaves skittering down the northern road, catching them in a whirlwind before scattering them once again. Fionn slunk after them, ignoring the route they always took.

"Fionn—not that way," Niall called out. "That isn't our road, and well you know it." Agitated, Fionn circled on the spot, a growly whine reaching Niall's ears.

And then Niall saw what had unsettled his wolfhound. The hairs lifted on the back of his nape.

The enemy tracks swung north.

NIALL SLOWED HIS MOUNT TO A HALT AT THE EDGE OF HIS UNCLE'S woods. Fionn crept forward, then tensed. The wind carried the acrid stench of ashes. A meadow stretched before him where nothing stirred, not even the flutter of a bird. Then he heard the distant cawing of crows. His horse shifted nervously under him. Fionn growled.

An alarm pealed in Niall's head.

He loosened his sword in its scabbard and checked the stag-horn dagger tucked into his belt. Motioning to Fionn, he started across the open field.

Every sense sharpened as he scoured the far woods for any sign of the enemy. His horse's hooves clomped against the winter-hardened ground and rang deafening in his ears. He urged the horse to move faster.

Niall reached the shelter of a copse where a solitary cow path led to the outbuildings. The greedy caw of crows grew louder as he approached. Ahead, through the tangled trees, the charred remains of his Uncle Mulriane's byre stole his breath. All but one valiant post lay in a pile, reduced to blackened timbers. Rage, cold and jagged, sliced through Niall. He clenched his gloved hands into fists; the reins dug into the worn leather.

English marauders. This stank of them. Niall had seen enough of their handiwork and recognised the fell signs.

They had passed this way.

Before, the English would never have dared venture so far from their garrison without a full regiment for fear that the Irish brigades would pick them off. But this winter, Irish strength was dwindling, and the English became emboldened.

Caution. The enemy could still be here. It took all of his training not to give in to panic and race to his uncle's manor.

At a quick glance, the courtyard appeared empty—none of the Mulriane servants putting things to rights. His attention focused on the manor. No trace of a cook fire rising from its chimneys, everything too still. One window had been shattered.

Niall rode around the byre, grimly taking in the wreckage, until he was clear of it and faced the courtyard.

Then he saw a cairn. Fear clawed at his gut. Crows flapped over the mound, picking at the spaces between the rocks, strands of hair caught in one beak.

Niall roared and kneed his horse, charging towards the cairn. Fionn shot ahead, scattering the birds and sending them in an angry blur of wings and shrieks. Niall launched himself from his mount and rushed to the cairn.

Not Mairead—please not my sister!

He snatched at the rocks, heaving them aside to dig through the cairn. Niall lifted a stone and then froze. A hand—a man's fingers contorted like claws. He cleared several more rocks to reveal a face.

Uncle Mulriane.

Niall dropped the stone he was holding.

His uncle's sightless eyes stared wide and milky. A once hearty man reduced to this. Niall braced his hands on his thighs and bowed his head, fighting to catch his breath. After a few moments, he shifted and, this time with more care, he dug out the other body. *Aunt*

Fi. She was tucked beside her husband as though she had fallen to sleep—except for the dried blood that stained the front of her dress.

How many cairns had he found, how many had he passed without giving thought to who lay beneath? But this one—this one was personal.

Niall reached over and smoothed her hair before he rose to his feet. "Where are the others?" he shouted at the watching crows, then lobbed a stone to scatter them. His cousins . . . their servants? *Dear God, where is Mairead?*

He hastily replaced the rocks and, when he straightened, caught a movement from the corner of his eye at one of the upper windows in the house. Had it been a bird's reflection—or were the whoresons still inside?

"Time for answers—or blood." He tethered his horse and headed for the manor. "Fionn, with me."

The hound followed, then shot ahead and disappeared around the corner to the front entrance. Fionn's whining and sharp barks spurred Niall forward. Drawing his sword, he approached, slightly crouched and coiled to spring.

He scanned the side of the manor and courtyard. Nothing stirred, not even a flash from the window. Fionn's whines grew more pleading.

Niall hurried around the corner and recoiled. Mounted on two spikes were a pair of bloody heads. As he drew closer, he recognised one—his cousin Diarmuid.

Mother of God.

Bile shot into his mouth, and Niall choked it down. "Bastards!" A curse on the lot of them.

Jaw clenched, Niall gripped his sword. A paper nailed to the iron-studded portal fluttered in the wind and caught his attention. He reached the door, and his eyes swept across the words. That they were written in Irish, not English, stirred Niall's outrage. A true Irishman would have had his throat cut before colluding with the enemy.

For the crime of harbouring and collaborating with the outlaw Tóraidhe, this manor and lands, including all associated chattels and outbuildings, have been seized in the name of the Commonwealth of England.

Niall ripped the proclamation from the door. "God damn them." He crushed it in his fist and yanked open the door, no longer caring what noise he made or if any soldiers had been left behind to guard their spoils.

Let them come.

The crows were hungry. Let them feast on rancid English flesh for once.

A scuffling echoed from somewhere inside the house. Niall canted his head, listening for the intruder. "Fionn, search," he whispered. The wolfhound set out without hesitation, leading Niall through one room to another, past broken and upturned furniture. The cold wrapped around him like a tomb. With every step he took, dread gripped him. What would he find in the next room?

From the floor above, a patter of footsteps darted across, then the creaking of the stairs. Fionn bolted ahead. Niall raced into the hallway and found the door to the kitchen swinging on its hinges. He plunged into the kitchen in time to see a shrouded figure reach for the fireplace poker and whirl around to face him. Their mantle fell away.

Niall skidded to a halt. A woman stood before him, panting and out of breath, her face pale against the vivid auburn of her hair. Her attention darted between the threat of the advancing wolfhound and Niall's drawn sword. She held the iron poker aloft, and it shook in her grip.

Niall lowered his weapon and motioned for Fionn to stop. "I mean you no harm."

The woman's shoulders slumped in relief. "You're not English." Her poker lowered, its tip striking the earthen floor.

"God forbid." Niall took a step closer, but the woman shrank back. Her gaze darted to the back door, and she edged towards the exit. "Wait—don't fly." He clamped down on his growing impatience, sensing that any moment she'd disappear, and then he'd learn nothing. "Are you alone?" He used a tone one would use on a skittish colt, even though he wanted to yell, *Where is everyone?*

Instead of putting her at ease, his question appeared to make her even more nervous, and she lifted the poker again. Fionn crept forward to inspect her closer, but she held her ground. "Down," Niall commanded. The wolfhound loomed before the slight maid, the top of his head easily reaching her chest. Strangely, she seemed more wary of Niall than the dog. "Who are you?"

She didn't answer right away, as though she weighed her answer. "Áine Callaghan," she said. "I'm a servant—the Mulrianes' dairymaid."

Hope flared in Niall. If there was one survivor, there were sure to be more. "Where are they? My kin—where's my sister?" Trust Mairead to have found a safe place to hide, clever girl.

"Your kin?"

"I'm Niall O'Coneill—"

"O'Coneill." Her eyes widened. "Mairead O'Coneill—"

"Where is she?" He looked around, as though expecting to see Mairead running into the kitchen. But the house was silent, and the maid, Áine, looked away. "She's not here, is she?"

Áine gave a slight shake of her head. Her eyes were bright with tears when she met his gaze.

"What happened to her?"

The maid's mouth quivered. "I can't say. I didn't see. Taken by the English, I suppose—they must have been all taken."

"You suppose?" His tone sharpened. "How do you suppose? Were you not here?"

Áine clutched the poker to her chest. "I saw nothing—"

"When did this happen? Can you tell me at least this?" The blood pounded in his temples. "A day ago, two?"

"A fortnight."

Niall sucked in his breath. *By Jesus.* So long? The trail would be cold. Where would he find her—if she still lived? Panic clawed at his gut. "She could still be near—"

"I searched the area for all of them," Áine said. "Every day I venture a little farther and still, I've seen no sign of them."

"Another cairn?" It hurt him to ask, but he had to. "A recently dug grave?"

"There is not another soul who could have done so. Your sister is gone—they are all gone. I've lost faith that they could be otherwise."

A sudden suspicion flared. "And how was it you survived?"

"I've hidden somewhere near. I only returned to see if I could find some scraps from the cellar."

Niall thought of the notice pinned on the front door, and his ire kindled again. A muscle pulsed in his jaw. "Did you betray them? Is that how you secured your freedom?"

A flare of outrage kindled in the maid's eyes, and she drew herself to her full height. "I betrayed no one. I would never have harmed a soul. I hid in the byre and barely escaped the fire. The smoke overwhelmed me, and I collapsed behind the peat stack." Her eyes welled with tears. She looked away, her chest rising and falling. "This is—was—my home."

Niall read the truth in her tone and realised she was as much a victim as his kin—as much a victim as Mairead. He stepped away, took in the cold, empty kitchen with stacks of empty crockery. Rage roiled inside his gut. This was to have been Mairead's safe haven, far from the threat of war, far from any garrison or port. The English should never have reached this estate.

By Jesus. What evil had befallen his sister? Niall thought of the bodies of women and children these past two years—left behind to spread fear and horror. The message clear: if they could do this to the most vulnerable, a hale and hearty man could expect a torturous death.

The pounding in his temples exploded, and his vision darkened. Fire rushed from his belly to his throat. With a roar, he upturned a table, then threw his head back and bellowed out his pain and grief.

As the pain receded, his blurred vision sharpened. He found the maid pressed against the hearth, round eyes filling her face and her hand pressed against her mouth. Seeing her naked fear, Niall struggled to master his anger, to replace the hot blood with ice. After a few moments, a colder, more purposeful fury filled him.

He would make the English pay.

CHAPTER 3

Áine still clutched the poker, her back pressed against the stone fireplace. She had never been more alarmed in her life to see a man materialise in her path. From experience, she gave them all distance. Niall O'Coneill had appeared, sprung from legend — a blazing warrior brandishing a gleaming sword, accompanied by a kingly wolfhound. He looked capable of hewing a giant in half. Were it not for his mud-splattered mantle, stubbled beard and dark shadows beneath his eyes, she'd believe him to be a figment of her fanciful imagination.

And then reality slammed her with the tide of his rage. With a fearsome bellow, he heaved the edge of the worktable, and it crashed onto its side, sending the crockery smashing upon the floor. Áine muffled a scream. Her shoulder scraped against the rough stone — she was pinned between the fireplace and the raging man. The old terror gripped her.

With his back turned to her, his shoulders rose and fell with each breath. Áine marshalled her scattered wits, determined to fly. Now was her chance, while this man and his wolfhound paid her no attention.

But then he faced her. Áine sucked in her breath, her stomach knotting. She was ten feet from the door—from safety—but with every heartbeat of hesitation, that distance stretched to impossible.

He took a step forward, and she flinched, braced for the force of a blow. She squeezed her eyes shut. *Please, not fists.*

"I'm sorry."

This hadn't come from Áine, though those same words had been running through her mind—a reflex she thought she had smothered. No, *he* had spoken those words.

Áine's eyes flew open. He stood a few feet away—jaw tense, hands balled into fists. "I'm sorry," he repeated tersely. "My anger is not with you."

She released the breath she had been holding and gave him an answering nod. Few had ever apologised to her. A part of her feared it might be a ruse.

The man ran a shaky hand through his dark hair and looked around the kitchen, a frown worrying his brow. "Gather what you will, Áine Callaghan. Supplies, any food. Especially food. We leave shortly."

"And where are we to be going?" Áine asked sharply.

"Away from here." He seemed deep in thought, his mind visibly whirring.

Áine had no intention of leaving with this man—any man, even. She had found herself a shepherd's hut to shelter in, and with the snares she had laid, she could stave off starvation. She knew how to survive.

She opened her mouth to correct him, but he startled her by reaching past her to pull a canister down from the shelf. He yanked off the top and, finding nothing, tossed it aside. Then he peered inside the bin where Cook kept the oats.

"Not much," he muttered as he rapped against the bin. "The bastards left barely enough for a mouse. Is there a sack we could use?" He glanced up and frowned at her. "You're not moving. Speed, woman. I'm counting on it."

And yet everything was moving too fast for her. "I'm not going with you."

26

Niall continued rummaging for supplies and did not look up. "You can't stay here."

She wasn't his concern. Why should he care? "Not here," Áine admitted but said nothing more. "I'll do very well on my own."

He frowned, as puzzled by her answer as she was by his refusal to leave her behind. Then he scowled. "Have you no care for your preservation, woman? I'll not leave you here alone and unprotected. What sort of man do you take me for?"

"I can't answer that—I don't know you."

"I'm not a rabid beast. I won't bite."

Áine's gaze slid to the fearsome hound, who sat on his haunches. His jaws were powerful enough to snap the neck of a wolf. Of the two, she was more inclined to trust the wolfhound. "Go with my blessing. I'll not fault you for it."

"Then allow me to see you safely to your kin," he said tersely.

There is no safety there. Before Áine could think of an excuse, the wolfhound cut in with a low, surly growl. Through the shattered windows came a clattering of hooves on the cobbled forecourt.

"Please tell me that's your horse," Áine whispered, praying he'd answer yes.

Niall swore under his breath, then dashed her hopes. "Not unless the beast multiplied himself tenfold over. Is there an exit in the back?"

"Through the scullery."

"Come on." He grabbed her wrist and hurried her towards the scullery.

Áine tried to pull away, but his grip was relentless. "I'll hide in the garret—they won't find me."

He rounded on her, nostrils flaring, his expression hard. "I left my horse tethered in the front. They know someone is here and will surely tear apart the manor looking for us. Your options have disappeared. We leave now."

Áine had been accused of many things in her life but never of being a fool. She gave up trying to disengage and instead quickened her pace to keep up with him.

They slipped through the scullery and outside into the walled kitchen garden. The wind had picked up, and storm-grey clouds released rain mixed with sleet. The wolfhound dashed ahead and was the first to reach the garden gate.

Niall crept out of the gate and then waved her through. "Head for the woods," he said to her. "Even if I fall behind, keep running. Ready? Go!"

Áine dashed for the fields. Now she was out in the open, an easy target for a predator to swoop in and pick her off. Her knees nearly buckled at the thought, but she pushed through her panic.

Keep running. Don't look back. Pretend you're invisible and they can't reach you.

Áine fixed her sights ahead to the sheltering woods. Niall kept pace alongside her, although she sensed he could have run faster. The wolfhound ran several lengths ahead of them.

Partway to the woods, Áine heard what she had been dreading — a shout from the manor. She threw a glance over her shoulder to see a dozen men swarming the courtyard, running for their horses.

"Faster!" Niall said. He grabbed her hand to speed her up.

They plunged into the woods as the English galloped across the field. The pounding of hooves grew louder, as loud as the blood rushing between her ears.

"This way." Niall pulled her off the trail, down into a small gully. They wove through a crowded stand of trees, jumping over roots and fallen boughs.

Behind them, the horsemen had reached the tree line and were charging into the woods. Hooves echoed from different directions — they were fanning out to search for them.

Niall stopped short, and Áine bumped into him. "We have to hide." Whirling around, he scanned the trees. They were tall in this part of the woods, their branches reaching upwards and well out of reach. "By Jesus," he hissed. "I'll never get you up there."

Áine struggled to catch her breath and looked around. She knew where they were. "No, this way." She ran down a slope with Niall now following her. They skidded their way down the hillside, hurried on by the thrashing sounds of pursuit.

Áine made straight for a giant of a tree with a yawning hollow.

She dropped to the ground and started crawling inside. "Hurry. Don't stand there," she called to him over her shoulder. Her words bounced off the interior of the tree. Without further encouragement, he squeezed in after her.

Áine scooted deeper into the trunk, drawing her knees up to her chest and making room for him next to her. He followed her lead and drew in his legs like a cramped nut.

"Where —" she started to ask about the wolfhound, but Niall cut her off, his hand pressed against her mouth.

Someone called from a distance and another answered, crystal clear and in their immediate area. Another joined in the call. Áine's heart lodged in her throat, and she held her breath, hoping the English soldiers would not come this far down into the gully. But wishes were not salvation.

A dull thud of hooves grew louder — a few horses, Áine guessed. Niall moved slightly and drew her gaze. He clutched a dagger, ready to strike.

"Come out, filthy bogtrotters," a man called out in guttural English. "We know you're here."

Niall tensed beside her, and she could see the pulse of a muscle in his jaw.

Áine shifted and pressed her thigh against his. She desperately tried to keep still and stop the involuntary trembling that tripped through her body.

Laughter rang out and drew closer. A pair of soldiers approached either side of their hiding spot. Áine's breath came in shallow gasps. Niall shifted so that he shielded her with his body. Áine drew herself into an even tighter ball. She heard the snapping of twigs, the falling sleet and the rush of blood in her ears.

Any second, they would be discovered. Áine clapped her hand against her mouth to prevent a terrified sob from escaping. Niall raised his dagger and leaned forward, ready to slash the soldier the moment he bent down to check the hollowed tree.

"Find anything?" a voice called.

"Nowt." That voice was close — too close. Loud in Áine's ears.

"The weather is getting dirty," the other said. "Circle back. The captain will need to be told."

After a long pause, "Aye."

One last shower of dirt tumbled over the opening, then the crunching of footsteps, fainter and fainter.

Áine sagged in relief against Niall's shoulder. When she realised she pressed against him, she lifted her head and found him looking at her curiously.

NIALL REMAINED TENSE LONG AFTER HE COULDN'T HEAR THE footsteps. Were they retreating, or was this a ploy to flush him out? That's what he would have done. He strained to pick out any foreign sounds from the whispers of the winter forest. The creaking of boughs in the wind gave nothing away.

Several more moments lapsed, and Áine began to squirm beside him. He leaned down to whisper against her temple, "I need to see if they've gone. Stay here."

The maid nodded. Niall eased from her side and crept out of the tree's hollow. He kept low to the ground and scanned the forest for any sign of movement. Nothing. As he searched for Fionn, a grey shadow shifted amongst the grey-brown undergrowth. Niall froze, then recognised Fionn wending his way through the trees. When the wolfhound spied him, he sprang into a run to reach Niall.

"Good lad," he said, scratching him behind the ears.

Niall scouted the immediate area. He found hoofprints that led back to the manor. Probably intent on looting. If he captured one of the troopers, he'd be sure to learn the plight of his sister—where they were holding her.

Niall returned to the hollow tree where Áine hid. Unthinkable to leave her there, but neither could he take her with him. A maid alone in the forest . . . But she hadn't wanted his help. Swearing under this breath, he dropped down to peer into the hollow. The maid was wrapped up in her mantle, a part of the shadows. Her grey eyes were luminous and stared back at him, wary. A single tress had escaped her plait and curled around her shoulder, gleaming copper-red.

"I'm going back to the manor to learn what I can," he said to her. After a pause, he added, "I'll return. Keep yourself hidden."

"Be careful," she responded softly.

Her words touched Niall. He didn't know why precisely, except that she was thinking more of his well-being than her own. "Promise me you'll still be here when I return?"

She bit her lip, as if debating her answer. Finally, she nodded. "For now."

Niall had the odd sense he had won a great boon. Turning to Fionn, he said, "Stay. Guard the maid." He didn't have to repeat himself. The wolfhound settled himself in the mouth of the tree's cavity.

He set off after the tracks, relishing his new role of hunter instead of hunted. The trail was clearly marked. A single set of hooves joined a few others before being swallowed up by several horses. All for two fugitives, Niall thought. *The English must be desperate for sport.*

When he reached the tree line, he halted within the shadow of the woods and scanned the surrounding field. Far in the distance, a section of his uncle's courtyard was visible, with horses tethered to a hitching post. He'd have a better view of the manor from the wreckage of the byre. Niall eyed the distance between himself and the charred byre. Might he make it before a sentry chanced to look his way?

The whoresons must all be inside the manor, looting the last of his uncle's goods, treasures that had been in the Mulriane family — his mother's family — for generations. What was the chance that these English soldiers, desperate to line their pockets, would pay more attention to an empty field instead of the pewter and cloth left behind?

Niall sprinted across the field towards the byre while keeping an eye on the manor. He reached the ruins without a shout of alarm or a single shot to the head and crouched behind a surviving section of collapsed roof.

Two soldiers stood sentry in the courtyard alongside a dozen horses, including Niall's. Their colours were clearly on display—green and gold.

"Now I'm short a horse. Grand," he muttered under his breath. He'd held no misconception that it would be otherwise, but he hated how crippled he'd be with the loss of his mount. At least he hadn't left O'Dwyer's dispatches in his saddlebag.

With both those sentries standing guard, he'd have no chance to sneak up on them. A diversion? Not unless he wanted to draw the rest of the soldiers out of the manor, spoiling for a fight. But if he drew one of these soldiers to him, he might at least learn about Mairead.

He looked around for where he might lure one out, but then four troopers entered the courtyard, and he ducked his head.

A man swaggered in the lead, wearing a buff coat and a wide-brimmed hat trimmed with a green band. His back was to Niall, but he had the look of a captain, too pleased by the scent of his own shite to be a lieutenant, but too out at the elbows to be anything superior. He moved around the courtyard as though he had the right to the place—no fear in the world that a larger beast would come in and rip the meat from his maw.

When he finally turned around, Niall inhaled sharply. He knew that man. Captain John Garret of Colonel Sankey's dragoons. He had captured that English bastard last year, but his commander had released the man and twenty others in a prisoner exchange three weeks later.

Niall sank back on his heels. The implication turned his stomach. By setting this man free, had he sown the seeds for his own kin's destruction?

Couldn't be. These men were opportunistic looters, while the English savages who had attacked his kin were long gone. But this argument tasted like ash in his mouth. Every wolf had his territory, and he had seen this pattern before. The English struck as quick as lightning and then circled back to gather the pickings.

Niall studied Garret with fresh eyes, burning every detail in his mind—from the dappled grey horse he went to check on to the slight limp in his left leg and the green scabbard that housed his sword.

That blade may well have been the weapon that had murdered his uncle and aunt and severed the head of his cousin Diarmuid. That *sword* might have the blood of Mairead on it. Bile rose in Niall's throat and soured his mouth. He dug the tip of his stag-horn dagger into the ground, imagining how he would plunge it into the man's gut. His vision darkened with rage.

Garret fired off a series of commands, but Niall couldn't make out what he said. A soldier pointed to the woods and shrugged. Niall held his breath, suddenly realising the risk to Áine if Garret sent them back to find the fugitives. She'd be alone. What if she mistook the searchers for his return and revealed herself?

The captain paused far too long for Niall's comfort. The bastard was weighing his options. A cold sweat trickled down Niall's forehead, and he wondered if there was any way to reach Áine in time.

Garret jerked his head and called out to those inside the manor. A few minutes later, men poured into the courtyard with several sacks of goods between them. They loaded up Niall's horse with the ill-gotten goods while Garret mounted his horse and surveyed the grounds. Niall crouched lower to avoid being seen.

The rest of the soldiers mounted their horses and, securing Niall's horse on a lead rope, left the manor and headed eastwards.

When the last rider disappeared from sight, Niall rose from his hiding spot, ready to howl his frustration. How was he to catch Garret without a horse? At least Niall was a keen tracker. If he had to hunt the English bastard all the way to hell, he'd see it done.

Niall broke out into a jog to hurry back to fetch Fionn and Áine. The sleet levelled off, turning into a steady drizzle, and there was only an hour left of daylight. A cold mist rose from the ground, obscuring the landmarks and his sense of direction. He retraced his footsteps back to the hollow tree. Niall found Fionn sniffing around the area. Catching his scent, the hound perked up before rushing to greet him.

"Well done, lad." Niall disengaged and called out to the tree. "You can come out." He expected to see her in the opening, but she didn't appear. "Áine?" A bad feeling washed over him. Had she fled after all? Niall drew closer and crouched down to peer inside the tree's cavity. "Áine?"

He heard a slight scuffle before the maid appeared at the entrance. Her auburn hair framed a heart-shaped face; her skin looked creamy against the grey bark. For a moment, Niall thought she was a faerie guarding the entrance to the Otherworld.

"Are they gone?" she asked, her voice soft and breathless.

"Ay. Our options have dwindled," he said, adjusting his mantle so that it covered his head. Twilight was fast approaching, and he dared not attempt to track Garret with fading light. If he missed signs of the troop changing direction, he'd never find them. "Where is this place you've been sheltering? Is it far?"

Áine hesitated.

"I'll not trouble you, upon my honour."

She wrapped her arms around herself, then gave him a curt nod. "It's a short distance. This way."

CHAPTER 4

ÁINE KNEW these woods in summer and winter, daybreak and night-fall, and could traverse them blindfolded. She led Niall with sure steps, all her senses alert for any changes in the natural rhythm of the woods. Overhead, a raven perched on a branch and cawed into the wind, as though he too were on watch.

The light faded, and twilight settled in. Áine kept glancing back to make sure that Niall still followed, for he advanced with stealth, as soundless as his wolfhound, who glided between the trees. Every so often, Niall paused to scan behind them. There was something wolfish about the way this man moved—lean and sure on his feet.

Many of the stories she loved involved a faerie messenger leading a hero on a quest, deep into an enchanted forest. For a fanciful moment, she thought of the stories about Fionn mac Cumhaill and the Fianna, outlaws fighting for their lives. But Niall O'Coneill was not one of the Fianna; he was a weary man who wanted to live through one more night. They were both in danger, and she'd do well to remember that.

She found the cow path and continued along its winding trail that looped around the southern edge of a birch grove.

"Where are we going?" Niall asked, breaking the silence. His voice sounded deep and rich. It surprised her that he allowed her to lead this long without comment. Few men would have been led beyond the hen cupboard.

"We're close," she assured him, bracing for an argument. But he held his tongue and gave no sign of impatience.

As the twilight deepened, they reached the rickety wooden structure that had sheltered Áine this past fortnight. Once, it had served as a shepherd's hut, barely large enough to shelter a couple of shepherds and a small flock of sheep for when the wolves came roaming.

"What is this place?" Niall asked. "Are we still on my uncle's lands?"

"Betwixt and between," she answered. "These lands lie between your uncle's and a neighbouring estate. There has been an ongoing dispute over this pastureland."

"This landowner, are you speaking of Eamon Grace?"

"You know him?" Áine said, then winced at how daft she sounded. Surely, the master's nephew would be acquainted with their closest neighbour.

Niall surprised her with a natural smile. "Ay. The man is a captain in our brigade. I've known Eamon well for years."

Áine sensed Niall held some affection for the man, so she spoke no more of him. She drew back the bolt and pushed the door open. The banked fire provided little light, and she needed a few moments for her eyes to adjust to the gloom. She groped for the tinderbox perched on a shelf near the door and one of the stubby tallow candles the shepherds had left behind. After a moment of fiddling, she struck the flint and coaxed a flame on the char cloth. She lit a candle and held it up for her to see. The hard contours of Niall's face came into sharp relief.

"Sure, this will do well enough." Niall took the candle from her and looked around.

Áine crossed the floor to the ring of hearthstones in the centre of the hut. She knelt on the hard-packed ground to stir the embers, blowing on them to awaken the flames. Directly overhead, a fist-sized hole in the thatch provided an ample draw for the smoke, but she was careful to keep the flames low.

She turned her head and watched as Niall examined the hut. He went straight to the collection of rabbit pelts she had draped over a wooden frame.

"You caught these?" he asked.

Áine stirred the fire. "I can lay snares."

Niall sank down to the ground beside her and slumped forward, exhaustion plain on his face. The faint glow of the fire traced the outlines of his jaw, and his dark hair appeared black in the firelight, falling in waves to his shoulders. His nearness made Áine nervous. She couldn't scoot away without drawing his notice, nor would she care to deal with his mockery if he did. Self-consciously, she held out her hands to catch the welcome heat while avoiding his gaze. Her skin tingled, and she felt his eyes on her—both exhilarating and terrifying. If he noticed the leaping pulse at her throat, he said nothing.

After the wolfhound explored every corner of the hut, he laid himself down beside Niall and settled his muzzle on his lap.

"What do you call him?" she said, itching to touch the good beast.

"Fionn, after Fionn mac Cumhaill."

Áine's eyes widened, suddenly embarrassed, as if he had been inside her head. She had been thinking of the mythic hero more than usual. Odd that this stranger would cross her path with a wolfhound named Fionn. A chill coursed down her spine. Perhaps not so odd. The Faerie Folk were not above interfering in the lives of mortals, especially in times of great need.

Nonsense, she thought impatiently. *The hound is just a hound, and you have a fanciful imagination.*

"A brave hero," she finally said. "It suits him."

After several moments, he asked, "Was it you who built the cairn?"

Áine nodded. "I wanted to protect them, keep them safe—" She couldn't go on as the memory of her lifeless mistress and master struck her afresh. "'Twas a simple blessing I gave them. I hope it gives you comfort."

Niall nodded, his gaze fixed on her. "It does, thank you." He ran his fingers through Fionn's bristly fur. "Was my uncle buried with his sword?"

Áine frowned. "I didn't see it, now that you mention it. He most definitely had his sword when he went out to confront the English."

"They must have taken it," Niall said flatly. "It was my grandfather's, Spanish wrought. One more tally against them." Then he fell silent.

It might have been the warmth of the fire, the excitement of the day or the strangeness of finding herself ensconced with a stranger, but tears pricked her eyes. "The Mulrianes were kind to me," she whispered. "Your sister too. I enjoyed her fiddle playing."

Niall's attention sharpened. "Tell me more."

"I think she missed home," Áine said after a little thought. "I overheard her speaking about her da and Galway a great deal. She liked to practise her fiddle in the early morning, and I'd often head down to the byre before I was needed only to hear her play. The music sometimes made me want to cry." She bit her lip, wishing to take her words back, for she had revealed a weakness. Áine knew better than to hand a man a weapon that could be used against her.

Instead of mocking her, Niall smiled wanly. "She did the same for my da, though he'd never admit it. I always preferred her lively tunes." He bent down to give his hound a scratch under the chin and kept his face averted for a few moments. When he looked up, his voice sounded harsh. "Why did the English make Diarmuid an example? Did he kill any of their soldiers when they threatened his father?"

"I can't say why they gave him such a gruesome death." Áine tried to close her mind to the grisly sight of the bloody head on a spike, but a shudder escaped her. "He hadn't been gone for long — they must have caught him when he was journeying."

Niall looked up and frowned. "Diarmuid was away?"

She nodded. "He left to join the Tóraidhe. I heard him saying he was going to offer his sword to Edmund O'Dwyer."

"Diarmuid was going to join our brigade?" Niall's eyes widened. "When — when was this?"

It did not surprise Áine to learn that Niall was with the Tóraidhe.

The man was an extension of his weapons, and his every movement had the focus of a warrior. "A fortnight before the English arrived."

Niall sat back and stared into the fire. "I didn't know . . . I was at Ross Castle at the time." He rubbed his jaw, his expression grim. "I saw troubling signs on the road. I came to ensure they were well—to see how Mairead was faring."

Áine wasn't sure how to reply. It seemed unfathomable to her that he had come this distance to find his sister. Many wouldn't have bothered unless there was a promise for gain.

"What of you?" he asked. The sudden change in topic surprised her. "Where's your kin? Are they far from here? I can see that you reach them safely."

"It's too great a distance."

"How far?"

Áine didn't understand why this would interest him, but she recognised a dogged determination to get an answer. "I was from Cork City once." She lowered her head and rubbed the puckered scar on the inside of her left wrist. The sneering face of her step-brother, Muiredach O'Keefe, flashed in her mind, his features contorted by drink or rage and often both. She tried to smother the memory, but traces of it nipped at her with sharp teeth. She was not above hoping that the beast had died in a tavern brawl.

"Cork? There's more than the problem of distance. You'll not be seeing me walk into an English garrison city."

"I didn't ask you to."

Niall's brows lifted. "No. You assuredly did not." After an uncomfortable silence, he said, "We can try to send word." Even he sounded doubtful.

The idea, however unlikely, turned her stomach. "No need. I am alone in the world."

"Have you no one?"

Áine thought of the Duggan family a few miles beyond the town walls. She had once stayed with them briefly. The sojourn had been as welcome as a warm blanket until Muiredach came looking for her in the night. The family had lied to shield her, but she daren't ask them to risk his wrath again. "No," she answered truthfully.

"I'll not leave you here on your own," he said. "I care for my conscience too well. Is there anyone you can shelter with?"

"I don't need people to care for me." This time Áine did not look away. "I belong to myself."

Niall's attention drifted around the hut, resting again on the rabbit pelts. Áine suspected he warred with his conscience. He didn't need a strange woman close on his heels but was loath to admit it. Finally, he said, "I must find my sister. The key is hunting down the English troop. If they didn't sack the manor, they'll know who did and where she might have been taken." He looked away, an angry muscle working in his jaw. When he spoke, he seemed once again in control of himself, but his voice sounded hard and brittle. "When the troop left, they were travelling east. They could be heading for any of their garrisons—Cashel, Dundrum or even farther south at Cahir. Either way, their route will take them through the Glen of Aherlow. A village stands at its eastern pass, a day's walk from here. I'll be sure to learn of Garret's movements from there, and O'Dwyer will be glad for any news. With luck, he may forgive my delay in bringing him his dispatches." When he faced Áine, she could tell that he had made up his mind, and she had an inkling that she wouldn't like what he would say next. "There's a public house in the village with a soft-hearted landlord. He won't turn you away, and the woman of the house will be happy to have another pair of hands to help with her work. You'll be safe there."

More strangers—impossible. She absolutely couldn't. Panic began to build. "I'll be staying here."

"Don't be foolish."

She sat up straighter. "I've survived this fortnight on my own."

"Do you keep all the pelts of the rabbits you snare?"

Áine frowned, puzzled by the odd question. "Of course."

"I count eight," he said. "Eight pelts. You've been here a fort-night. There must be days when you haven't caught your supper."

How provoking, but he was right. The rabbits were getting craftier at eluding her snares. Still, she wasn't prepared to admit defeat. "There's more food in this world than rabbit."

"You came to the manor to find supplies," he countered, sitting back and looking pleased with himself. "Wasn't that what you told me in the kitchen?"

Áine was not used to having a man listen to her, much less remember what she said. She'd be flattered if he wasn't using it against her. She didn't like the choice she faced, but she cared even less for starvation. "Very well," she said swallowing her pride and discomfort. "I'll go with you as far as the village."

Niall smiled. "We'll leave at first light so I can follow their tracks. Get some rest." He rose to stoke the fire. "I'll keep watch."

Wrapped in her mantle, Áine curled up on the ground. She should have been bone-weary, but her nerves were afire and struggled to calm. Niall walked around and checked the door latch. Near to her, the wolfhound lay down and rested his head on his forelegs.

As she listened to Niall's footsteps, her mind drifted, and she turned their conversation over in her head. The prospect of starting anew in a strange village set her on edge, but it had been the talk about Cork and belonging that had unsettled her most. Niall O'Coneill was a man surrounded all his life by strong bonds of kith and kin and could not fathom that familial ties did not always mean security, that sometimes those links cut and maimed instead of nurtured.

She could never explain to anyone how her stepbrother had . . . hurt her . . . and would tear her apart should she ever have the misfortune of crossing his drunken path again. Even after putting a distance of four years between them, the mere thought of that monster had the power of making her heart quail. She had fled Cork to save herself, and she'd never return there, either in this life or the next.

Áine kept shifting around until her mantle twisted around her. It was a long time before sleep claimed her.

NIALL SETTLED HIMSELF ON THE GROUND, HIS BACK BRACED against one post, knees drawn up. The length of his scabbard dug into his thigh, but he was too tired to unbuckle it. The fire gave off more warmth than expected and heated the wool of his mantle.

Long after Áine dropped off to sleep, he kept watch with his grief and fury. He wouldn't allow his anguish to overwhelm him, nor could he allow himself the luxury of hope. Niall wanted to dwell on the possibility that somehow Áine had been mistaken—that he'd find his sister sheltering in a hut like the one he found himself in now, but he knew better. He was a hardened soldier, one of the Tóraidhe. This bloody brutal war had turned him into a cold-hearted cynic.

Brace up, man. Keep your mind on strategy. You'll be no use to anyone running around as a mindless banshee. He must plan his next steps and find Mairead.

O'Dwyer's dispatches would have to wait.

He shifted his attention to what he had learned about Diarmuid. The maid's news still unsettled him, and the more he considered it, the more deeply troubled he became. He would have welcomed Diarmuid to O'Dwyer's camp and seen that his cousin was assigned to his own troop. The image of a bloody head impaled on a sharp spike seared his mind. Diarmuid's spirit must be wandering restlessly.

What happened to you, Diarmuid? Can you tell me that?

If Diarmuid had left to join O'Dwyer's brigade a fortnight before the English attack, why had he not left the area? There was more than enough time for him to have found his way to O'Dwyer.

An icy chill raced down Niall's spine—when the English captured his cousin, had they managed to extract the location of the Tóraidhe camp from him as well? Somehow Diarmuid must have known where O'Dwyer was situated in order to have left his father's home.

Either the English were closing in on O'Dwyer's position or they had already flushed them out.

Fionn nudged him with his wet nose and gave Niall an affectionate swipe on the chin. Niall buried his face in Fionn's coarse grey fur, inhaling the comforting scent of hound, mud and river water. The scent triggered a memory of him and his cousin Diarmuid charging into the manor, laughing and dripping wet with eager puppies at their heels. Diarmuid's sisters had squealed at the basket of frogs he had thrust out to them. But the one memory that truly stood out was how Mairead had held her ground, even though Niall knew she had been equally terrified.

Devil take me. An image of his sister as a captive of the English, shackled and abused, tormented him. Mairead would be sure to present a brave face, but the bastards could crush it out of her.

The thought nearly sent him howling.

Niall grimly stared at the fire. He was caught between a lightning storm and a tempest. If he rushed off to warn O'Dwyer, he'd lose any chance to find Mairead—her life would be a mark against his soul.

A loyal soldier would do his duty and rush back to camp. A brother would raze the ground for his sister, damn the rest.

He and his brethren-in-arms had long since squared with death. The Tóraidhe were all fighting men who took care of themselves. Mairead was not. If he could capture one of the marauders at his uncle's manor, he'd choke his sister's whereabouts out of them. He pictured them drunk on his uncle's wine cellar, sprawled on his aunt's embroidered linens.

He wouldn't rest until he tracked his sister down.

Niall's gaze drifted to Áine, curled up in her mantle. *What am I to do with the woman?* She was going to slow him down, but he couldn't leave her here to fend for herself, even if she had the ingenuity to trap an occasional rabbit for her dinner.

Firelight touched her auburn hair, lighting each strand with molten copper. He found it difficult to tear his eyes away and contented himself with watching the gentle rise and fall of her shoulders with every breath she took. She stirred, her lips parted, lashes fluttering for a moment before she buried herself deeper in the woollen folds.

The maid appeared fragile, easy to snap between his thumb and forefinger, and yet he sensed there might be more strength to her than appeared. She had kept her wits when they were fleeing from the English and had known where to hide. Niall knew first-hand how hard it was to keep from being overwhelmed by panic when the enemy was breathing down one's neck.

He had watched her carefully when she led him to this place, though he'd tried not to betray himself. The sureness of her steps spoke of an inner confidence that was missing whenever he asked her a simple question. *Shy*. That had to explain it. But as soon as he thought so, he reconsidered. There was more to it than that.

Áine had told him she wasn't his concern. Not his concern? Whether or not she liked it, she *became* his concern the moment he learned she had buried his uncle and aunt beneath a cairn. This woman knew his sister, had been moved by her music—something he had not been able to enjoy for years.

Niall owed a debt to see this woman safe. Áine Callaghan was the link to those who were closest to his heart—both living and dead.

CHAPTER 5

Áine woke before Niall and the wolfhound. She sat up, her body sore from the hard ground. It surprised her that she had managed to let her guard down enough to sleep at all. She must have been more exhausted than she had realised. The fire had died out, and the grey light of the new day became visible through the smoke hole.

Niall appeared to sleep soundly, his back propped against a post. But when she rose, his eyes opened immediately.

"Is it morn yet?" The timbre of his voice was low and deep.

"I believe so."

"Right. Let's get moving." As he stretched his back, his tunic pulled across his broad chest. Áine looked away, suddenly embarrassed and confused.

"Have you been awake long?" he asked.

"No." She snuck a sideways glance. He wasn't paying her any mind as he belted his scabbard around his waist. When he looked up, she quickly shifted her attention to gathering up her meagre supplies for the journey. She scooped up the tinderbox, twine and the last of the kindling.

"Don't forget the rabbit pelts." The corners of his mouth twitched.

"I'm unlikely to."

The first rays of dawn were streaking across the sky when they set off towards the manor house. Áine hung back a few paces, far enough for her own comfort, but not so far as to incur his impatience. The wolfhound, Fionn, seemed content to trot alongside her, and she welcomed his silent company. She reached out and touched his coarse fur. Her world had lurched beneath her feet, and events had smashed through the walls she had built around herself. Fionn's presence grounded her and kept her moving forward.

How had she ended up fleeing with this man? The world had once again proven how inconsequential and fragile her situation truly was.

"Stay close," Niall told her, eyeing the distance between them. "There may be enemy troops still about."

Áine wrapped her mantle more securely around her to not only ward off the cold, but to also form a shield of sorts. "I know how to pass through these woods unseen."

Niall gave her a long look. "I don't doubt it."

They backtracked until Niall picked up the enemy's trail outside the manor gates. Áine found she could not look at the courtyard, where the cairn stood out like a scar. Instead, she fixed on the stone wall and its iron gates. She touched them now as she had four years ago when she first arrived at the Mulrianes'.

It had been a bright summer day. The meadows had been a riot of wildflowers and flitting birds. Her nan had grown up with Mistress Mulriane's mam, and Áine had been fed on stories of the family. When Áine had walked through the gates and entered the grand courtyard, she had been choked with emotion. When Mistress Mulriane said she could stay, she'd broken down in tears. Fresh tears pricked her eyes now, though not for joy.

Áine stepped away from the gates and caught Niall staring at the courtyard, naked grief plain on his face. It was a single unguarded moment, and one that wrenched her heart. When he became aware of her interest, he squared his shoulders and whistled sharply to Fionn. The wolfhound ceased his sniffing and returned to his side.

"We'll need to set a brisk pace," Niall said.

Áine was determined not to fall behind, mostly out of pride. She sped after Niall and ignored the stitch that pinched her side. In one particular stretch along a steady incline, when her lungs were about to burst, Niall paused at the summit, cool and unruffled, and waited for her to catch up.

She braced herself for an insulting smirk or a sharp dig about keeping up, but he said nothing. Instead, he set an easier pace.

The trail was easy to follow at first. The troop kept to the main road that ran straight like a bowshot. Mountains rose on either side with the valley nestled in between. But two hours after they started, the tracks veered off the main road and ran down a lesser trail. This was when Niall's skills as a tracker shone. He took nothing for granted, pausing to examine the ground every hundred feet or so, lingering at a fork whenever another tract split off.

At one such juncture, Niall squatted down on his haunches and traced a muddled impression with his finger. His dark hair fell across his face as he studied it with the intensity that a master attended his craft. This piqued Áine's curiosity, and she ached to ask him how he could distinguish between tracks, especially over well-churned ground, but she held her tongue.

"A few split from the group." He looked in the direction of the left fork. "We'll stay with the main troop."

An hour before the sun reached its zenith, Niall halted by a running brook. "Best to rest here for a short time. You must be tired."

Áine weighed his statement but did not find his tone critical. "Thank you."

The sky was overcast and the air scented with rain. A pair of squirrels darted from one bough to another, chittering away at each other. Fionn explored farther down the stream, sniffing at rotting logs before quenching his own thirst.

Áine followed the wolfhound to the stream. She sat on her heels and leaned over to scoop water into her cupped hand. Fresh and cold, bone-chillingly so, the water made her teeth ache but was the very thing she needed.

She gazed at the grey-and-brown trees, naked in their glory. A raven observed her from the twisted branch of an alder tree.

Caw.

Áine frowned. The old stories held the raven was a cherished form of the Morrigan, the Goddess of War. "We need no more of that," she said aloud. In response, the bird flapped its wings and cawed again but remained on its perch.

She stayed thus, lost to the soothing world of trees, wind and birds, and didn't hear the crunching of boots.

Niall lowered himself to crouch beside her, so close she could touch him. He bent forward to quench his own thirst. When he finished, he stayed beside her, watching Fionn explore the riverbank. "We're making good time," he said, "but it may not be enough. They're moving quickly and are taking no rest."

He looked troubled and grim and self-reproachful, and Áine suspected he blamed himself for not catching up to them. If only she could reach out and brush aside a heavy lock of his dark brown hair and reassure him that he would surely find his sister. People did not simply vanish—most of the time. But Áine was not dreamer enough to believe in miracles, and she worried for the young miss's life. "You must truly care for your sister and fear for her."

Niall studied the muddy ground. "Ay," he said, his voice low. "Mairead always got herself into scrapes. I seem to have been given the job of minding her since she could walk. Cruel that this once bothered me."

Áine detected the grudging fondness in his tone. "She is quite fortunate to have your high esteem."

"I must find her—I'm not letting our da know that the English have snatched his only daughter. It would kill him."

Áine marvelled that Niall O'Coneill spoke of family and home as though they were a refuge and not a place to flee from. A deep craving gnawed inside that she could almost taste. How would it feel to have such a place, to belong to such a place?

"We best continue." Niall rose to his feet. He held out his hand to her, which only flustered Áine.

"One last drink," she said as an excuse, then scooped another handful of water. Instead of leaving, he stood there, waiting to help her up. She had no choice but to accept his hand and allow him this courtesy.

His skin was warm and roughened by calluses, but his fingers were tapered and sensitively shaped. This was a man who relied on his hands to survive. They were gentle now, but she had no doubt they could be deadly and deliver pain.

Áine pulled back her hand and self-consciously tucked a stray lock of hair into her plait. Her sleeve fell back, and she saw Niall's gaze settle on the burn scar on her exposed wrist. The scar started near her thumb and stretched up her arm, halfway to her elbow. As she was about to yank her sleeve down, he stopped her. His fingers brushed across the puckered scar and made her shiver.

"What is this?"

Áine pulled back as if his touch scalded. "Nothing. I hardly remember how it happened." She feigned a light tone.

"You're made of stern stuff, then. Looks like it had been painful."

Áine stood up. "Should we not be going?"

"Hand over the satchel," he said. "I'll carry it."

"I can manage."

He didn't reply immediately, as though weighing his options. Finally, he said, "Don't be shy to speak up if it becomes too much of a burden."

Niall set a brisk pace across the lower meadows, and Fionn shot ahead of him, stretching his legs. The wolfhound soon disappeared.

The trail narrowed, and the trees clustered together. With the arching branches forming a tight lattice, the light filtered to a gloom before it reached the forest floor.

"Stay close," Niall said. "There have been signs of wild boars."

"Very well," Áine said. Drawing her mantle close about her, she scanned the trees, fearing to see glowing eyes. She nervously adjusted the bag of kindling.

"A couple more hours," Niall assured her.

"Provided the weather holds," Áine said, eyeing the veil of advancing clouds skimming across the sky. "More rain is coming."

"I hope not," he grumbled.

His hopes were soon dashed by Áine's prediction. Within a quarter hour, the rain started, a cold, relentless drizzle that bit deep into her marrow.

"Sure, a bit of sun would not be remiss," he called out to her with a grimace. "Speak again, woman, and coax the clouds to part."

"I'll do my best." Her flippant answer earned her a wry grin.

Áine lost track of time and grew weary from the cold. The sack of kindling became heavier with every step. She kept adjusting the position to redistribute the weight. Clouds knitted across the sky, blotting out the moon and stars. The wind stoked up to a brisk pace, driving through her woollen mantle, biting deep into her bones. Her feet were frozen, and all she could think of was snuggling under a warm quilt. Several times she stumbled, and Niall steadied her before she fell.

"Nearly there. We should be approaching farmsteads."

His voice cut through Áine's stupor, and she focused all her attention on the man walking alongside her now. She would not embarrass herself by falling behind.

"Hand over the kindling," he said. "I'll not accept a 'no' this time."

With a sigh of relief, she unslung the sack and passed it over to him.

The sky began to lighten as the rain eased. Shapes became more distinct—naked trees, the rambling curve of a creek.

A grey shadow moved between the trees—was that Fionn? Then another followed closely.

Áine drew in a sharp breath and opened her mouth to warn Niall, but he had already stopped, tense and alert. He held out his hand in warning.

Yet another shadow flitted between the trees. Her heart leapt into her throat. Then a long howl echoed through the forest. The hairs on her nape lifted.

Wolves.

Niall drew his sword. "Keep calm." He gave a sharp whistle at Fionn. A snap of a twig and rustle of a fir sounded, then Fionn appeared with his hackles bristling. "Keep moving and don't stop."

Niall's tone was low and controlled, so at odds with how Áine felt, with her heart pounding like a bodhrán.

Áine prepared to bolt, but Niall sensed her move and seized her arm.

"Run, and they'll consider us all prey," he said. "If we stay together, the wolves won't be inclined to press their luck, not against a wolfhound and an armed man. Keep your head, Áine. Can you do that?"

She thrust the images of slavering wolves from her mind and nodded. "Ay." She spied a stout bough lying on the ground and rushed over to seize it. Áine hefted it in her hand, taking comfort in its weight.

"Brave girl," Niall said. His voice sounded warm, not mocking, so she took it as a compliment.

In a tight unit, they hurried through the forest with Fionn in the lead as though he were the leader of their small pack. The wolves kept a wary distance. Áine scanned the trees. Occasionally, she thought she saw a moving shadow between the trees, but then it vanished as quickly.

The path opened up, and with the growing light, a shape materialised. A single wolf stood in the centre of the trail, waiting. Niall silently motioned Áine to halt. Fionn advanced towards the wolf, a low growl rumbling through his chest. The wolfhound was bulkier and larger than the wolf. The two animals faced each other until the wolf gave a barking whine and backed away, ceding the path to Fionn.

"Press on," Niall ordered and hurried them along.

The hairs on the back of Áine's nape lifted as they passed the spot where the wolf had stood. She half expected the rest of the pack to be lying in wait for them, getting ready to lunge.

They continued along the way, going as fast as they dared. No howls. No barks or growls. The silence should have comforted her; instead, it unnerved her. She sensed the pack following them, and she kept close to Niall and Fionn.

The sky lightened, and Áine glimpsed a cottage in the distance. "There." She pointed. "Shelter."

"Pick up the pace," Niall called out to them, his tone sharp.

Áine hurried for the shelter with Niall close behind and Fionn guarding their rear. Trees thinned out, and they spilled into meadow-land. The farmhouse gate was still a distance away.

When they finally reached the safety of the farm gate, Áine slumped against the dry-stacked wall, light-headed with relief.

NIALL REACHED THE WALL THAT DIVIDED THE COTTAGE YARD FROM the field and halted. Between the winter fields and the house, a row of aspens served as a windbreak and partially screened their view. A byre stood a short distance away, its weathered wood scrubbed by wind and rain.

Áine drew up beside him and cast a worried glance towards the forest. "You said you saw signs of boar. How did you miss the wolves?"

Niall didn't respond. His attention was fixed on the cottage yard. Everything lay still and muffled. Wrong somehow. No birdsong — not even the clucking of hens. Only the distant caw of a raven. He glanced down at Áine, saw the gathering frown on her brow and realised she felt it too.

"It's best if you wait here until I've investigated," Niall said. "I've seen too many betray our countrymen to the English for the colour of a coin."

Áine stared at the shuttered cottage. "I don't think we need worry about that." She pointed to the roof. "There's no smoke."

That was what hadn't sat well with him. The maid was right. A cook fire should have been burning.

"Wait here." Niall climbed over the low wall and headed for the cottage with Fionn padding silently beside him.

At the door, he listened for movement before trying the handle. It swung open at his lightest push. He ducked his head to clear the lintel and entered the cottage.

The chill struck him first. Despite the stone walls, it felt colder inside than out. It took a moment for Niall's eyes to adjust to the dimness of the interior. Wooden plates and an overturned iron pot lay scattered across the earthen floor. A smashed chair had been tossed beside a pile of clay shards, and the hearth remained cold, a banked peat fire long since extinguished.

Nothing stirred—nothing but the sad remains of a household. Yet another empty house. Grimly, he returned to the door and waved Áine inside.

Áine's breath frosted in the cold air, and she rubbed her arms. She wandered through the room, then bent to pick up the iron pot. "They left hastily," she said, showing Niall the porridge caked at the bottom.

Niall ducked under a bunch of dried herbs suspended from the low beams. He flipped open a wooden box on a shelf and peered inside. "Oats," he said. "But barely enough to line a man's stomach."

Áine lifted the lid from an undamaged crock. "And a handful of split pease," she said with more enthusiasm. "A feast."

"Indeed," Niall said with a wry smile. "I'll check the byre." He left the cottage with Fionn beside him.

When he got close to the building, he saw the door hanging off its top hinges. As expected, all the animals were gone, but the place still smelled faintly of cattle.

A clear picture began to emerge. The English were expanding their reach through Tipperary well beyond strategic towns and strongholds. In the past, they had been careful not to spread their resources too thin, which was how the Irish brigades could wage a war of attrition. But this activity was brazen—a sign that the English either anticipated a flood of fresh troops to help them hold on to the new territories they were capturing or were expecting the Irish resistance to fade.

On a cold day in hell. If the English believed that, they seriously underestimated Irish resolve.

Niall hurried back to the cottage to find Áine wielding a broom. "Don't bother with that," he told her. "We won't be staying long. The village is not far from here, and I want to reach it before nightfall."

Áine slowed her sweeping but did not stop. "What did you find in the byre?"

"Empty. I suspect everyone left recently." He took a seat on a stool.

Áine stopped her labours and leaned on the broom. "I believe I shall stay here. The cottage is sturdy and well-built. It's surrounded by woodland, so I'd have plenty of fuel to keep a fire going, and the place is bound to be rich with rabbit warrens. If the people return, I shall at least have kept their home in tidy order."

"You don't owe these people anything, much less to keep their house. No good will come of a woman alone at such times," Niall said flatly.

"I'm adept at hiding," she said. "If I don't want to be seen, I shan't be."

"How so?" Niall was both appalled and amused at her naivety. "Are you one of the Faerie Folk to disappear in the forest dales?"

To his surprise, she visibly winced. "I have more mundane ways to accomplish it, I assure you. This is not the first time that I've had to manage it."

The maid was soft-spoken and appeared as delicate as a daisy, yet he suspected that she possessed the fortitude of a green reed. "The village would be safest," he told her.

"This is as far as I'll go," she replied with unmistakable finality. "You have a pressing need to reach the village, and I will only slow you down."

Niall threaded his fingers through his hair. He couldn't argue with her, but it still went against the grain to leave her on her own. That she kept her distance puzzled him. He had never been a vain man, but women had, at times, flattered him with their attention. An ogre he was not. And why was he thinking this? Finally, he said, "Very well, if you are bent on this course, I'll save my breath."

"Stay long enough for me to cook up the porridge," she said. "A meal would sustain you."

"I suppose."

Áine bent down to pick up a pot. Niall's eyes drew to her slender form. When he found his sister, he might very well pass by here. *Just to check on the maid.* Annoyed at where his musings were wandering, he rose from the stool abruptly and nearly tipped it over. "I'll get a fire started."

By midmorning, the cottage had warmed up and an appetising aroma filled it. Niall returned from foraging in a thicket, carrying a second armful of wood to feed the fire. A charged energy coursed through his veins. He was anxious to continue with his quest, but his conscience wouldn't allow him to leave until he settled Áine in the cottage. When he crossed the threshold with his bundle, he stopped in his tracks.

Áine stood at the hearth, stirring the contents of an iron cauldron while, with her other hand, she held her skirt back from the flames. The smoke from the cooking pot rose up through a hole in the roof. Fionn sat on his haunches beside her, the top of his head reaching nearly to her shoulder. Her plait had loosened, allowing tendrils of hair to curl around her neck. The fire highlighted the deep reds and copper of her hair and contrasted with the cool milkiness of her skin. Even Fionn's own grey coat appeared richer, made reddish by the light of the fire.

She spoke to Fionn in a low, melodious voice as she worked, "And the hounds were born of a human woman, but they were enchanted—"

Niall must have made a sound, for she glanced over her shoulder, startled. A flush warmed her cheeks.

"Go on," he said, laying the kindling on the ground. "This tale sounds interesting."

Áine cast him a wary glance before she applied a keen attention to the pot. "You haven't had a moment to rest."

Niall dropped to his haunches to feed the fire, aware of her standing near. The cooking aromas reached him, and his stomach growled. He couldn't remember the last hot meal he had eaten. "What's in your cauldron?" He peered into the pot and found a bubbling porridge. Her cheeks turned a deeper rose.

"I found more pease. Enough for a decent meal," she responded, reaching up to brush the strands of hair from her cheek. Niall's gaze followed the trail of her fingers before he tore his eyes away. "It's ready, if you care to have some."

"I'll not say no." He had been living rough in bogs and wild woodland with hunger an ever-present enemy. Niall reached over to pluck a pair of wooden bowls from a shelf and handed them to her. She divided the meagre pease porridge between themselves.

Áine settled herself across from him at the table. She ate slowly, lingering on every spoonful. Fionn, shameless creature that he was, crowded next to her, greedily eyeing the trail of her spoon from bowl to expressive mouth. The maid met the hound's imploring eyes and lowered her bowl to him. He lapped up the remaining portion and licked the bowl clean. When he finished, he rubbed his muzzle against her hand.

Niall couldn't help but smile. "You shouldn't encourage him."

Áine returned the smile. "He has pretty manners."

"Unlike his master?"

She shrugged but did not answer. They fell into awkward silence until she asked, "Tell me—how long have you been with Colonel O'Dwyer? You mentioned you were with his brigade."

"Nearly ten years, since I was eighteen," Niall replied. "The Rebellion had spread to Tipperary, and I could not stay in Galway counting bolts of woollen cloth when my countrymen were fighting Protestant Colonial forces for my rights as much as theirs. Ireland should be for all Irish, and not subject to an English colonial government." Niall thought back to his parting with his family. His father had tried to convince him to stay, having heard alarming stories of massacres and equally bloody reprisals coming in from Ulster in the north. "O'Dwyer had recently returned to Ireland after fighting for King Charles the First against the Scots, and the Confederate Irish Council had given O'Dwyer his own command to fight against the Colonial forces. Initially, that included raw-boned labourers and tradesmen but very few professional soldiers." Niall leaned on his folded arms and thought back to those days when he was still green as a sapling, untested in combat, and his only reliable skill the ability to stay on a horse. "O'Dwyer fashioned us all into fighting soldiers through discipline. We were well-prepared when Cromwell's troops spread through Munster. O'Dwyer's a fine leader—the very best—and it's my privilege to serve him. I've moved up in his regard, and he's given me the commission of captain and entrusted me with the command of a company."

"You counted yourself with the Confederates?" Áine asked. "You were a rebel, then."

Niall squared his shoulders. "I am a patriot."

"Is there a difference?" Her tone was even, but it provoked him just the same.

"Sure, I nearly forgot that you are from Cork. You sound like a Protestant, Áine Callaghan."

"I belong to myself alone, Niall O'Coneill." She bent down to pick up her empty bowl, averting her gaze.

"What is that to mean?" He pushed away from the table and stared at her. "Are you saying you're a Protestant?"

She looked up, and to his surprise, what he saw in her luminous grey depths wasn't anger or annoyance, only weariness. The same weariness he had felt when he had cut down that man hanging from the tree. To his relief, she shook her head. "No, I am not saying that." She studied the bowl before her. "There may be more porridge at the bottom of the pot, if you care to have it."

Her answer momentarily took him aback. Something rose in him to shake the weariness out of her, to kindle in her the same fire he had felt. He brought his stool closer and rested his elbows on the table. "Leave the pease to their pot and think about what should be. Everyone who was born in Ireland, even those whose family are new to these shores, should have all the rights and freedoms of all Irishmen. We are Éireannach."

"The porridge lines my stomach, but the more men argue of such things, the less we have to fill our bowls," Áine said. "I do not concern myself with such matters. I am not political."

"Everyone is political," Niall said, sweeping aside his empty bowl. "Even the cattle are political."

Áine gave him a pointed look. "You needn't bring in the cows to your argument. It matters naught to them who rules the land, whether it's from Dublin or elsewhere." She picked up the bowls and stacked them neatly. "Men always stirring trouble to mask their own inadequacies. It doesn't matter if they are great lords or lowly black-smiths, they are all the same. It's the rest of us who pay the price."

"Are you content, then, for an invader to sweep through this country and seize it for their own?"

"What happens then after hostilities cease, after we've driven the English from our shores?" she asked. "Will we go back to fighting amongst ourselves? Will this ever end?"

Niall rose to his feet and strode to the fire. Grabbing the iron poker, he jabbed the burning logs, causing a spray of embers. "I will fight for as long as I can grip a sword. Ireland is both my mother and my sire — I will defend her until my dying breath —"

The cottage door slammed on its hinges, and a whoosh of cold air swept inside. Niall whirled around to find the room empty. Áine had taken his wolfhound and left the cottage. He closed his slack jaw and settled again on the stool. Her leaving was as loud a rebuke as he had ever heard.

CHAPTER 6

ÁINE RUSHED OUT into the yard with Fionn close on her heels. That ridiculous argument! *Politics and religion*, she fumed. Politics made fools of men while women knitted the broken threads, and religion had never offered succour, only delivered strife.

I'm not political, she had said, but Muiredach had been. Her step-brother's hate for the Irish Confederacy had been like a sickness. Áine quickly learned that talk about the Confederates and their rebellion for an independent Ireland would set him off—usually on her, starting with open hand slaps and working up to fists as the drink and the night grew old.

During the early years of the rebellion, Cork City had been an isolated enclave of Protestant might, carved off from the rest of Munster. Had it not been for the unrest beyond the walled town, she would have left a couple of years earlier and escaped Muiredach's control. She should have feared him more.

Niall's questions about her religion had cut too close to the bone. She had not lied, nor had she been entirely honest with him.

The Callaghans were Catholic, and for the first six years of her life, there had been no question that Áine had been too—until her widowed mother had done the unthinkable and taken for her second husband a Protestant.

Áine hadn't understood the arguments between her nan and her mother. She'd hidden in the hen cupboard, frightened of their raised voices.

"Foolish woman," Nan had hissed. "His kind will never accept you, and you will be rejected by our own. I will never forgive you if you become a heretic and raise my granddaughter outside of our faith. Think of her soul."

"I have my daughter's best interests at heart," her mother had answered, tight-lipped and resolute.

Nan had been right. Áine had found herself betwixt and between, not accepted by either. Nor had Nan spoken more than a smattering of words to her own daughter in the years left to her, but to Áine she'd taught the old stories, to remind the child of who she was.

Áine's precarious situation only intensified after the Catholics had been purged from the city. Her family's acquaintances had resented her for remaining, while the Protestant townsfolk regarded her with suspicion. And Nan, dearest Nan, had been forced to leave too. Áine's one connection to her past had been cruelly severed.

A few years later, when she'd finally seized the courage to flee Cork City, she'd vowed to discard her past like a dirty, stained garment. No one, not the Mulrianes and especially not Roisin, had known that she'd been raised Protestant. Niall O'Coneill most assuredly did not need to know either.

She reached the far end of the yard and halted.

Breathe, Áine, breathe. She inhaled the damp air and willed its cleansing breath to ease her ruffled nerves.

She needed to be alone. Sometimes she only wanted to hear the blessed silence of the wind. It had always been this way for her. Loud voices made her cringe, and heated arguments shredded her nerves. This was why the byre had always held for her a place of refuge. Cows were placid, blessed beasts, uncomplicated and quiet.

Fionn pressed against her hip to remind her of his presence. Áine dropped her hand on his shoulder and scratched behind his ears.

"Unsettled your disposition too, did he?" The hound leaned closer into her. "I thought so."

The wolfhound must have sensed that she was feeling better, for he loped off to explore the grounds. *On the scent of a rabbit, no doubt,* she thought.

Áine headed for the byre, far smaller than the Mulriane's, and slipped inside through the postern door.

The faint scent of cow and manure teased her. She closed her eyes, but instead of being soothed by the familiar smells, an odd discordant note crept in, very much like sadness and loss. No lowing cows. No nervous nickering of horses. Silence. Only a shell.

This wasn't her byre and offered little solace, but it might be good for now.

Áine settled on a milking stool and looked around at the dark rafters stretched overhead. The snugness of the cottage reminded her of the Duggan farm, with its rafters stacked with spare woollens and old pots scrubbed until nearly worn through. She might be content here. Even if the English returned, the byre did not differ from the places she had hidden during her flight from Cork. While she had not dared to appear at a doorstep and beg a crust of bread or place by the fire for fear of being chased away, she had slept in byres until first light before moving on. She had managed without being seen then and could do so again. Perhaps the Faerie Folk watched over her, as people claimed. They had certainly led her to the Mulrianes' door. To be safe, she'd continue leaving them a saucer of milk, if she could manage it.

Áine began to regret the argument with Niall. The Mulrianes had shown nothing but kindness to her, and she had repaid the favour by being churlish with their nephew. She had allowed her own frustration to get the better of her.

Best to head back to the cottage. She could not hide here for long, and he'd be ready to leave soon. Better to part on good terms.

Áine closed the byre door and headed back to the cottage. She kept her eyes fixed on the ground as she walked, her head full of melancholy thoughts. Then a distant rumbling penetrated her distraction. Thunder? She glanced up to check the leaden sky, then realised it wasn't coming from the ground. Turning towards the lane, her heart plummeted into her stomach.

English troopers.

Áine's inner voice screamed, but her limbs remained locked. She watched in growing horror as three horsemen swooped towards her.

Run!

She whirled around and ran as fast as she could to reach the safety of the byre.

Behind her, the drumming of hooves grew louder. They were closing in—she was still several yards away. One bellowed an exultant cry.

A rider overtook her, then reined in directly before her path. Áine cried out and checked her flight. She darted to the left, but there was another trooper, and when she whirled around, the third horseman blocked her way.

The troopers circled around her, laughing as they penned her in. Áine searched for an opening, her panic rising.

"Our day just improved," one soldier said with a raucous laugh. "I'm partial to redheads."

"A tender bit, I wager," another said.

Áine's stomach flipped. She knew that leer and what it meant for her.

"This one will fetch us a good coin," the third said.

Áine grew desperate. She tried to dart past them, to reach the safety of the byre, but they laughed and crowded her in.

A grey blur streaked across the yard, head down and muscles bunching. With the soldiers facing Áine, none saw the wolfhound until he was upon them.

Fionn rounded on the nearest redcoat and sank his teeth into his shank. The thrashing man screamed as he was dragged from his mount. He slammed to the ground and howled when his leg gave a distinctive crack. Faced with a snarling wolfhound, the horse bolted towards the byre.

Fionn turned on the remaining English troopers, advancing on them with sharp teeth barred. The soldiers backed their mounts up, fighting to keep their own horses from unseating them.

To Áine's horror, the redcoat drew a carbine from his belt, primed it and took aim at the wolfhound.

"Run Fionn! *Fly!*" She threw herself between Fionn and the soldiers. "Don't fire," she sobbed, waving her arms. "Don't—"

Thwap.

Áine screamed.

Everything froze—the hound, the soldiers, even her heart. Then the carbine slipped from the soldier's hand, and he hit the ground. A dagger protruded from the base of his skull, and Niall stood behind him, twenty feet away, poised to throw another dagger.

The third soldier wheeled his mount around and scrambled to prime his carbine just as Niall threw the blade. One, two turns before it embedded itself in the man's shoulder. The man jerked back and fought to remain in his saddle.

Fionn lunged for him, but before the wolfhound could pull him down, the officer booted the animal in the chest. Niall tried to snatch the reins, but the horse sidestepped. Applying spurs to his horse's sides, the captain bolted past them and down the lane.

Niall whistled sharply to Fionn and set him to chase after the fleeing English soldier. Like an arrow, the wolfhound shot after him, but the horse galloped as though the hounds of hell were after it.

"Blight the bastard!" Niall shouted as the horse evaded Fionn and increased the distance between them. He swore again when the wolfhound gave up the chase and the horseman disappeared from sight.

Niall pried his stag-horn dagger from the dead soldier and wiped the blood on his breeches. He turned to Áine, who had not moved from her spot. "Are you harmed?"

She shook her head and clenched her chattering teeth. "They nearly killed Fionn."

"There will be an accounting." Niall turned to the remaining Englishman, who was attempting to drag himself away. As he scraped and crawled, the man kept looking over his shoulder, terror and pain contorting his face.

Niall reached the English trooper in several long strides. He grabbed him by the back of his coat and hauled him up before flinging him on his back. The soldier screamed in agony, clutching his bleeding and broken leg.

Drawing his sword, Niall pressed the tip against the man's throat. "Where is your camp? Are you holding prisoners?" When the man didn't answer, Niall slammed his foot on the man's broken leg, ignoring the gurgled scream that exploded from his mouth.

Áine covered her mouth and looked away.

Niall shouted at the soldier. "A pox on you. *Where are they?*"

"We have to leave," Áine gasped. "Before the soldier returns with reinforcements."

Niall ignored her. He bent down and looked the English soldier in the eye. "Who's your captain—is it Garret?"

"Aye," the man gritted between his teeth.

"Did you attack the manor at An Gallbhaile?" At first, the man looked at him blankly, but when Niall said, "Two leagues west of here. The lord and lady of the manor were murdered." The soldier's eyes rounded with fear. "That's what I thought."

Before Áine knew what he was about to do, Niall plunged his blade deep into the man's stomach. She muffled her shriek by clamping her mouth.

"This is how it will end," Niall said, surprisingly calm. "If you tell me what I need to know, I'll reward you with a quick death. Otherwise, I'll leave you to die slowly and painfully. Did Garret order the attack?"

The soldier panted, his face twisted in agony. "We were there— captain's orders." His gaze drifted to the direction the other soldier had fled. "Not my fault . . . war . . ."

Niall's expression hardened. He twisted the knife in the man's belly, and the man screamed. Áine covered her ears. "Where are they —the women, the servants from the manor? *Answer me!*"

The soldier gasped, "Sold . . . Captain sold them as indentured servants. . . shipped out of Cork."

Áine lowered her hands from her ears, not sure she had heard him right.

Niall's expression revealed his horror. "What?"

"Transported."

Niall paled. "God confound me, body and soul." He grabbed the man by the coat and shook him. "Transported where? Where were they sent?"

The man cried out in pain. "The colonies," he gasped.

Áine stared at the man in horror. Indentured? Taken away? All of them?

"Bastards," Niall screamed in his face.

The soldier's mouth twisted in pain. "Go to hell."

"God's curse upon you all, for as long as you seek to occupy this land," Niall said before driving his sword through the soldier's throat. Blood spurted through his life vein and soaked the ground.

Áine grew cold with shock. The blood, thick, sticky blood. She had seen so much violence in her life that she had thought herself numb to it, but she began to tremble, fighting against the scream that clawed at her throat.

When Niall straightened, Áine flinched. A feral wildness lit his eyes. "As the man said, this is war."

Áine closed her eyes, searching inside for a safe haven. What difference this than the heroic legends, tales of warriors and battles, that she had loved so well? What difference between Niall O'Coneill than either Cúchulainn or Fionn mac Cumhaill defending their people and vanquishing their enemies? "I understand," she assured him, then with strengthening conviction added, "I do."

Niall grabbed the only remaining horse by the bridle. "New direction," he said as though he were swallowing bile. "We're going to my camp. The English will swarm this place and damned if I'm going to put another innocent at risk." Before he mounted the animal, he turned to Áine and stretched out his hand to her. "You're coming with me."

This was not a question, nor was he giving her a choice. Áine wanted to weep in frustration, but he was right. The English would return to this place and with greater numbers, and if they caught her, she'd be sure to suffer the same fate as Niall's sister. The horror of that possibility could not be matched.

Áine took Niall's hand and, with his help, mounted the horse. He swung up behind her and gathered the reins. For a moment, Niall faced the direction the lone soldier had fled, eastwards down the Glen of Aherlow, where they had been heading. The urge to give chase surely warred inside him. Then, with an anguished expression, he turned his horse and headed south towards the mountains.

CHAPTER 7

SOLD. Indentured against her will.

God's curse upon them all.

Niall had heard stories of captured Irish prisoners being forcibly transported to the colonies, pressed against their will. Eight years of indentured servitude. Now the bastards had taken his sister, his bright, clever sister, and shipped her to one of their infernal colonies across a wide ocean, to serve the whims of an Englishman.

With each downstroke of his horse's hooves, fury pounded through Niall's head. He tried to smother the rage, keep it from tearing him apart.

The horse pulled against the bit and began to fight against Niall. Áine wobbled, and her gasp brought Niall to his senses. His arm curled around her, and he pressed her firmly against his chest to steady her.

Niall exhaled a ragged breath to clear his mind and slackened the reins—he had been clutching them in a punishing grip. First thing, he had to get them safely away. He was responsible for more than himself now.

Focus.

He now had confirmation that it had been Garret behind the

attack, behind his sister's wretched debasement. Niall clutched that information, imagined what he would do to Garret when the man was finally at Niall's mercy. But right now he needed to get them safely back to camp without leaving a broad enough trail that a blind Englishman could follow.

"Are we lost? We seem to be going around in circles," Áine said, tipping her head to study the direction of the sun.

"We're not lost, but this winding route is necessary." After a few moments, he said, "The camp has few comforts. We live rough on the ground."

"I'm not as frail as you may think," Áine said, and in a small voice added, "But I wish I could have stayed in the shepherd's hut."

Niall set a determined pace, only allowing for periods of brief rest to water and spare the horse. He often had to backtrack to confuse any possible pursuers before going a roundabout way south towards the Galtees.

Fionn loped ahead on the road before them, close enough to give Niall sufficient warning of danger. A couple of hours into their flight, the wolfhound stopped, his muscular body tensed. Niall checked his horse and led the animal off the road, making for a stand of yew trees that hid them from sight.

Niall handed the reins to Áine and swung down from their mount. "Wait here." He looked over his shoulder and added, "Do what you can to keep this nag quiet. Stay here no matter what happens."

"Don't do anything rash," Áine said in a small voice, no doubt fearing what would befall her if he didn't return.

"I won't."

Niall left Áine and crept back to the road, as close as he dared. He pulled his grey mantle over his head and hunkered down in a small gully, hidden behind a fallen tree. Fionn soon found him, and together they waited.

The rhythmic thudding of hooves sounded before a quarter troop of enemy horsemen came into view. They progressed at a steady canter, their colours brazenly flapping in the wind—red with the prominent Cross of St. George stitched on the canton. Niall scanned the soldiers but did not see Garret.

Garret. That bastard had pressed his sister into indentured service —or worse. Eight years of service may as well be a lifetime. Few ever returned.

White-hot rage shot through his veins. Mairead was beyond reach. Their father would never see his only daughter, never look upon her face and see his departed wife's likeness. If the captain rode past him at this moment, Niall would gladly dispatch him to hell, even if he had to deliver the whoreson there himself.

Niall gritted his teeth to keep from screaming his fury. A pale, terrified woman waited in a stand of trees, and he had promised her that he wouldn't do anything rash.

As the last troopers disappeared from sight, Niall made his way back to Áine. She was where he had left her, bent over the neck of the horse, trying to keep the animal quiet. When she saw him, relief washed over her face.

"You've returned."

Niall's single-minded focus softened when he took in her anxiousness. She had been through so much so far. This couldn't be easy for her. "I promised I'd return for you, Áine," he said in a softer tone, "and I'm a man of my word."

He mounted his horse, settling himself once more behind her. Instead of turning his horse back the way they came, he guided the animal farther into the forest. "The English have forced us to seek a different way."

They continued without rest. Niall was used to living on horseback, but this pace was taking its toll on Áine. She had not complained even once, but the droop of her shoulders and wan complexion spoke of her fatigue. Riding in front of him, her skirt bunched up mid-shin, giving Niall a glimpse of slim legs between the top of her worn shoes to the hem of her begrimed skirt. Loose tendrils of hair escaped her plait and brushed against his jaw, a red pennant lifting in the wind. He tried to put it from his mind, but the silky strands teased and beguiled.

When exhaustion had gotten the better of Áine and she

started to nod off, Niall tightened his hold around her waist, adjusting his seat so he could cushion her in his arms. He tucked the top of her head under his chin and, against his better judgment, savoured the warmth that seeped through her woollen mantle. His gaze dropped to the scar on her wrist, and, curiosity getting the better of him, he touched the burn. Áine jolted awake, her head knocking Niall under the chin. He grunted and rubbed away the pain as she glanced around in disorientation.

"Sorry," he told her thickly.

Áine looked around. "Should we not have arrived by now?"

"Nearly there." Provided the camp hadn't moved—or been attacked.

A coldness gripped Niall's belly at the thought. He had been away for over a month and didn't know what to expect, which was why he had taken a cautious approach. Their encampment was in Glengarra Woods, nestled within the mighty Galtee Mountains. The brigade had been forced to change location several times over the past year to avoid being discovered by English patrols. And now with Diarmuid's capture and murder, Niall needed to be prepared if the camp had been razed. For now, the maid didn't need to know of his fears.

The mountain passes were a crisscross of trails broken by running streams and gullies. Thick woods swallowed them up, leaf litter forming a carpet that muffled the sounds of their passage. The trail sloped upwards, and in places Niall was forced to dismount and guide the horse until the path levelled off again.

They finally reached the lower gorge, where the trail narrowed like the point of an arrow. As they approached the river, the sharp cry of a sparrowhawk rose in the wind. Up ahead, Fionn froze. He sniffed the air, then crept towards a stand of reeds.

Niall reined in his mount and handed the reins to Áine. Cupping his hands to his mouth, he mimicked the hoot of an owl—friend, all clear. A moment passed before he received an answering hoot. Fionn bounded ahead.

As they neared the reeds, a sentinel stirred amongst the brown stalks. A short, barrel-chested man lowered his musket and stepped into the open. "Niall?"

"Cormac." A great weight lifted from Niall. Cormac was his own lieutenant, and if the man stood at the first sentry point, the camp was still safe. "Never have I been more relieved to see your gnarly face." Despite all he had been through in the past couple of days, Niall broke into a tired smile.

"Glad to see you, finally," Cormac said. "Ruadhri wagered half the camp that you had been captured."

"Sorry to disappoint him."

"He now owes me a small fortune." Cormac grinned. What news of the road?"

"There were complications." Niall's gaze slid to Áine.

"Some complications may be easily borne." Cormac's gaze lingered on Áine, and his grin widened. "Figured you wouldn't be in a great hurry to end your sojourn at Ross Castle—proper beds and all." His smile deepened, revealing a crooked gap between his two front teeth. "But here you are, arriving like the blessed King of Connacht with a faerie bride."

"Jealous?"

"A little."

"You should be," Niall said.

Áine turned to look at Niall, her brow slightly arched. He held her gaze, causing her cheeks to blaze like the dawn. She lowered her head and fixed on Fionn, who had returned to their side.

"I'll be looking for that story over a cup of ale, O'Coneill," Cormac said, stepping aside.

"When you're released from duty, come find me at the fires," Niall said. "Until then." He whistled for Fionn and, with a nod, rode past Cormac.

As they neared camp, Niall spied more sentries, and he lifted a hand in greeting to those he knew. The way narrowed, lined on one side with scrubby trees and on the other a hillside buttressed with rocks. On the breeze, the familiar scent of burning wood from camp-fires beckoned Niall forward. Fionn lifted his nose to taste the air and set off ahead at a brisker pace.

When the trees thinned, the first rough shelters began to appear, haphazard lean-tos framed with cut branches and roofed by ever-green boughs. Campfires burned, scattered through the rough compound, with a few care-worn women tending the cook fires. Men bent at their tasks, repairing their equipment; sharpening blades scraped against the grit of whetstones, and anvil meeting steel rang out. Several young women drove a score of dairy cows, prodding them along with sticks.

Áine perked up at the sight, head turning as they passed the herd. "I expected only soldiers to be here," she said with clear relief. In the distance, more cattle grazed. "There's a sizeable herd here." Four score at least. "It reminds me of a booleying camp."

Niall hadn't considered it that way. "In addition to the soldiers, there are many here who were forced to leave their villages. We move around a great deal, but our needs are determined by avoiding the English, not finding the best summer pastures for the herd."

Áine craned her head as they passed a large group of men. "There are so many gathered here." She didn't sound awed as much as worried.

"The other camps are spread out through Glengarra Woods. It's a vast area with hidden glens and valleys. At this location, we have about a hundred and fifty horse and five hundred foot, but this is only a quarter of our strength."

Rather than taking comfort with these numbers, the maid chewed her lip and fell silent.

They rounded one of the larger shelters pushed up against a hillock, and a brawny man, another of Niall's men, appeared on the crest of the hill, his lime-washed hair white and braided in the fashion of a horse's mane. Calling down to Niall, he lifted his musket in a salute. "Took your sweet-arsed time returning, O'Coneill. I wagered we'd not see you again."

"Ruadhri." Normally, he'd have a countering quip for him, but Niall could not muster more than a brief nod. Old friends greeted him, and a few of the camp women called out ribald greetings. Áine shifted slightly to look at him, and he fixed on a point past her head, trying to avoid her quizzical stare.

Half a dozen soldiers were camped outside Colonel Edmund O'Dwyer's personal quarters, which was little more than a canvas tent stretched over poles made from stout tree limbs. The men were gathered around a small fire and a rowdy game of dice when Niall arrived.

Donogh O'Dwyer, the commander's cousin, detached himself from the game and strode to Niall, blinking as though doubting his own eyes. "Saints preserve us all. He's neither dead nor taken." Donogh bellowed in the direction of the tent. "Edmund! The prodigal returns."

A moment later, the tent flap parted and O'Dwyer stepped outside, clearly irritated. He was plainly dressed, and anyone who did not know better could have easily mistaken him for a lowly captain. But he wore his authority as effortlessly as another would a mantle. When he saw Niall, his irritation vanished.

"Niall," he said, a smile lurking behind his stern façade. "I'm eager to hear the news." His gaze slid to Áine. "All the news."

"Wait for me here," Niall said, handing Áine the reins. "I'll get you settled as soon as I finish."

Áine nodded, but her gaze darted to the men standing about. Niall couldn't help but notice how fiercely she clutched the leather reins and the frantic pulse that leapt in the hollow of her throat. The urge to gather her in his arms rose in him, and he nearly reached for her, but he remembered how she had recoiled from his touch in the shepherd's hut. "Every man here will be sure to behave, won't you lads?" This last he said loudly so his voice carried. After hearing a few grumbled agreements, he left Fionn with Áine and followed O'Dwyer into his quarters.

Niall ducked his head under the tent flap and squinted to adjust to the dimness of the room. A pallet of green reeds served as a bed in one corner, and a wide tree stump did duty as a table. A flask and four cups were placed on top.

"Drink?" O'Dwyer handed him a cup. All previous humour had fled, leaving him grim. A few silver threads shone against his black hair. "It's the last casket of *uisge beatha*."

Niall didn't hesitate. After pouring them both a healthy draught, he tossed his back. The liquor burned down his throat, and Niall welcomed the searing heat. A second brought a welcome numbing.

"That dire?" O'Dwyer asked.

Niall handed over the dispatch, sealed with Viscount Muskerry's coat of arms.

O'Dwyer broke the seal and read through the letter quickly. "Still no promised aid from the Duke of Lorraine." He sank down on a stool. "What the hell are we supposed to do now?" Their supplies were dangerously low, and without ammunition and weapons, they couldn't carry on against the English.

"The ships might still come," Niall said.

O'Dwyer shot him a dark look. "We should never have put all our faith in that quarter," he muttered under his breath. "Not that we had a choice."

The hard reality was that they could expect no assistance from their exiled king, Charles Stuart. His attempt to win back his crown had been trounced at Worcester when his Scottish army had been beaten, and he had barely escaped England with his life. Now he was in France, licking his wounds, while the French king, his cousin, re-evaluated his country's position with the new English Common-wealth. Only the Duke of Lorraine had been willing to bend his private fortune towards the aid of Ireland.

A month ago—a week even, Niall would have maintained his trust that aid was coming. A stupid, naive hope. Even if the ships were dispatched, anything could happen to them—intercepted by pirates or the English navy, beaten back by the weather. Winter seas were fickle.

And what if they don't come? Niall hadn't wanted to think of it before, had grown impatient when others would pester him with this dark possibility. But now there was no denying it. They couldn't go on.

"We're down to our remaining stores," O'Dwyer said. "Our ammunition is running low, and there's little fodder for the horses that are left to us." He glanced down at the letter again. "Muskerry has sent more pleas for supplies to France and Flanders and given instructions as to the safest ports in which to land." He crumpled the paper in his hand and snorted. "Assuming they haven't been playing us for fools all this time." O'Dwyer turned to Niall. "Tell me about Muskerry at Ross Castle. What's the state of his supplies?"

Niall shook his head. "The stronghold is secure, but his supplies are as depleted as ours. He has none to spare, else I would have brought back what I could. I delayed my return, hoping the ships would come—that I could bring you better news."

"What of the woman?" O'Dwyer asked. "Did you bring her from Ross?"

Niall scrubbed his hand against his stubbled chin. "I passed by my uncle's estate . . ." He had been living with the horror in his head, but now that he would have to speak of it, the words dried up. "On my way from Ross Castle, I saw some worrisome signs. Enemy troops ranging far from the security of their garrisons—on the other side of the Galtee Mountains. I thought to check in on my kin."

"You delayed my dispatches for a visit?"

"I had hoped to bring you more information," Niall said, deftly stepping around the sinking bog.

O'Dwyer's brow lifted, but he did not pursue it. "How did you find them—your kin?"

Niall's mind was filled with the charred remains of the byre and the cairn of rocks. He fell back on his soldier's training and pushed it from his mind. "Gone. Killed. Their property burned. Áine, the maid, was the only survivor. I could not leave her behind."

O'Dwyer was silent for a moment, then Niall felt the man's reassuring hand squeeze his shoulder. "I'm sorry."

"It was the work of Captain Garret."

"I know that name," O'Dwyer said, frowning.

"Captain John Garret of Colonel Sankey's dragoons. He was one of the English officers we ransomed last year."

"You sure he was responsible?" O'Dwyer asked.

Niall looked away. "He and his men returned to finish off the looting. They were heading with full speed back to Cashel." Then he explained how he had run into their scouts. "My sister . . . was taken prisoner by the English, along with the rest of my kin. She, and the others, have been pressed into indentured service—transported to one of the colonies."

"You have my deepest sympathies, Niall."

Niall's temper pricked. He needed more than just sympathy. "With all due respect, what I need is your blessing to take out a raiding party to track down Garret and his men. Cormac, Ruadhri—also Purcell, McTiege and any others we can spare. I'll set out at first light—"

"No."

"I wouldn't want to leave later."

"I'll rephrase it—request declined. You're not going anywhere."

Niall questioned his hearing. "What? Why?"

"There will be no roughshod raiding parties," O'Dwyer said. "We're barely surviving here. Supplies are at their lowest levels, and we need more than ammunition and weapons. We need grain and fodder for our suffering horses and to fill our bellies. Our focus must be on intercepting as many enemy supply wagons as possible. This is how we survive to fight the next day and the next, for as you can see, we're on our own."

"I'm not asking you to divert a regiment," Niall said. "A small company—my own men that you gave me to command and lead."

"I didn't give you command for you to use the men in your quest for vengeance. I will not allow you to throw away good men." The first stirrings of anger betrayed O'Dwyer. "You're thinking with your gut, not your head. Self-discipline wins battles—it wins the day."

"When have you known me not to be disciplined?"

"Never, but your people have never been directly attacked before," he replied.

Anger throbbed in Niall's temple. "If you are telling me to bury it, to forget, by God, I will not. I will have my vengeance for what they did to my family—what they've done to my sister. She is lost to me —" Niall's voice caught in his throat. "I know she's beyond my help, but for every tear they made her shed, by God, I will make them weep blood."

"Niall—"

"If this had happened to your family—to your wife—you would

have burnt down half of Tipperary. Deny it, and I'll call you out as a liar."

"O'Coneill," O'Dwyer's tone grew flint-hard.

"What are we fighting for? Inch by inch we give ground and swallow more and more defeat. Are we fighting for the mastery over bogs, or are we fighting for people?"

"That's enough," O'Dwyer snapped. "Our cause is greater than one man or one woman."

Niall glared, his nostrils flaring. "I will avenge my kin."

"We are your kin now." O'Dwyer came up to Niall and placed a hand on his shoulder. "You've been with me for ten years, and you're one of the best fighters I have." His hand curled around Niall's neck. "You've never failed to use your cunning and your wits. Use them now. Rush out now and the memory of your kin will die with you. Is this what you want?"

Niall felt the hot fury of his anger leach off, but it hardened into resolve. He knew O'Dwyer was right, knew that he'd get only once chance to get the bastard, and he'd have to gauge the time carefully. He gave a short shake of his head.

"Good." O'Dwyer's expression softened. "I'm not telling you to forget or to bury this assault. Boil down your rage until it's concentrated and focused, not resembling a scattered burst of grapeshot. Understood?"

"Ay." The admission was bitter on his tongue.

"Now get the maid sorted out and return in an hour for a council meeting. We have decisions to make."

Niall nodded and headed for the entrance. Before he left, he said, "I will get Garret. If it takes me the rest of my years, he will pay for this."

"Ay, but not today."

Áine read the poor news across Niall's darkened brow when he left his commander's tent. He spoke a few terse words to one of the soldiers before rejoining her.

"Is everything well?" she asked him.

Niall made a vague sound. "We'll need to get you settled. Eireen will give you a place at her hearth."

"You seem so sure when you haven't asked her yet," Áine said.

Niall quirked a wry glance. "I may not be sure of many things, Áine Callaghan, but I know Eireen won't fail me."

They made their way through the forest encampment until they reached a generous tent. Niall halted before the campfire and dismounted. He tied the reins to the trunk of an arched sapling. One young woman was stirring a pot while another was feeding the fire. Both stopped their labours to smile at Niall most prettily. Áine they ignored.

"Welcome back, Niall," one called out to him. She pressed the staff she held against her bosom and arched her back.

"We're glad to see you safe and hale," the other said, her face colouring.

Áine caught the quirk of his brow, but he managed to keep his tone even. "Thank you both. Is Eireen here?"

Before anyone could answer, a shriek sounded from inside the shelter. A young lad bolted out, chased by a tall, wiry woman armed with a round spoon and a clear determination to mete out justice. The lad collided straight into Niall and, before he could extricate himself, found the scruff of his neck seized by Eireen. He crammed a stolen oatcake into his mouth.

"If I catch you stealing once more, you little thief, I will drop your breeches and cane you blue," Eireen railed.

"I'm sorry, Eireen." The crumbs sprouting from the rascal's mouth ruined the contrite words.

Eireen clucked her tongue in disgust. She shook him for good measure. The lad squirmed out of her grasp and scampered off like a rabbit, but not before Áine noticed the slight bulge of contraband under his shirt.

Áine hid her smile and coughed into her hand. Niall looked up and exchanged an amused glance with her. A warmth spread through her at this shared moment.

Fionn rushed up to Eireen, and she started laughing a deep, rich chuckle that started in her belly and bubbled out from her lips.

"You've finally returned," she said to Niall as she fussed over Fionn. "Many were worried that something had happened to you."

Niall grimaced. "I hope you can make room for another, Eireen."

The matron fixed her sharp gaze to Áine, who squirmed in the saddle uncomfortably. "Where did you find her?"

"She was a dairymaid in my uncle's household."

"I can always use another dairymaid," Eireen said.

Niall offered his hand to help Áine dismount. His strong fingers curled around her waist, and he helped lift her from the horse. Áine could feel his touch even after he released her. When she looked up, she found that suddenly she was the centre of attention, with the women from the cook fires sending her riddling looks.

"If you don't mind working, you're welcome to stay. Mind your manners and your modesty. I won't be having the men sniffing around here like bees to honey."

"Now, Eireen, you do us ill," Niall said with a cajoling smile.

Áine found herself pulled in. *Sweet God Almighty. That smile is lethal.* Fionn brushed against her. Grateful for the distraction, she scratched behind his ears.

"Don't *now, Eireen* me, you rascal. It's a full-time job to protect my girls from the wandering eyes of your men, and well you know it. Besides, we need your men steady and focused, not lazy and slack."

Áine hung back, plucking self-consciously at her fingers. At the woman's words, she relaxed slightly. Already, she could tell the matron was fearsome. She only hoped that the force of this woman's protection would extend to her. "I would be grateful for your kindness, Eireen," she said softly. "I won't be causing you any trouble."

Eireen lifted her head and frowned at the maids who stood around idle. She planted her hands on her hips and glared at them. "And what's this? Have you all run out of work?" That was enough to scatter them like leaves on the wind.

Niall touched the small of Áine's back and drew her aside. "You'll do well with Eireen here."

Áine nodded and tried to tamp down her disappointment at being parted from him. She hadn't wanted to come with him, she reminded herself, and he was practically feral. "Thank you for your help—for everything."

"I will check in on you later," he said, clearing his throat.

"As you can," she said, oddly moved.

When Áine looked up, she noticed four young women gathered close, all ears and crackling attention. Waves of emotions radiated from them—some annoyed, others amused and all burning with a naked curiosity.

Niall whistled for Fionn. Áine seized one last pat before the wolfhound left her side.

The feeling of being cut adrift intensified as she watched Niall ride away. For the last few days, he had been central to her survival; now his world swallowed him whole. Although she was used to being solitary, this new absence felt strange to her—doubly alone.

Niall O'Coneill had done what he had promised to do, see her to safety, and now he had more pressing matters to consider than a homeless dairymaid. At best, she might run into him now and then, but eventually he would forget her name. Most usually did. She preferred it that way.

Áine pushed aside regret and, squaring her shoulders, faced these women. Eireen watched her as a hawk would a mouse.

"What do they call you?" Eireen asked her.

"Áine Callaghan."

"Are you his woman?"

Oh, the bluntness of old women. "Most assuredly no."

The young women relaxed slightly and exchanged smiles with one another, but Eireen's brow quirked. "You could do worse." When the old woman turned away, Áine thought she saw her smile.

Eireen clapped her hands, startling Áine, and set the girls to dashing about their work. "I don't coddle anyone who cares to stay under my roof." She glanced at the rough shelter and shrugged to herself. "Poverty waits at the gates of idleness." Handing two buckets to Áine, she said, "Fetch us some water, girl. The stream is yonder, past those aspens." She nodded to a southern sloping field. "And be quick about it. Lose an hour in the morning and you'll be looking for it all day." With a gentle push, Eireen nudged Áine towards the stream.

As Áine ventured through the camp, she became bewildered by the teeming mass of people. The shouting, the clanging of sword play, the grinding wheels sharpening blades. It was disorienting and alarming, and Áine's apprehension intensified to the point where her breathing became shallow gasps. Men stopped to look at her, their curiosity probing.

To get away from them, she dashed into the centre of a ring of patchwork tents and came up against a blazing campfire. A young lad stoked the fire while a blacksmith heated a length of iron. He pulled the red-hot metal from the flames and started hammering it atop a flat rock set up like an anvil.

Bang. Bang. With every fall of the hammer, the dull ringing sound cut through Áine. Her ears rang with it and her nostrils were assaulted by the stench of hot iron. She hurriedly backed away, then ran into a man carrying an armful of broken swords.

Ooff.

The man drew back and, in the process, dropped several of the swords. "Watch where you're going," he snarled.

"Sorry." Áine tried to bolt but came up hard against another man hauling a sack over his shoulder. She lifted her buckets in a defensive gesture and reeled backwards. She fought to keep her balance and keep herself upright, swinging the buckets as a counterweight. Her foot hooked on a stone, causing her to crash to the ground.

"Mind the fire, wench!" a woman screeched.

Áine felt the heat on her back and shrieked. She thrashed against her twisted skirt, but her legs only tangled further. She heaved herself to her knees and rose on shaky legs, edging away from the fire. Her gaze locked on the roaring flames, and she stared in sick fascination, unable to break its strange hold over her. The wind fanned over the burning logs, sending up a spray of sparks.

In that moment, she was back at the O'Keefe forge, attempting to evade her stepbrother, Muiredach. The memories rose to blind her to the present. Muiredach cornered her and feinted a lunge. She tried to dart past, but his hands clamped around her like a steel trap.

"Where are you going, kitten?" he whispered in her ear. His breath reeked of strong liquor, and she strained against him. "Forgot your manners?" He had never failed to twist her gut and make her feel unclean—wrong.

"Release me." *Must not cry. Must not show fear.*

"Or what?" He twisted her arm until she bit her lip and tasted blood. With an effort, she managed to slap him in the face.

Muiredach recoiled. "Slut! I'll teach you." He dragged her towards the forge. Áine dug her heels into the ground. She whimpered—fought to break free. He thrust her hand into the fire. *Curl your fingers. Make them small.*

Muiredach snarled. "Feel the heat. Be a good girl, or taste the flames."

Áine shrieked in pain. The flames burned her flesh—the pain went deeper.

Laughing, Muiredach released her, and she scrambled to the slack tub and plunged her burning hand into the tepid water.

"That's what happens when you defy me." Muiredach kicked the tub over, spilling the water. "Now fetch me more."

Cold water dashed over Áine's skirt and splashed into her face, jolting her out of her nightmarish memories. A woman holding a dripping basin came into focus. Áine looked down at her smoking skirt, horrified to see how close she had come to being burned. Again.

"What's the matter with you, daft girl?" the woman said, tamping out the remaining sparks on her skirt.

Áine focused on the harassed matron before her. A wide-swathed apron clung around the woman's middle, stained with dirt, blood and grease.

The matron's irritation softened to puzzlement. "Have you hurt yourself? Are you simple in the head, child?"

Áine shook her head before finding her voice. "My apologies— my . . . my thoughts were elsewhere." She grabbed her buckets and dashed off.

The incident had left Áine even more disoriented. She looked around for a view of the stream, but all she could see now were makeshift shelters.

Áine plunged towards the direction she supposed led to the stream and came upon a group of men wrestling in a muddy field. The shouts of encouragement and wagering thundered in her ears. Too much noise—far too much for her senses to bear.

A brawny man stepped into her path. His hair had been limed and braided to resemble a horse's mane. She immediately recognised him as one of the men greeting Niall earlier. "Just arrived, didn't you, sweet?"

Áine wasn't taken with his pleasant words; his tone was all wrong. Roving eyes and eager smile told a different tale.

"Not a haughty wench, are you?"

A bolder woman would have brazened this out and left the men laughing uproariously, declaring her a fine girl. But Áine did not have a glib tongue. What was she expected to do? Smile, and she'd only encourage them. Remain silent, and they'd deride her for a haughty snit.

Leave. Flee. Get away from here.

Áine tried to dart away, but Horse-Mane anticipated her move and blocked her way again. Áine backed away and bumped into someone who had come up behind her—a lanky, whiplike man.

The men began to crowd her in, studying her as though she were a wild and strange creature. They spoke over her to each other, commenting on her face and manner. Why didn't she smile? Was there something wrong with her that she wasn't more friendly? The circle closed in on her, and she whirled around like a cornered animal.

Áine shrank from them. She opened her mouth to tell them to back off but found her voice came out as a croak.

"What's your name, sweeting?" Horse-Mane tugged at her plait. "I admit to having a weakness for red-haired wenches. I don't see O'Coneill with you—he won't mind."

Áine pulled away. "Leave me alone." *Make them think I don't care, that I'll rip the throat out of anyone who dares to touch.* "Stay away."

But her bravado was met with guffaws. "I don't think she cares for you, Ruadhri," someone called out to Horse-Mane. "I'll wager a silver sixpence that you won't get her name from her."

"For that, I'll name her myself." Ruadhri thrust out his chest and laughed.

That pierced through Áine's distress. She was *not* anyone's to be named. It had been bad enough that she had been taunted and shamed most of her life. Strangeling. Touched by the Faerie Folk, others would sneer. She didn't need another label to be strung around her neck like a milestone.

A shame she didn't have Otherworld magic, else she could curse them into silence.

Words had power, and although she had never presumed to wield them, it wasn't too late to try. The men's rowdiness began to spiral out of control. Now or never. She fixed Ruadhri with an assessing gaze and took his measure. Vain braggart. In as commanding a voice as she could muster, she called out so everyone could hear, "Leave me be, or I'll invoke a curse." With her chief tormentor in mind, she continued, "To any who are foolish enough to persist in their harassment, may they be cursed to fade into nothing, like snow in summer."

Many drew back, giving a healthy space. A few even spat on the ground. "My nan was cursed by her neighbour," one man muttered. "She went blind soon after."

Ruadhri's expression mirrored his alarm. "Why would you do such a thing, being new here as you are?" he said to Áine. "Is this your concept of reaping endearments—threatening us with curses?"

Áine's first inclination was to brush it off as a harmless misunderstanding, but she hardened her heart. Weakness was easily manipulated, and she had no stomach for checking over her shoulder every time she went anywhere. "Best we understand each other clearly," she told him. "You seem to be a clever fellow who won't allow your own tongue to be the rope that hangs yourself."

Ruadhri rubbed the back of his neck. "A man needs to blow a little steam now and then," he said sullenly.

"Within reason," Áine said. She pressed her knees together to keep them from quaking.

Finally, he nodded. "No harm, then?"

"No harm." She glanced down at her empty buckets and wondered if she dared more? *Why not?* Lifting them, she said, "A blessing on anyone who can direct me to the stream. I can't seem to find it."

Ruadhri gave her a relieved grin. "We can all use a blessing. The water is that way."

Áine gave him a grave nod and set out for the stream. A disturbance rippled around her, making her pause. Several horsemen arrived in the encampment to calls of welcome and demands for news, with Ruadhri being the loudest. One of the men turned his head to respond to Ruadhri, and Áine got a clear view of him. She inhaled sharply and quickly pulled the edge of her mantle forward to cover her head.

Banan Molloy. Even at a distance, she recognised him.

While the two men greeted each other, laughing and exchanging bawdy jests, Áine melted into the background. If only she could disappear entirely.

An ill wind had blown Banan here. It had been four years since Áine had last seen the man, days before she had run away from Muiredach.

For a couple of years, Banan had been an inseparable companion to her stepbrother, each man goading the other on and bringing out the worst in their natures.

It was only a matter of time before Banan learned that she was here.

Sooner than later, there would be a reckoning.

And what could he do to her? Send word to Muiredach that his long-lost stepsister was in a soldier's camp? Not with an enemy army between here and Cork City, he couldn't. But the persistent churning of her stomach told her that his presence alone was bad enough.

Here was proof that the past could still hunt her down even in this isolated location.

CHAPTER 8

AFTER NIALL LEFT Áine with Eireen — he hoped she'd settle in — he led his newfound horse to the paddock to attend to its needs. He slid a feed bag over its head while he brushed the brown coat. Brushing the animal in long, rhythmic strokes helped to ease his unsettled mood, allowing him to think.

O'Dwyer would change his mind — *give him time*, he told himself. The man had only just received ill news. A few days would do it.

Niall continued his ministrations and found the nag in better shape than the other horses in the brigade, and this annoyed him to no end.

"And why should English horses get better fodder than our own?" he asked the beast. In answer, it flicked its tail. "Cheeky bastard."

No use looking a gift horse in the mouth. The brigade needed all the able mounts they could muster, and the fact that this one came from the enemy was sweet revenge.

"O'Coneill," a man called out. "Pleased to see you back."

Niall looked up to see Eamon Grace riding into the paddock ahead of several of his men and smiled. No tired garron for Eamon. The man had discriminating taste in horseflesh and spent a great deal of effort to care for the bay he rode now. The Graces had extensive pasture lands and had been neighbours to the Mulrianes for generations. Before the war, Eamon had been known for the quality of his stables. When Niall had visited with the Mulrianes as a youth, he and Diarmuid had pestered Eamon, nearly twenty years Niall's senior, to ride his newest colts.

"Eamon." Niall raised his hand in greeting. "You've just come in yourself."

"Patrols to the north and east. I've been a fortnight in the saddle, and if I don't get back on this nag in my lifetime," he said with obvious affection, "I'll be a happy man."

Eamon dismounted and handed the reins to one of the farriers. In a few strides, he reached Niall and drew him into a hearty embrace. "How was the trip to Kerry? I'd wager you were partaking of the pleasures Ross Castle afforded?" A wide grin split his face. "Do I have that right?"

Niall answered with a wan smile. "Enough of that for now. I have news for you, if you can spare a moment."

"By your sombre face, I'm already dreading it."

"Did you say you made it east? As far as Cashel?"

"In the shadow of the Rock itself," Eamon said. "What of it?"

"Do you recall one of the prisoners we captured last year south of Cashel—Captain Garret? He led a company of dragoons."

"Garret?" Eamon replied, mulling on the name. "Vaguely. Was he the crafty one? Always trying to cut a deal with O'Dwyer or anyone who would listen?"

"Ay, the very one," Niall said.

"What of him?"

"You won't like this," Niall warned, "but he was raiding around An Gallbhaile."

"What?" Eamon said sharply.

Niall studied the ground, his head canted slightly. "Garret and his dragoons struck my uncle's manor." He steeled himself for the rest. "My uncle and aunt are dead. His daughters and the servants were all taken. My sister, Mairead, had been there too."

"Mulriane is dead?" Eamon's voice faltered. "His womenfolk . . . captured? That can't be."

Niall rubbed his forehead to ease the pain that started to build. "I came across one of Garret's men. Before I sent him to his Maker, he confessed that the women and servants were indentured—transported by a merchant ship bound for their colonies."

"*What?*"

"They're all gone, Eamon." Niall's voice caught, and he cleared his throat. "The English nailed a proclamation to the door. They claimed my uncle comforted the enemy and his lands were forfeit. I'm sorry, Eamon, there was no time to pass by your own lands to see what state they were in."

Eamon nodded, his attention distant. "Of course. I wouldn't have expected you to linger there. His lands, you say? All of the lands?" Then he frowned. "How is it that you were in the area?"

"I saw some troubling signs and thought I'd extend my journey a few days to check on my kin."

"Devastating," Eamon said grimly. "I had a fondness for Mulriane's eldest girl. I had hoped to offer for her once this blasted war was over."

That surprised Niall, considering the difference in their ages. But Eamon was a fit man who did not look his years. "You've never mentioned this before."

"The alliance made sense for a number of reasons," Eamon said. After a moment, he asked, "What of Diarmuid? You've said nothing of him."

Niall exhaled slowly. "They killed him too. Mounted his head on a spike." Eamon maintained a grim silence, so Niall continued. "He was on his way to join the brigade."

"How do you know?"

"I found a survivor—Áine Callaghan, one of my uncle's maids."

Eamon drew in a sharp breath. "A survivor? How much did she see?"

"Very little," Niall admitted. "She said Diarmuid and a companion left to join the brigade a fortnight before the attack."

"Could she have been mistaken?" Eamon asked. "Young men often crow to inflate their worth."

"Ay, she was certain of it, and I've no cause to disbelieve her account. Diarmuid left a fortnight before the attack."

Eamon shook his head. "No one saw him here. I would have heard." He looked back to one of his men who stood attendance. "Banan, did you see any travellers lately? Two men searching to join the brigade?"

"Not I."

"There you have it," Eamon said. "Poor Diarmuid, struck down in his prime." He laid his hand on Niall's shoulder. "And I am sorry about your sister. An unexpected tragedy."

Niall nodded and looked away. He sniffed, then said, "I thank you for it, Eamon. When I catch Garret, I'll make certain he pays."

EVEN AFTER A FEW DAYS, ÁINE SLEPT POORLY UNDER EIREEN'S roof. It wasn't a true roof, only a shelter tucked under the sweeping boughs of a pair of spruce trees that shouldered each other. Evergreen branches were woven together to form a windbreak and, with the carpet of soft needles, made for a dry and warm bed. On her own, this might have made for a restful night, but the snoring and coughing, being pressed too close to complete strangers, even if they were all women, set Áine on edge.

Then there was Banan. Deep in the night, thoughts him plagued her mind and fuelled her apprehension. The prospect of running into him here, where she was alone and friendless, made her stomach lurch. Any close companion of her stepbrother hardly meant her well.

She couldn't remain here in camp, but where could she go when enemy forces were pressing close? Even Niall, trained and tested as a warrior, had trod with caution. Now she understood the desperation of a rabbit caught in a snare.

Only for a moment did she allow herself the luxury of wishing she could return to the Duggan family near Cork. They had been on her mind lately. Their cottage had been inviting, and Bridie Duggan had been a cheerful soul.

But no, she couldn't go there. It would cease to be a haven if Muiredach caught wind of it, as eventually he would.

Áine gave up the pretence of sleep the moment the sky began to lighten and rubbed the sleepless grit from her eyes. Her side ached as though she had lain atop a pile of pinecones. Stepping out of the bower, she stretched her muscles while gazing at the numerous shelters dotted before her. Men were rolled up in their woollen mantles with their feet nearest the banked fires. Eireen's hearth was situated on the edge of the camp, farthest away from most of these soldiers, and for that Áine was grateful.

Her gaze skimmed the dark shapes of the shelters, and she fretted about Banan. Was he close, a few campfires away, or had he moved on to the next camp farther into the mountains? She was never that fortunate.

When Banan had first arrived in Cork City, he had struck up a singular friendship with her stepbrother. That weasel Banan was the only Catholic Muiredach tolerated, for he presented himself as a reformed papist. The two men caroused together and partook of every diversion the underbelly of Cork had to offer. Áine thought fortune had finally taken pity on her and she'd be spared Muiredach's temperamental rages. A demon had always gnawed at her stepbrother. He hated the forge; he hated not having more wealth or power. She had been a convenient scapegoat.

For a short time, she had been spared—until Banan noticed her. Áine remembered how his head would turn when she entered the smithy carrying buckets of water, how he would try to speak to her behind Muiredach's back. He openly admired the colour of her hair, often comparing it to the forge's flames.

Her burn scar began to itch and throb as she remembered the lick of flames when Muiredach had thrust her hand into the fire. All because of Banan's interest. She hadn't even cared for Banan. Sobbing, she had tried to convince Muiredach of that, but he would not be moved. Banan had stood back, smirking and otherwise amused. No doubt, he had been tickled by her comeuppance for not paying enough attention to him.

The wretch.

"Early riser? 'Bout time someone is."

Áine started, not having heard Eireen rise. The woman gave a curt nod before she adjusted the linen kerchief that covered her hair and brushed the needles from her faded yellow skirt. "There's few that wake before me," Eireen continued. "Even my own girl, Maeve," she cast a withering glance at the black-haired woman still curled up in sleep, "can be a lazy slugabed. Takes after her late father, she does." She put her hands on her hips and studied Áine. "You haven't been sleeping well."

Áine hesitated before she gave a slight shrug. "I've never been a sound sleeper." Privacy had never been a privilege in Cork City, and she never cared to be so vulnerable.

Eireen snorted when she laughed. "A clever way of saying the accommodations are rough." The woman looked around at the sheltering trees and absently scratched her hip. "Best be grateful. We do as well as we can with what's been given us. Never know when we'll have to flee at a moment's notice—and often do."

"Flee?"

"The English are determined to flush us out of these mountains," Eireen said. "We've already moved three times before winter."

Áine grew uncomfortable at the thought. With all these soldiers about, she had hoped for safety in numbers.

"Wake up, slugabed," Eireen said, nudging Maeve. Áine thought she caught a tender expression on Eireen's face, but if so, it was fleeting and quickly replaced by a scowl. "Maeve, I'll string you up by your fingers if you don't get up now. The new girl is up before you, and it pains me that a daughter of mine is so lacking."

Maeve groaned and pushed herself up to her elbows. Her black hair stuck out at all angles from her plait. She popped open one eye and glared at Áine. "We need to talk—set some rules." Then she rubbed her eyes and yawned. "The others," she waved an airy hand at the three women only now stirring, "obligingly wait until the first cock crows."

Áine wanted to warm to Maeve, but she dared not. She remembered how Roisin had been rather sweet to her too when Áine first arrived at the Mulrianes. *Give Maeve a fortnight or two—then her true nature will surface.*

"Rise, you lazy maids, rise," Eireen scolded the other young women. "There's work to be done. A good start is half the work."

"But it's still dark," whined one.

"It must be midnight, Eireen," another pouted.

"Is this another test?" the third asked.

Áine had been quickly introduced to them when she arrived— Barbara, Brigid and Blanche—but for the life of her, she could not recall who was who, so she had taken to thinking of them collectively as the Triad.

Áine had quickly learned that the four young women living under Eireen's roof were known throughout camp as her daughters, but except for Maeve, none were of her blood. Eireen took in those in need, and all were united by one tragedy or another. One of the girls —the short, plump girl with the moon-like face—had once lived outside Limerick and had been caught in the crossfires of the siege. And another had been forced to leave when the English burned all their fields.

That Áine had arrived in a similar fashion, uprooted and alone, should have made the other young women more welcoming than they were. Instead, they watched her with open, though guarded, curiosity.

This group of maidens now clustered around Maeve, their leader in circumnavigating Eireen when the matron left to see to the goats. They shared conspiratorial whispers within their closed circle. One of the Triad said something that made Maeve toss her head and peal with laughter.

Áine busied herself with building the fire. Unsure of her footing, she studied the nuances of their expressions with painstaking diligence. A handy skill to have mastered and one she'd used to survive life under her stepbrother's roof, when a storm's early warning could be the difference between a split lip and a verbal thrashing.

"The cows need to be milked," Eireen said upon her return, scattering the maids with a threatening look. "Sure, the new maid has her priorities straight, keeping her mind on her work."

Áine. My name is Áine.

"Who left yesterday's milk in this cup?" Eireen asked, sharply.

Áine knelt before the fire and looked up. The woman was holding the cup that she had placed for the Faerie Folk. "I did," she said, rising. Should she not have?

Eireen had a strange expression on her face, and the other maids fell silent. Maeve was the first to speak up. "She didn't know, Mam." When she caught Áine's puzzled frown, Maeve said, "We haven't laid out the milk since being forced to leave our cottage."

"No good it did us then," Eireen said and poured the milk onto the ground, without even a respectful word of thanks or acknowledgment to the Faerie Folk who might still be watching. "Now get on with your day."

Áine rose and brushed the dirt from her skirts. Not needing more encouragement, she grabbed one of the milking pails and hurried off for the cattle pens without waiting for the others to lead. Even though the camp had not yet risen, she still took care to lift her mantle over her head . . . just in case Banan was about.

The closer she got to the pens, the more her spirits lifted. She had found it easier to get acquainted with Eireen's cattle than her daughters, with their vivacious and high-spirited ways. She had lingered there last night, making sure the cattle were snug and secure, chattering to them idly without fear of censure.

She enjoyed the walk alone down to the strip of meadowland. As far back as she remembered, she never minded her own company nor felt the need to chase others for conversation—a strength, but a failing as well.

Back in Cork City, this vein of independence had exposed her to slurs and the stain of superstition. Touched by the Faerie Folk, they had said of her, whispering to one another behind their hands whenever she passed them on the street or in the market. This had been Muiredach's wicked inspiration, an attempt to isolate and control her, but people were sheep, and when one started, the others bleated without rational thought.

How foolish of them all. Had she truly been a child of the Other-world, why would she have remained under that man's roof as long as she had been forced to endure?

The forest was dense with alder, birch and oak and filled with the musty scent of rich earth. From the direction of camp, a cock crowed, followed by another seeking to outdo him.

A guard had been set to protect the herd from wolves in the night. These dairy cows provided the main sustenance for the camp and were worth more than gold. When she drew closer, he jerked awake mid-snore. Upon seeing Áine and the light of dawn, he heaved himself to his feet and trudged off to the main camp.

Blessedly alone. Áine felt the tightness of her chest loosening. "Rise and shine, my lovelies," she said to the lowing cows nestled in their shelter. Áine didn't have time to tell them her latest story, as Eireen's maids were close behind with Maeve in the lead. Instead, Áine went to check on an ailing cow that had been cordoned off from the others. Murmuring softly the refrain of a favoured poem, she ran a light hand across its withers.

Maeve appeared across from her, on the other side of the cow. "What's this you're saying?"

"Nothing," Áine said quickly.

"If you're certain. I thought you might be singing a verse." Maeve gave the ill cow a pat on the head. "How's our darling girl today?"

Áine stroked the cow's hide before she lifted the rear leg to examine the hoof. She was relieved to see that the foot rot was greatly reduced. "The swelling has gone down."

"We weren't able to cure her lameness before, poor girl. You have a special touch."

Now it comes.

But instead of casting a slur, Maeve gave Áine a rueful smile. "Mam swears that had my attention to the herd been as keen as my interest in the soldiers of the camp, I would have minded the beastie better."

Maeve's ability to laugh at herself took Áine by surprise. In her experience, most people spent their time avoiding blame, not accepting it with grace. Áine opened her mouth to respond, but Maeve dashed off to get the milking started.

The early part of the morning passed in a usual flurry, and Áine was glad when she could finally stretch her legs as she and the others drove the cows to the stream.

Maeve fell in beside Áine and chattered on as they walked, sharing bits of gossip. "Brigid is sweet on Ruadhri—you met him the other day, the brawny man with the white braids."

"Hair set like a horse mane?"

"Ay, the very one. He's very proud of his braids."

"I remember him," Áine said. Ruadhri had come by, and when he had seen her with Eireen's maidens, he had made a hurried excuse to keep moving on.

"And Widow Lombard across the glade has brewed an elixir of violets. She guards it carefully, and there's many who swear it's a love potion."

"Truly?"

Maeve gave a broad wink. "I've heard that Eamon Grace is especially careful to only drink from his own flask."

As the woman trilled on, Áine began to doubt that very little happened in the camp without Maeve knowing about it. She had an uncomfortable thought—what might the young woman be saying about her? Ruadhri and his pack had minded themselves prettily enough, but backhanded gossip was a great deal more difficult to treat.

"Is it true that you come from Cork City?" Maeve asked, with no reason for her sudden change of topic.

Áine jerked her head up. "Where did you hear that?"

"You're not from there?"

"Many years ago," Áine said, wondering how she could divert Maeve from this conversation.

"Of course. A crime, it was, for those heretics to have purged good people of the true faith from the city walls. How frightened you must have been to have been forced from your home."

Áine grew uncomfortable with Maeve's questioning, caught between sharp rocks and unfathomable sea. She didn't know what would be worse—for the young woman to learn that Áine hadn't been forced to leave Cork City since she had been raised under a Protestant roof, or for Maeve to discover the true reason Áine had stolen away in the night. Fortunately, the woman had not noticed Áine's lack of response.

"What is Cork like? Are the city walls truly thicker than a man?"

Áine studied Maeve's expression, which remained open and curious. "Walls, yes, though I know nothing of their construction."

"I should have wanted to visit before the English claimed it. The city sounds like a grand place, but Mam calls it a wicked den of iniquity."

"Your mother is wise. How long have you been here at camp?"

"Well over a year—after the fall of Waterford," Maeve said, then grew silent for several moments. "This is as safe a place as any, and we're grateful for the protection of the brigade, and," she straightened and cast a glance at the other maids who chatted by the river, "others are glad for the company." She gave Áine a wide smile. "And some are even more grateful for a certain soldier who comes to visit in the evenings."

As promised, Niall had come by a couple of times to see that she had settled in, and God help her, she had felt a rush of pleasure during his visits. Áine wasn't oblivious to the flattering smiles the maids cast in his direction. She turned her head towards the stream, hoping to hide her flush from Maeve's sharp gaze. Best not expose herself to Maeve and give the young woman a weapon to use against her. Eventually, Niall O'Coneill would stop coming, and she would occupy less of his concern.

As though bidden from the force of her thoughts, Fionn appeared at the tree line, followed closely by his master, who carried a bow and a string of dead rabbits. Niall was wrapped in his mantle that brushed against his snug buff-coloured breeches. Dark, windblown hair fell to his wide shoulders. How had he grown even more attractive?

Handsome is that handsome does.

Áine tore her eyes away from the man—she could see Maeve's sharpened interest—and kept her attention on the wolfhound.

Fionn let out a low bark when he saw Áine and bounded straight for her.

Warmth flooded her, and she greeted the wolfhound like an old and welcome friend. "Oh, you dear boy," she said, scratching him fondly behind the ears. He tipped his head, and his pink tongue lolled out, clearly approving of the treatment. When she glanced up, she realised that the maids had gathered near.

"Look at how he sits for you," one of the Triad said. "Such pretty manners."

"The wolfhound has never acted like this with any of us," said another.

"He seems quite taken with you," Maeve said with a curious tilt to her head. "Be warned, Niall O'Coneill," she called out brazenly to the approaching man, "Áine may well steal your hound if you're not careful."

Niall reached the group of women, who closed around him. Not surprising to Áine, she found herself outside their circle.

"A fine catch you have there," one said archly, causing the others to fire off a series of breathless questions about where he had snared the rabbits and if he had found any other game on the trail.

Áine scuffed her shoe against the muddy pebbles of the river-bank. Betwixt and between, she had been clearly left out of the conversation, and there was no use in attempting to worm her way into their circle without looking pathetic. Instead, she thought of anywhere she could be except here. Had the herd taken their fill? Should they not be pasturing farther downstream? Fionn nudged her with his shoulder, and she touched his head for reassurance.

She sensed a gaze sliding over her, like a brush of cool wind over warm skin. Áine lifted her head to find Niall looking at her over the heads of the young maids clustered around him. He didn't immediately divert his attention, not even when Maeve asked him something and she had to repeat herself.

"Ay, a few of these are destined for your mam's cauldron," he assured Maeve. "I'll give her a couple more if she'll invite me to eat at her fire." Again, his gaze touched Áine.

"You're welcome anytime," Maeve answered with a broad smile.

"Áine Callaghan," Niall called out, startling Áine. "I see you've corrupted my hound. He's barely giving me the time of day."

Her hand had been running through Fionn's fur, and she stilled, suddenly aware of everyone's attention on her. "Do not call him fickle," she replied staunchly. "He's a brave lad who deserves affection."

Then he surprised her with a warm smile, causing her once again to forget how to breathe. "Sure, the same can be said for the rest of us poor lads. We'll not say no to a little fuss now and then." Though his words could, without reservation, apply to the entire camp, beleaguered, cold and hungry as they all were, the way he spoke them made Áine feel that they were reserved for her. Judging by the looks darting in her direction, the other maids sensed the same current.

Niall must have sensed it and moved to quickly extricate himself. "The lads will be waiting to break their fast. I'll see you all later tonight." With a sharp whistle, he called for Fionn and headed for camp. Just before he disappeared in the woods, he paused and turned around. Though the shadows had nearly swallowed him, she knew his gaze found hers. He lifted a hand in farewell before melting into the trees.

CHAPTER 9

FOR A WEEK, regular patrols rode out from camp, but Niall and his men were instead assigned the mundane task of saddle maintenance. The equipment was old and shabby, and there was no shortage of work.

"I'd rather be sitting sentry in a bog," Cormac said. "Mind-numbing though that be."

Purcell, the youngest member of the troop, despite his proud moustache muttered his agreement, but Ruadhri held his tongue as he focused, nearly cross-eyed, on stitching leather.

Niall ignored them all. His mind travelled along different paths. As he rubbed tallow into the cracked leather and stitched up frayed ends, he was free to imagine what he would do to Garret once he found him.

A shot through the heart was too quick and merciful for the English captain. Hanging? Niall had seen more than his fair share of those and knew that they could be quick depending on how the noose was tied and if it was a long drop. Usually, it took a good twenty minutes of misery while the body gasped for air and life. Twenty minutes would give Garret time to consider his actions before meeting his Maker. But a sword through the gut, there was a slow and agonising death. Let him suffer well and truly. The man deserved it.

"Young O'Coneill, if you keep rubbing that saddle so fiercely, you'll bore a hole right through it."

Niall looked up to find Donogh, O'Dwyer's cousin. Although the man was a colonel and the brother of the late O'Dwyer chief, Donogh never stood on ceremony and was often to be found drinking and dicing with the men. He lived hard and fought hard and had been involved in the rebellion for Ireland's independence longer than any of them.

Niall rose to his feet to give him his due. A few paces behind Donogh stood three men carrying saddles. "You can put them down over there," he said to the men, nodding to the other saddles waiting to be repaired. They did so and left, but Donogh remained. Fionn rose to greet him, and Donogh bent to scratch the wolfhound behind the ears.

"Have you come to inspect our progress?" Niall asked ruefully.

"I have better things to do with my time, young O'Coneill, than inspect saddle repair."

Niall winced at the rebuke.

"I was on my way down to the paddock," Donogh said, his attention on Fionn.

A twinge of envy stung Niall. If only he could ride out, unfettered and free to hunt his quarry, but he was tethered to camp.

"A handsome lad. I had a wolfhound once from my grandsire." Donogh ruffled Fionn's fur before he straightened. "I wanted to offer my condolences on the injustice against your kin. I know how you must burn to avenge them."

A sudden thought occurred to Niall. The organisation of patrols and schedules were Donogh's realm. O'Dwyer's orders were for Niall to get these tedious tasks done; he'd never actually forbidden Niall to go out on patrol.

"Donogh . . ."

"What?"

"We're nearly done with the repairs—"

"No, you're not," Donogh said. "The lads who dropped off those saddles will return with more."

Niall smothered a groan. "You have good, clever lads who know their way around a repair kit. Give me and my men leave to go on patrol for a couple of days. Your men can take our place with these repairs."

"Sorry?"

"I know it sounds mad, but I'll make it worth your while."

Then Donogh started to laugh. "You don't have enough to tempt me, O'Coneill."

Niall considered Donogh's interest in his wolfhound. "I'll let you take Fionn out hunting. You must be getting tired of rabbit meat. With Fionn, you'll be roasting fresh venison this very night. I can smell it now. The charred aroma of roast meat—juices dripping into the fire. He'll bring back good memories of your grandsire."

Donogh narrowed his eyes. "And how do you propose I explain to our commander that I let you off the leash?"

"Did he order you to keep me here?" Niall asked, affronted.

"He didn't use those words, no." Donogh chewed his bottom lip. "Fionn, then? I'd want him for at least a week."

"Four days, and to be clear, he stays with me unless you're hunting." Fionn became a puppy at the prospect of going out on a leisurely hunt, so it wouldn't be any hardship for him, but Niall didn't like the thought of the hound being with anyone else for long.

"Then you can stay with the saddles."

Cormac nudged Niall from behind. "Make the deal," he said in an undertone.

"A sennight," Niall agreed. "Deal."

Both men spit in their own hands and shook on it. Before Niall could step away, Donogh's grip tightened and he leaned in. "You're only to patrol the borders of Glengarra Woods. Stay clear of the English garrisons, and I expect you to return before the sun sets on the second day. O'Dwyer is due back from his inspection of the other camp at that time. Understood?"

"Ay."

"If you don't, I'll have Fionn as a forfeit." Donogh smiled, the kind one gave when his opponent fell into their trap.

"Before the sun sets," Niall agreed.

It didn't matter that Donogh had outmanoeuvred him. Niall's blood coursed with excitement at the thought of his own hunt, though he'd be after different game.

NIALL AND A SELECT GROUP OF HIS MEN — CORMAC, RUADHRI AND Purcell — set out for the eastern borders of Glengarra Woods. There, the foothills of the Galtee Mountains spilled down to Cahir Castle on the River Suir. From there, he intended to continue northwards to reach the Glen of Aherlow, where he had last encountered Garret's men. He prayed he could pick up the bastard's trail again.

They reached the foothills as the sky began to darken to an ominous slate. Niall rode at the head of the column, keeping under cover of the tree line as he searched for signs of riders having passed this way. Through the thinning trees, the towers of Cahir Castle were visible, light grey stone skirted by a muddy-brown river.

No sign of enemy patrols. Niall caught a glimpse of the main road leading to the castle. A man leading a plough horse and cart lumbered towards the village — nothing more.

Clouds lowered to touch the treetops, mirroring Niall's churning mood and growing doubt. Should they use their short time instead to explore around Cahir or head as quickly as they could to the Rock of Cashel, where they had captured Garret a year earlier? Would Niall find him there?

Stay the course. A good tracker returns to the place where he last found his quarry.

"Have you lost the power of speech?" Cormac asked, catching up to Niall and leaving Ruadhri and Purcell behind.

"I've been thinking."

"Never a good sign," Cormac said.

Niall didn't respond. His attention rested solely on the trail ahead.

"About that woman you brought back with you," Cormac said.

"What about her?" Niall's attention snapped back to Cormac.

"Ruadhri wants to know where he could get one." Cormac's shoulders shook with a silent laugh.

"I do not," Ruadhri called out gruffly. Nothing wrong with his ears. "The minx nearly cursed me. She's a proper menace."

"Áine is not a minx," Niall said, thinking of the fawnlike quality of the woman. He half turned in the saddle to glare back at Ruadhri. "I've no doubt you must have deserved it."

"And now he's on his best behaviour." Purcell's glorious moustache twitched a moment before he laughed. "She did us all a good turn, I say."

Ruadhri growled, "Mind your tongue."

While the two continued to bicker, Cormac began to hum the well-known tune of a favourite bawdy song, one about a wandering traveller and an enchanted woman.

"Must you?" Niall interrupted him.

"You've never minded my songs before." Cormac feigned hurt. "Or would you prefer Purcell's bodhrán?"

"He doesn't want you to scare away the English, and neither do I," Ruadhri said, squaring his shoulders and elevating his chin. "We haven't had a proper skirmish in over two months."

"I doubt we've scared anyone away," Purcell said dryly, "but with all this loud discourse, we may have invited their curiosity."

Niall grimaced. "Purcell is right. If there's to be a skirmish, I'd rather be the one setting the trap."

By midmorning, they came upon horse tracks that merged with the main trail at a juncture. Niall dismounted and examined the ground. "Six or seven horsemen passed this way several hours after the last rain." He touched the ridge of one of the tracks. The hoofprints were sunk deep into congealing mud. "Travelling fast, by their depth. They must have passed here in the early morning, I wager."

"English horses?" Cormac asked.

Niall traced his finger around the imprint of one horseshoe. "Ay." When he rose, another set of tracks a few feet away caught his attention. These were different. Narrower. "Irish mounts too. Not packhorses either. The depth of the hoofprint is equal to the other tracks."

"The English must have captured more of our horses," Ruadhri said, looking as though he'd tasted something sour.

"Perhaps." Niall scanned the surrounding trees, imagining the enemy lying in wait. "We had better press on. At least we now have a trail to follow."

Let it be Garret.

They did not get far before a steady drizzle of rain started and soon intensified to a furious downpour. Visibility worsened, and their horses, heads bent low, struggled against the channels of rainwater cutting a swath through the trail.

Cormac hollered to Niall over the moan of the wind. "This is impossible. We need to find shelter."

Niall swore. Any tracks were literally being washed away. Icy cold, the rain bit deep into his very bones. Soon the horses would stiffen and lose their footing. They couldn't afford to lose even a single mount.

"The Gleeson cottage is a mile away," Niall shouted back. They had all travelled this way before and knew whose doors would open for them. Most of the people in the barony of Clanwilliam honoured their ancestral ties to the O'Dwyers.

The rain slanted horizontal and came down in sheets by the time they reached the cottage.

Niall dismounted, his muscles stiff with cold, and dashed for the door. "Farmer Gleeson," he called out as he knocked on the door. He heard scraping and scuffling from within, but the door remained shut. "It's Niall O'Coneill."

The door cracked open, and Farmer Gleeson's squinting eye became visible through the gap. The moment he saw Niall, the man swung open the door.

"Ooh, I've not seen such dirty weather. Come in, come in," Gleeson said. His glance swept to the rest of the men with Niall. "You're all welcome. Any man of O'Dwyer's is welcome. Bring the animals out of this dirty weather. We'll make room for them."

Niall led his horse into the warmth of the cottage, and Gleeson's eldest lad helped bring in the animals. Near the fire, Gleeson's elderly mother sat at her spinning wheel with her grandchildren gathered around her. The far end of the cottage was roomy enough to house a dozen animals, but now contained only one in-calf cow, a pig, three sheep and a new lamb.

"God save all here," Niall called out to the family.

"And to you all," Gleeson said. "Meggie," he called out to his wife above in the sleeping loft. "Bring down some clean blankets." And to his mother, who scooted one of the children to settle the hens in their cupboard, he said, "Mother, you remember these good men."

"I do, I do." The old woman motioned for Niall to come closer. She had a weathered face, heavily lined, with strands of white hair that escaped her kerchief. "You keep me company." She patted the stool beside her.

Meggie Gleeson appeared with a wealth of blankets, her round face beaming and her cream-coloured kerchief bringing out the rose in her cheeks. As she handed them out, her oldest daughter, a girl of twelve, was already grinding a handful of oats with quern stones.

"You must be famished," Farmer Gleeson said. "Meggie will cook up some oatcakes for your supper. We don't have much these days, but you're welcome to share what we have."

Meggie offered them a cup of fresh sheep's milk.

Niall glanced at the four children, all looking thinner than he had last seen them, and declined the offer. "We'll take some water if it's not too much trouble," he said, giving a pointed look to all his men.

"Water will be grand," Cormac said.

"Well, if you insist," the woman said, reaching for a jug of water. He caught a glimpse of her relief.

While Meggie settled herself by the fire to grill their oatcakes, Gleeson hunkered down with his guests.

"How have you been keeping?" Niall asked the man.

"We do well as can be expected," Gleeson said.

"Getting rickety in the knees," the old woman shot out.

"Let the men talk, Mother." Gleeson splayed his roughened hands over his knees. "Truth be, I was just saying to Meggie the other day, I wonder how O'Dwyer's brigade has been faring. Haven't seen any of the lads stop by since after the feast of Saint

Nicholas, and we began to worry. Heard news of the English routing one of our brigades north of here."

Niall exchanged a look with Cormac. "Ay, that was Fitz-patrick's brigade, not our own. The English threw everything they had to flush them out. Hundreds of good lads were killed or captured. It beggared belief." Word had been swift in coming to O'Dwyer from the survivors. What was left of Fitzpatrick's brigade had been broken up and scattered through northern Tipperary. They were left with no supplies or livestock with which to feed themselves.

"They fought like heroes," Ruadhri said with an admiring dip of his head.

"They fought as proud Irishmen." Niall lifted his cup in a silent toast.

The first steaming oatcakes were passed around by Gleeson's eldest, and Niall and his men set into them gratefully. While they were eating, Meggie saw that their cups were refilled with water.

"What brings you this way, and in such fine weather?" Gleeson asked them.

"We're tracking down an English troop. One in particular," Niall said. "Their captain wears a wide-brimmed hat trimmed with a green band. The troop's colours are green and gold."

Gleeson bobbed his head. "I know that one. He has made his presence known on a few occasions, with the last being a month ago."

"If I was younger, I'd have bent him over my knee," the old woman said.

"Mother—"

Purcell leaned forward. "What happened?"

"Made off with three of our best cows," Gleeson said. "Good milkers."

"And he took my treasure—a brooch I was saving for my daugh-ter's dowry," Meggie said, twisting the edge of her apron in her hands. "I had it wrapped up in linen and hidden in the oat bin. One of his men found it when they were rooting for food. The captain fancied it and smiled to my face as he dared me to kick up a fuss."

"I should have stopped him," Gleeson muttered, his face flushed red.

"He'd have skewered us if you had," his wife said. "And then where would we have been?"

The old woman nudged Niall. "He's a magpie. Drawn to shiny objects."

"Which direction was he heading to? North to the Glen of Aherlow?"

"Don't believe so," Gleeson said. "East towards Cashel."

"You need to find a woman, Niall O'Coneill," the old woman interrupted loudly, thumping Niall's leg with her blackthorn cane.

Cormac burst out laughing.

"Mother," Gleeson hissed.

"We could all use a woman," Ruadhri grumbled. "What do you say about me, Old Mother?"

"Keep looking," the woman said with a toothless grin, waggling her finger at him.

"Old Mother, our Niall has already found one," Cormac said between guffaws.

"Áine's not my woman," Niall said.

Cormac leaned in. "Then you won't mind one of us courting her."

"Give it over, Cormac. You're a dog with a bone." Never would Niall admit that bitter distaste rose at the thought of someone courting Áine.

"Notice that he hasn't answered," Purcell said, smoothing his moustache thoughtfully.

Before Niall could retort, Old Mother Gleeson tapped him on the shoulder to get his attention, then pressed her finger against his chest. Her little black eyes bored into him, and she no longer smiled. "There's a hole there," she told him. "One that wasn't there before. A woman was the cause of it. A woman may help you mend it. You need to find her."

Niall stared at her, unable to speak. She had been speaking of Mairead, he was certain of it. He didn't know how she knew, but she somehow saw through it all. He looked around the fire, seeing the Gleesons comfortably housed together, and a lump formed in his throat. When he had set out for his uncle's manor, he longed only for a warm meal in his belly and the company of kin around a fire.

"May the Almighty guide you and bless the road at your feet," the old woman said. Then she settled herself at her spindle and draped her shoulders with a shawl.

No one spoke. Cormac had sobered and cast questioning looks to Niall, and Ruadhri crossed himself.

A scuffle sounded outside and then a sharp rap on the door. Niall inhaled sharply and stared at the door, unable to move. For a wild moment, he expected Mairead to burst into the cottage. But Ruadhri and Cormac proved to be more sensible, having risen to their feet and drawn their swords.

Gleeson was at the door questioning who was there, and after an indistinct exchange, the farmer slid the door's bolt. Two dripping travellers, muffled in their mantles, hurried inside the cottage leading their weary mounts. While Gleeson secured the door behind them, the men lowered their mantles and revealed themselves to be Eamon and one of his men, Banan.

"Meggie, bring more blankets," Gleeson called out, beaming. "Eamon Grace won't be catching his death on my doorstep."

"Look who's washed in with the rain," Cormac called out, sheathing his sword.

"What the devil are you all doing here? And you, my lad," Eamon squinted at Niall, "who let you off the lead? Does O'Dwyer know you're here?"

Niall offered Eamon his place by the fire. "I appealed to Donogh's better nature."

"And Donogh's better nature had a price—Fionn," Cormac said.

"You gave away your hound?" Banan asked, ending with a wheezing laugh. He combed his fingers through his tangled beard. "I'd have made an offer for him."

"I didn't give Fionn away. I'm not a complete bastard," Niall said and quickly added before Banan could open his mouth, "and no, I will not entertain offers." The man had pestered him enough in the past to sell him Fionn. "I've only allowed Donogh to have him for a week's hunting."

"Still a generous offer," Eamon said. In the firelight, his greying beard shone like silver. When Meggie offered him a cup of milk and an oatcake, he bestowed upon her his most winning smile. "Ah, Mistress Gleeson, you are a paragon of hospitality." The woman flushed, pleased.

"If my daughter-in-law is a paragon, what, pray, am I?" asked the old woman from her seat at the spindle.

Eamon rose and gave her a courtly bow. "Unparalleled."

"Away with you." The woman dismissed him with a wave of her hand, but it was plain she was amused by Eamon's flirtation.

Once the laughter faded into lingering smiles, Eamon settled back on his stool and turned to Niall. "Was it truly worth Fionn just to range on horseback in poor weather?"

All humour fled Niall. "It's more than a jaunt."

"Ah, Garret," Eamon said with a nod.

Banan bumped into Meggie, sending a batch of oatcakes flying to the ground. The pig, which had been evicted from its stall to make room for the extra horses, darted after the cakes before anyone could stop it. Meggie shrieked at the animal, and the children helped to herd it elsewhere.

"Which direction did you come from?" Niall asked Eamon when the commotion died down. "Where's the rest of your party?"

Eamon bit into an oatcake and washed it down with a draught before answering. "We made it as far as the Rock of Cashel. I've sent the others to do a sweep through the lands east of there. Cover more distance that way."

"Any joy in the hunt?" Ruadhri asked.

"Nothing," Eamon replied. "And where are you headed?"

"To the Glen of Aherlow," Niall said. "Ours is a short tour — we're due to return back tomorrow by sundown."

Eamon shook his head and made a soft clucking of his tongue. "The roads are washed out." He reached for a second oatcake. "You'll be swimming upriver."

Cormac nudged Niall. "If it's as he says, there's no sense in continuing. The roads will be a misery, and we'll need the extra time even from here."

If only Niall hadn't agreed to Donogh's restriction, he'd chance the roads, but he neither wanted to risk losing Fionn nor explain to O'Dwyer why he wasn't polishing saddles. Niall grimaced, not yet willing to admit defeat. "We'll see in the morning."

"The night won't improve things, I tell you. There will be other opportunities," Eamon said to reassure him. "O'Dwyer won't keep you tied to his apron strings for long. If he does prove to be stubbornly adamant, I'll keep an eye out for Garret for you. You have my pledge."

"I appreciate that, Eamon."

The conversation continued into the night until one by one the men sought their rest where they could. Niall held off seeking his own comfort—as long as he was past exhaustion, nightmares wouldn't plague him. Lately, those nightmares involved his dead kinsmen and pleading sister.

Eamon stayed with him, in no hurry either to end the night. The Gleesons had climbed up to their sleeping loft, leaving the two men to their own company. The fire had died down, but it still gave off the rich, earthy scent of peat. Niall studied Eamon. It might have been the light, but he looked more weathered, and the lines around his eyes were more deeply etched.

He had known Eamon Grace for a number of years, since Niall was a twelve-year-old exploring the fields around his uncle's estate with seven-year-old Diarmuid. Those had been treasured summers when he'd been allowed a visit, and the Grace stables had been a lure too appealing to resist. Eamon's son, Hugh, was the same age as Diarmuid and a willing conspirator, arranging to sneak out some of his father's prized horseflesh for their own amusements.

Rather than the memories offering comfort, they bit sharply into Niall. He rubbed his eyes with the heels of his palms.

"Are you well, Niall? You're not yourself."

Niall tried to fix a brave smile on his face, but it faltered. His shoulders sagged by the weight of his grief. He couldn't pretend, not with Eamon. "It's hard. Damned hard." He raked his fingers through his hair. "If only I had arrived sooner and not tarried as long at Ross Castle . . . I might have saved them."

Eamon brought his stool closer. He reached over and placed his hand on Niall's shoulder. "It's a tragedy, what happened, but nothing you could have done would have stopped this, my lad. You were never your cousin's keeper, and Mulriane was an able swordsman with a household of servants to do his bidding. This is war, Niall. You know it. But Garret overstepped his bounds as a soldier when he imprisoned the womenfolk and took Mulriane's lands. He had no right." Eamon's brow furrowed, and his mouth pressed into a thin line. "For that, there will be an accounting."

Eamon was right. Niall needed to push away the guilt that ate at him and concentrate on Garret. There would be an accounting and it would be Niall who carved out the payment.

"I can't help thinking of Diarmuid," Niall admitted in a low voice. "The adventures we would get up to, though I suspect you don't remember them so fondly given the mischief we caused."

Eamon waved his hand abruptly. "Speak no more of Diarmuid. I don't want to hear any confessions you care to make." His voice softened, easing the sharper corners of what he had said. "It's too painful."

Niall nodded his understanding. Diarmuid had been close to Eamon's son, who had died before he reached his prime. Diarmuid's end would not be a welcome reminder to Eamon.

While Niall had been focused on his troubles, he had given very little thought to Eamon's worries for his own lands. There was every chance that Garret had already stripped Eamon's holdings bare.

"It must be vexing not knowing the condition of your own estate," Niall said.

Eamon toyed with a piece of rush that he'd picked up from the ground. He twirled it between his thumb and forefinger and watched it turn this way and that. "My stables I prized most highly, and over the last several years I had to face my best horseflesh be used as war horses. There's little the English can touch me on that score. Nor can they threaten me on those who are dear to me. I lost my wife years ago to smallpox, and my only son was brought low by a fever of the brain. I'm past caring for treasures and comforts. Chairs and tables or fine linens preserved in a chest are of no concern. But the land . . .

111

the land is everything. It's the only legacy I have left." He said this with the fierceness of a hawk. "If my lands were threatened, there's little I wouldn't do to wrest them from my enemies."

Niall met Eamon's gaze. They shared a similar passion. "And there's nothing I won't do to avenge my kin." He'd bide his time and wait for Garret to eventually show himself, then Niall would strike and strike hard.

They stayed up a little longer, indulging in shared memories of an easier time, until exhaustion and the late hour claimed them. Niall rolled himself up in his mantle and immediately dropped off the moment his head touched the green rushes.

In the morning, Niall and his men decided on an early start to return to camp, for it was apparent that the night's storm had defeated them. Eamon and Banan had left earlier still, well before the cock crowed.

"Thank you for your hospitality," Niall said, offering his hand to Gleeson.

"My door is always open."

Mother Gleeson reached up to cup Niall's face. "You mind what I said, and may your journey be a safe one." She tapped his cheek before stepping away.

They rode away from the cottage, and the last view Niall had of the Gleesons was Meggie scattering seed for the chickens.

As Cormac had predicted, the heavy rains had washed out the trails and taken a healthy bite out of many of the lesser tracts that Niall had counted on as a shortcut to camp. The thick mud wore down their horses and drained them of energy. At times, Niall and the others had to dismount and slog alongside their tired mounts. With each passing hour, Niall was getting more anxious to reach camp in time and reclaim Fionn from Donogh. He watched the downwards passage of the sun with an anxious eye.

Finally, just as the sun was sinking behind the largest treetops, Niall rode into camp and nearly collapsed outside Donogh's shelter.

CHAPTER 10

O'DWYER HAD NOT WARMED to the news of Niall's excursion when he was made aware of it.

"Since you crave activity more than honest work," he'd said sternly, "I'll put your aggression to good use. The men could use sparring practice, and you will lead them."

After three days of shouting out instructions to combatants with wooden staves, Niall grabbed a sparring sword and challenged Cormac to a fight. The moment they stepped into the ring, Ruadhri, that cunning sharper, was open for wagers.

Niall seized the offensive, forcing Cormac to scramble in defence. With each strike of their wooden swords, Niall sought an opening to score a point, but Cormac held his own, deflecting each blow with the skill of a seasoned swordsman.

Strike and parry. Feint and lunge. Then a small hesitation, the dip of Cormac's sword too prolonged. Niall reacted instantly, jabbing his weapon into his opponent's exposed side. A cheer went up from the men ringing the field.

"God's wounds, man." Cormac jumped back. He rubbed his side while glaring at Niall. "A little more force and you'll impale me with that damned stick."

"Be quicker next time," Niall said tersely. He knocked the flat of his wooden sword against one boot and then the other before rolling his shoulders and settling into his fighting stance.

Onlookers formed a broad perimeter around them. Ruadhri stood at the front accepting odds. Even from this distance, Niall understood that the wagers were going against Cormac.

"Quicker? I'll show you quicker, pretty boy." Cormac launched into a fresh attack with a bloodcurdling yell.

Now Niall found himself on the defensive. Cormac's wooden stave smashed against Niall's. Muscles straining, Niall focused on forcing him back. He shifted his weight slightly, causing Cormac to lose his balance before he jumped aside, laughing.

They circled each other to the mounting excitement of the onlookers. A flash of red hair at the corner of his vision caught Niall's attention—Áine at the edge of the crowd. She gripped a milking pail and seemed to be on her way to where they pastured the herd, along with the other maids. How vivid her hair blazed in the mist of this grey morn. Her pale face shone like a beacon.

A hard blow to his shoulder followed by a punishing jab to the stomach snapped Niall's wandering attention. Cormac smashed the stave from Niall's hand and, with a swift hook of his foot, sent Niall sprawling backwards to the ground. Cormac stood over him with a triumphant smirk—the blunt tip of his sword pressed against his throat.

"Victory!" Cormac danced in a circle, brandishing his stave over his head.

A burst of cheers mixed with roars of frustration.

Niall pushed aside the wooden sword and struck the ground with the flat of his hand. He rose to a sitting position in time to see Áine disappear down the lane. *Stupid fool.* The last thing he wanted Áine to see was him getting knocked flat on his arse.

Meanwhile, Cormac danced a victory jig, brandishing his sword in the air. "The mighty Niall O'Coneill goes down in defeat. A grand day it is!"

"There's a first for everything," Niall said, rising to his feet and wiping his muddy hands against his breeches. While Cormac lapped up the accolades, Niall stared in the direction Áine had taken.

Ruadhri knocked Niall on the arm. "You've cost me, O'Coneill, fighting like a wench."

"When did you become a fishwife?" Niall tossed him his wooden sword. "Here—you take a turn against Cormac. See if you can do better."

As the two men prepared for a new match, Niall walked off the field, whistling for Fionn. Frustration had made him irritable. Confined to camp, he'd never find Garret. At least he had Eamon's word to search for the bastard.

"Trust in my eyes," Eamon had told him. "I'm as eager to find Garret as you." But as yet, Eamon had found nothing.

Niall had to do something, anything but fight with wooden staves. Cormac plied him with drink, and while that took the edge off his rage for the span of a night, with the day came the stark reminder that Garret remained at large and free to destroy more lives as he had Mairead's.

The whoreson must pay. And with blood.

Niall kept walking, without any thought as to where his feet were leading him. He looked around to find that he was near Eireen's quarters.

Again.

This seemed to be a daily occurrence with him, he realised, and he offered various excuses. At first, the truth—he wanted to check in on Áine and see that she was well. Then when that wore thin, the subterfuge. "This side of the shelter is a bit sparse—I can sort that for you, if you like." But the extra work didn't grant him any opportunity for a few minutes alone with Áine, which was what he was hoping for.

Niall scratched his stubbled chin. This was useless. He had better things to do than haunt Eireen's campfire.

Besides, she wouldn't be at Eireen's now. She had been heading down to the cattle pens. He considered that a moment. The paddock *was* near the cattle enclosures. It might be a good opportunity to check on his new horse.

While he was debating this with himself like an untried lad, one of Donogh's men arrived, riding a tawny-coloured piebald garron that shuffled along in a disjointed gait.

"McTiege," Niall called out to him and hurried over to greet him. "Well met."

"O'Coneill!" He reined in his horse and dismounted to embrace Niall. McTiege was a brawny man with dark hair braided in a similar fashion as Ruadhri's. Although his face had a craggy, hardened cast from having once been afflicted with smallpox, a few of the pretty girls in the camp still tried to win his attention. A good drinking companion, McTiege spent more of his off-duty time with Niall's men than his own troop.

"I haven't seen you since I left for Ross Castle," Niall said. "Have you only returned now?"

"Ay, and looking forward to washing the grit of the road from my mouth with a bit of ale, if there's any left." McTiege bent to greet Fionn, who was sniffing at his hands. Normally, Fionn would have jumped all over the man and ploughed him exuberantly to the ground, but this time he was surprisingly subdued. It then occurred to Niall just how strained McTiege appeared.

"Donogh's been running you ragged, has he?" Niall said. "Where did you come from? Any news on the English?"

"Here and there," McTiege answered. "Nothing to mention." Then he said, "Is your kinsman well? Did he arrive in good health?"

"My kinsman?"

"Ay, with his friend, a boastful fella. The pair of them were having trouble finding the camp, wandering on the northern fringe of the Galtees—where we were a few moves ago. Said he was your cousin, Diarmuid Mulriane."

"Diarmuid?" Niall struggled to make sense of the words. "You met Diarmuid?"

McTiege frowned. "Ay. Is he not here?"

"No. No, he's not . . ." Niall's voice trailed off. Diarmuid had been more than halfway here. "He was captured by the English and his head mounted on a spike on the doorstep of his father's home. He and that boastful fella you mentioned."

McTiege winced. "My sympathies, Niall. Was it you who found him?"

"Ay." Niall explained what happened. "The English must have captured them shortly after you left them." Diarmuid hadn't given up O'Dwyer's location, not even to bargain for his life. *Brave lad.*

McTiege frowned. "I don't understand. They severed his head from his body? I've only seen them do that when they capture one of us and we've pushed them too far. Why would the English have troubled themselves for your kinsman? They could have left the two men for the carrion and have done with it."

This question hadn't occurred to Niall before. He had seen more than his share of bloody English reprisals and had been numb to the whys of this one. Diarmuid hadn't pledged himself to O'Dwyer, and yet the English had given his cousin an Irish death.

"Your uncle's manor was not close? They went to a great deal of trouble for him."

"They were greedy swine and no doubt saw the possibility for profit in this." Niall recalled the note posted on the door. "They seized the opportunity to enrich themselves with plunder. All the ills lie at Captain Garret's feet."

"Garret?" McTiege said sharply.

"Ay, you recall the man? He was one of the prisoners we released last year."

McTiege grimaced. "Ay."

"Promise me, McTiege, if you ever come across him, if the opportunity ever presents itself, bring me Garret's head on a spike."

McTiege's gaze shifted away. "I'll do my best."

THE FIRST STARS GLEAMED IN A DARKENING SKY WHEN ÁINE joined Eireen's family and their friends around a central campfire for an evening of companionship.

Maeve herded Áine into the gathering, giving her no opportunity to escape into the shadows. She didn't want to run into Banan, and she feared this would be a gathering that would have drawn him like a moth to flame. To her relief, he wasn't there.

Seated by the fire, Cormac and Ruadhri were holding court, racing each other to the bottom of their respective cups. A burst of applause erupted when Ruadhri finished first, and he pumped his victory into the air. Áine shifted nervously. Drink never brought out the best in men. While everyone focused on the colourful pair, a silent and solitary figure captured Áine's attention.

Niall sat apart from the others with Fionn lying at his feet. Áine hadn't intended to stare, but when he lifted his head and their gazes locked, all modest intentions dissolved and she couldn't turn away. How tired he looked, so weary. Her fingers itched to ease the tension written on his brow.

Áine replayed over and over in her mind how he had appeared in the sparring ring. The way he had moved, fluid and sure, had made her catch her breath in admiration. Even though he had lost his round, her esteem had not wavered. A reminder that he was a flesh-and-blood man, not a heroic figment of her imagination, made him all the more appealing.

"Here's a place we can sit," Maeve said, breaking Áine's wandering thoughts. The young woman grabbed Áine by the wrist and drew her to an available log situated directly across from Niall.

Self-consciously, Áine smoothed out her skirt, fussing over every wrinkle. When she finally lifted her head, Niall still stared at her, his expression inscrutable. Áine gathered her courage and said, "A fine night it is."

He nodded gravely, softening slightly. "Have you kept well, Áine?"

She gave him an answering smile, then tucked away her response when two of the Triad wandered over to greet Niall. The young women, presenting a wall of swishing skirts, effectively screened her view.

Áine tore her gaze away. Maeve wasn't paying attention, being deep in conversation with the rugged and intimidating McTiege. Someone started playing a tune on a pipe while another clapped in time to the beat.

The music calmed her, and she felt herself relaxing, but she still kept sneaking glances over at Niall. He was now speaking to

Cormac. Fionn seemed content to remain at his feet, and Niall's hand strayed now and then to touch the hound.

Áine grew short with herself after she once more snuck another glance. *What is the matter with me?* Would she be constantly checking to see if Niall was paying her any attention for the entire evening? She just couldn't, she decided. Better to remove herself from this and seek some solitude.

She rose, intending to let Maeve know she was leaving, but the woman's head was bent close to McTiege's. Maeve was idly twirling a lock of her hair around her finger. Neither looked as though they'd welcome an interruption. Áine took a step forward when Niall's deep, stirring voice stopped her.

"Why are you leaving, Áine Callaghan?" He asked. "Won't you stay?" He spoke as though they were alone, but there was no question that they weren't, and there was nothing wrong with everyone's hearing.

Áine felt the weight of everyone's attention, but Niall's encouragement heartened her. He wasn't being polite. She knew the look of someone saying the right things for courtesy's sake—their shifting attention gave them away every time; his was steadfast and earnest.

"Very well." Reclaiming her spot on the log, she plucked at her skirts again.

His gaze felt like a physical touch, and not knowing how she should react, she scanned the campfire.

Across from her stood O'Dwyer, as imposing a figure as a lord from the Otherworld. Áine had studied his manner during his interactions with his men. His command seemed to be built through the relationships he had forged—with all the men, not only those who directly reported to him. To Áine, he took a keen interest in each soldier who wielded a sword in his name. Though he may not have been the chief of the O'Dwyers, Edmund O'Dwyer was undoubtedly the chief of this brigade.

Conversation soon flowed around Niall. Áine followed the talk but did not contribute. Twilight deepened, the pearly light swallowed by a spreading deep blue. This was a magical moment between day and night—the magical time when anything could happen and one could wish on their heart's desire.

In the gloaming, the ruddy tones of the campfire defined Niall's chiselled features and rounded out his broad shoulders. This was a moment she wanted to impress in her mind, to be taken out later. So consumed was she with this perfect moment that Áine missed Maeve's question.

"We do want to hear the tale, Cormac," Maeve said, nudging Áine with her elbow. "Agree, Áine, or we won't hear it."

"Let us hear it, then," Áine said quickly.

Niall leaned forward, resting his elbows on his knees. "Make it good, Cormac."

Cormac cleared his throat and rose to his feet. Someone refilled his cup. "Half a draught of ale? My thirst is greater than this." But he still tossed it back and wiped his mouth with the back of his hand.

"I'll pour you another if your storytelling skills are as good as you claim," Ruadhri told him.

Cormac narrowed his eyes and wagged his finger at Ruadhri. "Sure, it will be grand." He glanced around the campfire, commanding everyone's attention. "In these days of invasion with an enemy threatening close, let us be reminded of the tale of Cúchulainn and how he defended Ulster from an invasion by Connacht. Who hasn't heard how Medb of Connacht brought her warriors to steal the Brown Bull of Cúailnge?"

Áine clasped her hands, eager for the tale. Though she had heard the *Táin Bó Cúailnge* many times before, she had never tired of it.

"The might of Medb's army aligned themselves along Ulster's border," Cormac started in a singsong voice. "But most of the Ulstermen were afflicted with their mysterious pangs, leaving only one to stand for them—Cúchulainn. Were it anyone else, Queen Medb's army would have crossed uncontested, but this was Cúchulainn they faced, one of Ulster's greatest warriors."

He continued the tale, describing how Medb sent three times fifty of her best warriors to beat Cúchulainn, and he defeated every one of them in single-handed combat until he came up against his foster brother, Ferdia.

To Áine's disappointment, Cormac rushed over Cúchulainn's reluctance to fight against one so beloved to him and instead replayed every vicious thrust and bloody parry using a stick he had picked up from the ground.

"Then cunning Ferdia impaled Cúchulainn through the heart." Cormac thrust his stick into the ground.

The breast, Áine corrected him in her mind.

"Not the heart," Niall called out, startling Áine. Was he reading her thoughts? "He speared him in the breast."

Cormac glowered at Niall. "I'm telling this story, O'Coneill, am I not?" After Niall waved him to continue, he finished the story. "In the end, Cúchulainn's charioteer saved him when he threw a magic spear, the *gae bola*, to his dying master. Cúchulainn grabbed the *gae bola* and thrust it through Ferdia's *heart*, killing him instantly. Queen Medb's army was driven back and Ulster saved."

When Cormac finished, he swept a gallant bow to warm applause. When he straightened, his attention landed on Áine, who hadn't clapped. She was still thinking of everything he had left out.

"Did you not enjoy the story?" Cormac asked, drawing attention to her.

Everyone stared at Áine, many with impatient expressions, and she found herself tongue-tied. Eventually, she answered, "I enjoyed it well enough."

"You did not," Cormac said. "Admit it." He tried to sound jovial, but it came out as petulant.

"Leave off, Cormac, and take your accolades where they are freely offered," Niall said, holding out his cup. "Admit it, you missed a few sections; the maid is right. What about the part where Medb still managed to steal the bull through trickery?"

"That's another tale," Cormac huffed, but he still accepted the cup. He took a long draught, then smacked his lips, swiped his hand across his mouth and nodded his thanks. But he wasn't finished with Áine. "A fine thing it is to be a critic. Being a bard is a calling, an art."

"I never said I didn't like it." Áine grew uncomfortable, now wishing she had pretended to enjoy the telling. But it was too late.

"These are important stories, and they deserve to be remembered correctly."

Cormac laughed and shook his lank hair over his eyes. But he was still a dog with a bone. "I would hear the woman try it." He lowered himself to his seat, propping his elbows on his knees as he leaned in. "Tell us a story. Go on."

Áine heard the challenge, and her heart sank. She could either accept or be laughed back to the cottage and into next week. Either way, she'd be ridiculed.

"Not easy, is it?" Cormac said with a satisfied smirk.

"Leave it, Cormac," Niall said in a warning tone.

Fionn sat up and left Niall's side to plant himself in front of Áine, giving no concern that his back was facing the others. Grateful, Áine cupped the hound's muzzle before scratching behind his ears.

"Well?" Cormac asked.

"Sit down and mind your tongue," Niall called out. The campfire company was threatening to splinter, with many arguing for Cormac.

Could she dare? The hound seemed to be speaking to her, his liquid eyes warm and encouraging. Were these men not very like the Fianna, outlaw warriors of yore?

Courage.

Áine started her tale. "Attend the Fenian cycle of heroes and giants and mighty foes." Voices lowered, even Cormac's.

The terror nearly overwhelmed her, and she found it hard to breathe. Her voice wobbled, and she almost gave up and buried her face in Fionn's fur. The hound gave her hand an encouraging lick, and she breathed deeply. She could do this—she had been telling the Mulriane herd her tales for years. So as not to falter, Áine focused on Fionn—she didn't dare lift her eyes to see his master.

"Fionn mac Cumhaill was one of Ireland's greatest heroes, a giant amongst men, and there has never been his like before or since. There have been so many songs of his daring, but this is the tale of how he saved Tara from invasion by battling Aillen of the Tuatha Dé Danann on a faerie mound."

Áine rose to her feet and imagined the misty forests of years ago, greener than new leaves and bewitched with silvery moonlight. "A long time ago, when the world of man and the Otherworld were not sealed off to each other, the Tuatha Dé Danann made Éire their home. Brightly enchanted kings and queens, they kindled the wonders of sword, spear, stone and cauldron. But with the light, there is also the dark, and not all of the Tuatha Dé Danann had men's best interests at heart."

She threw herself into the story, tasting every word on her tongue. "Every Samhain, Aillen of the Tuatha Dé Danann would rise from the underworld to lull the men of Tara into an enchanted sleep before burning that blessed place with his hellfire. 'Who will defend Tara from this scourge?' the high king demanded." Her voice rang with the authority of the ruler of Tara, and she held up her hand as though she were invoking the gods.

As though he had sprung up before her, Áine saw the hero Fionn standing before the High King of Éire, vowing to defend Tara with his very lifeblood. Only now he bore the face of Niall O'Coneill. Inspiration carried her, giving flavour to her tale.

All were silent around her. And then Áine lifted her eyes and met Niall's intense gaze. A bolt of energy, as enchanted as Aillen's fire, shot through her. He leaned slightly forward, hanging on every word. Her words.

Áine's mind froze, and her tongue stumbled on the narrative. She mentally tried to snatch at the words, but they dispersed like will-o'-the-wisps. Panic bubbled up until Niall nodded at her as though to say he believed in her.

She refocused her story and now directed the rest of her narrative to Niall. Everyone else faded into the shadows. With Niall as her inspiration, she took her audience through every dramatic setback and twist. By the time she reached the dramatic battle, the only other sound was the crackling of the fire.

"Fionn mac Cumhaill faced Aillen with his enchanted spear, the Birga, in one hand and in the other, his great shield that was three times the size of the largest shield ever constructed." Her words took on shape; even her fingers tingled when Aillen shot the fury of hellfire down on Fionn, who deflected it with his shield. Then the great warrior delivered the killing blow. "With Aillen's defeat, Fionn was allowed to claim his father's lordship of the Fianna and take his place, a leader amongst them."

Áine bowed her head with the last line. Silence. Swallowing nervously, she kept her head down, terrified to look up and see their scorn. Her face burned hot.

Then a burst of applause erupted, and she lifted her head in surprise. They weren't mocking her—they were cheering. Even Cormac clapped, with a look of grudging respect. But it was Niall that made her heart overflow. He had risen to his feet and clapped the loudest, his eyes shining for her.

"Well done, Áine." He handed her his own cup, and his fingers brushed hers when she took it. Áine smiled and couldn't look away.

Someone stood up and began to play their bagpipes, the drone of them stretching across the camp like an otherworldly lament. Áine shivered. She was aware of Niall's nearness, and the song of the pipes stirred too many emotions. Rising, she intended to slip quietly away, but Niall stood up as well.

"Where are you going?" he asked her.

"The hour is late," she replied. "I need to rise before the sun."

"As do I," Niall said. "I'll walk you back to Eireen's." He stepped aside, allowing Áine to proceed. His hand touched the small of her back before dropping away.

Slowly, they walked in silence away from the campfires, Fionn melting into the shadows. A full moon soared in a cloudless midnight-blue sky. Eireen's tent was not far.

"You astonish me, Áine," he said.

The use of her name brought a thrill to her, not the least because his tone decidedly softened over it, as though he were savouring the taste.

Don't overreact, Áine. "I do?"

"You're different than anyone else I've met."

Her heart lurched, and she struggled with whether to ask what he meant or remain quiet and allow herself to remain ignorant. But she was still lifted with the euphoria of the story and so braved, "How so?"

"You have the soul of a poet," he answered. "The light of a bard shone on your face when you spoke. You bewitched us all."

The soul of a poet. A golden compliment, an unexpected treasure. "Thank you." For the first time, she had a desire to unburden herself. "Not everyone cares for different. It makes for misunderstandings."

"And you care to please those people? They are sheep and not worthy of your trouble. We all have different gifts, and there is no shame in that. The only shame would be to not follow the courage of our gift. Had Fionn mac Cumhaill wanted an easy life, he would have become a blacksmith. Look up, never down, Áine Callaghan."

She was overwhelmed by this man, and all she could say was, "Thank you."

"I must tell you that I anticipated another story instead of the one you gave us."

"Which one?"

They reached Eireen's shelter. Niall stopped and canted his head. Even though his face was half in shadows, she could see a smile playing across his lips. "The tale of how Fionn mac Cumhaill found an enchanted maiden in the depths of a forest."

Áine flushed, her cheeks growing hot. Again, he had read her thoughts. There was a moment when she had considered that very story but had quickly discounted it—wishful thinking on her part, and she didn't want to expose herself to ridicule.

"The group preferred the taste of battles, not fanciful tales."

Niall smiled and tipped his head back, studying the stars in the night sky. "Not all tales are fanciful. There's truth if you know where to look for it." He stopped and faced her. Áine's breath hitched in her throat. "What would you say if I told you I want to kiss you?"

Her eyes widened, and she felt her cheeks flooding with heat. Áine's sense fled and she was incapable of forming a coherent thought. Instead of replying with a witty phrase, she blurted, "Why?"

Niall stepped closer. "Because you are the fairest maid I've seen, Áine Callaghan."

"That can't be true."

"You would call me a liar?" He lifted her chin with his finger and bent closer to her, his lips hovering inches away from hers. "May I?"

Áine was certain he would be able to hear her heart pounding violently in her throat. This was madness, but she found herself wondering what his touch would be like. She gave a small nod.

She wasn't sure what to expect, never having been truly kissed before, but when his lips touched hers, a tumble of emotions assailed her. She felt herself unfurl like a new bud, shyly at first. Their breaths merged. Áine's world constricted to his taste, scent and touch. Niall's mouth slanted across hers, gently probing, and her lips parted tentatively. It was an intimate moment, and Áine felt herself especially shattered.

When Niall lifted his head, his expression mirrored how she felt. For a moment, she thought he might kiss her again, but instead his thumb passed gently over her parted lips. A simple touch and yet one that she felt to her toes and parts in between.

"Goodnight, Áine Callaghan." His throaty voice sent shivers rippling through her.

He stepped away from her, his expression unfathomable. With a sharp whistle to Fionn, he headed down the lane.

Áine watched him go, watched the darkness close in around him. She grazed her lips with her fingertips. "Good night."

CHAPTER 11

ÁINE SLIPPED OUT of Eireen's shelter before the first rays lightened the sky and the cock crowed. Having slept fitfully through the night, she welcomed the coolness of the mist to clear her muddled head. Her intention, when she had slipped on her mantle and tiptoed past the sleeping women, was to head for the river and watch the current flowing past. But now that she found herself alone in the mist-shrouded forest, she couldn't bring herself to leave. Silence clung all around her, and her thoughts did not need to fight against the clamouring world.

She sat down on a dwindling stack of firewood, brushed her shoes against the damp grass and thought about the hours she had spent tossing and turning last night. The sweetened green rushes that served as a pallet may as well have been crushed stones for the good they did her rest, but the cause of her restlessness was no mystery.

Áine could still feel the press of Niall's mouth against her own, the tingle of her skin, rubbed sweetly raw by the scratch of his stubble. The encounter last night had been a dream, a glorious dream spun of starlight and secret longing, a dream that no woman would want to wake from.

She had never been more terrified.

Was that how a man's regard felt? Glorious. Unsettling. Had her mother ever felt this way for her second husband, the man who had become Áine's stepfather? She thought of his red-rimmed eyes and sour breath. Had he ever been so attentive and gentle when he courted her mother? At what point had he changed from the man who would cause her mother to abandon her faith to become the mould for his son?

A note of sadness crept into her breast. So much that Niall did not know about her—must never know about her. And yet, did she not deserve just a little happiness?

In the grey light of early morn and through the thinning mist, a man with a wolfhound approached, his mantle billowing behind him. Áine's breath hitched in her throat, and she blinked to clear her vision. Both hound and man appeared to have stepped out of the verses of a myth—a lord of the *sidhe* walking between the worlds betwixt morning and night.

The spell was broken the moment Fionn bounded at her with an excited bark. Áine squealed in pleasure as she fended off his exuberance.

Niall whistled and called, "Fionn, down." The hound obeyed, but he still bounced around her legs. He greeted her with a warm smile, and Áine felt the blush on her cheeks mount.

"You have risen early, Niall O'Coneill." For the first time, she noticed that he carried a canvas satchel.

"As have you. Are the others still abed?" He glanced past her shoulder to the cottage.

"If they are, they will be rising soon. Eireen will be after them."

"That's a shame." Niall's low voice sent shivers rippling through her. He reached up to toy with a loose tress that had escaped her plait. He wound her hair between thumb and forefinger, his expression thoughtful. "Has anyone ever told you that your hair is magnificent, Áine Callaghan? Each strand rivals the brilliance of the rising sun." When she shook her head, he added, "Blind fools."

He glanced again at the hut before leaning in to brush his lips across hers. Áine forgot her earlier fears and worries—everything except the taste and smell of him.

Then, from within the shelter, someone coughed loudly. Áine pulled back, suddenly aflutter. Niall still fixed his attention on her and didn't bother to look up.

"Good morning, Eireen," he called out in a loud voice.

"You've come to give us a hand, have you?" she said, her capable hands resting firmly on her hips.

Niall shifted the satchel that rested on his shoulder. "There's a greater claim on me this day. I finally have leave to ride out on patrol."

"It's about time O'Dwyer relented. You've been agitating like a caged wolf." Eireen lifted her brow and sniffed. "Go on, or you'll be feeding my chickens."

Niall's mouth turned up in a wry smile. "On my way."

Eireen released a large harumph and rattled around the yard until she headed around the cottage towards the chicken coop.

"Will you be travelling far?" Áine asked, finding it hard to hide her disappointment.

"Only to the foothills," he said with a grimace. "Ensuring our borders are secure."

Áine frowned, suddenly concerned. "You'll be careful—not take unnecessary chances?"

Niall took her in his arms. "You needn't worry. I'll return soon." He tilted his head and captured her lips in a slow, stirring kiss.

"Promise?" she breathed against his mouth.

"Promise."

Áine heard the scratching of the tent flap, followed by a hushed giggle and a muffled shriek.

"I believe there's a nest of starlings in the trees," he commented with a grin.

"I'm afraid so."

"I'd better leave." He sighed. Unmindful of the eyes that were surely spying on them, he touched her errant lock one more time. "I'll see you in a few days."

"Three days?"

He smiled. "Not a day longer."

"I'll hold you to your word," she replied. When had she become so bold?

Niall winked at Áine, then stepped away and whistled for Fionn, who was sniffing around the yard. The hound came back, but instead of falling in step beside his master, he settled himself on his haunches beside Áine.

"Come." Niall slapped his thigh, but Fionn remained fixed where he was. Instead of listening, the hound behaved as though he had gone deaf and blind, examining the sky with cool nonchalance. "Fionn." Niall's tone hardened, but still, his loyal, ever-present companion was having none of it.

In the distance, shouts sounded. The call to gather. Niall snapped his fingers and whistled again.

"Go on, Fionn, your master is waiting," Áine said, scratching his neck. The hound fixed her with his warm, liquid eyes and whimpered under his breath. Instead of obeying, he lay down on the ground at her feet.

"Ungrateful wretch," Niall swore.

"I'll watch out for him," Áine said, her voice betraying her laughter. "A reason for you to return."

"I already had one," Niall said, his smile deepening for her. With a final wave, he headed down the lane in the direction of the paddock.

Áine watched until he disappeared from view. Then she heard the patter of footsteps running behind her. Maeve pounced on her.

With a sharp elbow to her ribs, Maeve said, "So glad that there isn't *much* to talk about today. Milking will be so much more interesting, I suspect."

Áine saw the questioning incline of Maeve's head and the quirk of her brows. "Ah, I have to fetch water."

"Dash the water —"

"The girl will be doing my bidding, Maeve. I will thank you to remember that," Eireen called out sharply to her daughter. "Run along now and see to the milking. Áine, you were on your way to fetch the water, were you not? Hurry along, then. Work is better than talk."

Eireen kept Áine running on her feet all morning and far away from Maeve and her eager gossip. Fionn followed wherever she went, becoming her shadow. Áine couldn't be upset about the arrangement and welcomed the reprieve. She hadn't missed the speculative glances from the Triad, and while Maeve might be pure in her enthusiasm, she wasn't sure about the other dairymaids. Áine preferred to keep Niall like a treasure clutched at her breast, not willing to share when she did not know how long this euphoria would last.

In her experience, joy was reserved for others more deserving and never for herself.

"Hand me that twine." While Eireen focused on the swollen hoof of an ill cow, she held out her hand to Áine.

"She was improving last week," Áine said, placing the boiled twine in the woman's hand. Her heart went out to the poor beastie. In her head, she went through everything they had done for the animal, wondering what they could have missed. It had been an otherwise rewarding week, with a successful start to the calving season.

Eireen mumbled a concerned, "Hmm," and continued to work on the cow's hoof without comment. She had a deft hand, and the animal did not balk as she rubbed the twine between the cow's diseased toes. The twine had been soaked with healing herbs, and the paste she applied to the area had also been infused with those same herbs. When Eireen finished, she sat back on her heels and examined her handiwork. "Best we can do, considering. What this poor animal needs is a dry byre in which to recover. But she won't getting anything half so comfortable, will she?" Eireen wiped her hands on her apron with quick, irritated movements.

"We can all use a dry cottage to get out of the damp," Áine said. "Comfort is all well and good, but there are worse things in this world than a bit of damp."

"Not when you're a cow." Eireen's attention shifted past Áine's shoulder, and she narrowed her eyes. "Speaking of worse things."

Áine turned around to find Widow Lombard marching towards the cattle pens. She had seen the woman several times around the encampment, and it seemed to her the widow only moved at one speed—brisk.

Maeve appeared at Áine's elbow, startling her with the sudden appearance. The young woman had been set to milking, but she rarely sat in one place for long. "What do you suppose she's come here for?" she asked archly.

"Mind your manners," Eireen said, then in a low tone added, "Woman has ears like a bat."

"Eireen, my dear," Widow Lombard called out with a wave of her hand. She entered the cattle pens, dancing around a trail of cowpats.

"Tilde, my love," Eireen said with a fixed smile. "Have you come to offer my girls assistance? The milk is flowing, and we have a few heifers who'll be calving soon."

"They're all very capable, I'm sure, being under your tutelage." The widow then glanced over at Áine and affected an air of surprise. "Is this the new girl?"

Eireen leaned slightly forward, as though about to impart a great secret. "I have it on good authority that her name is Áine."

"Your wit is a beacon in the night," the widow said dryly. "Well, well." She fixed her unwavering attention on Áine. "A very pretty girl. You'll have your work, Eireen, dear, keeping her out of trouble. She's bound to stir interest, make no mistake."

"She already has," one of the Triad piped in. "A prize, no less." The other two drifted closer and exchanged pointed glances with one another.

Áine squirmed under the attention that swivelled in her direction and saw the wisdom of being elsewhere. "If you'll excuse me. I have to help Maeve." But Maeve ignored the hint and made no move to return to the milking. Instead, she watched the two matrons with obvious relish.

"Maeve," Eireen said sternly. "Those cows do not milk themselves. Off you two go—"

"Why the rush, Eireen?" The widow's smile showed to her advantage and proved that she still was a handsome woman, even if her looks were marred by the sharpness of her tongue. "I've heard stories." She waggled her finger meaningfully at Áine.

Áine shifted uncomfortably. *This can only turn ill.*

"When have you not?" Eireen muttered in a low tone that only Áine, standing closest, could hear.

"What was that?"

"Nothing, Tilde, my love."

"Escaped an English attack, I've heard," the widow said. "Your master and mistress both murdered. How horrifying."

Áine thought back to the cairn she had built for them. Every stone she had laid, no matter how small, had been a burden. "It was a tragedy, and one I'd like to forget," she replied in a tight voice.

"And you were the only survivor? How could you possibly have escaped?"

Áine looked around. Maeve and the Triad had moved closer. They had tried to fish for information before, but Áine had managed to avoid the subject. Now they were all attentiveness. "I was fortunate."

"Fortunate?" The widow's mouth pressed into a curious smile. "Some might call it opportune."

"Really, Tilde," Eireen cut in. "Have you nothing better to do? We have more than enough work and no time for this nonsense."

"Does it not worry you that her former mistress was brutally killed and yet she somehow managed to escape? Do you not think it odd? I have the right to know who she is and whether I should fear having my throat cut in my sleep. How do we even know if the English were truly behind the attack?"

"Tilde," Eireen warned. "You are stirring trouble where there is none."

Maeve nudged Áine with her elbow and motioned her to follow, drawing her away from the arguing matrons. "Best we give them distance. Feathers will be flying soon."

She saw the wisdom of Maeve's words. The woman was determined to stir the pot of discord, and nothing Áine could say in her own defence could divert the widow from her course. There were some who thrived on controversy.

Áine picked up her pail and milking stool and headed across the paddock, as far away from the arguing women as she could. The cows had taken note of the disturbance and were becoming quite anxious. As she tried to soothe the herd, a man was walking by, leading his horse to the paddock. She didn't register that it was Eamon Grace until he halted alongside her.

"What is all that commotion?" He gripped his horse's lead in his gloved hands. It was a fine beast, far too grand against the other horses in the brigade.

"I can't truly say, my lord." Áine was about to lead one of the cows away when he halted her with a question.

"You're the Mulrianes' dairymaid, are you not?"

"I am."

"I recall seeing you when I had occasion to visit the Mulrianes. Hovering near the byre."

That surprised her. During the rare occasions he would arrive for a visit, his exacting attention had been directed to the stable hand tasked to care of his mount.

"A tragedy, what happened to the Mulrianes," he said, shaking his head. "I can hardly believe it. Niall O'Coneill is taking it hard."

Áine wondered what he meant by speaking to her so openly, but his concern for Niall seemed genuine. "I understand he loved them dearly."

Eamon Grace nodded. "They were his mother's folk and the last connection to her after she passed." He frowned, as though realising that he might be speaking out of turn. "I trust you've given him all the information you have on the attack? It will help him find the ones responsible."

"I have, although it's poor information and not terribly helpful."

He nodded. The horse nudged his shoulder, and he looked up fondly. "Better get this nag to the paddock, where a ration of oats awaits." He clicked his tongue and led his horse away.

Shortly after his departure, the widow sailed out of the pens, her head held high. Eireen followed in the woman's wake, stopping at the perimeter where Áine stood.

"And a good day to you too," Eireen called out to the widow.

"That woman." She took a deep breath and exhaled slowly. After a moment, she appeared less flustered. "Tilde Lombard is a meddling witch."

"Why did she bother to come if all she wanted was to spread discord?"

"To show how clever she is." Eireen glanced down at Áine's wrist. "I am curious. How is that you left Cork and found yourself in Tipperary? Run away from a father, or was it a husband?"

Áine hid her wrist behind her back, dismayed at the question. Widow Lombard had had her moment after all. "I'm not married, and my father died when I was a babe."

Eireen looked as though she wanted to ask another question, but she merely nodded. "Very well. Get back to work."

CHAPTER 12

NIALL RETURNED from his patrol on the third day, finding no sign of Garret. The earth may as well have swallowed the bastard whole. It didn't help that Donogh had kept Niall on a tight leash, sending him out with a troop of his own dragoons to scout out their borders. His only consolation was being able to see Áine again. He had thought often of her kiss in the quiet of the night, with the sounds of the night forest lulling him to sleep.

On his way to the paddock, a horseman cantered past. One of O'Dwyer's messengers. As the man swept by, Niall saw his weariness, the mud-splattered cloak and the foam flecked on the horse's mouth.

"Where are you coming from?" Niall called out.

"Ross Castle."

The ships!

Niall hurried the remaining distance to the paddock and tossed his reins to the farrier. "Take care of my horse and I'll owe you a good turn." Before the man could protest, Niall ran after the messenger.

Crowds began to gather in the horseman's wake, slowing Niall down, but he finally reached O'Dwyer's quarters just as the messenger was dismounting. Eamon saw Niall and motioned him forward.

Niall pushed his way through the crowd and entered the tent in time to hear O'Dwyer questioning the messenger. "From Viscount Muskerry?"

"Ay, from his very hand."

O'Dwyer cracked the seal and unfolded the letter. Even from his vantage point, Niall could see that it was a lengthy missive. When O'Dwyer finally finished, he said, "Eamon, shut the tent flap behind you."

"What news?" Donogh said impatiently.

O'Dwyer would normally have handed the letter to Donogh, but instead he kept it. "Ships arrived."

Niall wanted to shout with relief and joy, but O'Dwyer's expression stalled him. Donogh, however, released a low whoop and slapped Eamon on the back, unmindful of the gathering chill in the room. "The Duke of Lorraine came through. Finally!" Then his enthusiasm cooled. "Why don't you look pleased, Edmund?"

"How many arrived?" Niall asked.

"Three supply ships and a frigate," O'Dwyer said grimly. Were it not for the angry muscle pulsing in his jaw, Niall would have thought him dispassionate. "One arrived at the Aran Islands while the other two and the frigate landed far off the west coast at Inishbofin."

"What of the others?" Donogh asked, his voice sharpening. "What of the other dozen or more that the duke offered?"

"There are no others," O'Dwyer replied.

"Impossible," Eamon said. "Where there are three, there must be more. They must have been delayed—"

"There are no more," O'Dwyer barked. "That's it. That's all we get."

No one spoke. Niall's mind reeled. Sweet Almighty. What good were three ships to them? How much time would that buy them—a few weeks? A couple more months? Less. Muskerry had his own troops to fortify. "And the supplies?"

"A thousand muskets, thirty barrels of gunpowder," O'Dwyer said. "Most of the barrels of rye were spoiled by seawater."

Niall shut his eyes and exhaled slowly. A thousand muskets. There were nearly three times that many in O'Dwyer's brigade and the same under Muskerry. The gunpowder would be used in no time. "God save us all." At least they still had the support of the people in the barony.

Donogh started growling like a bear, lumbering back and forth, his expression getting darker and darker. Then with an enraged bellow, he smashed his fist on the table. "Feckless bastards!"

O'Dwyer kept a tight leash on his temper while Niall wanted to howl like Donogh. Finally, O'Dwyer squared his shoulders and addressed the group. "The message is clear. We're on our own. It's up to us to survive, lads. Gather your men to prey upon the roads leading to Colonel Sankey's base in Clonmel. Approach from the north, west and east. Seize any supplies and captives you can. We'll ransom prisoners for food and ammunition." His gaze cut to Niall. "Time to bloody Sankey's nose. Are you up for that, O'Coneill?"

Niall gave a wolfish smile. "You know I am."

ÁINE STRAINED THE LAST OF THE FRESH MILK INTO A JUG, careful to avoid spillage. Maeve and the Triad had already taken the herd to the lower pastures, leaving her alone to finish off in the cattle pens. While she worked, she couldn't help but notice the sudden activity in the horse enclosure. Men were swarming all over, saddling horses and preparing to ride out.

A prickling rippled down her spine, and she stopped what she was doing to look around. No one seemed to be paying her any mind; they had saddles to secure and packs to load up. Still, she raised the top of her mantle to cover her head while casting a wary glance at the gathering men.

The crunch of footsteps approached her from behind. Áine checked the flow of milk and glanced over her shoulder. The pail nearly slipped from her hands.

Banan stood several feet away, staring at her in astonishment. "Áine? Áine Callaghan? I thought I saw you earlier, and clear as the dawn, here you are."

For a wild moment, Áine considered playing simple and denying who she was. After all, it had been four years since he had last seen her, and she must have changed a great deal, even if he had not. His eyes were still too large and widely spaced and his face still too long, made more so by an unkempt brown beard. Even his hair had grown thinner, which she expected would be a source of irritation to him—how Banan had prized his thick nut-brown hair.

Feigning ignorance would not fool him, and her ruse would only invite mockery. The man had never been one to hold back his derision.

Áine straightened her spine and forced herself to meet his gaze with a steadiness she did not feel. "Banan Molloy," she acknowledged. The only thing that betrayed her was the white-knuckled grip she used to clutch the milk pail. "I thought you would still be in Cork."

Banan laughed, an unpleasantly high-pitched sound laced with the knowledge of slugs and things best left under a heavy rock. "I left shortly after you disappeared." His voice trailed off expectantly, no doubt hoping she'd fill in the gaps of her story. She'd rather die.

Áine knew what was coming, and she prayed the earth would cave in and swallow Banan whole before he could utter another word. "If you'll excuse me," she said, "I have work to finish." She tried to still her shaking hands and poured the last of the milk through the strainer. Silently, she willed him to leave. But Banan never considered anyone other than himself.

"I've been with Eamon Grace these past few years. When this war is over, I've been assured the living of head groomsman in his estate."

"That should please you," Áine said, not entirely surprised. She picked up the milk jug and clutched it tight in her arms, preparing to leave. "Good day to you, Banan."

"Does Muiredach know you're here?"

That name, especially spoken aloud, had the strength to bind her. Áine couldn't move. She couldn't breathe. She could only swallow, and barely so. The name hung on the bracing air between them like a frozen puff of mist. "It's none of your business." She tried to brush past him, but he stepped in her way.

"Muiredach," he began, and she flinched again, "he was certain you found your way into a brothel."

Áine gaped at him. "What?"

"Sure, in the first weeks, he visited every one to flush you out."

As though he needed an excuse. The two men had always goaded each other to prove which one could be more audacious than the other.

"Which brothel was it?" Banan said, his attention sharpening. His eyes grazed across her breasts and down the curve of her waist. His meaning made her gasp.

"Is that what you think?" Áine's voice came out strangled. As if she could ever let men with ale-soaked breath and calloused hands touch her—hurt her. The thought made her want to vomit. It was on the tip of her tongue to say that she would never have lowered herself, but she bit it back. These decisions were rarely a woman's to make. "I *never* entered a house of sin."

Banan burst out laughing, a suggestive, insolent reminder that he knew more than he should

"Move aside," she said, almost pleading. His continued laughter lashed her pride.

"Surely, do you expect me to believe that you're not giving comfort to these good lads?" He waved his hand vaguely towards the camp. "How is that possible?"

Áine closed her eyes against a fresh memory of Mistress Mulriane. That kind woman had taken her in and saved her from the life that Banan accused her of. "I've been blessed."

"Or charmed?" Banan said with a smirk.

"Good-bye, Banan." She tried to skirt around him, but he jumped in her path and crowded her. His closeness made her sick. Oily, bitter ash wafted from his pores.

"There's no shame in giving comfort." His tongue darted out to wet his lips. "I've always had a fondness for you, chick." He cupped her chin, rubbing a calloused thumb across her jaw line.

Áine jerked away. Milk sloshed against the sides of the pail. "Do not touch me." She intended to dump its contents on him, but she caught herself in time. She had more respect for the cow than that. "Keep away from me."

"Hard to do so in this camp," he said with a sly smile.

"What is going on?" Niall stood at the edge of the enclosure with Fionn. He wasn't smiling, his piercing stare was directed to Banan. "All right, Áine?"

A rush of gratitude and relief swept through Áine. Fionn rushed over to her and managed to wedge himself between her and Banan. The man took a cautious step back.

"We're old acquaintances, O'Coneill," Banan called out. "No call for heroics today. She's fine."

Fine? When had been the last time she could say that she was fine? She had been safe these past four years—a brief respite, nothing more. But fine? She hadn't been fine, not for a long time.

"Áine? You know this man?" Niall had reached her side. His glance was a reassuring touch.

New panic set in. She couldn't let Niall question Banan more— what if he found out about Muiredach? She'd be less fearful of him finding out that she had been raised a Protestant. Áine couldn't bear to see his manner towards her change. "I do know him. I was only startled to see him here."

"I'm an old friend of her brother's," Banan said tersely. "I told you, we're acquainted. Have you suffered a knock that's affected your hearing?"

"Her brother?" Niall turned to Áine, "You have a brother?"

Áine heard the sharpness in his tone and recognised the hole she found herself in. The very thing she did not want him to know.

"Áine, girl, did you not tell him about Muiredach?" Banan said archly.

Fionn flattened his ears, and a low growl rumbled in his throat.

Banan took a step backwards. "Call off the wolfhound, there's a lad."

"No need. You'll be on your way," Niall said. "Eamon's looking for you."

"Is he now?" Banan's eyes narrowed. "You're at his beck and call? I thought you were only wiping O'Dwyer's arse."

"Should I enlighten Eamon that you're reluctant to obey his orders and will be remaining in camp with the women?" Niall asked coldly.

Fionn showed his teeth, and the man retreated several paces. "Best be going, as you say. Patrol awaits." Banan lifted his hand as a mock-salute to Áine before heading out of the enclosure. Before he left, he stopped and turned around. "Your brother will be glad to hear that you've been found, Áine," he called out to her. "He's fretted for your safety long enough. As soon as I can, I'll be sure to send word to him."

Her knees grew weak, and they nearly buckled under her.

"Áine?" Niall asked. "You're as pale as a sheet."

She pressed her hand against her cheek, finding her skin clammy, and stared after the direction Banan had taken. He couldn't mean what he just said. "'Tis naught. A chill, perhaps."

"I came to see you before I set off—didn't want to leave without letting you know. I may be gone a fortnight."

Áine felt herself softening, but she couldn't allow herself this vulnerability. Banan's presence made it impossible to pretend that she could have a future. She wrenched her gaze away from Niall and ducked her head. "Godspeed and safe journey."

"If Banan is distressing you . . . if you need—"

"I'm well." It came out shrill. She took a steadying breath and said, "I had not expected to see him here."

"You care for him?" Now his voice had a sharp edge. "Did he mean something to you?"

Her head snapped up. "No!"

Niall looked over his shoulder towards the direction Banan had taken. Then he frowned. "You told me you were alone in this world."

He looked hurt and disappointed. Áine bit her lip, hating to be caught in a lie by this man.

"My stepbrother is dead to me. There's nothing more to say."

Fionn's wet nose nudged her hand, and before she knew it, she was scratching behind his ears. The wolfhound's brown eyes eased her tension.

Niall appeared troubled. "While I'm gone, stay close to Eireen.

No one crosses her. And if Banan troubles you again, you'll let me know."

Not a question. An expectation. Áine wasn't sure how she felt—flattered yet horrified. "This isn't your cause." No, she definitely did not want him entangled in her past.

"Áine—"

"I told you before—I belong to myself alone."

"Do you, Áine-my-Áine?"

Her heart lurched and tears pricked her eyes, but she blinked them away. There were pieces of her that were too broken to be shared. "Godspeed, Niall."

CHAPTER 13

NIALL and his handpicked raiding party were the first to ride out of camp. No more patrol duty. He was a soldier, first and foremost, and thrived on the opportunity to strike a blow against the enemy. Only now every victory against the English would represent for him a strike against Captain Garret.

Before they left, Eamon had embraced Niall and given him an affectionate pat on the back. When he'd released him, Eamon had said, "Be safe, my lad. No unnecessary risks. I want to share a draught of *uisege beatha* with you. I'm saving a flask."

"I'll look forward to that."

Niall and his men headed for Clonmel, a fortified town lying nearly thirty miles to the southeast. There, the English commander, Colonel Sankey, maintained a sizeable garrison where he quartered the bulk of his troops. Heavily guarded convoys often travelled between Waterford and Clonmel and from there spread like a spider's web to other garrisons as needed. Niall and his men had captured several along this route over the past couple of years. Capturing them was relatively simple. Getting the spoils back to camp was another matter. Niall's company was to approach the town from the northern road while Eamon and Donogh's men would swing farther south and approach from the eastern and western roads.

Now that he had a mission, he had renewed purpose. Soldiering was his profession and would always be, even if that meant years of raiding parties or a last stand on the field with his sword gripped in his hand.

Passage through the mountains proved to be slow and difficult. The trails were mired in mud and the rivers swollen from the February rains, and they had to backtrack and find alternate routes to safely ford the raging waters.

Niall should have been focused on his mission with the single-minded attention of a wolfhound after a stag, but his mind kept drifting back to Áine. The tension between her and Banan had been a taut rope strained to its limit. A moment before he had alerted them to his presence, he had seen her naked fear. She had the look of a hunted animal backed against a cliff.

Nor had Niall missed the appraising gleam in Banan's eye. Niall had itched to wipe that mocking smirk from the man's face. That insolent grin hinted that he knew more about Áine than Niall did. That Banan might have been right rankled the most. Áine had constructed a wall around herself, and it hurt Niall that she pushed him away too. Niall didn't understand why, but the brother was central to her distress. It didn't take a seer to divine.

"You're doing it again," Cormac said.

"Doing what?"

"Brooding."

"I'm thinking," Niall said with a great deal of truth.

"Brooding," Cormac said firmly. "McTiege here must be influencing you." He nodded to the silent man on his tawny garron. "Sure, McTiege's lost the power of speech at times. Don't allow that happen to you, O'Coneill."

Niall exchanged a glance with McTiege, who had joined them for this trip. The man shrugged and said in his gravelly voice, "When I have something to say, you'll be the first to hear it."

To Niall's surprise, Cormac let it rest.

"Better be coming up with a plan to defeat the English. They've become tiresome," Ruadhri tossed over his shoulder, riding ahead of them. His freshly limed hair stood out in stiff white waves, and he carried himself with the majesty of the ancient High King of Ireland Brian Boru.

"You should tell them so yourself," Purcell called out to Ruadhri. "They'd appreciate your honesty."

Ruadhri half turned in his seat and bared his teeth. The two had been playing cat and dog for years.

"Easy now, wenches," Cormac called out to them. "Sharpen your claws later."

By early afternoon, they had left the mountain trails and reached the foothills tumbling towards Cahir Castle and headed south. They kept to the tree line and, to disguise their numbers from anyone following their trail, they rode in single file.

Niall now rode ahead, watching for signs of the enemy passing this way. Fionn caught a scent and bolted after a fleeing fox, and the flash of copper caught Niall's eye. His thoughts drifted to the flame-haired woman, slim as a reed, who lately occupied his mind. What was Áine doing right now? Knowing Eireen, the maid was more than earning her keep.

If everything had gone as planned and Garret's men had not found them at the cottage, Áine would've been at the Glen of Aher-low, settling down in the comfort of an inn instead of their wooded camp. They'd have parted ways . . .

Niall shook his head at his drifting thoughts. *Keep your mind on the mission.*

They reached a verdant valley and were forced to abandon the wooded trails. They made their way along a stretch rich in heather and gorse. The roads grew wider, and they soon came across well-churned roads, suggesting that a number of horses and heavy wagons had passed this way.

Cormac dismounted and examined the ground, studying the thick-set tracks. "A week old."

Niall scanned the horizon—thickly wooded stretches obscured his vision. It felt like they were chasing ghosts. "There's a village not far from here. We may learn more there."

They linked up with another wooded stretch and once again kept to the tree line, keeping the main road in the distance within their sights. Empty. Still empty. Even as they drew closer to the village, not a single rider could be found.

And then, as they detected the first waft of peat fires, Niall drew up. "Cormac and I will go this last mile into the village on foot. The rest of you remain here." He swung down from his horse and tied the reins to a sapling. Fionn sniffed around the area. "McTiege, I'd ask you to join us, but that garron of yours—"

"Too distinctive," McTiege mumbled in agreement. He stoked the aged horse and gave the animal an indulgent smile.

"The landlord is a good soul, but I can't vouch for others who may carry tales," Niall said.

"Must you ride the only yellow horse in Tipperary?" Cormac asked.

"Leave Broom alone. We suit each other well."

Niall unstrapped his sword from his belt and handed it to McTiege. "Keep that safe."

"You can trust in that."

Nail lifted his mantle to cover his head, and he and Cormac started on the way to the village. He felt exposed not having a mount and the easy means to fly if needed. Fionn bounded after Niall, refusing to stay behind even with McTiege whistling for him.

He and Cormac reached the village just as the rain started. A row of cottages and shops hugged either side of the street, occasionally breaking to reveal a glimpse of a river beyond. A drover cut his small herd across their path, forcing Niall to wait until they passed. Following in the rear, a young woman led the straggling cattle, a long switch touching them now and then to keep their pace.

Niall stared at the girl as the last of the herd passed. She had similar colouring to Áine, although more muted. It was the difference between staring at a fire directly or peering at it through a thick glass.

A family plodded behind the herd in a wagon pulled by a grey garron. A mother and four small children rode in a wagon with their possessions loaded beside them. Niall watched the procession,

147

puzzled. They were headed out of the village. He noticed a couple more families with bedding, chairs and cookware piled behind old carts. Furtive, worried glances were cast in his direction.

Where were they going?

He had been in this village several times, and normally the place was a bustling crossroads. Now it was nearly deserted.

Niall and Cormac found the public house at the other end of the town.

"Let's investigate the stables," Niall said. "See if there are any English mounts."

Around back, they entered a sprawling courtyard that led to the stables on one side and a series of storehouses on the other. No stable hands could be seen. Even the landlord did not hover at the door.

Cormac popped into the stables and quickly returned, giving a shake of his head. "Only two horses, and sorry ones at that."

"A horse is a horse," Niall said, not sure if he was disappointed or relieved. *We're here to get our bearings. Patience.*

The stale air of tobacco and spilled ale faintly hung in the room. Instead of the press of bodies, laughter and chinking cups, the common room was empty save for the landlord, who sat by the fire, his feet propped on a chair to catch the heat. The man jumped up when he saw Niall and Cormac and rushed over to them. "You should not be here, O'Coneill," he said in a low tone. "If the English find you, we will all pay."

"What happened? When were they here? I've never seen the town this way."

"More than a week ago, but they will return. They delivered an order—they've set up protected areas, within a few miles of their garrison. Everyone is required to move into those quarters before the last day of February."

"Or else?" Cormac demanded.

"They'll be treated as enemies—they can be taken, slain, any goods destroyed. And their cattle confiscated."

"We saw a few families leaving town," Niall said, still trying to grasp the impossibility of the situation.

"Most left for Clonmel over a week ago when the order came.

Others intended to resist but are now reconsidering. They'll be on the road soon enough. May the rains not mire them down."

Niall swore, his anger clenching like a fist. "Within a few miles of a garrison?" At the landlord's nod, Niall ground out, "The better to cut off our aid." He swore again.

"They're tightening the noose, curse them to hell," Cormac said.

First their aid from Lorraine had not materialised and now this. For the past two years, they had survived thanks to the good graces of their own people. As long as an O'Dwyer led the resistance against the English, the people of Tipperary would be there to help them. Until now.

"And yourself?" Niall asked tersely. "I do not see you leaving."

"I am by myself and will wait until the others leave. Please," the poor fellow implored, "you must go. Now."

"It's a ruse," Cormac exploded. "They wouldn't dare."

"That's what we thought," the landlord said miserably. "They started a few weeks ago with the saddlers, blacksmiths and any tradesmen useful to them. Not everyone left, so an English troop swept through here and seized their equipment, then herded them towards Clonmel."

"What colours were they flying?" Niall asked sharply.

"I don't know," the man blurted, then frowned. "Green. I think. No, wait—"

"And yellow?"

"That's it. Green and gold."

Around the time that his uncle's manor had been sacked.

"We'll not trouble you any longer," Niall said to the landlord. "Be safe."

He and Cormac left the public house and slipped out of the village. Neither said a word until the last cottage had been lost from sight.

"What now?" Cormac asked.

"It can go either way. The English need their supplies, and with the villagers crowding the road, they may be more vulnerable."

"From your lips to God's ears."

"Then let Garret be on the road," Niall muttered.

They returned to their troop, and Cormac quickly filled them in, drawing bursts of outrage from the men.

"Stealing our herds, burning our fields and now they hold our people hostage." Ruadhri scowled, black as thunder.

"We desperately need to find one of the enemy's convoys," McTiege muttered.

A bracing wind whistled down the valley as they set out again. As before, Niall's company kept to the tree line. It was even more important for them to be careful the closer they got to Clonmel. They encountered a no-man's land of abandoned cottages and empty fields. Rich farmland and rolling hills left fallow.

All abandoned.

People uprooted and forced to relocate.

There would be no one to plough the fields. Who would feed these families in the protected areas? How would they keep themselves come next winter with no crops?

They reached a long hillock where the north road was visible. Niall peered over the grasses and viewed the road below.

Villagers were making their way along the main road. Carts laden with crates of chickens and squealing pigs trundled along with a small herd of cattle following in their wake. Household stuff piled on the backs of wagons—stools, baskets. They reminded him of herdsmen looking for fresher pastures, but this was not summer, and rich pastures were not what they were searching for. The grim faces of the men and the harried women trying to keep their children hushed told a different story. They were driven by the threat of English violence on the innocent, people who never raised a weapon against them, people who only wanted a safe roof to shelter their families.

"These aren't the convoys we expected," Cormac said.

"No, they are not," Niall agreed.

All of those goods would be within their enemy's reach. Their brigade would not be able to rely on a kind farmer like Gleeson to open his door and his matronly wife to give them a bowl of bonny clabber to line their stomachs. Niall had always been grateful for the support they had found during these past couple of years, but until this moment he'd never appreciated how reliant they had been on the villagers and the farmers, even for a safe night's shelter.

Now the English had taken this from them too. How much more would they be allowed to get away with?

AFTER A FORTNIGHT, NIALL AND HIS COMPANY HEADED BACK TO camp—a fortnight with nothing to show for it. Low spirits sank their teeth into Niall, and he couldn't shake the sight of the villagers and their uncertain future.

They were a few miles away from the encampment when they reached the crossroads. Though eager to return this night and see Áine again, Niall had no choice but to call a halt. A thick layer of fog was quickly settling in with the night. Only the foolhardy continued in such conditions when a wrong footing would mean injury or death.

"We need to find a sheltered place before the light fails us," he called out to his men. His announcement caused a few groans and grumbles but no arguments. They were all aware of the dangers of proceeding in the dark.

"There's a glade not far from here," McTiege said.

They followed a stream as it wound its way deeper into a shallow gorge. The wind picked up and gusted past grey boughs and budding tree limbs.

Fionn lifted his head and sniffed the air. Niall could smell it too. His nose twitched with the sweet, acrid scent of charred wood and flames. He held up his hand to call a silent halt. He dismounted and handed his horse's reins to Purcell. He drew the dagger from his belt. Cormac, Ruadhri and McTiege followed his lead. Together, they fanned out on foot.

Careful not to make a sound, Niall crept through the forest with Fionn treading softly beside him. The woods swallowed them up.

The land sloped upwards to a stand of hawthorn topping a hill. As he drew closer, he saw the orange glow of a campfire through the sweeping boughs. Horses were hobbled a short distance away. One nickered nervously, no doubt picking up Fionn's scent.

The wind shifted, carrying with it the unmistakable aroma of roasting meat. Niall's nose quivered, and his empty stomach groaned. Through the trees, he saw shadows of men gathered around the fire and heard the low tones of conversation. Niall's grip tightened on his stag-horn dagger.

Then a high-pitched, wheezing laugh rose over the sound of crackling wood. Niall knew that grating laugh.

"Banan Molloy," he muttered under his breath.

Niall's tension should have eased, but he found himself irritated. Fionn let out a deep woof and bounded for the campfire.

"Niall O'Coneill?" Eamon called out. "Come out of the shadows, man."

"Ay," he replied. No help for it. Niall cupped his hands and imitated the hoot of an owl, their all-clear signal. An answering hoot sounded, and then the woods stirred with his men.

Niall entered Eamon's camp to find him and half a dozen of his men gathered around a fire with a haunch of meat roasting on a hazel spit.

"You've posted no guards," Niall told him. "The English could have found you."

"Let them come," Banan said with a wide, gap-toothed grin. He was snapping his fingers to get Fionn's attention. Niall gave a sharp whistle, and the wolfhound darted to his side.

"Hard to attract nothing," Eamon said. "The English are hunkered down in Clonmel. We've gone days without seeing a patrol or a convoy. And you?"

Niall shook his head. "Only villagers answering the summons to relocate to English-controlled areas."

Eamon nodded. "Same on the eastern road."

Just then Cormac crashed into the clearing. He stared in amazement at the haunch of meat roasting on a spit. "Where. Did. You. Get. That?"

"You'd do well to keep with us, Cormac," Banan wheezed a chuckle again. "Not sure we should share."

"Oh, you'll share," Cormac said, rubbing his hands together. "Move over." He plopped himself beside one of the men and forced him to scoot over on the log. "Is that mutton?"

"The remains of one."

"Where did you get it?" Niall asked, his eyes narrowing.

"Who cares?" Ruadhri said. "The question we need to ask is if there's any more. I could devour this on my own."

Niall watched his men carve out a share from the haunch to the grumbles of Eamon's men. Something didn't sit well with Niall. There were no farms in the immediate area, and in these times it would be unlikely that a farmer would part with one of his live-stock—*willingly*. He thought of the families trudging along with their dearest possessions. Crates of chickens, a few sheep, all crammed in the back of a wagon. They could ill afford to lose even one.

"This didn't come from one of our own, did it?" he asked.

"Of course not," Banan answered.

Niall did not miss the silent exchange shared between Banan and his companions. Niall's own men had their heads down and were more interested in blowing their fingers and stuffing their faces with the steaming meat. "That's what I thought."

Eamon leaned in closer to Niall. "You insult my generous hospi-tality, O'Coneill. Don't you know that it's rude to question where your host went hunting?"

Eamon's tone surprised Niall. The silent warning was clear —back off.

"Better hurry, or it will be all gone," Cormac said, finally looking up. Juices ran down his beard. He sliced another hunk of steaming meat and held it out to Niall at the tip of his blade.

"Not hungry," Niall said with a shake of his head. His appetite had fled. The sheep was dead, and there was no giving it back to whoever it was owed to. Let his men fill their bellies, leaving less for Eamon's men. But he still couldn't touch it. "You have my share."

"Ay. I'll not offer again," Cormac said, stuffing mutton into his mouth.

"Free with our food, aren't you Cormac?" Eamon said.

"We're brethren-in-arms, are we not?" Cormac said, wiping the dripping juices with the back of his hand.

"Our mission is to bring back more supplies to camp," Niall said sharply. "Tell me you found more than this."

"There was more, but it didn't last," Banan said with a snicker.

Niall sank to the ground near the fire, drew his legs up and wrapped his mantle around himself. The warmth felt good.

Banan left his perch and took a place beside him. Niall had never cared for the man. He could never lay his finger on it, only that Banan rubbed him the wrong way. Perhaps it was how he was always grinning, like he savoured a secret. Or how he fawned over Eamon.

And yet Niall seemed to be the only one who had an objection with the man. Banan was generally good for a laugh and a ribald tale and was a sought-out drinking companion. Even Cormac liked the man.

But Fionn did not. The wolfhound avoided Banan's outstretched hand and ignored every entreaty. Even when Banan tried to lure Fionn over with a morsel of mutton, the wolfhound didn't budge, even though his nose twitched.

Niall rose to slice off a generous hunk of mutton and offered the wolfhound the morsel from his own hand. Then he settled back to his spot. He did not miss Banan's scowl, which vanished when Niall faced him. Banan grinned and popped the meat into his own mouth, then scooted closer.

"I heard about your kin," Banan said. Niall remained silent, but the words grated. "To return home to find death and destruction." Taking Niall's silence as encouragement, Banan pressed on, "To find your kinsman's head on a spike. Gruesome bastards."

Niall motioned to Cormac to pass him the flask of *uisge beatha* that was being shared. He took a swig, savouring the burning liquor as it trickled down his throat.

"You've kept yourself together," Banan blithely continued. "I would have razed half of Munster in my grief."

"There's still time," Niall said grimly. He handed the flask back to Cormac.

Banan started laughing uproariously. "Can't help but notice you picked up a strange token from that adventure."

Niall kept his expression blank, warring with himself whether he should ask the man's meaning or ignore the bait and leave, claiming he needed to relieve himself. The latter won out. Niall started to rise to his feet, but he was halted by Banan's next words, "You know, Áine Callaghan."

Niall reclaimed his seat. "What about her?"

Banan's smirk widened. His mouth twisted as though he relished a juicy titbit. "She's a comely one, isn't she? But like fire, I'd warn caution."

"How do you know her?"

"I knew her stepbrother in Cork. I knew them both when I finished off my apprenticeship there several years ago. People called her strangeling. Muiredach had fits when she left Cork without his blessing. He'll be relieved to hear that she's been found."

"He is a friend of yours?" Niall asked. Already he didn't like the man.

"Ay. You can't put Muiredach down. But he was mighty put out when she slipped her jesses. My thoughts—he's better off without her. She is an odd one, mark my words."

By now, others had leaned in to hear their conversation.

Niall bristled. "What are you on about?"

"I'm only repeating what I heard," Banan said, spreading his hands wide and looking the picture of an innocent messenger. He looked around to get encouragement before ploughing on. "They say she talks to the dumb beasts, and she nearly cursed Ruadhri. Isn't that so, Ruadhri?"

"Nearly," Ruadhri said before catching Niall's eye. "But we're good now."

"What about the cows? Heard that a couple have sickened," one of Banan's companions said.

"You make it sound like this has never happened before," Niall said.

"We never had a problem before she arrived in camp."

"We've never had such a shortage of supplies," Cormac called out, then belched, ruining the effect. The men laughed. He cleared his throat and added, "The herd is skin and bones, naught enough meat for a wolf to pick through. It's a marvel they have any milk in them at all. You don't have to look much farther for signs."

That got a few nods, and the interest in the subject began to wane. Niall, however, studied Banan.

But Banan hadn't had his fill of tales. He leaned in to Niall. "When she left her brother's house, she took whatever coin he had in the shop. A dishonest, spiteful wench. It's the quiet ones you need to watch your back with." Banan sat back with the gravity of a seer. "Mark my words."

Niall didn't answer. He'd not take Banan's word on anything, much less his slanted views on Áine. Although Niall might not know Áine well, he refused to believe that she was dishonest or spiteful. But there was a mystery here surrounding the maid, and he was determined to mine it further.

CHAPTER 14

ÁINE KNELT beside the prone cow while her fingers stroked its fore-head. The poor beastie had taken its last breath only a few moments ago. She wasn't an old cow and hadn't been ill beyond a couple of days ago. The cow had ailed suddenly, and nothing Áine or the others could do had stopped her fast decline. This was their third death in the cattle pens this week.

Maeve returned from the fields and lowered herself to the ground across from Áine. "Oh," she said with a catch, "is she dead?"

"Just now." The words felt heavy on Áine's tongue. "I don't know what caused this." The other cows had died of similar symp-toms. "I've not seen anything like this before."

"The girls are making a sweep of the pasture where the herd grazed this week. We wonder if there may be something poisonous growing there that some of the cattle got into?"

"We should find a new meadow, to be safe." If they could. In Glengarra Woods, open meadowland was not abundant. Áine rose to her feet and brushed the dirt from her palms against her skirt. *Poor, gentle beast.*

"It's a shame that we won't be able to use the meat," Maeve said in a more practical vein. "No one would dare eat it for fear of sickening. Soldiers worry more about taking an ill turn than dying by musket fire."

Áine had a passing inclination to tease Maeve and ask if her knowledge had come from McTiege, but she didn't have it in her right now. Besides, the foraging parties had not returned, and the woman would not appreciate being reminded of McTiege's absence. Nor would Áine about Niall.

"Come," Maeve said, linking her arm through Áine's. "There's nothing you could have done." The girl's touch was surprisingly pleasant, and it left Áine wondering if she'd ever truly had a friend before. "We'll fetch one of the drovers to help us with the animal. None of the others are ailing, so pray that we've seen the last of this."

Later that morning, the Triad came back from the cattle pens, no closer to finding an explanation for what had sickened the herd.

"It has to be something." Eireen clucked her tongue and handed Maeve the ladle to mind the kettle. "Barbara, Brigid and Blanche, this way." And without a backwards glance, she marched towards the meadow. The Triad sighed and grumbled, but they scurried after Eireen's wake.

Áine held her silence. She hadn't put out a dram of milk for the Faerie Folk after Eireen had forbidden the practice. *I hope they aren't being spiteful over it.* She feared they were. Many times that morning she considered sharing her concerns with Maeve, but she didn't want Eireen to hear of it. Quietly, so as not to draw Maeve's attention, Áine filled a small saucer of milk and hid it behind the wood pile.

Eireen trudged back with the Triad at midday, baffled and frustrated. The girls slumped down on a log and picked out bits of grass from their skirts and fair hair. Áine could only imagine where, and how thoroughly, Eireen had them search.

"No other cows have the signs of the malady," Eireen said. "There's that at least."

Later in the afternoon, Áine and the other maids returned to the cattle pens to finish the day's milking. As usual, they worked methodically through the animals, isolating those who still needed attention. When they were nearly finished, Áine stood up to stretch her back, and for the first time since they had started, it occurred to her that something wasn't quite right. There seemed to be fewer cows than the morning. Had more fallen ill?

She began counting the cattle but had to start again when Maeve came up to her. "What's the matter?"

"Does it seem that we're missing cows?" Áine asked, shading eyes with her hand. Both women started counting together. "Three are gone."

Maeve bit her lip and counted them herself. "They must have wandered off, and the drovers missed them."

Áine's skin tingled, and an uncomfortable feeling settled over her. "I don't like this. We're almost done here—I think I'll go search for them."

"Only with me." Maeve called out to the Triad, "We'll be back soon."

Áine led the way to the pasture, but they found the meadow empty save for a few blackbirds flitting about. The two women continued along a cattle trail that led to the river, but again found no signs of the missing cows.

Maeve crouched down to drink from the water while Áine looked around, considering where next to look. "They couldn't have gone far on their own. Someone must have taken them."

"Why on earth would anyone steal three cows? The entire herd provides for all," Maeve said. "Let's keep looking."

Instead of going back the way they came, Áine picked another path, a wooded trail high along a steep ridge.

"You wouldn't think it possible they came around here, do you?" Maeve asked her. "The trees are too crowded."

Áine knew it was improbable and highly unlikely, but a strange feeling still pulled her along. It spurred her steps, and an urgency seized her.

"Slow down—you'll fall and break your neck," Maeve called after her. "They can't possibly have come this way."

Áine did stop, but not because of Maeve's entreaties. Another trail merged with the one they were on, and at the juncture branches were snapped in a wide swath and hoofprints were clearly visible. It didn't take Niall's tracking skills to tell Áine that the cows had come this way.

They continued along, now with clear tracks to follow. The trail narrowed and sloped downwards, forcing them to mind their footing. Áine and Maeve finally reached a section in the path where the earth had caved in, as though something had taken a bite out of the ridge. The tracks had stopped.

At the bottom of the gully, three cows lay dead, their legs splayed in unnatural angles.

Tears sprang to Áine's eyes. First the illness, now this tragedy.

Maeve was the first to look away. "We had better get back," she said, her voice thick. "Whatever drove them over might still be lurking around." She looked around at the dim woods. "Wolves might be about."

Áine shivered and edged away from the ridge. She doubted that wolves were at fault. Something or someone must have led the cows here, so far from the rest of the herd—something, perhaps, more dangerous than wolves.

Neither woman spoke as they made their way back to the encampment. They reached the cattle pens just in time to help the Triad finish up, and Áine was glad for the chance to divert her mind from the sight of the dead cows.

Áine topped the last milk can with steaming milk and sealed it. Together, the women hauled the cans to Eireen's and set them in their usual places, a short distance from the cook fire.

"Mam," Maeve said, drawing her mother aside, "we have bad news."

Eireen listened grimly. Her silence unnerved Áine more than if she were shouting. "These things have been known to happen," she finally said, her voice hard. "Girls, get the dinner started. Work is better than talk."

But she had not factored in talk of a different nature. Widow Lombard marched straight up to Eireen's shelter holding a small jug, as determined as a galley sailing into harbour.

"Eireen. You gave me spoiled milk again when I specifically demanded fresh." She held up the jug and thrust it in her face.

"The milk was fresh when it left here," Eireen said, showing the woman her back. Her mouth worked into an annoyed line. "But if it soured, then maybe you allowed it to sit too long."

"I did *not* allow it to sit too long." The widow planted her hands on her hips indignantly. "*Perhaps* you drew the milk from those dying cows."

"Nonsense. We do not milk sick animals. Check with the men who delivered you the milk. Perhaps they gave you two-day-old milk instead," Eireen said. "Either way, use it for bonny clabber."

Widow Lombard was not amused, much less mollified. She screeched at Eireen, and while Eireen's sloping shoulders and lined face spoke of fatigue and worry, she held up her end of the argument. Old disagreements were freshly churned and festering grievances eagerly aired. Their verbal sparring match drew an amused crowd of men. A few even wagered when the two women would finally come to blows.

"Go, then," Eireen said to her opponent in a scathing tone and pointed to the milk cans. "Get another ration of milk, if that is what will take to leave me in peace. Girls, fill this hoyden's jug."

"I'll do it myself." Widow Lombard stomped away from Eireen and brushed rudely past Áine. The lid was ajar, and the woman pulled it off to scoop out the milk. Then she recoiled. A horrified cry escaped her, and she dropped the cup.

"What's the matter now?" Eireen hurried over. When she peered into the milk can, her eyes widened. She whirled around and faced the maids, though to Áine it seemed as though she was looking straight at her. "How did *blood* get into the milk?"

The women rushed to take a look. Áine peered over Maeve's shoulder to see—sure enough, a thick ribbon of blood had been swirled into the milk. Her stomach twisted with fear. They had just filled those cans with new milk. Where had the blood come from? Then Áine remembered the jug's lid had been ajar. She was certain it had been firmly closed.

"Well it's clear what has happened," Widow Lombard said when she recovered her power to speak. "You have a spiteful, evil wretch under your care." She levelled an accusing finger to Áine. "Look no further than this new girl."

Áine picked her way through the forest, putting the sounds and activity of the camp behind her. She closed her ears to the metal ring of hammer against steel and tried to focus on the wind through the trees.

Her nerves were a discordant knot as she foraged for dry wood. With every stick she gathered, her despondency grew. Eireen had banned her from the milking pens over the rumours swelling around her.

"This will blow away like chaff," Eireen had told her. Áine knew better. There might not be much weight to chaff, but a spark could ignite it just the same. And Widow Lombard was the wind needed to fan the flames.

Two more cows had sickened in the same number of days. Even a daily saucer of milk did not appease the Faerie Folk, but Áine was past thinking that their troubles came from an Otherworldly source.

The obvious answer was that the cattle had poor forage over a cold winter, but that wasn't the answer that they wanted. Such an answer would remind them that their own conditions were dire, and who was to be blamed then? Better to cast side-glances at the newest dairymaid, cross themselves for protection, then blame her for their ills. A whispered question became common knowledge. It had been she who had spoiled their milk. It had been her who had caused hoof and stomach ailments for their herd. Their neighbour over at the next campfire was sure of it. It must be so.

Áine took a long branch with both hands and cracked it over her knee. She still had more wood to gather.

Even though Banan had been away with the patrols for the past fortnight, he had sown the seeds well before he had left. His name was never mentioned, but Áine recognised the crisscrossed trails that led to him. Members of his own company, those who had been left behind, were mentioned frequently as a knowing source despite the fact that they had never bothered with the cattle pens before nor spoken a word to Áine. And even more telling, a few started calling her strangeling, a name she hadn't heard since leaving Cork.

Too many men were tired of thinking about the war and turned instead to wild speculations. The longer they drank by the campfires and gave their imagination free rein, the sooner they would conclude that the entire English invasion had been brought on by Áine Callaghan.

Eireen had taken Áine aside just that morning when Áine grabbed her milking pail. "Mind, I do not believe that nonsense that you cursed the herd. But I'm a practical woman, and there's a great deal more that can sour relations than milk. I can't have anyone questioning the source of their food. A single refusal spreads to two, then three, then half the camp. Soon it becomes more contagious than what's affecting the herd."

"What would you have me do?" Áine had asked.

Eireen had taken the milk pail from her, right in front of Maeve and the Triad. Áine had flushed in embarrassment. "Tend the fires and odd jobs around our shelters. Start with gathering more wood."

It smarted that the girls had been there to hear this.

Áine continued her foraging farther down the ravine. It was wetter here, being closer to the streams, and she found it difficult to find dry wood. Tears pricked her eyes as she thought of the futility of trying so hard. Eireen had been kindly to her, but the needs of her family and the soldiers who protected them came first.

What if Niall returned and the rumours poisoned him against her? She couldn't bear it. Things would only get worse, especially when the news that flowed into the encampment was fouler by the day. Perhaps, it might be better to leave before such a thing happened.

Where could she go?

Returning to the Duggans of Cork was not an option. She had succeeded in travelling north unmolested years ago, but enemy forces had not occupied the territory between them. Áine thought back on the little cottage in the Glen of Aherlow, but it was outside the protected areas. If another patrol came to investigate the smoke coming from the cottage, the consequences for a woman alone would be horrifying.

She had no choice. Though she hated to be the source of a whisper campaign, she'd just need to bear up and face it with as much grace as she could muster. At least her person would be safe even if her reputation was in tatters.

"Where are you, Niall?" she whispered to the trees, as if the wind could answer her. "Are you safe?" If the wind knew, it held its counsel.

He still had not returned from his expedition, even though the first troop had returned the other day. Had something happened to him? An image of Niall lying at the foot of a gully, sightless, lifeless, a broken shell, scared her more than she could have fathomed.

A movement through the trees suddenly drew her attention—a man leading his horse towards the stream. His shoulders were slouched forward, suggesting a deep weariness. Áine could not see his face, for his mantle covered his head like a cowl.

She stood still so as not to draw attention to herself. The wood in her arms began to feel heavier. The man paused a moment, canted his head as though he were listening for a faint sound and then continued down the slope to the stream. Then, from down the same trail he had come from, came the sound of branches snapping and scattered leaves. A low bark broke the silence, and a wolfhound charged through the trees after the man. He turned at the sound, and his mantle dropped.

Niall.

Relief flooded Áine. He had returned. Safe and unharmed.

Niall lifted his gaze past the energetic hound and saw her. Áine could feel his surprise even from where she stood.

Fionn spotted Áine and gave another resounding bark before he bounded for her. He jumped up and nearly sent her crashing backwards. Áine dropped her armful of wood and fought to keep her balance while she laughed between swipes of a long pink tongue.

A whistle pierced the air, and Fionn dropped to his haunches, although he still danced around Áine's feet.

"Give our girl a bit of space, you great big bear," Niall admonished.

Our girl. That had a nice ring to it.

An urge to fling her arms around him nearly carried Áine forward, but she forced herself to remain calm. "When did you arrive?" She hoped her voice didn't sound as breathless as she felt.

"Just now," Niall said. His horse nudged him in the shoulder, and he shook his head. "I promised him a drink. Walk with me to the water?"

Áine nodded and fell into step beside him. Fionn darted ahead as though to show them the way. "Was the trip successful?"

Niall made a face. "Not hardly." Then he noticed the scattered kindling just as Áine bent to gather everything up. Niall quickly dropped down to give her a hand. "I expected to find you at the cattle pens," he said. "I went there first when I arrived."

Áine averted her head, pretending not to hear his unspoken question of why she wasn't there. "Eireen needed firewood."

Niall nodded as if satisfied with the answer, though she thought his jaw tightened. He took the wood she had collected and strapped it together using rope from his pack. Instead of securing it to his pack, he left the bundle by a rock. "Eireen can wait for her firewood. I want to show you something."

Áine chewed her bottom lip and glanced in the direction of the camp.

"I'll help you gather the rest, don't worry. She won't have any cause to scold you."

"Where are we going?"

He gave her a tired smile. "It's a surprise. I had a vague notion of going there before I saw you, and now you've determined the matter."

"Very well. Only for a little time."

He hoisted her atop the horse and settled comfortably behind her. A thought struck her, and she half turned to look at him. "You must be tired, riding all this time."

Niall's arms tightened around her, and he whispered in her ear. "I find myself restored."

Áine smiled to herself. She was aware of his warmth and the earthy scent of man mingled with leather. His arms encircled her, and she wanted to lean back and burrow deeper into his embrace.

It was a short ride upstream along a sloping trail that ran towards the mountains. The woods were alive with chittering, flitting birds. Sunlight filtered through an interlace of trees ready to bud.

They reached a glade filled with the tinkling of running water. Presiding over a shallow pool, water tumbled over moss-covered rock into a basin. The grass was a bright lime green—a sheltered spot untouched by winter's fading breath.

"How beautiful," Áine said as Niall helped her down from the horse.

"I thought you'd like it." He sounded pleased. While she explored a little, he tied the horse's lead to a sapling.

"How did you find this place?"

"Fionn once chased a fox all the way here," Niall said.

Áine looked around, imagining the wolfhound squared off against a cornered animal. She shivered. This wasn't a place for death, but for life.

"Don't worry, the fox got the better of Fionn. He simply disappeared," he said, apparently reading her thoughts. Niall stretched out on his side on the turf with his body propped up on his elbow.

"I'm glad." She settled down on the grass beside him.

The lines of his face were more pronounced in the sunlight. She could see the tightness around his eyes, and she wanted to touch his brow and ease the tension built there.

"When was the last time you slept well?" she asked.

"Nine years ago."

"Since you became a soldier. But your father was a merchant?" At his nod, she asked, "What made you decide to take up the sword?"

Niall tipped his head to the crown of branches above them. "I have an older brother who is content to continue in the family trade and several younger brothers who are more than willing to help. But I hungered to be a soldier instead of the quartermaster in my father's store. As far back as I can remember." He toyed with a

166

blade of grass, then plucked it, examined it closely. "There was an old codger in Galway market who would sell stacks of chapbooks. He displayed his stories like other merchants would display fine cloth or spools of ribbon. Stories of travel—a bookseller's account of London or the accounts of a Spanish rogue." He smiled at the thought. "Near the end of the day, if you were to catch him in a good mood, he'd crack open one of the chapbooks and read a selection from it."

"I'd have liked to hear that."

"Every week I'd go to his stall hoping to hear a story." He frowned at the blade of grass that he now twirled between his fingers. "I'd have the minding of my sister those days, and she always wanted to dawdle. I kept trying to hurry her through the market so I could hear the latest stories. Always chasing adventure."

Áine found herself caught up in his memory. How must it have been for him as a child with the freedom of the market? She could imagine his dark hair falling across a boyish face. The memory of him sparring with wooden staves merged with that image. "Will you return to Galway when the fighting ends?"

"I'm a soldier, Áine."

"Yes, of course," she said. "But the war will end eventually."

"In our favour, I hope," he said in a low voice. "If not, I can't say what will happen."

"But if we did succeed against the English, what then?"

Niall sat up. "Some of the men in the brigade were tenant farmers and have come on the word of an O'Dwyer, no matter that Edmund O'Dwyer was not head of the clan. May the Almighty see them safe to their homes when the time comes. For the rest of us, this is our profession. There are many in the brigade who spent years on the Continent cutting their teeth in foreign wars. If we survive, there will always be a new war to fight. This is my life."

She wanted to ask about family and how he might have one if he fought in one war after another, but he would misinterpret her question and think she was asking for herself. It seemed to Áine that for a man who cared so much for family, it would be a profound shame if he didn't have one of his own. But perhaps that was the way of things — those who shouldn't have one did, while those who should be there to shape lives could not.

NIALL WATCHED ÁINE MULL ON HIS WORDS, COULD SEE THAT SHE wanted to ask more. He hoped she'd let it lie. Would there ever be a time they weren't fighting? Before Cromwell's invasion, the country had been embroiled in a civil war, Irish Catholic against Irish Protestant, that eased into an uneasy truce a few years later. Nothing had been solved. The king's needs in England made temporary allies of most Irishmen. Who could say what would happen if they succeeded in driving away the invaders? A man hanging on his last length of rope would never give thought to how high he'd climb the next time.

What Niall wanted right now was to forget. For a moment, just forget. He did not want to think about the villagers making their way to an English garrison with all their belongings. He did not want to think about the cairn of rocks where his uncle lay or the strange land where his sister was sentenced to serve. He most especially did not want to think about how frustratingly elusive Garret was and whether he would ever catch him at all.

Niall closed his eyes and leaned back again on the grass. To forget.

"Tell me a story, Áine-my-Áine."

She didn't answer at first. Niall opened his eyes and studied her expression. She was frowning, no doubt considering her options. Would she choose a tale of the great heroes — Fionn mac Cumhaill and the Fianna or the undefeated warrior Cúchulainn? Then she smiled, and he caught his breath. Her face lit up, no less than the sunlight that brought out the bright copper of her hair.

"I do have a curious tale." She settled herself more comfortably on the ground and rested her hands in her lap. "This is a story that comes from Ancient Greece."

Niall wanted to ask her how she knew those tales, but then he remembered she came from Cork, as busy a port as Galway was. Foreign ships carried more than just goods. "Will it be the Fall of Troy? For if so, I have no stomach for that one."

Áine smiled, and Niall was once again lost in her brightness. "You needn't worry. But it is about one of the Greek heroes at Troy."

"Not Achilles. He was an arse."

Áine's smile deepened in agreement. Were her eyes grey? He had always thought so, but they were picking up green. "It may be faster if you would allow me to start the story," she said, interrupting his musings. "Otherwise, we'll be here all day."

That would hardly be a hardship. "As you wish, I won't interrupt."

Áine cleared her throat and sat up straighter. "Odysseus was not only a great hero and king, but he had been renowned in his life for being a clever and wise man." She paused, expecting another comment, but he remained dutifully silent. "When he passed away, his soul descended into Hades to await his next life. The day for selecting new lives came along, and all the souls were to choose lots to determine who would be the first and who would be the last.

"All the souls chose, and by poor fortune, Odysseus chose the last lot. All the souls laughed at his expense, for it was clear that he would be left with the life no one wanted. The lives of kings, emperors and majestic lions were the first to be taken."

"Lions?"

"And great eagles," Áine added. "They continued selecting new lives until it was Odysseus's turn. As expected, there was one life left, one that everyone had spurned."

"And it was?" Niall's undivided attention was focused on Áine.

"An ordinary man."

Niall frowned. "An ordinary man?"

"That's what I said."

"Like a farmer? A cutler? A shoemaker?"

"I'm not sure, but some would consider them ordinary. A king would, I'm sure," she said.

Niall thought of their exiled young king who had no country and was living on the largesse of his French relatives. Perhaps he would have a different perspective. "Very well, go on."

"All the souls laughed at Odysseus and ridiculed his poor

fortune. That such a great man had been so reduced did not invite their pity, only their scorn."

"I can understand that," Niall admitted. "What happened?"

"Odysseus called them arseworms."

Niall grinned, delighted by her wit. "He didn't."

"No, but he did call them louts and misguided fools. Then he told him that he had been the fortunate one, for had he been given the first choice, he would have chosen the life of an ordinary man."

Niall lifted a brow. "I will have to challenge you on that one. He had fame, fortune. Songs were sung about him. We're remembering him now, how many centuries later? He can't possibly have wanted to be obscure."

"It had brought him nothing but misery, you see. He barely knew his wife or son; there was always a king who commanded his service and pulled him away from the land he loved so much. For the next life, he wanted nothing more than to wake up in the morning beside his wife and watch his children grow."

A moral lesson disguised as a story, Niall thought. He didn't quite believe that's what would have happened. "Where did you learn this story? I've never heard it before."

"I heard it a long time ago, but I can't say from where," Áine answered. "Perhaps I learned it in the cradle. My father—my true father—had been a scrivener and entertained us with stories."

"And your stepfather?"

"He had no use for learning, much less when it was wasted on a woman." She was rubbing her wrist again.

"It's a good story. I thank you for it." Niall reached out and plucked her hand from her lap. He wove his fingers through hers and studied them. They were beautifully shaped, and he began to imagine them tracing a path down his bare chest and stomach. He felt himself go hot and hard. He sat up, and, casting a quick glance around, he said, "Tell me again how Odysseus wanted to wake up beside his woman."

Niall watched her face flush, and she nibbled on the bottom of her lip, making it as red as ripe berries. Her eyes glowed silver-green. Niall brushed aside a lock of copper hair that curled upon her throat and leaned in to kiss her.

Áine's lips parted under his, and she moved in closer. Her breasts brushed against his chest, and the feel of them shot down to his manhood. She smelled of honey and violets and spring air.

"I missed you," he whispered against her lips.

"I missed you too," she said shyly.

Niall pulled her in for another kiss, but his appetite had stirred, and he wanted more. His tongue explored her mouth and heightened his need to explore other parts of her. He wanted to take his time, worship her on this swath of grass like she was the first woman and the very last.

His hand cupped her breast, revelling in the feel of her in his hands, her nipple growing hard.

Áine froze before she jerked away. Her eyes were no longer grey and glowing; now they were dark and full of fear. *Fear of him?* She scrambled to her feet and backed away. The change in her was startling and confusing. It reminded him of when he'd had her backed against the fireplace and she'd brandished a poker to keep him at bay.

"I'm sorry," he said, rising to his feet. She was a maid, that was clear, but she was curious about him. She had not said or done anything to push him away. How had he misjudged this so badly?

"We should be returning," she said, her voice shrill and strained. "Eireen will be wondering where I've gotten to."

"We all live in fear of Eireen's tongue-lashing."

"She's fearsome," Áine said with an awkward laugh. Again, she was tugging on her fingers.

"Besides, I've promised to help you with the wood. We'd better get to that, then."

After a moment, she said, "I'm sorry." Her voice was small and pitiful, and it made him want to gather her in his arms. But she was hugging herself fiercely.

"No need." Niall whistled for Fionn, and while he waited for the wolfhound to return from his rambles, he helped Áine atop the horse.

Instead of settling behind her in the manner they had ridden here, he walked the horse.

"You don't want to ride?" she asked, a little dismayed. If it was anyone else, he would have considered she was playing coy with him, but this was Áine. He could tell she was genuinely distressed and conflicted.

Niall thought of his heated blood and knew this was the safer course. "There are some steep parts on the way back and mostly downhill," he gave as an excuse. "It's better if I walk this nag." Along the way, he kept wondering how deep the stream was and if the water was as cold as he hoped.

CHAPTER 15

SOUNDS INTRUDED NIALL'S SLEEP. He sensed movement swirling around him. Low, urgent voices.

"Up. Wake up—"

"—get the horses."

Niall awoke in an instant. In the predawn light, the camp was in an uproar. Men scrambled to snatch their gear, waking those still wrapped in sleep. He rolled to his feet and grabbed his weapons. Ruadhri was already up and buckling his sword.

Cormac ran over to them with the news. "An English troop," he said. "Spotted at the lower gorge.

They had been found . . . again.

Everyone knew what to do—they had done this before, each time the English discovered their camp. The infantry would help drive the cattle and sheep to safety while the cavalry would delay the English as long as possible.

Niall kicked dirt over the low fire. Shadows and darkness were the few tools left to them.

The brigade had been found before, but a different alarm bell rang in his head. Their camp was burrowed deeper into Glengarra Woods than any other previous encampment. They should have been safe from casual English patrols roaming the lower woods. All the branching trails, streams and gorges could have diverted a scouting party, and yet the bastards had unerringly found their location . . .

Niall stopped one of the men running past. "How far have they gotten? What are their numbers?"

"A full company—past the lower gorge by now."

No mere scouting party. Damn. About a mile and a half away. How had the enemy managed to get so close? They needed time. More time to evacuate everyone. "The sentries?"

"Only one made it back." Before Niall could question him further, the man bolted away.

One man out of five sentries. Niall's mouth pressed in a grim line. It was no use looking for O'Dwyer. When they selected this camp, they had already marked out defensive positions. Everyone knew their part and had their standing orders.

"A full company comes this way," Niall called out to his men. "We need to delay them as long as we can. Gather at the upper river."

"To the upper river!" Cormac bellowed.

"To the river!" rippled from man to man in their troop.

Niall grabbed one of his men. "Find Áine Callaghan—she'll be with Eireen. Tell her . . ." he trailed off, thinking of what message he could deliver.

"Niall. What are you waiting for?" Cormac shouted at him.

Niall ignored him. "Tell her to be safe." How ridiculous. As though she wouldn't safeguard herself. "Tell her I expect a story when I return. That's all. Away with you now."

The darkness was easing when Niall reached the horse pens. Fionn was already there, waiting with the gathered men. Niall mounted quickly and joined his men. The upper river was a quarter mile away—they had to lay their trap before the English reached it.

They passed the doused campfires, their progress checked by fleeing foot soldiers. Niall felt as though he were swimming upstream, and instead of the spring runoff waters that hindered their progress, it was the runoff of fear—fear of being cut down by the enemy, taken prisoner or worse, having their necks stretched by a hanging rope.

Niall's company joined others rushing to take their positions. They plunged down the trails. Some splintered off into side paths, melting into the forest to provide a last line of defence before the camp.

Niall and his men continued to the river. All was clear. The English had not made it this far yet.

A week of heavy rains had swollen the river, and now the waters were high and treacherous. Combined with the darkness, crossing proved to be difficult. Niall led the way across the river, keeping a tight grip on the reins. His horse lost his footing a couple of times, but the beast kept its head and ploughed through the surging waters. Even with the state of the river, the defenders would still have to rely on sheer grit and resolve to prevent the English from crossing.

On the other side, Niall and Cormac split up the men to melt into the shadowed woods crowding opposite sides of the river path. The road leading to the river narrowed like the point of an arrow. For the English to reach the camp, they had to breach the river defences, but first the enemy would have to get past Niall and the others.

An expectant silence wrapped around Niall as his horse shifted uneasily beneath him. Even the rushing waters had dulled. He strained to hear the enemy approaching, strained to see a torchlight betraying their presence. Fionn stood, his ears pricked to attention.

Then he heard it—the steady rumble of thunder. Horses. The drumming grew louder. There had to be a hundred troopers coming their way.

"Spread the word—we fire when they reach that stand of birch a hundred yards away," Niall whispered to Ruadhri beside him. "Cut the bastards down." The order rippled through his men.

Niall peered into the shadows, hoping to see Captain Garret leading the English horse. *Let him be here.*

The sound of advancing horses grew louder, and a dark mass moved towards them, guided by a few torches.

Niall focused on his task. His men were spread out along the length of the woods. Low on shot and powder, they had one chance to cut them down at the knees. Everything depended on taking down the enemy's vanguard.

The English drew closer. Niall checked his carbine while others levelled muskets and carbines. He held up his fist and waited, gauging the enemy approach. He scanned for sign of Garret, praying to see his flamboyant hat with its band of green.

A hundred feet away . . . fifty . . . twenty.

Niall dropped his hand. *Now!*

Irish muskets fired in unison. Puffs of acrid smoke stung Niall's vision. He blinked back the smarting tears before reloading his own carbine.

Horses screamed, and several men fell to the ground only to be trampled by their own panicked mounts. Some of the horses reared and tried to bolt. Shouts drowned out barked orders.

So assured of your welcome. "Not today," he yelled.

Before the English could organise themselves and fire back, another round of musket fire discharged, this time from Cormac's side of the path.

Horses reared, and the English advance faltered in the face of a crossfire. Men fought to remain in the saddle, where they had a chance to survive. They recovered quickly enough to fire back, though their muskets discharged blindly into the forest.

A shot whizzed past Niall's head, shattering a tree branch inches away. Splintered wood struck his cheek. He ignored the stinging and returned his attention to firing another round with his second carbine.

Rather than retreating, the English pressed forward and threatened to sweep past them. Niall released an angry bellow and with his men rushed out of the tree line to attack, his sword flashing. Cormac's men charged at the same time in a move intended to crush the English within their snapping maws.

The ferocity of the Irish attack checked the English advance, sending their horsemen into a mad scramble to regroup.

Long months of hiding and melting into the shadows had taken their toll on Niall. Now he threw himself into the relief of fighting in the open. With every swing of his sword, with every rasp of steel against steel, his blood surged. In every opponent, he saw a man who had debased his sister, and in every sword a man who had driven a blade into his uncle's belly and murdered his aunt. A fierceness drove Niall past fear, past exhaustion. The rage that he had kept tightly controlled burst through the dam, and he drove his horse deep into the melee.

For once, Niall gave no thought to his own personal safety. He wanted to burn them all down, mow them like a sickle to grass and trample them all.

And then he saw him—Garret, hovering at the back of his line, clear of the fighting as he shouted orders.

Niall bellowed his rage and fought his way towards the English captain. He slashed and swung his sword in an arc, slicing through muscle and bone. Across the battlefield, Garret's eyes met Niall's. The moment hung in the air. Did the bastard feel a moment of fear— did he realise the depth of Niall's enraged determination?

With a blink of an eye, the tide turned against Niall's men, and they found themselves pressed in on all sides. Niall narrowly avoided getting his head bashed in with the butt end of a musket. He kicked the side of his horse, causing the animal to sidestep away. Fionn darted in to shield Niall. The wolfhound nipped at the flanks of the English horses, causing the animals to crash into each other in an attempt to get away from the grey-furred threat.

Niall raked his gaze around the field for Garret. He roared his frustration. The bastard must be somewhere—he could not let him escape.

"Retreat!" Cormac bellowed from over the fighting. His brow was streaked with sweat and blood. "To the river. Retreat!"

Niall swore. Cormac was right. They had no choice, they had to fall back to the river. "Pull back!" he shouted. Word spread around like wildfire, and the Irish troops fell back to the river.

He leaned forward in the saddle and willed the animal to run as fast as he could to cross the river. They plunged into the icy water. His horse trembled under him, exhaustion sapping his strength. Niall pushed the animal's reserves and made it to the other side of the bank just as the English vanguard charged into the river.

When the first English horses reached the other side, a deafening bellow erupted from the Irish. O'Dwyer's reserves poured out of the trees and slammed into the English who, too late, realised the trap laid out for them. Now it was time for the English to retreat as they reversed their direction and attempted to cross to the safety of the far bank.

Battle lust gripped Niall, and he turned his labouring horse to give chase. Had it not been for Cormac, who intercepted him, Niall would have lost his head and crossed the river after them.

The English were now being routed. Their slowest were cut down while a few managed to slip away from the tightening noose and flee back the way they had come. Several of O'Dwyer's men chased after them with the vengeance of banshees.

Niall dismounted and advanced on one of the fallen enemy soldiers who crawled out of the river and onto the bank. His face was obscured by a wide-brimmed hat. The man struggled to get to his feet, his head and arm bleeding, but he could not rise. The soldier lifted his head, and Garett's face swam before Niall's eyes. Hate pulsed through Niall's veins. He lifted his sword, preparing to drive the blade through the man's neck.

"Quarter! I plead quarter." Garett's face disappeared, leaving an unknown English soldier kneeling at his feet. "I plead quarter."

"Quarter?" Niall ground out. He gripped his sword and held it poised, ready to strike. He wanted blood. He wanted to sever this man's tendons and muscles. He wanted his bloody quarter pound of flesh. It didn't matter that this wasn't Garret, Niall wanted retribution. He needed to make someone pay.

A hand clamped around Niall's wrist. O'Dwyer forced Niall to lower his sword. "Enough, O'Coneill. Your quick thinking saved the camp. Don't let blood rule you now."

Addressing the others, O'Dwyer gave quick orders. "Gather up the prisoners and any weapons or shot you can find. We'll turn this to our advantage."

Niall looked around at the dead and wounded on both sides. About twenty enemy soldiers were gathered up and herded back to camp. None were Garret.

· · ·

THE CALL TO EVACUATE RIPPED THROUGH THE CAMP, AND ÁINE found herself being pulled this way and that.

It's happening. Again. The English are coming.

Maeve shoved blankets into Áine's arms while the Triad scooped up all the cooking pots. Meanwhile, Eireen directed the operation with the authority of O'Dwyer himself.

"Pile everything up on that ass," Eireen called out to the erstwhile urchin who now was helping them upend their world and hurry along with the infantry.

To where? Áine's mind fumbled wildly. The English were coming. Again. Where could they possibly go that would escape this enemy who hunted them with the tenacity of the *sidhe* from the Otherworld?

Preserve us all. They'll be upon us any moment.

They would attack, burn everything in sight. They would kill. *Capture.* The words of the English soldier, dying at Niall's feet back at the cottage, came sharp to Áine's ears. *Indentured. Transported to the colonies.*

Upended. Torn from Ireland. Upended again and again.

The only safe haven Áine had ever known had been with the Mulrianes, and that had been torn from her. Burned down to ash, blood soaking the ground.

Áine worked as quickly as she could through her mounting fears. She had never thought of the camp as safe, not with all the men and with no connection to rely on except Niall. But until this moment, she hadn't realised how much she counted on their shielding her from the English.

Was there any place that was truly safe? Áine wanted to curl up into a ball and weep. What was the point of fighting, of running? They would only come again and again. Like Muiredach assaulting her, again and again.

"Áine, hurry." Maeve dragged her away from the ass. "The lad will take care of that. The herd—we'll need your help." She pinched Áine's arm. "What's the matter with you?" Maeve's sharpness cut through Áine's panic. She spun Áine around, her fingers digging into her arms. "Gather your wits. We need your help!"

Yes, the herd. "I'm fine. I'll be fine." Áine dashed after Maeve, running as fast as she could to the cattle pens. She shut out the fear that gripped her heart and focused instead on leading the cows and their calves to safety—she hadn't been able to save the Mulriane herd, but she wouldn't let this one fall into English hands.

Donogh's men led the way deeper into the mountains and helped drive the cows. In the distance, Áine heard the repeated pop of musket fire and the clash of fighting.

"They're fending them off to give us time," Maeve called over to Áine.

It was a hurried flight. The terrain grew more treacherous, with dips and gullies and broken land. Dark hills rose on either side of her. The trail narrowed into a slim passageway. It took all their skill to funnel the herd through that narrow stretch. Áine kept looking up, expecting to see the enemy cresting the hills and sealing them within. That had to have been the fear of many of Donogh's men, for their urgent calls to get moving faster rose sharp in the wind.

The way finally opened up, and the ground sloped downwards. Áine's ears picked up the sound of running water. They were farther upstream than where the battle was currently raging.

Everyone came to a halt, but Áine didn't understand why. Then word reached her and Maeve. The waters were much higher than normal, but they had no choice other than to make the crossing.

"This is how we'll do it," Maeve said to Áine. "We lead them three abreast. The largest, strongest cows upriver and the weakest and smallest downriver."

The current was surprisingly strong, and men struggled to wade across with the water reaching their waists. Men lined up in the water as the cows were urged across, wading through icy-cold water. A few balked and tried to backtrack, but Áine, Maeve and the Triad were there to keep them going forward.

Then a shout and a frantic splashing. One of the men slipped, lost his footing and went under. Another man lost his balance trying to fish him out. The cows that were mid-stream panicked at the violent thrashing in the water and balked. A calf floundered, and it looked as though it would be swept under.

Áine rushed into the river to reach it. The animal flailed about, eyes rolling in its head. She could feel panic rolling off its back. The water was so cold that her legs grew numb.

She looped her arm around the calf's neck. Despite the urgency to get the animal across to the safety of the bank, she made no attempt to rush it. Instead, she bent her head to its ear and started murmuring soft words. The words were nonsensical. They did not belong to a poem or a song or any story that she knew, but the unhurried nature of their pattern soothed the animal. Then, when it stopped trembling, Áine led the shaking calf gently across the river.

Others rushed over to take the animal. Áine's knees buckled. She nearly lost her balance, but Eireen was there to lend her a helping hand. The matron gave her a private smile.

But the warmth of that gesture faded when Áine became aware of the looks directed to her. Her ears caught their whispers, that the words she had cooed to the calf were not from this world but from the other. Even Maeve hung back and gave her strange looks.

"Best to keep going," Eireen said, stepping in and shielding Áine. "Never mind them."

They travelled for a couple of hours, and Áine lost all sense of direction. Finally, when the sun was cresting the tops of the trees, they reached an expansive clearing and Donogh called a halt.

Makeshift cattle pens were set up downstream from camp, and when they took a tally, they discovered that they had lost over a dozen animals in the evacuation.

Áine sank to the ground, exhausted and chilled to the bone. Maeve and the Triad, for once, said not a word. Even Eireen held her tongue. Shelter-building would have to wait. If they didn't move again.

For the rest of the morning, weary survivors gathered wood and carved out areas for shelters. The soldiers set up sentry points on the trails leading to the new camp. Áine kept looking in the direction from which they had come, hoping to see their men return in victory.

Hoping to see Niall. But the hours dragged on, and even Donogh could not rest. He sent runners down for news.

When she thought she couldn't take it any longer, she saw movement on the trail below. Soldiers! O'Dwyer's men. The wounded were mounted on horseback, some slumped forward, others draped over the saddles. Those who could walk led the horses.

Áine scanned the men walking into the clearing, searching for Niall. She saw smudged and wearied faces, bloodied men, but none of them were Niall. She hurried forward, wending her way through the advancing soldiers.

Where is Niall? Dear God. Where is he?

Near the end of the column, she saw Fionn trotting along, his muscular shoulders drooping. Then she saw Niall. His face was scratched and bleeding, his skin grey with the residue of powder and sweat. Dark hair was plastered to his skull.

He was absolutely the most beautiful sight she had ever seen.

Before she could think, she flung herself in his arms. He gathered her up tightly and buried his face in her shoulder.

"Áine-my-Áine," he murmured into her hair.

CHAPTER 16

Niall whispered a prayer of thanks that Áine had survived the attack. When he had reached the new encampment and seen her, with muddy clothes and tangled hair but unharmed, he had nearly sunk to his knees in relief. He still felt the sweet clasp of her arms around him.

He would have liked nothing more than to have remained with her, pillow his head on her lap and sink into a dreamless sleep, but his work was not done.

After giving his report to O'Dwyer and taking stock of their casualties, Niall and a party set out to search for their missing sentries. Only one of the five had been accounted for, and he had been the one who had raised the alarm. No one had had time to look for them earlier.

"Pray that they've regrouped near the old camp," Cormac said, mounting his horse. "They won't know where we've uprooted to."

"Unless they're hurt," Purcell said.

"Or worse," Ruadhri added, giving one last tug to cinch the saddle.

Cormac led the way, and they set out and passed through the old camp. A deserted, churned-up clearing with pots and gear strewn across the ground. A trio of crows squawked and took sudden flight, their black wings a dark blur. But no sentries.

They continued down to the lower gorge. Purcell had taken the lead and ranged fifty feet ahead when he suddenly reined in his horse.

"Here!" he called out over the rushing waters.

There, propped against an old willow tree, one of their sentries lay, throat slit and shirt drenched with blood.

They continued their search and found two more, both dead, one also with his throat cut and the other shot through the chest.

"Here's where the first sentry should have been," Purcell said, leading them farther down to a stand of empty bullrushes.

Niall examined the soft ground. "Who was posted here, do we know?"

"Banan," Purcell replied.

Niall glanced up sharply. "He rarely does sentry duty."

Cormac shrugged. "He volunteered this time."

"Ill timing, poor bastard," Ruadhri said.

Niall searched the immediate area but found nothing. He explored farther along where the ground sloped upwards and stood firmer. "Grasses have been pulled out in clumps here, and the ground has been kicked up. Looks like a fight."

"Could he have been taken as hostage?" Cormac asked.

Why him and not the others? "Keep looking."

The men fanned out to search the area. Twenty paces in, Ruadhri called out. "Here." Hidden by a clump of tall grasses, Banan lay facedown.

Cormac bent over him. "He's alive!" He rolled Banan over to find his head crusted in blood and a swelling near his temple the size of a goose egg. Banan groaned and tried to open his eyes, but they were swollen shut.

Niall crouched down and held a flask of water to Banan's lips. "Here, try to drink this." Much of the water dribbled down Banan's chin, but he did manage to drink some.

"Can you speak? What happened?" Niall asked.

Banan struggled to answer, but all he managed was a groan. His expression twisted in pain.

"Help me get him on one of the horses," Cormac said.

After they hoisted the wounded man on the horse and the group prepared to return to their new location, Niall held back. "Go ahead without me. I want to look around more."

The others headed back with Banan, and Niall examined the area. Only one set of tracks, and they were Banan's. The man must have made it to the clump of grass on his own. He was damned fortunate to be alive.

Niall returned to the camp in the late afternoon. By now, several rough shelters had been erected as well as makeshift pens for the animals. His shoulder blades were as knotted as old oak, reminding him that he hadn't rested in a full day and night. God, he needed to see Áine again.

After seeing to his horse's needs, he passed by Eireen's and found Áine stirring the contents of an iron pot over the cook fire, not in a gentle, rhythmic motion, but vigorously, as though she were whipping up thick custard. Fionn sat in the grass at her feet, watching.

Niall sank to the ground beside Fionn, exhausted. After a few moments, he raised his head. She still worked with furious energy. "Are you well, Áine?"

"We're fortunate to have saved this pot," she answered. "Otherwise, what would we have used to cook our supper?"

"The English care nothing for cooking pots," he said gently, puzzling over her manner. "We would have gone back to the old camp and scavenged what we could after they left—this is what we've done before."

"Of course, it's happened before." She whirled on him, holding out the ladle. She had a wary, feral expression, similar to when she had held an iron poker against him in his aunt's kitchen.

"You're safe now, my Áine," Niall said.

Eireen, hovering near, caught his eye and shook her head. "Áine, lamb, why don't you go get some rest for now? Maeve will take over the porridge for you, won't you?"

"Certainly," Maeve said, taking the ladle from Áine and leading her inside the makeshift shelter.

"Come later," Eireen told Niall. "She'll feel better then."

Niall stared at the shelter. The urge to follow after her, demand to know what was wrong gripped him. "I can't leave her like this." He took a step forward, but Eireen moved to block his path.

"Go," she said. "She's had a shock—don't tell me that all soldiers react the same way after a skirmish? I didn't think so. Give the woman some space."

"Ay," he said.

Eireen looked grim. "There are strange whispers swirling about."

"What kind of whispers?

"If you have to ask, then you need to listen more carefully."

Niall thought of Banan and his poisoned tongue. A chill pierced his heart. For Eireen to be warning him, things must have worsened. He had been away from camp so often, consumed with finding Garret, he had paid very little attention to gossip. "Watch her for me."

"You know I will. Off with you."

Niall found his men and, having no energy to build a shelter, simply wrapped his mantle around him. His legs were restless, riddled by tiny jolts of energy. It was a long time before blessed sleep claimed him.

THE NEXT MORNING, BLEARY-EYED AND ACHING ALL OVER, NIALL made his way to the new paddock, with Fionn padding beside him. The horses were kept in a small clearing not far from a stream. Bright sunlight sparkled over the flowing water, beckoning him. "If I took a plunge," he asked Fionn, "will everyone think I've gone mad?" Fionn lifted his head. "Ay. That's what I thought."

Still, the urge persisted, and while Niall was brushing his horse, he allowed his thoughts to drift to Galway, where he and his brothers had often played like otters. He was so caught up in his memories that he hadn't realised anyone approaching until Eamon placed his hand on his horse's neck.

"You look like shite, my lad."

Niall snorted. "And good morning to you, Eamon."

"I suppose." Eamon looked around. "It could have been worse, the skirmish. The English might have routed us like they did Fitzpatrick's brigade to the north and captured O'Dwyer. Then where would we be?"

"We'd be suing for peace." The thought soured Niall's stomach.

Eamon made a sound of agreement. "You heard about Banan? By rights, he should be dead."

"Has he said anything yet?" Niall said.

"No. I've set my own men to watch him," Eamon said. He nodded to a group entering the paddock. Under his breath, he said, "O'Dwyer needs to speak to us on a matter."

"Ay?"

"Come with me." Eamon led him away from the horses and the main camp. He struck a winding trail that climbed the side of a hillock. In sections, the incline was steep and rocky.

When they finally reached the summit, Niall found O'Dwyer standing with Donogh and another of his officers. The precipice overlooked a hillside of trees and falling slopes that ran to the glen below. The men stood close together, deep in conversation. When they saw Niall and Eamon, they broke off their talk suddenly.

"Niall, you fought well at the ford yesterday," O'Dwyer said.

He nodded his thanks and waited to hear why he had been brought here. This was a great view, but he didn't think O'Dwyer cared for rocks and a bird's-eye view of treetops.

"The English took a bite out of us today," O'Dwyer said. "Even with the hostages we gained, we lost twenty good men, and another fifty have been seriously injured. As for the animals, we lost thirty garrons, half the sheep and several cows."

"What of the other camps?" Niall thought of O'Dwyer's forces spread throughout Glengarra Woods.

"Not a ripple," Eamon said. "But they'll uproot and relocate, just in case."

"The English have found us before," Niall said. Not an unusual occurrence during the fighting season. In fact, during those months they shifted camp every few days, rarely staying in the same place for more than a week at a time, but never in winter. "The English activity has been more pronounced everywhere, not just here."

"They smell desperation," O'Dwyer said flatly. A few moments of silence stretched uncomfortably. Finally, O'Dwyer looked each man in the eye. "What we discuss here doesn't leave this place."

"Agreed," Niall and the other men said.

"What do you think of the attack?" This question was directed straight to Niall.

"Close. Too close," he answered. "If we hadn't stopped them at the river, we'd have lost everything." The camp wouldn't have had enough time to get away. The thought of Áine captured by the English twisted his insides.

O'Dwyer nodded. "What else?"

Again, Niall was surprised that the question was directed to him, as though O'Dwyer expected him to know something he wasn't saying. Niall sorted his thoughts, thinking back to the river and his subsequent search of the area. Something had been bothering him all day. "They knew where we were. Precisely where we were encamped."

"Go on," O'Dwyer said.

"There were a number of trails they might have taken, but there was no sign of the English deviating from their route. If they suspected that we were in the area but didn't know exactly where to find us, we should have found tracks heading down other trails. But we didn't." Niall paused, thinking back to when he and his men had first reached the river. "They came with only a few torches before first light." The implication settled on him like a dead weight. He knew O'Dwyer's next words.

"We have a traitor in our midst."

"Someone gave up our location," Donogh added.

Niall's anger stirred. The brigade was more than a fighting unit, it was kinship. These men whom he had served with for years were closer to him than his own brothers. They were the Fianna of the old stories, united and committed. The possibility that there was a traitor in the brigade was an abhorrent thought. And yet O'Dwyer spoke sense. "Who do we think it is?"

O'Dwyer, Donogh and Eamon all looked at him.

"You think I did it?"

"Of course not," O'Dwyer assured him quickly. "I trust you as my own. You wouldn't be here otherwise."

"But we wonder, young Niall," Donogh said, "what do you know of the woman, Áine Callaghan?"

"Áine?" Niall expected Donogh to break into a wide grin and nudge him good-naturedly in the arm, saying, "Only jesting." But Donogh did not smile, and everyone else, especially O'Dwyer, waited for Niall's answer. "You think Áine is responsible? That's nonsense."

"Why? Because she's a woman?" Donogh asked. "They're not all softness and innocence."

"With all respect, I'm not a complete fool," Niall said.

"No, but you *are* smitten with her," Eamon said.

Before Niall could retort, O'Dwyer cut in, "I hear that this Áine is from Cork—a notorious Protestant stronghold. What do you know of her people?" His jaw was set in a determined line.

Niall floundered. He didn't want to admit that he knew very little. Áine had been evasive about her life before she joined his uncle's household. She had not even told him about having a step-brother. But there was a good reason for it, he was certain. "She left Cork four years ago and has no intention of returning there. Her nan was an old family connection to my Aunt Fi. Look, Áine cares nothing for politics."

"This is what she told you?" Donogh said.

"What does that mean?"

"The maid was the only survivor," Donogh answered. "Rather careless of Captain Garret."

"What you're suggesting is vile," Niall snapped.

"Eamon recalled her being at the Mulrianes. Said she was odd," Donogh said.

Niall faced Eamon. "Did you now?"

"I only meant that she was skittish," Eamon said. "Look, Niall, we mean nothing by it. But we have to ask."

"If you are serious about finding the traitor, you'll put aside these ridiculous questions about Áine and focus on who has the means and the will to betray us," Niall said, looking pointedly at each of the men.

"Any other suspicions as to who it could be?" O'Dwyer asked.

"What of Banan?" Niall said. "He was at the first sentry point, and yet he survived when three others didn't."

"The man nearly died," Eamon said. "Are you suggesting that he bashed his own head in?"

"Are you saying, Eamon, that a dairymaid has the means and the will to spy for the English? How do you suppose she's sending them messages? Whispering to the magpies?"

"Protestants have their means," Donogh said grimly.

"What the hell is *that* supposed to mean?"

"You didn't know that she's a Protestant?" Donogh asked. "She's a bloody heretic."

"That's ridiculous."

"You know this to be true?" Donogh frowned, his eyes narrowing shrewdly. "I've heard credible accounts that she remained in Cork City after the Catholics were purged. Her family were Protestants, young O'Coneill. If she said otherwise, she lied to you."

"She's been accused of being the bloody Queen of the Faeries," Niall cried. "Tell me you believe those stories too, *old* Donogh."

"Enough," O'Dwyer said sharply. "No use fighting amongst ourselves. I want the traitor found, plain and simple. Put your heads together and come up with a plan to catch the bastard. Whoever it may be."

"A cornered animal is a dangerous brute," Niall said tersely, "but it covers its tracks poorly. We'll find the traitor, and he will be brought to justice. You have my word on it."

He left with a bitter taste in his mouth, frustrated and disappointed that O'Dwyer would have even given credence to wild rumours. It was imperative for him to find the traitor as soon as possible.

Eireen was right. The rumours were spiralling out of control. Áine had told him herself that she wasn't Protestant, and that was good enough for him.

Niall halted mid-stride.

Was that what she had actually told him, back in the cottage in the Glen of Aherlow? He frowned, trying to recall how she had answered the question he had thrown at her. Her exact words came to him now, settling as an uncomfortable pit in his stomach. She hadn't truly denied it.

ÁINE SAT BEFORE THE FIRE, HUGGING HER KNEES AS SHE WATCHED Maeve and the Triad finish a screen of green branches for their new shelter. This was the first opportunity Áine had had to rest the long day, and even Eireen did not begrudge her this respite.

It was the gloaming, and the sky darkened from a washed out grey to a deep azure. This should have been a peaceful time for her, for she enjoyed the quietness of twilight more than any other time, but the attack on the camp and how close they had been to being captured rendered her nerves into shattered glass.

And another magpie had crossed her path.

A movement drew her attention in the trees. Áine saw Fionn nosing toward their fire.

Dear Fionn. She was glad that nothing ill had befallen him.

Smiling, she rose to greet him, taking care to scratch him where he enjoyed it the most. "Where's your master?"

"He's right here." Niall entered the fire's circle.

Áine was used to seeing him strained, and the last couple of days had been grim, but this time his expression bordered on troubled. "What's the matter?"

Niall lifted his head and noticed the women's attention. "I would have a private word with you, Áine."

"Certainly." What was the matter with him?

"Come, Fionn," Maeve called out. "We've saved you an oatcake."

Áine followed Niall away from the shelter, and he kept walking a fair distance, even when there were clear of earshot. He didn't try to touch her or hold her hand, and with each silent, passing moment, she grew alarmed.

Finally, she refused to go farther. "Where are we going?"

Niall stopped and faced her. "My commander was enquiring about you."

"O'Dwyer?" Áine asked. "Why should he concern himself with me?"

"His concern is the safety of the brigade."

"Then I don't understand why I matter to him."

Niall gave her a searching look. "Because you matter to me, and these are dangerous times for our survival. He has heard some troubling reports."

A chill went down Áine's spine. "What reports?"

"He heard you were Protestant and wondered how I didn't know." Even in the deepening twilight, she could see the plea in his eyes.

Áine stilled. Her mouth went dry, and the earth beneath her feet felt unsteady. "What did you say?"

"That the rumours were untrue and he was mistaken," Niall continued, flatly. "You once told me you weren't Protestant, and the woman I care about wouldn't lie to me, would she?" No apologetic smiles, no soft words, not even a gentle touch to reassure her that he had taken care of this. By the hardness of his tone, he knew. "Why are you not saying anything?"

"What would you like me to say?"

"Tell me I haven't given a lie to a man I've always been honest with."

Was this all she needed to do—reassure him that these were all lies—and mayhap he'd believe her? But she wasn't that woman. " I can't," she said in a whisper, but she might as well have shouted.

Niall looked away and shook his head ruefully. "As I feared." He paced a short distance, then stopped and whirled to face her. "How could you have lied to me?"

"I didn't lie—not entirely." She tugged at her fingers and wished she was anywhere but here.

"Which is it, Áine? How can you not entirely give me a falsehood

nor entirely the truth either? The truth, woman, is one or the other."
Even in the fading light, she could see the angry tic in his jaw. "Or
have you become a clever Dublin barrister, parsing words to suit
yourself?" He marched back to her, not bothering to hide his anger
and disappointment. That last cut right through her. "I remember
exactly what you told me. I asked if you were saying that you were a
Protestant, and your precise words were . . . ?" When she didn't
answer, he did so for her, "That you weren't saying that. What did
you expect me to believe?"

"I can explain." She tugged at her fingers. "I was Catholic once
upon a time until my mother remarried a Protestant blacksmith."

"And then you weren't." Niall raked his fingers through his hair.
"You were raised Protestant?"

"I suppose."

"You were or you were not, Áine. Which is it?"

"I was," she admitted. Her heart sank when he turned his head.
"I was but a child when she married him. My nan tried to teach me
her ways, but . . . my stepfather wouldn't hear of it."

"So a lie of omission," he said. "You led me to believe you were
one of us."

One of us.

A sharp blow. Too sharp. Betwixt and between once again but
belonging to neither.

"I am not one of you. I never will be, clearly." She gave a bitter
laugh. "This has been my fate, to belong to no one. There is a reason
why I belong to myself alone." She choked back the tears that
pricked her eyes. Now was not the time to indulge them. "You ask
why I didn't tell you when you asked? *I didn't know you.* I found
myself alone with a complete stranger, and my life was in danger.
You wore your beliefs for the world to see, a proud Irish Confederate
soldier."

"You make that sound like a sin."

"It is when you're a hypocrite."

"Sorry?" He drew back, outraged. "You're accusing *me* of being
false?"

"How well you remember *my* words but conveniently forget your own," she said. "Did you not yourself say that Ireland should be for all Irish? What corner of this ideal world will you reserve for people like me?"

"You're turning my words against me. This is not about ideology —it's about trust."

"And yet you've already judged me," she cried. "What would you have done had I confessed I was raised in a Protestant household, that I stopped being Catholic when I was just a child? That I haven't given a fig for being one or the other and saw no love from either?" A sob escaped her, and she turned away. "That the priests offered no help or solace for a woman alone without protection." *That they maintained a piousness when I came to them about Muiredach but blamed me for my situation?*

"Were you never going to tell me?"

The hurt in his tone nearly undid her. "I hoped not to."

"Is that how you handle inconvenient truths, like your brother?"

Áine drew back. "What of him?"

"The brother you never told me you had until Banan revealed it," Niall said.

"He's. Dead. To. Me."

"What are you hiding?"

"I have nothing more to say about this." Áine whirled around and headed for the shelter, but he grabbed her arm and held her back.

"How do you think it feels for Banan to know more about you than I do?" Niall said, leaning closer, making her flinch."

"It is my misfortune that he does, and it wasn't by choice," Áine said. "How maddening that he could ingratiate himself with my step-brother and other Protestants in the city yet not be accused of lying."

Niall scowled. "I'm not interested in Banan, nor do I trust him to claim it's day when the sun is up. But I don't like to be made a fool."

He still held her, and his grip on her arm was tightening. Anger switched to fear. "Release me."

Niall frowned, looked at her arm in sudden confusion, then released her immediately.

Áine didn't waste a moment. She bolted through the woods as far away as she could.

CHAPTER 17

IN EVERY RUMOUR, there was a grain of truth. Niall couldn't stop thinking about their argument. Áine may not have entirely lied, but she had kept things from him and allowed him to believe what he would. And still she refused to answer any questions about her family.

What was she not telling him?

One thing he did know, and he'd wager his life on it, she had not betrayed the brigade even if she had betrayed his trust.

After Áine had dashed off, Niall had left to lick his wounded pride alone. He hadn't returned in the morning to talk with her either. He wasn't yet ready to face her.

Meanwhile, he had a traitor to uncover.

The realisation that there was a traitor disgusted him. It wouldn't be the first time a coward chose his own self-interests over the lives of his countrymen or the honour of his country. He thought back to the note that was nailed to his uncle's door. It had been written in Irish—the work of collaborators. They were everywhere. Niall did not fool himself to think otherwise, but it was even more galling to know that one of O'Dwyer's men was craven enough to work against the brigade.

Niall was still aghast that O'Dwyer should think Áine was somehow connected. All because of those damned rumours. They had taken a life of their own and attracted the suspicions of their commander. He had to find the traitor before things became more out of hand—but how?

Niall spent time around the paddock, but it became quickly apparent that there was too much coming and going. Daily, a few scouting patrols went out to sweep the area—parties of five or seven. From experience, they didn't often stay close together and usually split up to cover a wider area. Any one of them could have the opportunity to be the spy.

His thoughts kept drifting back to Banan. How had the man survived a stealth attack that had claimed three others?

It was time he learned.

Niall found Banan sitting up before a campfire with a couple of men in his troop keeping him company. When he happened to step on a twig and it snapped, Banan startled.

"Sneaking up on me, are you, O'Coneill?" Banan said with a trailing laugh. He touched the linen wrapped around his head and winced. His colour looked sallow, made more so by the dark purple bruises around his eyes.

"Didn't mean to." Niall lowered himself to the ground across from Banan.

"If you're looking for Eamon, I haven't seen him," Banan said.

"I'm not. I wanted to see how you were faring."

Banan's eyes narrowed. "Someone nearly bashed my head in. How do you suppose I'm faring?" He gave him an exaggerated grin. "But I thank you for your concern."

Niall gritted his teeth, willing himself to be patient. "Humour me, Banan. Do you remember aught of that night?"

"Nothing." Banan grimaced and looked away.

"Were you attacked at your post or where we found you?"

"I was unconscious, O'Coneill. How on the Almighty's green earth am I to know where I was found?"

Niall stroked Fionn's fur as he considered Banan. The man couldn't look him in the eye. "You don't recall if you were attacked at your post? Surely, you can answer that . . . unless you want to think of another way to put me off my questions?"

Banan touched his bandage. "I'm dizzy. Think it best if I get myself some rest."

Niall studied the man carefully. He felt a prickling in his fingertips. "What are you hiding, Banan?"

"Go away. Leave me be." He waved a dismissive hand. "I can't say what happened. It was dark, and my mind has been scrambled."

One of Banan's friends, a thick-necked brute known as Bull, called out from across the fire, "O'Coneill, you got anything better to do than bother a wounded man?"

"Ignore him, Bull. I usually do," Banan answered. "The man is bewitched and addled in the head. It's no mystery who's done it either."

Niall's hackles rose. "Meaning what?"

Banan turned his head, though a slight smirk betrayed him. "Afternoon, O'Coneill."

Niall glared at Banan. The man was hiding something, he was certain of it. He leaned forward, unconcerned if anyone heard. "If I find out you're behind the poisonous rumours circulating around the camp about Áine, I'll make you wish the English did you in after all. Fair warning. You only get one." With a curt nod to the others, he left the fireside with Fionn at his side.

Seething, Niall headed for the river to clear his head. That oily bastard needed to have the conceit knocked out of him. And if Banan proved to be the traitor, he'd take great satisfaction to nail his hide to a tree.

Near the water, a crowd had gathered around a commotion. A scrap was breaking out, and Niall was in just the mood to join in.

Fionn started whining, nudged Niall before shooting off towards the crowd. Niall whistled for him to return, but the wolfhound ignored the command and barrelled through the men, scattering a few like partridges. As Fionn parted the crowd, Niall saw straight through to the centre of the commotion.

Áine.

In an instant, he perceived it all—her terror at being hemmed in by a jeering crowd, her growing panic at not being able to break free.

Niall sprinted across and pushed his way through the crowd to reach her.

"What the hell is going on here?" Niall placed himself between the men and Áine.

"She's cursed us all." One man pointed a grubby finger at her.

"I have not," she gasped behind Niall, but her words were mainly drowned out by the shouts of agreement to the man's accusations.

"She hasn't cursed anyone," Niall said. "You're letting superstition poison your mind."

"I wouldn't put it past any Englishwoman," another snarled.

"English? She's not English, man. She's a good Irish woman." Had they gone all mad?

"English. English. English." A man started chanting and stoking the crowd further. Soon everyone was chanting the same thing. They had indeed gone mad.

The taunting continued. "English, English, English."

Then something cut through the chants, "English spy."

Niall whipped around to find Bull standing there. The man had his arms crossed over his husky chest, and a self-satisfied grin twisted his mouth.

"Say that again," Niall called out to him as he loosened his sword in his scabbard. "Go on. Repeat it. Unless you have peas for bollocks."

Bull's grin disappeared. His nostrils flared, and he too went for his sword. The crowd hushed immediately and backed away to give the two men space. Anger had shifted to eager anticipation of a bloodletting.

Niall and Bull circled each other, swords drawn. He cleared his mind and focused on his hulking opponent. This was no sparring match with wooden staves. What was on the line here was not just his life, but Áine's.

"Let's see if your blade is sharper than the lies you spread," Niall called out to the man.

Bull barred his teeth and bellowed before swinging his sword in a wide arc. Niall arched backwards and jumped aside. The man's blade cleared him by inches.

"Your aim needs improvement." Before Bull could recover, Niall launched his offensive. Lunge, parry, thrust and, at the final pass, Niall sliced through the fleshy part of the man's arm. The man stumbled back and howled.

Niall settled his stance in a defensive position. "If you were one of my men, you'd be spending more time in the sparring ring."

"Shut up, O'Coneill. Are you here to fight?"

"I'm fighting. You're bleeding." Niall smiled grimly and motioned him forward.

Bull's attack came swift and fierce, but Niall held his ground, giving his opponent no opening. The man had strength but no finesse, and as Niall continued deflecting the man's sword thrusts, he grew increasingly irritated. That this brute could stir up trouble so effortlessly for Áine fuelled Niall's anger. He darted in, then leapt to the side, scoring a nick here and there—on Bull's forearm, his left side and even his thigh.

Niall could feel Bull slowing down, trying to overcompensate with harder thrusts. He waited for his moment. Bull extended his blade and held it forward a moment too long. Niall shifted his weight and slid his sword down his opponent's blade, connecting with the hilt. With a quick flick of his own wrist, Niall disarmed the man and sent the sword skittering to the ground. Before Bull could react, Niall had the tip of his own blade pressed against his throat.

"I yield." He stared at the length of steel.

"Not before you speak the truth," Niall said. "Tell them she's not a spy."

Bull's mouth pressed in a stubborn line. His gaze dipped back down to the sword at his throat before he finally gave a curt nod. "She's not a spy."

"Louder, so they can hear it in Dublin."

"She's not an English spy."

Niall lowered his sword, but instead of stepping away, he shifted his weight and seized Bull by the scruff of the neck. "You tell Banan the next time I'll come for him." Then he pushed the man away from him in disgust.

Grumbling over the fight being over so soon, the crowd began to disburse. Niall found Áine standing beside Fionn, who growled at anyone who got too close to her. Her arms were wrapped tightly around herself, and her eyes were enormous and filled with uncertainty.

Their gazes met.

Niall took her in his arms. He felt her tension ease slightly, but she was still rigid with fear. He brushed a kiss on her bright hair and rubbed her back.

"It's over," he murmured, not only speaking of the fight.

"I'm so sorry that I deceived you. I couldn't bear to let you know." A tremor went through Áine's body, and Niall held her tighter.

"I reacted badly. You were right—I've been a damned hypocrite," Niall said. "We'll speak no more of it." Her body relaxed against him. "What happened here?"

"I went to the river to fetch water," she said in a small voice.

Niall now noticed the empty tin buckets spilled on the ground. "Never mind that. I'll get it for you. Come, I'll see you back to Eireen's."

She didn't answer, but she allowed him to lead her. Niall stayed long after Eireen had settled Áine with a soothing cup of milk and sent her into their bower to get some rest. The first stars had appeared in the evening sky when he finally thought to leave.

"She was lucky you were there," Eireen told him in a low voice, so as not to carry to Áine's ears.

"It won't happen again," Niall said.

Eireen's brow raised in a silent rebuke. "Don't be a fool, Niall O'Coneill. This is hardly over."

THE SOUR MOOD IN THE CAMP BURROWED DEEP INTO NIALL, leaving him both exhausted and too unsettled to sleep. He passed a poor night—he doubted that he had more than a few hours of rest.

When the first rays of dawn stretched across the sky, he rose from the lumpy ground with relief.

He needed to clear his head with a speeding horse beneath him and the wind whipping in his face. On his way to the paddock, Niall passed by Banan's campfire. He maintained a healthy distance, but he could see Banan still rolled up in his mantle, with Bull and two others not far.

Eireen was right. A single sword fight hadn't ended the nonsense. It wasn't over yet.

Niall reached the paddock and was surprised to find McTiege saddling up his mount, the oddly tawny piebald with the disjointed gait. McTiege fawned over the yellow beastie as though she were a pure white chariot steed.

"Where are you going so early and on your own?" Niall asked.

"Dispatches. O'Dwyer's orders," McTiege said curtly. His jaw was clenched, and he fussed overly long with his horse's saddle.

"Why you?" Niall asked, his pique rising. "It's me who carries his dispatches." If O'Dwyer had decided to displace him because of Áine, he could have the decency to be a man and tell Niall.

McTiege turned to face him. "Go on, ask him yourself." The vehemence in McTiege's tone surprised Niall. *Not him too.* Niall's pride wouldn't allow him to question O'Dwyer's orders, to hear that even after years of faultless service, one baseless rumour would make his commander reconsider Niall's abilities.

"Piss off," Niall said.

An uncomfortable silence grew between them. After a moment, Niall relented. "If you're going to Muskerry in Ross Castle, take the southern route. I've never been troubled by English patrols travelling through Mitchelstown."

McTiege sighed, then he nodded. "Thanks," he said before mounting his horse.

Troubled, Niall watch him go, and he didn't hear Donogh approach until the man was close.

"I heard what happened with Banan yesterday and that display of swordsmanship later," Donogh said. "It didn't help the girl's cause."

"She's innocent," Niall said flatly. "Of all accusations."

Donogh looked across the fields and squinted. Deep lines appeared on his face, and more grey hairs had threaded through his dark temples. "Rumours gather faster under the spurs of fear and superstition. Will you battle every man who repeats what he's heard?"

"If I need to, ay."

"Fancy yourself as Cúchulainn standing alone against the might of Queen Medb's Connacht warriors?"

"Even if three times fifty were to stand before me."

"We aren't living in the days of an epic poem." Donogh faced him. "Keep your head, young O'Coneill. Dark times are on the horizon."

ÁINE HAD TO LEAVE. *I'M NOT SAFE* DRUMMED IN HER MIND OVER and over again until she thought she'd go mad. She couldn't sleep. She couldn't eat. Every moment felt like she was fighting an invisible opponent, one that chipped away at her. Worry wore her down, made her want to weep, even though she could not shed a single tear.

The English attack had terrified her, but what had shaken her more were the rumours that were fermenting in the camp. Banan's lies had spread and taken an ominously dark turn.

She heard the whispers. Some blamed her for the attack, calling her English whore and Protestant Jezebel. Others swore she had cursed them all, by incantations whispered under the last full moon or some such nonsense.

And now O'Dwyer was questioning Niall about her. She must not be the reason that he lost the trust of his commander. He was a professional soldier—fighting under O'Dwyer's banner was his life.

Flight was her only option—even if it meant she'd have to leave Niall. Even if it meant that she would cut her heart out of her chest. Better now before he learned the truth of her. She'd disappear, and people would swear that the Faerie Folk had reclaimed her. Niall might search for her, but eventually he would wonder if the rumours were true; eventually, he'd forget the strange woman he'd found in a ransacked estate.

A few hours after moonrise, Áine crept past a sleeping Eireen, careful not to wake the sharp-eared woman. She had saved part of last night's supper—a couple of oatcakes and half a small wedge of cheese—and wrapped it in a square of linen. She put the food into her satchel along with the tinderbox and snares.

Maeve and the Triad were in an exhausted slumber after the additional work needed to set up new shelters for the animals as well as their own.

Eireen twitched in her sleep. Áine froze and held her breath. *Don't wake. Don't wake.* She didn't want to face the woman's questions.

After a few agonising moments, the matron settled down and her chest rose and fell to the sound of soft snores. Áine released her breath and ducked under the overhanging branches of the shelter.

The bracing wind brought immediate relief. It cleared the cobwebs from her mind but left her uncomfortable enough so as not to dawdle. She studied the early morning stars and determined the direction she needed to take—back to the last place she had felt safe, the shepherd's hut.

It was better this way . . . for Niall. For herself, she was heartsore over the prospect of never seeing him again. To never lose herself in serious hazel eyes that sometimes softened into a smile, or touch the thickness of his dark hair, or delight in the way his head tilted when he listened to her—truly, truly listened to her.

Áine's steps faltered, but she hardened her heart and forced herself to continue. Niall's fascination with her would not last beyond these fraught days. Even if the war ended in his favour, he was the lord's nephew, his father a prosperous merchant in Galway and he, himself, a soldier. She, on the other hand, was damaged, strange and misunderstood.

She left the encampment behind and made her way down to the river a quarter mile away. If she followed it upstream, north towards Cashel, it was bound to lead her out of the forest and through the foothills. Once clear of the hills, she'd head west through the Glen of Aherlow, the same route Niall had taken to get them here.

I can do this.

She had done it once before when she had fled from Cork. As long as she kept off the main travel routes and exercised caution as to who she asked for aid, she stood a chance.

The air was cooler by the river. Moonlight rippled along the flowing waters. From somewhere upstream, she heard a splash like a fish would make in the shallows.

After a few hours of walking, dawn came bright and hard. Long shadows stretched across the forest floor. Áine took a few moments to splash her face and scoop a handful of water to drink. With the sunrise, she realised that she had travelled farther east than she had expected. If she continued along this route, she'd reach the English garrison at Cahir Castle instead of the northern pass out of the mountains.

She adjusted her course, keeping the sun over her right shoulder. Her mind drifted back to the camp. Eireen would be furious at Áine's disappearance. The Triad would be annoyed at having to face the brunt of Eireen's wrath and being forced to do Áine's share. Maeve alone would be worried, but until the immediate needs of the herd had been met, no one would be actively searching for her. Unless Niall stopped by in the early morning before setting off on patrol. She needed to get farther away before that happened.

The sunlight warmed the forest. Áine paused to loosen her mantle. Her feet dragged and her limbs had turned to iron, locked on the ground. Their power leached into the carpet of needles and last year's rotted leaves. The furious energy that had spurred her this far drained from her. Áine leaned against a tree trunk and closed her eyes.

Birdsong played high up in the trees, a soothing, calming concert. Áine's tense shoulders relaxed. For the first time in days, silence enveloped her like a warm hug. A single tear welled in her eyes and slipped through her closed lashes to trace down her cheek. And with that tear came another and another, then a flood. She gathered her knees tightly to her chest and sobbed into the folds of her skirt. These tears did not bring weakness; they silenced the gnawing fears and subdued the anxiousness that had been crushing her.

Áine wasn't sure how long she cried, but when there were no more tears, she felt both empty and strangely full. She swiped her wet face with the back of her hand and dried herself with a corner of her mantle.

Always isolating herself, always fleeing for safer ground. How had that served her before? Being alone and cut off from people never worked. That was what Muiredach had used to control her, and he had burned it into her consciousness. Even here and now, his memory controlled her—if she allowed it.

Her life would always be a struggle—that she couldn't change. This world was an uncertain, dangerous place, and there was no safe haven to be found except through the people who cared. There would always be those who whispered about her, and yet, if there were a few who did believe in her, like Niall and Eireen, people who saw *her* for who she was, then she'd be content.

Niall did not think her strange. He cared for her, and he was hers —for how long, she wasn't sure. But every day was a blessing, and she'd do well to never squander that. Perhaps Niall, Eireen, Maeve and the Triad were the closest family that she had ever had.

If she continued to run now, it would only solidify her guilt to her accusers. She couldn't do that to Niall, not after he had risked his future with his commander by standing up for her innocence.

She rose to her feet and brushed the twigs and wet leaves that clung to her mantle. Flight was the coward's way. She had fled enough times in her life. It was time she learned to stand her ground.

Áine started back to camp, already feeling lighter in spirit with each passing step.

In the distance, she spied a movement through the trees. A horseman, trotting slowly along the trail. Áine dropped to the ground. Pulling up her mantle to form a cowl, she crouched behind the trunk and made herself as small as she could.

The clip-clops grew louder, then the horse nickered. Áine lifted her head just enough to peer over the trunk. Following a well-worn trail, the horseman rode a tawny piebald garron.

Áine knew that horse, had seen it in the paddock. When the rider drew closer, she recognised the intimidating McTiege.

She watched as he continued on his way. O'Dwyer's men routinely scouted the areas surrounding the enemy garrisons, but there was something about McTiege's plodding pace that told Áine he wasn't scouting. He wasn't paying any attention to the woods around him. It was as though he did not fear enemy attack.

He rode out of sight, north towards the east.

Áine rose from her hiding spot and continued towards camp. She walked a mile before another rider appeared on the trail, this time with a grey wolfhound. Her heart leapt in her chest, and a lump of emotion lodged in her throat.

He had come for her. Tears pricked her eyes.

Niall drew his horse before Áine but remained astride. Fionn was jumping all over her with joy, but his master looked far from joyful, only relieved and exasperated in equal measure.

"Where are you going?" he asked.

Áine smiled. "Back to the encampment."

Niall gave her a pointed look. "Are you certain?"

"Give me a ride," she said, holding up her hand.

Niall shook his head, then bent down to help her up. "Sure, you are a trying woman, Áine Callaghan."

She settled herself behind him and looped her arms around his waist, squeezing tight. The familiar scent of Niall, of horse and leather, filled her senses.

"Did Eireen send you?"

"I do not need Eireen to send me after you," he said. "But she alerted me that you were gone."

"How did you find me?"

Niall glanced back over his shoulder at her. "For a slip of a maid, you leave a broad trail." He urged his horse forward.

"Not possible. I couldn't have stirred a leaf."

He gave a small laugh. "I'm an excellent tracker."

Áine rested her cheek on his back. "McTiege was better, it seems, since he passed this way first." Now she knew what the man had been doing out here on his own.

"Sorry?"

"McTiege," Áine said, looking behind her. "Perhaps we should find him and let him know."

Niall reined in his horse and twisted around so he could look at her. "You saw McTiege? Here?"

"He passed this way some time ago, though he didn't see me."

Niall frowned and looked around. "Which direction was he travelling?"

"East."

Niall didn't say anything, but it was clear that he was troubled. "Did you not send him to help find me?" she asked.

"No." After a moment, he added, "He should have been heading southwest towards County Kerry, not east towards Cahir Castle."

CHAPTER 18

W HY WAS McTiege heading towards an enemy garrison?

Niall sat before Eireen's campfire, oblivious to the soft women's talk that flowed around him. McTiege was heading in the opposite direction from Ross Castle. Why had he allowed Niall to believe he was off to Kerry? Niall considered different reasons, but he kept returning to one possibility. Was McTiege the traitor?

McTiege had been acting oddly the last time Niall had seen him. Curt. Irritated, like a man having to do a distasteful task. Niall puzzled some more and realised that McTiege had been off lately. He searched his memory—where had McTiege been during the attack? Everything had happened so quickly, with men running here and there. Niall couldn't be sure, but he didn't recall seeing McTiege with his men.

Unease burrowed into Niall.

It was possible that O'Dwyer had sent McTiege to Fitzpatrick's brigade in northern Tipperary. That would explain it—except Fitzpatrick had been thoroughly routed a few months ago, and his brigade was running for their lives.

There had to be another explanation.

Niall shifted his attention to Áine, who sat on her heels, cooking oatcakes in a sizzling pan. Fionn was stretched out beside her, watching the process with studied intensity.

Áine smiled at him with a warmth he felt down to his toes. "There's a deep frown on your brow. Didn't your nan tell you that if you scowl like that, it may become permanent?"

"How is it you've stolen the affections of my hound?" he asked, forcing himself to relax. It wasn't hard with Áine. "Lately, he's been with you far more than me."

Áine patted Fionn's head. "I'm glad for the company."

Niall reached across to snatch an oatcake while her attention was diverted to the wolfhound.

"I saw that, Niall O'Coneill," Eireen called from inside the shelter.

"The woman has eyes everywhere," Niall whispered to Áine after devouring the cake.

"And she has ears like a bat," Maeve said, suddenly behind them.

Áine tried to hide her smile, but her eyes shone a clear grey.

"Now don't you go eating all our oatcakes." Maeve swatted Niall with the back of her hand. "Others are counting on them too."

Niall leaned back, enjoying the nearness of Áine, the cool of the grass and the early spring breezes that were blowing. He tried to shut his mind to the other pressing matters. "And who is more deserving than me?"

"Cormac is perhaps not as deserving, but he's certainly as eager," Áine said. "He'll be bound to smell the cakes cooking."

"A shame that McTiege will miss them," Maeve said, her face colouring.

Áine exchanged a glance with Niall. His tension flooded back, and he felt his brow gathering again. "Has he not returned yet?" she asked casually as she reached out to flip an oatcake on the hot skillet. "Do you know when you expect him back, Maeve?"

"I can't say," she replied. "He didn't even tell me where he was going."

Niall rose. He couldn't sit here any longer eating oatcakes. He had promised O'Dwyer that he'd uncover the traitor, no matter who it proved to be. He owed it to Áine to find the bastard and clear the shadow of suspicion that followed her everywhere. He couldn't keep asking Cormac, Ruadhri or Purcell to sit as guard outside Eireen's shelter in the event the mood in camp further soured. Niall finally had a track to follow. It was about time he found his quarry.

Absently, he brushed his fingers along the curve of Áine's cheek. "I had better be going. I'll see you later."

Without a backwards glance, he headed for O'Dwyer's quarters. He was halfway there when Eamon caught up with him.

"There you are, lad," the man said. "Where are you going in such a hurry?"

Niall considered sharing his concerns with Eamon, but he pushed the thought away. Until he was certain of McTiege, he'd not say anything except to O'Dwyer. He knew only too well how rumours could escalate. "It's nothing."

"I heard you were over to speak to Banan." Eamon cast him a reproachful look.

"Ay," Niall said, folding his arms across his chest. "I suppose I could have been friendlier."

Eamon snorted. "It's no secret that you dislike the man."

"He's a serpent."

"The serpent was banished from Eden for telling the truth," Eamon said.

Niall turned on him, aghast. "The serpent is a deceiver and twists the truth for his own gain. I'll not sit by and—"

"Settle yourself, lad. I did not come here to stir the hornet's nest," Eamon said. He fell into silence. To Niall, he had something heavy on his mind.

"What is it, Eamon?"

The man sighed, then after a lengthy moment, said, "I must insist on your discretion." He waited until Niall gave him a crisp nod. "How comfortable are you with O'Dwyer's judgment?"

"What do you mean?" Niall asked. "The man is a good soldier and excellent commander."

"I'm not speaking of his military skills, which are formidable, no one can deny." Eamon scratched his chin.

"I'd follow him anywhere."

"Even as far as to treat with the English?"

"What?" Niall's skin prickled.

"O'Dwyer is negotiating terms for a treaty with the English commander, Colonel Sankey."

The words struck Niall with the force of a hammer striking an anvil. They left him gasping to find a logical meaning other than the obvious. "That's not possible."

"I'm afraid it is."

"He can't be—he wouldn't do that," Niall said, but his own protest fell flat on his tongue. No supplies. No aid. O'Dwyer had, in essence, told them that they had no choice. But there was a world of difference between acknowledging a dire situation and capitulating. Handing over Tipperary and Waterford. To the English. "Impossible." They hadn't given up on Lorraine and the aid he had promised. They had made it through the winter—they had not done enough.

"I'm not to blame, Niall. You should be aware of what's happening, to protect your interests. I fear our commander may be too soft with the English. He may not negotiate favourably. You remember how well he treated the English prisoners last year when your Captain Garret had been captured? Who can say, but the soft treatment might have contributed to Garret believing that he was above consequences."

Niall felt the blood draining from his face. "No."

"You should not be ignorant of these negotiations," Eamon said with sympathy. "O'Dwyer's inclination is to uphold his nobility, but we need the wiles of a fox to ensure the settlement favours us all. He'll be seeking terms for his own benefit, not yours or mine. He will keep his lands when all this is done, but what of the rest of us who live under the shadow of uncertainty? You can be sure that our birthrights will not be considered."

Niall reeled as though he had been delivered a death blow. This was not possible. Eamon must have misunderstood. It was probable that he heard a few words and jumped to the wrong conclusion.

O'Dwyer could *not* be considering handing over Tipperary to the invaders. Eamon continued to natter on about treaties and land claims, as though that was all that mattered. "I have to go."

Niall did not hesitate. He headed straight for O'Dwyer's quarters only to be told by his servant that the commander was not in.

"I'll wait," he said.

"It may be hours," the servant said.

"I said I'll wait."

O'Dwyer returned with Donogh before Niall had worn a gully with his pacing.

"A word alone, if you will," Niall said to O'Dwyer.

As Donogh opened his mouth, O'Dwyer silenced him with a nod. "We'll continue later, Donogh."

Niall plunged into the tent without waiting for an invitation. When O'Dwyer stepped inside, Niall whirled around. "Is it true? Tell me it's naught but a vicious rumour," he begged. It couldn't be true. The rumours around camp had been particularly vile lately, borne of frustration and idleness. This had to be one of them.

"Rumours?" O'Dwyer poured himself a draught of ale and offered a cup to Niall, who refused. O'Dwyer shrugged, but the slight lift of his brow signalled he was not entirely immune to the insult. "Since when do you heed such things?"

Niall felt the sharpness of a well-aimed barb. "If untrue, they will easily be laid to rest and I'll plead your forgiveness."

"It's my patience you're testing, O'Coneill."

Niall ignored the warning. "Tell me you're not treating with the enemy."

"Where did you hear that?" O'Dwyer scowled, his voice laced with irritation.

Niall almost breathed a sigh of relief, nearly, but not yet. Eamon had been sure of his facts. "It's a lie, then?" *Say it's untrue.*

O'Dwyer's expression shifted, suddenly guarded.

By Jesus. Eamon had not been mistaken. Niall felt his gut wrench. "You *are* treating with the enemy."

O'Dwyer swore. "I had hoped no one would find out. Not yet."

"You're selling us out to Colonel Sankey."

"I am not selling anyone out. We are down to our last supplies. There is no aid forthcoming, and the English hound us at every step. We can't continue this fight the way we are."

"Since when does Edmund O'Dwyer surrender? That isn't the man I admired—not the man I believed in." It was as though the ground beneath Niall's feet had become marshland. "We are not cowards. We'd rather die fighting than capitulate to the English."

"I will not have the blood of my men on my soul. I'm looking for the best terms," O'Dwyer said. "For all of us."

"So we can live to fight another day, right?" Niall said, grasping to make meaning out of this. "Tell me that this is but a ruse to lure the English into easing their vigilance."

O'Dwyer shook his head. "If I give my word not to raise arms, I will not break my oath, nor will any man under me."

Damn his oath. Damn his morals. Niall wanted blood. Eamon's words rang in his head and spurred his tongue. "This isn't about us." He leaned closer and spat, "This is about you wanting the best terms for yourself—so you can save your lands and go back to the way you were before the English violated our shores." It came tumbling out of his mouth, and the words blackened the space between them. Niall had gone too far.

O'Dwyer's face blazed in anger, his dark eyes turning pitch-black. "How dare you? You haven't earned the right to talk to me that way. O'Dwyers have been fighting for Ireland since the days of Brian Boru. We survived to this day by knowing how to use our swords and when to use our minds. I learned how to wield a sword from the cradle and cut my teeth on strategy at my father's knees. I led men into battle well before you had learned how to acquit yourself with a blade. You presume far too much, Niall O'Coneill. The son of a Galway merchant will not lecture me on war."

Niall drew back from the sting of O'Dwyer's words. "And what do you expect me to do? Bow to these invaders, these men who torched my kin's home, who spirited my sister away? Beg their forgiveness?"

O'Dwyer's anger hardened into cold resolve. "I expect you to survive. You'll do no one any good lying cold in a cairn."

"I'll bring them all down in flame and fury before I capitulate."

"If you live under my banner, you will do as I say," O'Dwyer said. "Think, O'Coneill. We cannot afford to be coming into these discussions crippled. Sankey will offer the best terms only if he perceives us to be strong."

"Did you negotiate where our prison will be, or will they transport us to one of their infernal colonies?" Niall asked bitterly.

O'Dwyer's brow darkened. "Mind your tongue, O'Coneill." After a moment, he relented and said, "We'll be free to leave for the Continent as a mercenary force, provided we don't take up arms against England. Spain is looking for soldiers."

Niall bit back a retort. "It sounds like you've settled it, then."

"I'm negotiating in good faith."

The tent was stifling, and Niall needed to get away. Without saying another word, he spun on his heels and stormed out.

He gave no thought to where he was going. He didn't care.

Niall pushed past men and ran into Donogh but spared him no explanation.

Donogh must have known too.

The gall of having to beg forgiveness rose in his throat—to give his word to the men who had destroyed his family, the men who had forcibly indentured his sister and shipped her far from her homeland. He couldn't do it—he'd rather cut off his tongue and sever his hand so he could not speak a lie or put his signature to a travesty.

Niall didn't mind where he was going and charged into Cormac.

"What's the matter with you?" Cormac said, righting himself. "You look wild around the eyes."

Niall backed away. "I don't want to talk about it." He took a few steps, halted and turned to Cormac. "We need to talk." His gaze flicked to the men within earshot. "Not here." He grabbed Cormac by the arm and herded him away. When he felt they were a safe distance from straining ears, he stopped. But he couldn't say it. He couldn't form the galling words.

"What the hell is going on, O'Coneill?" Cormac asked. "You're acting like someone has murdered—"

Niall didn't need him to finish the expression. "They have." And then he found his words. "O'Dwyer is engaged in talks with Sankey." He expected a burst of disbelief and shock from Cormac, but it didn't come. Another blow. "You knew?" Niall snarled and grabbed Cormac's shirt. "Why in the name of God's own bones didn't you tell me?"

"Because you'd have acted badly."

"Badly?" Niall's rueful laugh ended in a snarl. "Like this?" He drew his fist back and threw a punch.

Cormac arched backwards and dodged the blow.

Niall swung again, but Cormac feinted and ploughed his fist into Niall's chin.

The pain only fuelled Niall's rage. "What else are you keeping from me?" He lunged again, but his rage made him sloppy. Cormac easily darted behind him, locked his arm around Niall's neck and held fast.

A group of men ran over, drawn to the spectacle like flies on shite.

Cormac hissed, "Not here. I'm going to release you, but you're coming with me."

Niall tried to throw him off, but Cormac's hold tightened.

"We're not airing this in front of everyone. Understand?" Cormac said. "Shut your mouth, or I'll put my fist down your throat."

"Fine," Niall gasped.

Cormac released him but kept his hands raised in readiness. Niall glared at Cormac and pressed his balled fists to his sides. "This way," Cormac told Niall and, without waiting to see if he was coming, strode away from the gathered crowd. When there was no fear of being overheard, he faced Niall. "Why didn't I tell you? It wasn't my place." His nostrils flared, and his jaw was in a hard line. "And I'm as frustrated and cross as you are." His expression became weary. "But it's the only thing left for us to do."

"What the hell does that mean? After what they did to my family—"

"Precisely," Cormac said. "You're not looking at this the right way. What could you have done? How would you have changed things if you knew? There would be no convincing you—"

"You agree with this?" So much worse than he'd thought. Betrayal everywhere.

"Ay—it's the sensible thing to do. Best to seek terms before the English realise how crippled we are."

"They already do," Niall muttered. When Cormac looked at him curiously, he added, "We have a traitor. Someone has betrayed our location."

"And look who's keeping secrets," Cormac said. "Never mind. O'Dwyer was right to get ahead of this. It's a good thing we repelled the last attack, otherwise we'd have no leverage. At least there's still hope."

"You call this hope?" Niall said.

"I understand your pain, but we're all tired of this. We can't go on."

Niall's fury pulsed in his neck. He wanted to bury his fist into someone's skull, and at this point he didn't care whose. He backed away from Cormac. Who was this man he thought he knew? "You can all go to hell with your treaty and your politics and your damned leverage." Then he stormed away.

ÁINE HAD DISCOVERED A SMALL WATERFALL A SHORT DISTANCE from camp, sheltered from view by a stand of newly leafed black-thorn. Crystal water tumbled into a small creek that fed into a larger stream. She lingered there, drinking in the pearly twilight, not wanting to return to Eireen's, not just yet at least.

For the rest of the day, she had thrown herself into the endless work that was needed to care for the remaining animals and to gather sufficient firewood for their own needs. She was bone-weary, and yet the work had helped shut out the undercurrents of discontent that permeated through the camp.

Niall had not returned as promised, and she felt his absence keenly. His horse was still in the paddock, so he couldn't be far. *Oh, to have the boldness to march through the camp and seek him out.* The

216

thought of encountering hostile stares and insolent grins tamped down that wish.

A splash interrupted her thoughts, followed by the sound of a man's muttered cursing. Áine leapt to her feet, preparing to dart deeper into the woods when she heard, "Devil take me."

Niall?

Áine scrambled down the small slope buttressed by rocks and emerged on the banks of the stream. She found Niall crouched at the water's edge, his shoulders hunched forward while he splashed water on his face. Under her feet, a twig snapped. Before she could blink, he was on his feet with his stag-horn dagger in hand.

"Áine?" His voice was low and gravelly. He relaxed his stance and tucked away the blade. But something did not sit well with Áine.

"Is all well?" She drew closer and searched his face. His light hazel-green eyes were now dark and turbulent, like the muddy waters of a churning stream. She lifted her hand to touch his cut jaw, but his fingers wrapped around her wrist tightly to stall her.

"Leave it," he said. "'Tis the least of my troubles."

"What happened?" Áine looked at his hand. His knuckles were grazed and raw. "You've been fighting."

"Not nearly enough." He hung his head and groaned. Pain furrowed on his forehead. He remained silent for a few moments, then said in a low voice. "Capitulated. O'Dwyer . . . even Cormac. Capitulated." Niall's shoulders slumped forward, and his throat swallowed convulsively. His eyes were overly bright before he averted his gaze.

Áine was becoming increasingly alarmed. The last time she had seen him so distraught had been when she'd told him about his kin.

Niall muttered a few more disjointed words she couldn't connect. He wasn't making any sense, but she felt his deep sorrow. Áine wrapped her arm around his shoulders and tipped her head to peer into his face. He wouldn't look at her. "I've failed." Only a whisper, Áine wasn't sure she'd heard correctly.

"Failed? Unthinkable. How have you failed, Niall?" Her heart ached for him. Was he still flaying himself for not being able to save his family?

"It has all been for nothing. All of this. Naught." Bitterness laced each word.

"What do you mean?" She brushed a wet lock from his forehead. His skin burned beneath her cold fingertips.

He did not answer at first. Then he said, "O'Dwyer is seeking terms. With the English. Surrender. Do you understand?" He turned to her, his face stark and hard.

Áine's eyes widened. No more fighting. She searched her feelings for the same depth of rage and despair that Niall now displayed, but she could not find it in her. Relief. *Please, God, that it might finally be over.* She'd be willing to swallow her pride, again, as long as it meant survival.

But Niall was different, and she feared for him. She did not fool herself that the English would be merciful to him and to anyone who raised a weapon against them.

"What does this mean for you?"

He threw his head back and barked a hollow laugh. "I've failed. These bastards will have won. They have ravished this land and our people—my kin—and they will have gotten away with it. Curse them and their descendants." He half stood and yelled, "Curse you all."

Áine grabbed his arm, alarmed. "Be wary of curses. They may come back to cross you."

"I don't care," he said. "It's over."

"I do care," she said. "For you."

The planes of his face softened. "Áine-my-Áine." His arm curled around her waist, and he pulled her against his chest. His hair dripped, and his shirt and mantle were damp. At first, he held her as though she were his support, as if she weren't here, he'd crumble to the ground. She stroked his hair and murmured reassuring sounds. Then he lifted his head and looked at her. The misery was still there, but there was something more.

Strong fingers curled in her hair before his mouth slanted over hers. This kiss differed from any of the others. It was hard, demanding . . . desperate. Áine's mind reeled. Part of her warmed to his touch, his taste and the woodsy scent of him. But a part of her trembled at his passion, recognising the undercurrent of anger that coursed through him.

Anger is not passion.

Áine stiffened. She pressed her hand against his chest to disengage herself from his embrace.

Niall tore his mouth away from hers but did not release her. "I need you," he whispered against her ear.

I can do this.

He trailed ardent kisses down her throat, exploring, claiming. Áine's breath hitched in her throat, and her heart slammed against her chest.

Niall cupped her breast, kneading and squeezing, while he ground the hardness of his groin into her. He lowered them both to the ground, and loose pebbles bit into her back.

You'll get what you deserve. The words exploded in her head, and Muiredach's twisted leer flashed before her eyes. A mewling panic burst from her lips. She no longer saw the face of Niall.

"Stop. Stop." She pounded against his chest.

Niall released her and pulled away. Her breath came in sharp gasps as she sat up and drew herself into a tight ball. Cold beads of perspiration coated her skin; blood coursed between her ears.

"Niall—" She scrambled to her feet and edged away from him. "I can't—"

"Áine, I'm sorry. What—"

"I can't—" She bolted for the stream. She dreaded to hear the crunching of footsteps behind her. Would he chase her, grab her—force himself on her?

She plunged into the forest, trying to get as far away as possible. She found a hollowed-out tree and crawled into its cavity. Her entire body trembled, no matter how tightly she wrapped her arms around herself.

The memories assaulted her. The old fears were real and present. Bile rose in her throat. She wanted to vomit. That Muiredach's leering face would impose on her mind over Niall's beautiful, kind face made her absolutely sick.

Áine scrubbed at her face, her arms and thighs, but she couldn't cleanse the memory. She may have physically escaped from Muiredach, but she would *never* be free.

Sobs tore at her throat.

Soiled. Unclean. Would a man's touch always make her feel this way? Would it always remind her of Muiredach's hands gripping her, pinning her—hurting her in monstrous ways?

It had started with isolation, a desire to control her. Muiredach had always beaten her. She could not avoid him. She had nowhere to go. No blood kin to take her in. Surrounded by strangers who thought she was fey. Unnatural.

Then the fondling started. Cornering her in the hallway, the sour stench of ale on his breath, and that provoking grin. "What's the matter, kitten?" He'd treat her as though she were overreacting, that she misunderstood his good graces. It would not have progressed—on this, she was nearly certain, were it not for Banan. He filled Muiredach's ears with lies—lies of stealing kisses from her, with her eagerness for him.

One night, after a long-drawn drinking session with Banan, Muiredach descended on her in a fury. He reeked of strong liquor, and his hands were determined, purposeful. He hit her when she cried and pleaded with him to stop, which only seemed to fuel his passion. She retreated inside herself until he finished.

Later that night, when he lay snoring on his pallet, his tunic stained with dried vomit, she pried his key from his belt—she nearly threw up having to touch him—and took the coins from his strongbox. She then gathered what food she could find and bolted from the house.

Áine covered her face with her hands. Would her body, her mind, ever allow herself to forget?

Her trembling began to ease, and her fear shifted to deep sadness. It was too late for them. She was broken, and Niall wouldn't have the patience to bind the pieces together. He would only see the cracks, but he'd never understand how those cracks had been made.

Áine didn't know how long she sat there, hugging her knees. As the sun was setting, the shadows lengthened. Twilight would soon follow.

She had to make it back to Eireen's before night settled, but she dreaded seeing anyone—especially Niall. She waited until she could wait no longer.

Áine crawled out of the hollowed tree. The sound of rushing water guided her back to the stream. When she emerged onto the pebbled shore, her breath caught in her throat.

Niall had not left after all. He sat on a boulder by the water's edge, facing in her direction. When he saw her, he rose to his feet. Gone were the warring emotions of anger and passion. All that remained was concern.

"You waited for me?" Áine hugged herself.

Niall's eyes were the hazel-green that she dearly loved. "Always." He walked to where she hovered, on the edge of something that terrified her. "Áine?" He tilted his head to see her better. "I'm sorry that I—"

"It wasn't your fault," she blurted. "I wanted . . . You did nothing wrong." She closed her eyes and allowed the bubbling of the stream to soothe her. She wanted him to know what happened. He should know. To not tell him would be the same as a lie. "Someone hurt me once." She stared at the pebbles on the ground—every one of them a dull shade of grey. "My stepbrother . . . Muiredach was not a good man," she said, rubbing her wrist. "Particularly when he drank, which was often. The slaps and punches could be endured. Bruises faded. Then he hurt me in ways a brother never should—touched me where he had no right to. Took what was never his to take."

Áine couldn't go on. Niall's silence struck her as a resounding rebuke, and her courage faltered. She had just destroyed every chance at happiness. "I'm sorry—"

Niall's finger touched her lips, stilling her words. She lifted her gaze to see not disgust or outrage, but concern. "You have nothing to apologise for."

Tears welled in her eyes, blurring her vision. "But I should have . . . should have known . . . what he would do." Tears streaked down her cheeks.

Niall's arms encircled her. She melted against him and grabbed fistfuls of his tunic as she sobbed. The sluice had been opened, and all her grief now poured out.

He did not speak for a long time, and she felt his tenseness under her palms. "Oh, Áine." Then he held her even tighter. "You have no reason to blame yourself, my Áine," he whispered against her hair. "He won't hurt you ever again."

CHAPTER 19

AFTER ÁINE RETURNED to Eireen's, Niall passed a restless night away from camp, under the boughs of a tree. Fionn lay curled up beside him. Too many things chased away sleep. The treaty he couldn't avoid. The traitor who eluded him. The woman whose pain he now owned.

He rose before dawn, clear on the path he needed to take and set on a grim purpose. Niall couldn't help Áine against Muiredach, and he couldn't save Mairead from indentureship, but he would make Captain Garret pay.

Niall was through biding his time and obeying orders. No more raging at the useless moon. Caution died on the altar of necessity.

Time to hunt down Captain Garret. Niall wouldn't return until the man was dead.

If O'Dwyer sealed his treaty with the English, Niall's chance to avenge his kin would be forever lost. He couldn't rest if he allowed his chance to slip away. Although O'Dwyer would be enraged when he found out, Niall would cross that bridge when he reached it.

Niall headed back to camp and found men still rolled up in their mantles around banked fires. He crept lightly to his own shelter, his footsteps masked by the sound of snoring. He stared at an empty patch of ground where Cormac normally slept. His fury over Cormac's silence eased, replaced by wounded feelings and a sour taste of betrayal.

Strange to be setting out alone. He and Cormac had been friends these last ten years—in fighting years, a lifetime. At least Niall wouldn't need to fend off questions about where he was going.

Quietly, he gathered his gear—gunpowder, shot, weapons, twine for making snares. Fionn sniffed around, looking for old scraps while Niall packed his things. Niall hefted his saddle and headed for the horse pens.

Only a few of the horses were awake, but when Fionn dashed up to Niall's horse, the wolfhound's movements caused the rest to waken and edge away, alarmed.

"Easy, Fionn," Niall said in a hard whisper. He reached his horse and spent the next few moments trying to soothe it. His tone still carried a sharp edge, and it took longer to get the animal saddled than usual. When he was finished, he led the beast around, stopping when he saw Cormac and Purcell at the entrance.

"Where are you going?" Cormac asked flatly.

"It's my business alone," Niall said, walking his horse past them.

"You're going after Garret."

Niall halted and faced Cormac. "And if I were?"

"I know when to keep a secret," Cormac snapped.

Niall tightened his grip on the bridle. "Why do you care if I am going after Garret?"

"So I know how much powder to pack," Cormac said. Before Niall could respond, he said to Purcell, "Gather what supplies you can, even if you have to steal a few flasks."

Niall lifted a brow but did not comment as Cormac took charge. His pride wanted to lash out and tell Cormac he presumed too much, but he firmly squelched it. A weight lifted off his shoulders. He'd be glad for the company and the help.

Cormac continued, "And bring Ruadhri and Mc—"

"Not McTiege," Niall interjected. Until he could be sure of McTiege, he'd be careful of the information the man was given.

Cormac frowned, but to Niall's surprise, he nodded. "Not

McTiege. But no excuses from the others. We'll expect you back here in ten minutes, no later."

After Purcell left, Niall said to Cormac, "You're a fool."

"Ay."

"There's no turning back where we're going," Niall warned. "You're going to regret this."

"I already do," Cormac scoffed. "We've both shed blood for one another. Nothing has changed."

Niall finally smiled. "Nothing has changed." He spat in his hand and offered it to Cormac, who did the same. He canted his head to the lightening sky. Time was running out. "I have one other matter to attend to before we leave. Wait for me at the riverbank." Niall mounted his horse, then motioned to Fionn. Together, they headed for Eireen's shelter. He needed to see Áine before he left—if things went ill for him, he wouldn't return.

The first fingers of dawn were tracing across the night sky when he arrived at Eireen's shelter and found Áine stoking the fire. She looked magnificent. Her copper tresses spilled around her shoulders and picked up the bright firelight. He wanted to lose himself in those soft waves.

Fionn bolted ahead to greet her. A smile tugged at her lips as she petted the hound, but her eyes fastened on Niall with uncertainty. Her trust was a fragile bird, and he would need to nurture it gently.

He tilted his head to see into her eyes. "Did you sleep well, Áine?"

She shrugged. "As well as I could." Then she gave him a wry smile. "Maeve snores. Don't tell her I told you."

"Not ever." Niall took her hand and threaded his fingers through hers. Áine's skin was warm, and he wished he could stay this way for the rest of the day. He cleared his throat. "I can't stay. Cormac and the others are waiting for me at the river."

"You're leaving?" Her emotions were written plain on her face— alarm, confusion and dismay. "Where?"

"I have matters to settle with Captain Garret," he answered.

"Oh." Her brow furrowed. Niall longed to kiss the creases away. Instead, he brushed away a bright lock from her cheek.

"Can I count on your discretion?"

"Always." She flung her arms around him. "Please be careful."

Niall wrapped his arms around her, gathering her tightly against him. Her hair smelled of springtime air just after a cool rain. He rested his chin on the top of her head and revelled in the feel of her. "Áine-my-Áine." Fionn's whining to set off brought him to his senses. His men were waiting. "I have to go."

Before he could step away, she rose on her tiptoes and pressed a light kiss on his mouth. "Return safely."

Her breath brushed his lips, and her scent filled his senses. He locked eyes with her and lowered his mouth to hers, showing her what a true farewell kiss was.

Fionn's whines grew more anxious. Niall pulled away from her and touched his forehead to hers. "Whatever happens, stay close to Eireen." And with one last parting glance, he mounted his horse and hurried to join Cormac and the others.

NIALL AND THE MEN STARTED RAZING ABANDONED BYRES ALONG the protected borders east of Cahir, working their way north towards Cashel. He was in essence raising his standard in smoke and in flames.

Each time they torched another building, they withdrew to a sheltered area to wait. It took a couple of byres to finally pique English interest, but the troop that came to investigate was not Garret's. Though Niall spoiled for a good fight, he held himself back. His mission was to capture Garret, and he wouldn't allow himself to be diverted. Instead, he and his band melted into the shadows and baited the next trap.

On the fifth day, they came upon a substantial farmhouse north-east of Cashel outside the protected zone. The byre and outbuildings had already been destroyed. The main house appeared to have been ransacked for more than food stores. Linens had been pulled out of drawers and strewn across the floor. From the pattern of muddy footprints circling the pile, it looked like they had been picked through. A cupboard door had been torn from its hinges and dangled like a drunken lout. Only a few earthenware bowls remained.

Valuables taken—items that couldn't be eaten or stuffed down the bore of a musket, nothing that could have been an advantage to the Irish brigades if left behind. The scene sharply reminded Niall of his uncle's manor—it reeked of Garret. The man was a magpie gathering shiny treasures or exchanging prisoners for gold.

Niall ran out of the house and joined the others outside the byre. "He's been here."

Cormac was kneeling on the ground, examining a charred ridgepole. He rose and dusted off damp earth and ash from his breeches. "This was recently done. A few days, no more."

Ruadhri returned from a search of the lanes and courtyards with Purcell. "Less than a dozen horse," he said. "They're heading farther into the unprotected areas."

"Looking for easy pickings," Niall said, even more convinced that they had come across Garret's trail. "We need to find a plum they haven't plucked yet."

"There's the country home of a Dublin wool merchant a league from here," Cormac said. "It's west of the route the English are taking, closer to the protected area. If we're fortunate, they haven't found it yet."

"Or it's already been stripped like a carcass." Niall was conflicted. He had a reasonable trail to follow that might lead him to Garret, but he'd always be a few steps behind. To beat this man, he needed to be ahead of him. "Lead the way."

The wool merchant's home proved to be deserted of people, animals and remaining food stores and showed no evidence that Garret had swept through the place. The manor stood bracketed between broken, hilly ground and a winding river, with one passable road leading to it. Cart and wagon tracks led away in an orderly procession.

Some distance from the manor, in the centre of a large clearing, a large wooden byre stood. It was solidly built with aged timbers and must have been in the owner's family for generations. Very like the Mulrianes' byre.

Niall faced the prospect of inflicting the same destruction upon another man's property as had been done to his own. He pushed aside the distaste that rose sharp and bitter in his mouth and steeled himself. It must be done.

"Torch it."

They piled whatever furniture they could easily break up into the centre of the byre, including bedding and linens and anything that could be set alight to produce as much smoke as possible. "I want this to be seen as far away as the Rock of Cashel."

Then they made their preparations, hobbling their horses a distance off and securing their positions. A well-trodden trail wended through the woodland, and they selected a section with a deep bend in the road to lay their trap. Rushes flanked either side, and they dragged a fallen tree across the span of the road. Meanwhile, Purcell served as lookout farther up the trail.

Garret was in the area. Niall felt this deep in his bones. The man's curiosity would drive him to investigate, and he'd enter Niall's trap as easily as a rabbit would trip a snare.

A couple of hours passed with no alert from Purcell. The fire had long since burned down, although thick trails of smoke were still visible in the sky. Niall grew increasingly frustrated at Garret's absence. At first, Fionn patrolled the woods, but eventually he gave up and curled down for a nap.

Garret has to be near.

Doubts gnawed at Niall, and he began to question his reason. He had wagered everything based on a farmhouse that could have been looted by anyone, Irish brigands included. Garret wasn't the only greedy bastard taking advantage of the confusion of war.

Had they burned down a perfectly good byre for nothing?

Garret must be near. And if he wasn't? Niall would torch every byre in Munster to draw him out.

The scream of a sparrowhawk broke through Niall's thoughts. Purcell's signal—*enemy sighted.*

Niall held his breath, waiting for the next call, which would tell them the way the wind blew. The caw of a raven meant hide, retreat —grossly outnumbered and with no hope of winning the day. But the piercing cry of a goshawk signalled something entirely different —it meant that the game was afoot.

Niall prayed he wouldn't hear the caw of the raven. He didn't think he could bear it if Garret came with a full company and they were forced to stand aside and allow the whoreson the freedom of the road. *Let it not be the raven.*

Another moment passed, and still no sound from Purcell. What was he waiting for? And then the second warning came—the eager scream of the goshawk.

Niall smothered a whoop of triumph. Cupping his mouth, he gave an answering cry. An acknowledging call sounded from Ruadhri's position farther down the trail, where the fallen tree barred the way.

Purcell and one other in the rear. Ruadhri with another in the front. Niall glanced to his left—Cormac stood in place—then across the road, only visible because Niall had stared at that patch of spindly shrubs for hours, two more of his men. Fionn crept beside Niall, ears pricked and sensing the hunt. Niall primed his pistols and loosened his daggers. He'd get two shots in, so his blades must count.

Word swept down from Purcell. A company of eleven, including Garret. Niall watched the trail with hawkish attention. Eleven men to their eight. It was rare for the English to ride out this far from a garrison with fewer than twenty-five riders. The fact that Garret risked it confirmed what Niall had suspected—the man was up to mischief and not under orders. Fewer men meant fewer tongues wagging and less chance of any tales being carried back to Colonel Sankey. The English commander had a reputation for being scrupu-lously godly and did not hold with looting.

The faint drumming of horse hooves disturbed the stillness of the forest, growing louder by the moment. Niall laid a restraining hand on Fionn's ruff, silently commanding the wolfhound to hold.

The advance guard appeared down the road—two men riding cautiously, their hands hovering close to their swords. Niall waited for them to canter past and disappear around the bend.

The forest held its breath. Then a cry of alarm cut short and the dull ring of steel on steel. A horse whinnied, followed by the unmistakable thud of something hitting the ground and then another. Niall did not need to hear the soft yip of a goshawk to know that Ruadhri had taken out the advance guard.

Nine more riders came into sight, stretched out a distance apart from each other. Their blood-red coats were a slash of colour against the greening woods, their pewter helmets dented and dull. And in their midst rode a man in a stained and patched buff coat with a wide-brimmed hat trimmed with green pulled low over his forehead.

Garret.

Niall lifted his carbine, aimed and fired. Through the burst of smoke, he saw the soldier beside Garret take the shot instead.

And then everything happened at once.

Cormac released a bloodcurdling scream a second before he fired his musket. A spit of gunfire erupted from their men across the road. A horseman farther ahead bolted for Ruadhri's position, and his screams of alarm proved they were pinned between Ruadhri, the boggy verge and the obstructing tree. From down the road, Purcell and his watcher were rushing towards the skirmish, creating as much noise and confusion as an entire brigade. The English horses began to panic, whirling around for an opening and rearing in fright.

Niall fired again, taking out a soldier who stood between him and Garret. Before the carbine stopped smoking, he was running to reach Garret, Fionn charging beside him. Two enemy troopers saw his move and cut him off with their horses. One fired; the shot grazed past Niall's ear. Fionn launched himself on the other soldier and unsettled him so that the man's carbine fired harmlessly into the air.

Garret was shouting orders to his men. Niall heard none of that with his ear ringing and his blood coursing. The English drew their swords, not having enough time to reload their carbines. Ruadhri launched himself into the fray, roaring like a madman before plunging his sword into his opponent's breast and unseating him from his horse.

Garret now used the riderless horse as a shield. Wheeling his own mount around, he looked for a path away from the skirmish. He fired wildly, then used the butt end as a cudgel.

One of the English soldiers charged at Niall, sword drawn. Niall deflected the blow, catching his blade against his own. Fionn bounded in to support Niall, harrowing the soldier's horse until the man lost control of it and fell from the saddle. With a swift slice through the windpipe, Niall leapt over him to advance on his true quarry.

Four men still surrounded Garret, fighting hard for their lives. With every square foot of ground Niall gained, it seemed that Garret swept two feet beyond his reach. Niall tried to hack his way to Garret. He had the bastard in a trap that the devil himself couldn't have slipped from. But the man fought like a demon, and at any moment his horse would break free from the melee and race to freedom.

Niall's vision flooded with red—the red of his uncle's blood soaking the ground; the red of his aunt's lifeblood staining her smock; the red blaze of fear that his sister would have surely felt when these vicious bastards had loaded her on board a ship and cursed her to a hard life in a hellish land.

He looked around for Garret—the man's horse crashed into one of his own to flee. The distance between them widened, and he was about to slip away. Niall pulled out his dagger—the distance was greater than he'd ever attempted—took quick aim and let the dagger fly. The blade turned twice before glancing off Garret's shoulder and falling to the ground.

Another shot cracked, and Garret's horse screamed. The man had barely enough time to kick his stirrups and launch himself from the thrashing horse. Garret fell to the ground and rolled aside. The fall jarred the sword from his grip, and it landed a few feet away.

This gave Niall the precious few moments to reach his quarry. Just as Garret scrambled to his feet, Niall levelled his sword at the man's quivering throat.

"I yield," Garret gasped, the whites of his eyes shining. "I am—"

"Captain John Garret of Colonel Sankey's regiment of dragoons. I know you for the devil," Niall gritted out. Sweat stung his eyes, and his breath was ragged. He fought for control, to keep from skewering the bastard here on the spot and giving him the blessing of a quick death.

Garret narrowed his eyes. "I know you. You're one of O'Dwyer's men."

"Ay, I captured you the last time, but you can be sure I won't be releasing you now." A surge of anger coursed through Niall. "May the curse of the Almighty blight you and your family through their generations."

"I demand to be taken to Colonel O'Dwyer," Garret said to Cormac, who hovered close.

Niall lowered his sword, gave a bleak smile, then smashed his fist into Garret's jaw. Garret's head snapped back, and he fell to the ground. Niall stood over him. "Think again."

"What do you want?" Garret cried, rolling to his side and struggling up. He pressed his hand to his bleeding mouth.

"My kin back. I want my sister restored to her family from whatever heathenish place you sent her and my uncle hearty and hale by a warming fire with his wife and daughters around him."

"What are you on about?"

Niall hauled Garret to his feet, then drove him against the bole of a tree, his grip tightening around the bastard's throat. Garret's eyes bulged out, and he struggled to throw Niall off. Niall would not let go. "What I am going on about, you piece of shite," he snarled, "is the family you destroyed. Does the name Mulriane prod your memory?"

Panic flared in Garret's eyes. "I don't know who you're talking about." His voice came out in an unconvincing gurgle.

Niall reversed his sword and drove his fist and the pommel into Garret's stomach. With a sickening whoosh, the man crumpled. Niall stepped back, then kicked Garret hard in the side. "You rounded up my uncle's household and indentured the lot of them to a merchant bound for the colonies. My sister was one of them. Don't pretend you don't remember."

Garret moaned. He pushed himself up. "I never did such a thing." He was visibly sweating.

"How much did you make from each defenceless woman?" The

tip of Niall's sword hovered near the man's throat. "Tell me so I can carve that exact amount from your flesh."

"I didn't—it wasn't me.

"Liar."

"There are a number of troops patrolling that area," Garret said in a rush. "It wasn't me or my men."

A worm of doubt burrowed into Niall. What if Garret spoke the truth? Niall had assumed that it had been Garret after seeing him cleaning out the last of the Mulrianes' treasures. *What if you have it all wrong?*

Garret must have seen his hesitation, and he launched himself into action. Too late, Niall saw that the Englishman clutched a rock in his fist, which he smashed against the side of Niall's blade, knocking it aside. Then Garret dove for his own sword, which still lay on the ground. But Cormac was already there, barring his way.

"He's not finished with you yet," Cormac said, motioning to Garret with the tip of his blade and forcing the Englishman to back up a few paces.

Niall's attention drew to Garret's sword. The basket hilt was elaborately scrolled and spoke of a Spanish design. *That design.* Niall bent down and picked up the sword. The hilt's knuckle guard tapered at the end to resemble a serpent's head; the counterguards, used to protect the hand, twisted around each other like a trio of snakes. The balance was perfect and the blade's edge lovingly sharpened. But not by Garret's hand. This sword, fashioned by a Spanish craftsman, had once belonged to his uncle.

"Where did you get this?" Niall crossed the short distance to Garret and showed it to him.

"It's mine—"

Niall grabbed Garret by the hair and yanked his head back. "You know very well from whose hand you ripped this out." He tightened his grip and twisted. "This sword belonged to my kinsman, Brian Mulriane. I would know it anywhere." Niall placed the edge of his uncle's sword against Garret's quivering neck. All he needed to do was slice it across his throat and his kin would be avenged.

"It's war—we're at war," Garret babbled.

CRYSSA BAZOS

Something snapped inside Niall. "You dare give me the excuse of a coward?" Niall backhanded Garret with all the force he had. Garret coughed up blood and teeth, but it did nothing to appease Niall's own pain. He drew his fist back and slammed it into Garret's face, but the crunch of bone meeting bone did not ease his rage. Niall snarled like a wolf, thrashing and tearing apart his prey.

Garret was screaming, shouting meaningless words that did not penetrate Niall's rage or still his fists. Then Niall found his arm yanked back, and he was pulled away from Garret.

"Cease," Cormac shouted in his ear. "Niall, stop! Listen to what he's saying."

Niall's chest heaved, and his breath came in ragged gasps, but he couldn't speak.

"He says he has information," Cormac added.

Niall wrenched himself free. "They always have information. What the hell do I care how much ordinance or muskets they have?" He tried to lunge again for Garret, to finish him off, when Ruadhri caught him and hauled him back.

"He says there's a traitor in the camp," Ruadhri said.

Niall's rage drained away. "He's lying. He's done it before. The worm will swear upon the second coming."

"I know who the spy is," Garret said, then, seeing Niall hesitate, he laughed. His bleeding face leered in a macabre fashion. "How else do you think we found your location?"

Niall cursed. "Who is it?"

"Take me to O'Dwyer. I'll only tell him."

"We're not playing this game." Niall twisted his uncle's blade against Garret's neck. This time the Englishman did not flinch.

"Enough. It's no longer your call," Cormac said. "We're taking him back to O'Dwyer. You can kill him later."

Niall bent low and spoke to Garret in a low voice. "You can have your meeting with O'Dwyer, if that be your final request. Then I'll hang you myself."

234

CHAPTER 20

NIALL GRIPPED the rope with enough force to crush a windpipe. Tethered to the other end, Captain Garret stumbled along blindfolded, blood seeping from his wounds and his hands lashed together. When O'Dwyer agreed to hang him, this would be the rope that would snap his neck.

Niall kept the line taut and allowed no slack, forcing the prisoner to keep to his pace over broken trails. He did not stop, even it meant dragging Garret bloody and broken back to the fastness of their encampment.

Cormac and Ruadhri led two blindfolded English soldiers. Niall blocked out their moans, his ears seeking the sound of Garret's distress, but the bastard withheld that from him.

Niall gave a sharp yank on the rope, jerking Garret off balance. The man struggled to right himself, scrabbling for purchase, but he remained on his feet. Sharp disappointment bit Niall. Let the rocks below his feet, the upthrust roots and raw earth dig into the man's flesh for Ireland to scar him as he deserved. The thought burned into his mind—was this how Garret had treated Mairead as she was marched across enemy-held territory to reach a ship that would take her away from their home? Did she beg for mercy—*no, she'd never have done that*. She would have taken this torture without a cry, dry-eyed and with a brave face. The thought that she might have faced more than she could endure, that she would have broken down, made him want to howl.

As they approached camp, word spread quickly from the first sentinel, and by the time Niall rode into the enclave, a sizeable crowd had gathered, with O'Dwyer at the forefront. Niall jumped down from his horse, drew his blade and sliced the blindfold from Garret's head. The man flinched from the stab of sunlight.

Cormac hustled the other two to take their places beside Garret.

Niall kicked Garret behind the knees and drove him to the ground. "A present for you, Commander. This one," he said, "claims he has information."

O'Dwyer peered at the man and frowned. "I know you."

"I'm Captain John Garret of Colonel Sankey's regiment of dragoons," he replied with a raspy voice. "You showed me courtesy last summer when I was your . . . guest. I appeal to your sense of honour, sir, and ask that you show me the same courtesy this time."

"Where did you find these men, O'Coneill?" O'Dwyer asked in a deceptively mild tone.

Niall sensed the man's gathering irritation. He had been attuned to the colonel's moods for years. "We were on patrol."

O'Dwyer's gaze slid to Cormac. "Have you a more detailed report?"

Cormac shifted from one foot to the other. "We caught them on the edge of the occupied area, halfway between Cahir and Cashel."

"Is that all?"

"More or less."

"You left without orders." O'Dwyer's gaze drilled into Niall.

"It was necessary."

O'Dwyer's jaw tightened, but he did not question Niall further. Instead, he approached Garret. "What's this about information?"

"In exchange for my life," Garret said.

Niall snorted. He did not miss Garret's omission—his bargain clearly did not extend to his own men.

O'Dwyer moved to stand beside Niall. In a voice low enough not to carry, he asked, "What information?"

"He claims he knows the spy in our camp," Niall said tersely.

O'Dwyer's brows lifted a fraction. He looked around at the gathering crowd. "Very well. Bring them all to my quarters."

Niall grabbed Garret by the arm and half marched, half dragged him to the canvas shelter reserved for O'Dwyer. Cormac and Ruadhri brought the others. By the time they reached the enclosed area, Donogh and Eamon had joined them, Banan and McTiege both following closely behind.

Garret's step faltered, and he tripped, but Niall jerked him upright, shoving him inside the colonel's tent.

Niall forced Garret to his knees at the centre of the room, and the other two prisoners joined him. His uncle's sword hovered a few inches away from the back of the Englishman's neck. His hand twitched, as though it fought against its better nature, for Niall longed to plunge the blade into his enemy's flesh.

Garret didn't move. He looked around at the officers who were gathered there, then stared resolutely at the ground.

Outside, O'Dwyer said a few words to his servant, then ducked his head and entered his quarters. A moment later, the servant rushed in with a bucket of water and three cups.

"Captain, you and your men must be parched." O'Dwyer waited as his servant handed cups of water to the prisoners.

Niall clenched his teeth in irritation. He looked up when O'Dwyer tarried beside him. "Water will be wasted on them."

"We're not barbarians, O'Coneill," the colonel said in a warning tone.

Nor are we fools, Niall thought, but he wisely held his tongue.

O'Dwyer pulled up a stool and settled in front of the prisoners, hands braced on knees. "Captain Garret, my officer says that you have information to share. Unburden yourself."

Garret's gaze darted to the men gathered inside the shelter. His mouth pressed into a thin line. "Colonel Sankey has not forgotten your courtesy last year when you treated with his men with the grace of a gentleman. Sankey has always expressed the highest regard for you, sir. He considers your word as your bond."

"*Virtus sola nobilitas,*" O'Dwyer said, referring to his family's motto. *Virtue alone enables.*

"Virtue is lost on Garret," Niall said impatiently. "He'll admit to being a saint if it's to his advantage."

O'Dwyer silenced Niall with a stern look. "And what is this information you have promised me, Captain Garret, or have you come here only to flatter?"

"Only this—I'm well aware of the treaty you are negotiating with Colonel Sankey to bring an end to these unfortunate hostilities—"

"Unfortunate hostilities?" Niall burst out. "Pray, what about the unfortunate prisoners you treated with such *considerate* honour?"

"O'Coneill," O'Dwyer's voice sharpened in warning. "Continue, Captain, and you had better quickly get to the point."

"Colonel Sankey will only give fair consideration to your terms if he believes you will continue to act with honour. How you treat me and my men will be certain to either reinforce his favourable impression of you or," Garret shot Niall a dark look, "cause him to reject your overtures and instead demand blood for blood."

"We are still at war, Captain," O'Dwyer said, "and you are at my mercy. I will not be manipulated into abandoning my duty."

"Colonel Sankey has a great deal of pressure not to give you favourable terms. Oliver Cromwell himself has not forgotten the Irish atrocities against English settlers during the Rebellion and watches what unfolds here with keen interest. Cromwell craves vengeance on behalf of the dead and has little patience for my colonel's more moderate perspective."

"A simple solution," Niall said. "If he's dead, he disappears. Sankey can't blame you for it."

Garret continued to ignore Niall and focus his attention on O'Dwyer. He was a drowning man and O'Dwyer his only rope. "I've exchanged messages with your courier."

This surprised Niall. Garret had been a link in this treaty negotiation? Had O'Dwyer been aware of it all this time?

"If I disappear," Garret continued, "Colonel Sankey will assume you had me killed."

O'Dwyer rubbed his beard and considered Garret. "Was that it? This was the information you promised for your life? I doubt it, if O'Coneill's expression is a weather gauge."

Niall pressed his blade against Garret's skin. "Tell him the rest."

"There's nothing more," Garret replied.

O'Dwyer looked around the tent at the gathered men. "A moment of privacy, gentlemen."

Eamon hovered a moment at the exit, staring at Niall as though he wanted to give him a warning, but instead he followed after Donogh.

O'Dwyer faced the prisoners. "I understand you can tell me who is spying for Sankey. I'll be grateful for this intelligence and will reward you accordingly."

"He's my prisoner—"

"O'Coneill," O'Dwyer said in a warning tone.

Niall tightened his grip on the sword. A muscle in his jaw twitched.

Garret squared his shoulders. "I appreciate that, Colonel, but I have no additional information."

Niall hauled Garret on his feet. "Then there's no reason to delay your hanging."

O'Dwyer lifted his hand and halted Niall with a dark look. "I'm not finished with these men."

For the next half hour, O'Dwyer questioned Garret and each of the men separately, but none would name the traitor. Niall believed the other two didn't know, but Garret, he was certain, was stubbornly refusing to reveal what he knew.

"I throw myself upon your mercy, Colonel O'Dwyer," Garret said at the end of the questioning. "I beg your assurance that no harm shall befall me."

"Niall, a word." O'Dwyer drew him aside. "Did any of them hint at the man's identity?"

Niall shook his head. "I suspect he was lying. He made the claim when we were engaged."

"Engaged? I take it that accounted for his injuries."

"Don't waste a thought for that piece of shite." Niall showed him the hilt of his uncle's sword. "This man was responsible for the death of my kinsmen, for forcing my sister into indentured servitude and transporting her to the English colonies. He has blood on his hands. I have the right of vengeance."

"I'll not deny that. If it were my kin, I'd be eager for blood. But," O'Dwyer said, "he's more valuable alive."

"This is about the negotiation, isn't it?" Niall nearly spat.

"This is about our survival," O'Dwyer said. "We've lost this war. Now is the time to secure a raft so we don't sink. This captain is leverage. You must see that."

"Don't believe what he says. By his logic, all actions we take against the English will seal our doom. We are still at war until the last trumpet sounds, and we'll do what must be done until the final note is silenced."

"I'll not kill a valuable prisoner only to satisfy your thirst for vengeance."

"You can't possibly expect me to allow this man to walk out of here alive. He will win, and I can't live with that. I want my blood due. You don't know what you are asking."

"I do, and you will follow my orders."

"Damn your negotiation," Niall spat, not caring for the consequences of speaking that way to O'Dwyer. "Give Sankey the other two. That should content him."

"I can't let you have Garret. That's my final decision." O'Dwyer stepped away from Niall and returned to Garret. "I offer you quarter. You will remain my prisoners until I come to adequate terms with your colonel. Upon my honour, none shall harm you."

Niall roared in frustration. "After everything he's done to me and my own, I will not be bound by this." He pointed a finger at Garret. "I will have my vengeance. I will see you laid low and your body fed to the carrion birds.

"O'Coneill." O'Dwyer's tone was sharp as a blade. "Consider well the next words you utter. I have given my bond, and you and every man here will be bound by it. Break my orders, and I swear you'll learn what justice truly is."

Niall looked at O'Dwyer bitterly. "I don't know who you are." He stepped away from O'Dwyer and wouldn't look at Garret. To do so would have been the same as having a dagger plunged into his chest. Niall spun on his heels and stormed out of the tent with Fionn close on his heels.

Niall got halfway to the woods before Eamon overtook him. Fionn started growling when Eamon grabbed Niall by the arm to stop him.

"What has gone on in there?" Eamon asked.

"Nothing," Niall snapped. "Absolutely nothing."

"Everyone heard you shouting at O'Dwyer. He will not let your insolence go unpunished."

"I don't care, neither do I give a shite for his bloody treaty." Niall shrugged off Eamon's restraining hand. "Leave me."

"Where are you going?"

"Away."

"Don't do anything rash," Eamon said.

Niall paused. "This isn't finished. Not until Garret is carrion food." And with that, he headed for the mountain trail.

DAWN WAS AWAKENING WHEN ÁINE HEADED DOWN TO THE stream. A heavy bank of clouds sat above the horizon, leaving only a small band of clear sky to herald the new day. Pale blue gave way to crimson red.

She carried two empty buckets, but instead of the most direct route to the water, she selected a winding path away from the main camp. This, she'd found, was the best way to avoid Banan. After sufficiently recovering from his injuries, he had regained his second wind and continued to stir up trouble for her. He seemed to be everywhere she turned.

Áine was halfway to the stream when a small flock of black-and-white birds flew past, their wings flashing iridescent violet-blue. Áine drew up short. *Were those —?* And then as if in answer to her unspoken question, a single magpie alighted on a branch directly in front of her.

One foretells sorrow.

An icy chill trickled down her spine. Áine hesitated—her path took her straight past the magpie, but to head back would mean the certainty of seeing Banan. As she passed the bird, its beady eyes assessed her, studied her. She took a deep breath and continued on. It would not find her wanting.

Áine forced herself to keep a steady and unhurried pace until she was well shot of the magpie. Then she hurried. The camp would begin to stir soon, and she wanted to be back before then.

It was only when she was nearly there that she realised her path would take her straight past where O'Dwyer's men kept the English prisoners. Maeve had told her that these were the soldiers who had torched the Mulrianes' estate and killed the master. After finally capturing the brute, Niall hadn't brought her the news himself. Áine felt deeply hurt by that. She kept expecting him to come around, but he hadn't. In fact, he was nowhere to be found after the argument he had with the commander. The news of that had spread through the encampment like a spark upon dry tinder.

Áine saw the three prisoners, each tied to a tree, all three slumped forward in sleep. But where were the guards? The prisoners' heads rested in such odd angles. Dark stains soaked the front of their coats and tunics. Cold goosebumps lifted on her skin.

Blood.

Áine recoiled and dropped her buckets. They clanked and rattled when they hit the ground and bounced a few feet away. A flutter of birds alit, their wings beating—startled.

The prisoners' throats had been cut.

She clamped a hand over her mouth to stop the building shriek. Bitter bile flooded her mouth, and she turned away, her stomach threatening to heave its contents.

When she straightened, she saw a pair of legs sticking out of a bush. One of the guards—he should have been on sentry duty. Áine rushed up to him, hoping to only find him knocked out, but the sharp, metallic scent of blood hit her nostrils. She parted the branches and drew back in shock.

Banan lay dead, his throat slashed open.

Áine didn't remember screaming, but she must have because men suddenly were there. Angry and fearful shouts erupted. Someone touched her arm, and she drew away. Maeve stood before her, her expression questioning, concerned.

Eireen arrived and immediately took control. "Maeve, take the girl away. This is no place for either of you."

But Áine stood rooted to the spot. All around her, men were blaming Niall for this horror. They had found a bloody dagger discarded near Banan and swore it belonged to Niall. Cormac and Ruadhri came running. As men babbled around them, hovering near the dead guard, Cormac's manner changed from anger to confusion to horror. Ruadhri said nothing, only looked bleak. Someone held up the dagger for the others to see, and she recognised the stag-horn hilt.

"It can't be." Áine shook her head and repeated louder, "He couldn't." She grabbed Maeve's arm. "He would not."

Eireen clucked her tongue and looked grim. "Maybe he did, and maybe he didn't. Only the Almighty can know for sure. Niall never hid his desire to avenge his kin."

"Not this way." Áine felt sick.

"I'm not saying he did it," Maeve said, holding her hands up to forestall Áine's protest, "but no one else swore a blood vengeance against these men."

Eireen drew Áine and Maeve aside. "A blood vengeance could be forgiven," she said in a low voice. "Even O'Dwyer. Oh, he'll bluster and posture and claim Niall overstepped and challenged his authority, but in the end, they are three English soldiers who deserved no mercy, and there's not a man in all of Glengarra who would say otherwise. But it didn't end there. Everyone in camp knew there was no love lost between Niall and Banan."

Was this her fault? Had he killed Banan for her? Or had the man pushed him beyond endurance?

No. Despite the circumstances against him, Áine refused to

CRYSSA BAZOS

believe it could have been Niall. No matter Eireen's assurances that
he was justified for those murders, Niall would never, could never be
so cold-hearted as to kill defenceless men who were bound and
helpless.

Not Niall.

But who else? whispered a cold voice that knew the worst in a man.
Who else hated these men with as much passion, who hated Banan
for her sake? *What do you really know of Niall?* hissed that cold voice.

It was as though she had stepped on firm ground only to discover
that a bog lay beneath. Had she allowed herself to be lulled by a few
kisses and kind words?

There were many in Cork who thought the world of Muiredach.
When he had a mind, he could charm the faerie queen Mab. What if
Niall was no better than her stepbrother—what if he had shown to
Áine the same side that Muiredach showed Cork? Heat flooded her
cheeks as she remembered his passionate embrace and where his
kisses were leading her.

No! She wrenched herself from that cold, smug voice. She
wouldn't believe this of Niall. Actions spoke louder than words. He
had been kind before there was any advantage for him. He had been
protective of her when she meant nothing to him.

Niall O'Coneill might be thirsting for the blood of his enemies,
but he would have slaked it through honourable means and not cut
their throats like a coward, and he certainly would never have killed
one of his own. Niall O'Coneill was no coward, and this massacre
could only have been committed by the hand of one.

He was innocent, Áine would swear to it on her soul.

CHAPTER 21

ÁINE SPENT the morning searching the glens for Niall. It seemed that half the encampment had left to hunt him down, which made her even more desperate to find him first. Her own progress was hampered by having to hide behind boulders, rocks or fallen trunks whenever a fresh search party passed. She didn't want to be seen, to unwittingly lead them to wherever Niall sheltered.

Where would he go?

The answer came to her clear as a moon mirrored on a still lake. The enchanted glade. Their sanctuary.

As she trudged up hills and climbed over rotted trees, she grew more convinced that she would find him there. But when she reached the tumbling brook and entered the clearing, she found it empty. Not even a songbird greeted her.

Áine sank to the ground and stared at the green grass. She had been so sure that he would be waiting for her here, even if it was to tell her farewell. Áine had even imagined what she would say to him —*my path runs where you go*. Niall would try to convince her to stay, that she was safer with Eireen than wandering the wilderness with an outlaw such as himself. She would cup his face and silence him with a fierce kiss.

But he wasn't here and, judging by the fresh grass, unflattened by a man's footsteps, he hadn't ever been.

Áine returned to the encampment before midday, bowed down and heartsore.

SUNLIGHT STABBED AT NIALL'S GUMMED EYELIDS. GROANING, HE buried his head into warm fur. He pried one eye open, then the other. Fionn slept, moulded against his master.

Niall's tongue felt twice as thick as normal and three times as fuzzy. The cloying taste of strong spirits coated the inside of his mouth. Fumes oozed from his pores.

Devil take me. He pushed himself upright and shook his head to clear the mist. The dull throbbing in his head only magnified, and he gritted his teeth against the pain.

How much had he drunk? His head couldn't have felt worse had he consumed an entire hogshead of spirits. Niall probed his memory, but all he could remember was a black haze and the burning rage in his belly.

He laid down again and closed his eyes. Fragments pricked and teased but offered no inkling as to how they were connected. Just as he grabbed a thread, it slipped from his fingers. Niall had a memory of Eamon giving him a flask of spirits to ease the pain — this he did remember, possibly because it was a luxury more dear for having survived the last English raid. Then vague images of Banan offering him jugs of ale flitted through his befuddled mind like flashes of light on a grey pond. After that, everything went dark.

Why would he drink himself into oblivion with Banan? He loathed the worm. Niall looked around. Except for Fionn, he was now alone in the woods, and he had no idea where he was. Nothing looked familiar.

Niall rose on unsteady feet and staggered towards the sound of running water. His raging thirst was a physical, snarling beast. He sank to his knees by the edge of a creek and splashed his face. The bracing water did nothing to clear his head. It felt sluggish and suffocated by layers of wool. When he cupped his hands for a drink, he discovered a number of fresh cuts and dried blood.

What happened last night?

Niall threaded his fingers through his hair as he marshalled his thoughts. He must have gotten into a scrap—not surprising considering his frame of mind when he'd left O'Dwyer. And with that thought, all the outrage over Garret flooded back. He had to get himself together and return to camp to offer an accounting.

A twig snapped. Niall spun around and reached for the stag-horn dagger at his belt, but it wasn't there. Fionn gave a deep woof and bounded towards the disturbance.

Cormac and Ruadhri appeared, but instead of a friendly greeting and a good-natured jest over his rough appearance, they looked relieved—and something else Niall could not name, guarded?

"Thank the Almighty we found you first," Ruadhri said. "We've been hunting these woods for you."

"Where are we?"

"A mile and a half north of camp," Ruadhri said. "Don't you know?"

Niall shook his head and immediately regretted it.

"You look like shite," Cormac said.

"Feel worse." Niall's voice came out as harsh as a rasp. He scrubbed his face with his hand.

"O'Dwyer is demanding your head," Cormac said grimly, adjusting the sack he had slung over his shoulder. "His lads are combing the woods."

"His pride is bruised." Niall didn't bother hiding the bitterness.

"Pride?" Cormac seemed genuinely shocked, then he darkened in anger. "Were you intending to tweak O'Dwyer's manhood when you cut the throats of those bound prisoners after he promised them quarter? If so, you should have stopped before moving on to Banan. The poor bastard was the sentry on duty."

Niall struggled to follow what they said as though they spoke from the depths of a bog. "What did you say?"

"What's the matter with him?" Ruadhri asked. "He's not quite right."

"Throats cut. Garret dead. Banan killed," Cormac yelled at Niall. "Do you follow now?"

Niall opened his mouth to answer, then Cormac's meaning finally sank in. *Throats cut?* "What? Garret's dead? Banan —"

Cormac's expression hardened. "All murdered. Call it for what it is."

Niall gaped, desperately trying to understand. "I didn't do it." When his friends looked unconvinced, he said more forcibly, "Not by my blade." His hand fell to his dagger, and he remembered that he didn't have it. He turned his palms upwards and stared at the cuts and abrasions with growing horror. Had he killed Garret and his men and then, in a bloodlust, finished Banan?

"I'm not faulting you for the English, although it was a cowardly thing to have done when they didn't have a chance to defend themselves," Ruadhri said. "But Banan, though he was an oily bastard, was still one of us. Talk is that you did it over Áine."

Garret was dead. Niall should have been relieved that the man would be worm fodder, but none of that came. "I'm innocent of this."

"Then how is it that your dagger was found near Banan's slashed throat?"

"What?"

Cormac looked at Niall's empty belt and growled, "You went too far. Your thirst for vengeance has consumed you. And we all know how Banan has been plaguing your woman."

"Poor girl. It was Áine who found them too," Ruadhri said gently.

"Áine?" His Áine had to find these men slaughtered? After everything she had been through, to have witnessed that.

Something rebelled in Niall. Even befuddled with drink, he couldn't have stooped to cold-blooded murder. He had no idea how he had gotten the cuts on his hands, but he would swear on his everlasting soul that he had not murdered anyone.

Cormac shrugged off the canvas sack and thrust it into Niall's hands. "There's a wedge of cheese, some oatcakes and a few other supplies. Get as far away from O'Dwyer as you can. He's vowed to string you up by your bollocks."

Niall's ire kindled and cut through the fog. "You truly think I'm capable of this? After all the years we guarded each other's backs, when we fought alongside each other like brothers?"

Before either Cormac or Ruadhri could respond, the snap and crash of approaching men echoed through the forest. Then a shout, "There he is!"

Cormac swore and pushed him towards the trees. "Go—get out of here!" But Niall didn't have the chance to take more than a few steps before he found himself ringed in by Eamon's men. Their carbines were primed and drawn, levelled at him. Though he saw more than a few familiar men, they were no longer smiling comrades willing to offer good cheer.

Into this circle, Eamon stepped forward. He glanced at Cormac and Ruadhri without surprise, and it occurred to Niall that Eamon must have followed their trail to find him.

Eamon was sober, mournful even. "Why did you do it, Niall? I know you had your differences with Banan, but to have killed him in that fashion . . ."

Niall forced himself to meet Eamon in the eye and ignore the threat of the carbines. "Eamon, you have to believe me—I know nothing of this crime." When Eamon didn't reply, he added, "How could I have done this? You were with me last night."

"Not I," Eamon said.

"Why do you say that? We shared a flask of spirit—'twas from your own stash."

Eamon shook his head. "I took pity on you and gave you a flask, ay. I had hoped to dull your thirst for vengeance, for you spoke of nothing else, and I grew alarmed at what you might do." Eamon's grim expression cracked, and he looked as though he was close to tears. "We shared but a cup before I was called away. I curse the hour that Donogh demanded to see me for a trifling matter. I could have stopped you from doing your worst."

"I was passed out in a fog of fumes," Niall cried out, frustrated. "Eamon, how can you believe this of me? After all these years?" First Cormac and Ruadhri and now Eamon. If his friends didn't believe him, all was lost. For a wild moment, he wondered if they weren't all

249

right—that he had actually done it. The Good Lord knew he'd wanted to throttle Banan on more than one occasion, and Garret . . . How could he not have remembered? Niall rubbed his forehead with his palm, as though to massage the memories free from whatever prison they were locked within his mind.

Eamon's attention shifted to Niall's hands. "Your hands are cut. How did you get those wounds?" He moved closer. "Did Banan get in a few cuts before you killed him? You should not have left your dagger near Banan's poor body."

"I lost my dagger," Niall said, feeling the noose tightening around his neck. "Someone must have stolen it when I was passed out."

"Niall," Eamon said, shaking his head.

"Look, Eamon, there's no reason to discuss this here," Cormac said, standing now beside Niall. "Let O'Dwyer do the questioning himself. Or is it your intent to stand a trial here? Are you here on O'Dwyer's orders to bring O'Coneill back, or do you wish to act as judge? Because these lads are champing on the bit to tear the man to shreds at the first sign from you."

Eamon's expression hardened. "Cormac O'Shea, should I be asking you what you're doing here with O'Coneill? Do you know more about what happened last night than what you are willing to say?"

Niall grabbed Cormac's arm to hold him back and shook his head. "Leave it, Cormac." Angry murmurs spread through Eamon's men. "I was alone last night." He smothered images of Banan that floated in his head like a spectre. "Your quarrel is with me."

"We're taking you back to O'Dwyer," Eamon said. "Don't make this unpleasant."

Niall felt the weight of their condemnation pressing down. He couldn't flee—they'd shoot him in an instant. His only hope now lay with O'Dwyer. "I'll not give you trouble."

Eamon motioned to one of his men, who lashed Niall's hands tightly, leaving barely enough room for circulation. Niall gritted his teeth against the pain but refused to cry out. The man gave one final tug, a spiteful satisfaction written in his face. Then he spat on Niall.

Spittle ran down his chin, but Niall held himself in check.

Outwardly, he did not flinch from the hatred, but inside he was trembling with outrage and fury.

They marched Niall back to camp. On either side of him, men flanked him with swords drawn and ready in the event he managed to bolt. Fionn stayed close to his master, hanging on his footsteps, and would not be urged away.

As they approached camp, a crowd began to gather. Niall didn't know if he hoped to see Áine's beautiful face or feared to. He couldn't stand it if she saw him now, in this state.

Many stared as he walked past, silent and with open disbelief. Others, friends and companions of Banan, jeered and called out insults. It didn't take long before their anger stoked the uncertain. Clods of earth and cow pats began to be hurled at him. Niall kept his head bent, trying to evade the missiles. A rock struck him above the eye, cutting his brow. A stream of blood ran down his face.

It didn't matter that Cormac and Ruadhri barked at the crowd to back off, the damage had already been done and there was no reasoning with them. The pair might as well be trying to part the waters of the Shannon.

Close to O'Dwyer's quarters, Eamon called out to their commander, "We have him!"

O'Dwyer did not immediately leave his quarters, but when he did, anticipation charged the air. Arms folded across his chest, he studied Niall, revealing nothing of what he was thinking. Finally, he said, "Inside."

Niall was hauled into the shelter and forced to his knees. Someone gripped the back of his neck like a vise.

"What do you have to say for yourself, O'Coneill?" O'Dwyer's tone was clipped and jagged, as though it had been torn from him.

"It wasn't me," Niall replied flatly. "You can't believe that I would do this?"

"You vowed your vengeance against Garret openly and before me," O'Dwyer said flatly. "Was there anyone else who had a greater hatred for those prisoners than you?" Niall was painfully aware of the answer to that question and that it only pointed to him. "And Banan, what did he do to deserve his fate?"

Banan had spread vile rumours of Áine, but to admit this would surely seal Niall's fate. But it was hardly a secret. The entire camp had all partaken of Banan's salacious gossip and knew that Niall cared for the woman. A sickening feeling settled in his gut, that Áine would be swept up in this by her association with him. "I am innocent of these killings. I never touched any of them. I swear it upon everything I hold dear."

O'Dwyer bent down and looked Niall in the eye. "You have to give me something better than that, especially after that display of insubordination yesterday. Where were you last night? Can anyone vouch for you?"

Niall could see that O'Dwyer was holding on to a thread of hope, but he had nothing and his own protests had worn flimsy. He shook his head, wincing. "I must have drunk too much." In truth, his head still felt muffled with wool.

"That's your excuse? The drink urged your hand?"

"I didn't do it," Niall said, his ire spurred by frustration.

"And your dagger? We found it near Banan's body."

Niall seized on that, hoping he could turn it in his favour. "Am I such a fool to have killed someone, then left my own dagger behind to inform against me? Someone must have stolen it from me while I was passed out, to blame me for their crime." Niall lowered his voice so that it carried no farther than O'Dwyer. "The traitor in our midst—"

"Enough," O'Dwyer roared, incandescent with rage. "There's only one man before me who has betrayed my trust. I gave the English prisoners my assurance—the word of an O'Dwyer—that they would not be harmed. My honour is the only thing I have left, and you've made a liar of me."

"I didn't do it—I couldn't have."

"Upon your word, Garret was a dead man. Did you make a liar out of yourself too? Did Banan challenge you, and as you already had blood on your hands, you thought to deal with him too?"

"I don't bloody well know what happened."

"You don't know or don't want to remember?" O'Dwyer asked with scorn. "I can believe that after you killed the English, you realised the situation you put us in. Garret had the right of it — if Sankey finds out that his men have been killed while under my protection, we're all dead men. You've sealed our fates." O'Dwyer straightened and began pacing, his agitation evident with every step he made. "Donogh thought you were unready to lead a company, that I should have chosen another, but I didn't listen to him. You thought yourself untouchable, but no more. I never make the same mistake twice." He halted before Niall. An angry muscle worked in his jaw. O'Dwyer's brown eyes shone nearly black, and he appeared to be struggling with his temper. Finally, when he had mastered himself, he lifted his voice so that everyone could hear. "I sentence you, Niall O'Coneill, to death. On the morrow, you will be hanged until the breath leaves your body. May the Almighty have mercy upon your soul."

As they were hauling Niall away, he dug his heels into the earth and forced them to stop. "Edmund O'Dwyer, I swear on the bones of my kin and the life of my sister, Mairead O'Coneill, that I did *not* kill those men."

O'Dwyer lifted his head. His gaze locked with Niall's. Then one of the guards yanked Niall forward and dragged him outside.

CHAPTER 22

EIREEN HAD KEPT Áine especially busy to distract her from what had happened, and Áine stumbled through the tasks with her mind elsewhere. It was when she was churning butter with Maeve that Eamon and his men brought Niall into camp.

Niall looked rough and haggard, as if he had been turned inside out. Though his hands were bound, he walked with dignity, his broad shoulders thrown back. Fionn trotted beside him, as magnificent a hound as any king of Ireland would have had.

This was the image she held in her mind just before the crowd became ugly. They snarled at Niall, behaving like a pack of rabid wolves. Áine cried out, feeling every assault they rained upon Niall. His head bowed, and she felt the strain he must be struggling with to keep going.

Preserve us. Áine swallowed back a ragged sob.

Maeve pried Áine's hands from the stilled butter staff and called out to one of the Triad to take their place at the churn.

"You'll be no use to us here in the state you're in," Maeve said gently. "Go on, luv. We'll cover for you."

"Thank you." Áine squeezed Maeve's hand in gratitude and quickly hurried off.

Her progress was hampered by the clog of people that followed after Niall like an inrush of water. Men all around her were talking about what had been found. Had she not seen the bodies with her own eyes, she would have been convinced that the men had been sliced into little pieces and their offal fed to the birds. The stories became wilder and more divergent with each group of men she passed, but all agreed on one thing—Niall had succumbed to madness and killed them all.

"He was a good lad before," one man said.

Áine's ears perked up. A supporter. But before she could approach the man in gratitude, she heard him say, "Of course, before he brought that faerie woman back to camp with him. She bewitched him well and good."

"Ay, stole his soul and offered it to Queen Mab so she could stay on this side of the veil."

Both men stopped their chatter when they realised that Áine stood within earshot. She gave them a withering look and had the grim satisfaction of seeing these two sturdy men squirm and look away.

"Shame on you," she told them. "Continue to talk like that and your tongues will blacken and shrivel up in your mouths."

They muttered something under their breaths and pushed their way through the crowd to get away from her.

Áine wished she could savour the reaction, but it weighed heavily on her. Inevitably, this is what would be spoken. Supporters would blame her for Niall's fall. Enemies would spread the blame equally between them.

She edged her way through the crowd towards the front. She ducked and squeezed through gaps in the men, hearing scraps of news that filtered down from O'Dwyer's quarters.

"He's still defiant," one man muttered.

"Won't admit to the rise of the moon."

"O'Dwyer will break it out of him."

Finally, she reached a boundary that could not be breached. Donogh's men were holding the line and keeping everyone at bay. Áine craned her neck to peer past their shoulders and caught a glimpse of Cormac and Ruadhri standing just outside O'Dwyer's tent. She stood on her tiptoes and lifted her hand to flag their attention, but some commotion happened in the tent, and they rushed inside.

The drone of voices fell to a hush, as though everyone collectively held their breath. Áine's heart pounded so hard against her chest that surely everyone could hear.

"He's to be hanged. Hanged on the morrow."

Áine heard this from someone, and then another repeated it more loudly until the words became a hateful chant.

No! Áine clapped her hands over her ears. *It can't be*, she moaned. They heard it wrong—they had to have. She pushed through the crowd to reach Cormac. He was close by to hear what O'Dwyer really said. Surely, they were all wrong.

But when Áine reached the front of the crowd and saw Cormac restraining Fionn, she knew the horrible truth. A moment later, the soldiers hauled Niall out of the tent and dragged him away, past his howling wolfhound.

Áine could not speak. She had lost the power of words. Her limbs felt heavy, and she wanted nothing more than to scream her pain to the world. How was this justice when men like Garret had shown themselves to be monsters who destroyed innocent women? How was this justice when a man like Banan hid a blackness inside that corrupted and stained? There was someone out there who had done this deed, and she would not judge them for it, but it had not been Niall.

Áine closed the distance between herself and Cormac and Ruadhri. By the time she reached them, she had regained her voice, though it came out wildly. "He is innocent."

Cormac and Ruadhri exchanged a look, and Ruadhri asked, "Were you with him the entire night, girl? Tell us you were. No shame if it saves the man."

Áine would have gladly told a falsehood to save Niall, but her lie would have been easily uncovered. "I wasn't," she admitted bitterly. "But I know still the same."

They didn't seem at all convinced, and that stirred Áine's outrage.

"You don't believe him? How could you doubt him, after all this time you've shared the same meals, slept on the same ground, even guarded each other's life?"

"I believe him." Ruadhri gave a pointed glare to Cormac.

"Ay, I do too," Cormac agreed, almost reluctantly. "Ay. I do," he added with more spirit. "But they won't take the word of a fair maid, more's the pity, and our gentle feelings on the matter will mean naught," he said grimly. "The evidence is too damning."

"It was meant to be," Ruadhri said darkly.

"Where are they taking him?" Áine asked, her voice catching.

"Donogh's tent," Ruadhri said. "They'll be holding him under guard there until—"

"Until the morning," Cormac finished.

The morning. Then they would hang him.

Áine couldn't let that happen.

One magpie foretells sorrow,
Two promise joy . . .

Áine crouched behind a shrub in the darkness beside Maeve, as close as they dared to Donogh's quarters and outside the circle of light made by the dying campfire. His men were starting to settle down for the night.

She and Maeve waited for the signal. Not for the chirp of a magpie; instead, she waited for the warble of a more exotic bird.

"What is keeping them?" Maeve hissed in Áine's ear. "Slugabeds."

If Áine wasn't a tightly wound bundle of nerves, she would have smiled at Maeve's exasperation. The young woman was more like her mother than she would have admitted.

"Soon," Áine whispered back. She glanced at the sky. Moonrise was due soon, and she wanted to be well away from here before then.

And then she heard the first strains they had been waiting for—

clear, trilling laughter, followed by a loud shush and more muffled giggling. The Triad had arrived. Áine risked a peek over the shrubs and saw the three young women illuminated by the campfire. They looked especially enticing, with their hair flowing down their backs. The firelight brought out the sheen of their locks and drew the interest of Donogh's men. Rugged soldiers transformed instantly into fluttering moths.

The Triad behaved as though they had been caught in a late-night stroll. They teased and flirted, first with the soldiers who were lounging around the campfire closest to the tent, then they cast artful lures to the men guarding the tent where Niall was held.

The plan was working beautifully. Ruadhri had thought to start a diversion—his mind went instantly to a fight, and Cormac was all for it, but Eireen had stepped in with the pragmatism of a mature woman. "Bait the trap with honey, not blood. The nights have been cold, and we need to put them to mind a different sport."

"Blanche is being too obvious." Maeve clicked her tongue softly. "She should follow Brigid's lead. I'll be sure to tell her so."

"Never mind that," Áine murmured. "We have work to do."

The two women kept to the shadows and made their way to the rear of the tent. Áine canted her head and tried to detect any sounds from within. Donogh was reported to be in O'Dwyer's tent, but he could have left someone else with Niall.

Maeve nudged her arm and mouthed, "Hurry."

Áine took a breath and, with a sharp blade, started sawing through the canvas, two feet from the bottom. It was harder than she'd expected, but she bit her bottom lip and concentrated on cutting through the rough material as Maeve kept watch.

The last inch was the hardest to cut through since the strength of the canvas was bound there. Finally, with the sound of a loud tear that made Áine wince, she succeeded.

Áine parted the flap she had fashioned and ducked her head inside. It was darker here than outside, with the rising moon and the indistinct glow of the campfire. She waited a moment to adjust to the gloom, her heart beating in her throat. Her muscles tensed in anticipation of strong hands grabbing her and hauling her to her feet for a reckoning.

Dark shapes detached from darker shadows until she saw Niall sitting in the centre. He was alone. His knees were drawn to his chest, and his arms were bound behind him. Even in the darkness, she could tell he sat straight and alert.

"Who's there?" he whispered.

She rushed over to him and heard his quick intake of breath. "Áine-my-Áine?" Then his tone sharpened. "What are you doing here?"

"Freeing you." Áine gave his arm a reassuring squeeze before she applied the blade on the ropes that lashed his wrists together.

"You should not be here."

"Nor should you," she said simply. "Now stop talking, or they'll hear you." She finished cutting through the threads, and the ties fell apart and dropped to the ground.

The moment he was free, Niall pulled her into his embrace and kissed her hard, with the desperation of a starved man. "I didn't think I'd ever be able to do that again," he whispered against her lips.

"I don't want that to be our last kiss," she said breathlessly and then stepped away. "We have very little time." She gathered any materials she could find—firewood, bed linens and rush mats—then arranged everything down the centre of a pallet and covered them with her mantle. At a quick glance, it would look like a sleeping form.

"Clever girl."

"This way." Áine led him to the cut section of the tent, and Niall knelt before the flap, ready to crawl through the opening. Before he could, there was a sharp rap on the tent.

Maeve's signal.

Áine pulled him back and pressed a hand to his mouth in warning. "Someone must be coming," she whispered in his ear. Carefully, she pressed the two cut sections together, holding them in place so they appeared to still be knitted to the rest of the canvas wall.

Áine heard the crunch of approaching footsteps. She prayed that

Maeve had managed to slip safely away after she had given the warning.

The footsteps seemed to be moving back and forth across a short length, and it seemed to Áine that whoever they belonged to was searching for something. She imagined them bending down and seeing the cut canvas. Niall took the blade she had used and crouched low, prepared to lunge.

Just when Áine was certain that the stranger was going to find the hole, a screech, loud enough to awaken the Underworld, sounded in the front of the tent.

Eireen!

"What is this nonsense?" Her voice carried crisp as a bell, even to inside the tent. "Maeve was right to alert me that you girls were up to no good."

Áine exhaled in relief, not only because there was no doubt that Maeve got away, but the footsteps outside quickly retreated.

"But Eireen, we did nothing wrong," one of the Triad protested.

"We only stopped for a moment," another said, her voice petulant and pouty.

"Do you take me for a fool?" Eireen cried. "And you soldiers should know better. I've warned you before." The woman launched into a heated tirade, and Áine knew this was their chance to escape.

Niall crawled out first, made sure it was clear, then helped Áine out. They hurried to the cluster of shrubs where Áine and Maeve had previously hidden and dove for cover.

"We need to make it to the paddock. Cormac and Ruadhri are waiting for us there," Áine said.

Niall shook his head. "This is madness. You'll all be held to blame for this."

"It won't matter," Áine said. "It's all been sorted out."

They turned their backs on the conflict still raging at Donogh's tent. She hoped that Eireen knew to wind it down before the commotion drew Donogh and O'Dwyer over to investigate. It wouldn't take much for someone to think about checking on the prisoner, and Niall needed to be far from this place before that happened.

When they got a little distance from Donogh's tent, Niall pulled her aside. "Áine, you have to know—I have no memory of what happened, but I swear I didn't—"

She placed her fingers on his lips. "You didn't do it. I know."

"But I wanted to carve them up. I would have relished their death."

"I know the evil that lurks in men," she said, "but your soul is not blackened by it."

When they reached the horse pens, they found Cormac waiting with Ruadhri and Purcell. They had readied the horses, including Niall's. Fionn jumped up on him, nearly knocking him over. The wolfhound made whining noises, and Niall had to shush him so that he wouldn't alert anyone. When Fionn calmed down, Niall faced the gathered men.

"Unsaddle your horses. No one is coming with me," Niall said grimly. "If you leave here with me, you'll all be outlaws. Not only from the English, but also from our own. O'Dwyer will hunt you down himself. It's not too late to feign a drunken revelry and deny anything to do with my escape."

"This isn't a merry jaunt we'll be going on," Cormac said. "We have a traitor to find."

"Get on the horse," Ruadhri said, folding his arms across his chest. "We have a plan."

"And that is . . . ?"

"Purcell will stay behind to spread a rumour that your wits have been restored and you know who the traitor is," Ruadhri answered.

"If I knew who it was, I'd tell O'Dwyer, not run away like a brigand in the night."

"Ay?" Cormac squinted one eye and looked at him. "And how golden is your word these days?"

Niall grimaced. "Right."

"You'll be away securing the proof you need," Cormac added.

"It still doesn't signify. O'Dwyer wants my head. I can be no threat under those circumstances."

"That's where you're wrong," Cormac said. "You'll eat away at the traitor's peace of mind every moment of the day, and he'll be living in fear of you revealing his identity. He'll be obsessing over any loose threads, reconsidering the faithfulness of those closest to him. There's always someone who knows where the shite is buried."

"He'll come after you if I leave a broad trail," Purcell said.

Niall rubbed his forehead. "Fine. Makes sense," he said curtly. Then he turned to Áine, and she immediately knew that his hesitancy sprang from her. "I'm not leaving Áine behind. She'll be blamed for this."

She slipped under his arm and pressed a hand to his chest. "For once, you will listen to me — I'm staying here. I'll be safe with Eireen, but *you* won't be if she's gone to all this trouble to set you free and you're still caught —"

Niall pulled her into his arms and gave her a long kiss that made her weak in the knees. It hardly mattered that they had witnesses. "I will return to you as soon as I am able," he said. "Remain with Eireen so I'll know how to find you." When he released her, he bent down to ruffle Fionn's fur. "Stay with Áine," he told the wolfhound. "Stay. Guard her."

Fionn looked up at Áine, and he seemed to understand his task. He whined a little, but he did not bolt away from her side.

Áine watched as Niall, Cormac and Ruadhri rode away and the darkness swallowed them up. "Keep him safe," she whispered to the night air and to any friendly Folk who might be listening. "Anything you desire will be yours if you bring him back to me safely." For now, he was wanted from both sides.

CHAPTER 23

THE ENGLISH HAD FINALLY DONE Niall a favour. By forcing Irish families to relocate into the protected areas, the garrison towns became besieged by a community of displaced villagers. Overnight, tents, wagons and an invading army of cattle, sheep and chickens sprang up like toadstools. By the time Niall, Cormac and Ruadhri arrived within the shadow of Cahir Castle, three travellers didn't generate any interest.

Cahir Castle was an intimidating fortress situated on a rocky island in the River Suir, strategically at the crossroads between Clonmel, Dublin and Limerick. It could have easily withstood against the might of Cromwell's forces; instead, it had been surrendered without a single shot being fired.

Such a waste, Niall thought as he studied its defences. The prospect of Ireland's defeat had been paved with an accumulation of missteps and craven choices.

Niall scanned the distant ramparts and picked out the dull grey helmets that betrayed the English sentries who kept watch. What could they be looking for, with the numbers of displaced people on their eastern banks multiplying daily?

Niall thought it unnatural to be riding openly within sight of the

English garrison instead of slinking past its stone walls like a brigand. Ruadhri, on the other hand, found the possibilities amusing.

"Why hasn't O'Dwyer thought of this?" Ruadhri asked as they walked past a woman feeding her chickens. "Most of the camp could relocate here, and the English wouldn't know. I wager we could even infiltrate the castle. Consider the havoc we could wreak."

Ruadhri had an excellent point, Niall thought as he looked around at the wagons that had been turned to sleeping quarters and the dizzying number of people clustered around them. "Mention it again later—after we capture the traitor."

It did not take them long to find families who had once sheltered and fed them and who were willing to further aid them. Niall sprinkled his plans to visit the public house in the village like seed on fertile soil. A select few he swore to secrecy and received their solemn oath, "None will hear it from my lips."

Niall thanked them and continued on his way with Cormac and Ruadhri. "One hour before everyone knows."

"Less," Cormac said.

Ruadhri lit up. "I'll make you a wager. By the time we reach the public house, someone will welcome O'Coneill by name."

"Find another fool," Cormac said.

They found the landlord of the public house completely overwhelmed with the influx of refugees in a village that could not sustain them. When they rode into the courtyard, the harried man was ushering out a woman who held a bowl in her arms. "I have no scraps for your swine, woman." He nodded at Niall. "O'Coneill. Heard you were coming. My girl will see you settled."

"This plan will work well enough," Niall exchanged a wry glance with Cormac before pulling the landlord aside. "Is the room over the stables available for a night or two?"

"I have better rooms in the house for your ease," the landlord said.

"The loft will suit us well," Niall assured him. They had stayed there before and knew it commanded a good view of the central square. The last time he had made use of it, he had been keeping watch for English soldiers. This time he hoped to uncover the traitor.

"Leave the room unlocked, and we'll find our own way. But tell no one."

The landlord chewed his bottom lip before nodding. "As you wish."

Niall, Cormac and Ruadhri crossed the courtyard and entered the public house.

The benches were crammed with patrons, but true to the landlord's word, the daughter was already preparing a table for them in a snug corner of the common room. Niall slid into the seat across from Cormac and Ruadhri just as the woman of the house directed to their table oatcakes and earthenware pitchers of ale. The matron appeared with a linen kerchief wrapped around her head and stood at their table clasping her plump hands.

"We have a tasty dish of stewed rabbit," she told them as Ruadhri dove into the fare like a famished wolf.

"Forgive his manners," Niall said to her with a pained smile. "Anything will be grand." He slipped a few coins into her apron.

When she bustled off to fetch the food, Niall went to take a sip of ale, and its scent soured his stomach. He lowered the untouched cup on the table. His stomach hadn't been right since he had awoken from his drunken spree, nor had his head. Niall still hadn't regained his memories of that night, but the few snatches he could pick out started to solidify. As Cormac refilled Ruadhri's cup, a vivid memory of Banan plying Niall with ale came sharp and vivid. Banan's laughing face, with his too-large eyes that seemed odder than usual. A voice inviting Banan to join them. Where had that come from? Niall focused on the voice, which eluded him. Then Banan's wheezing laugh—the man had seemed relieved, as though some matter had finally been resolved. Or had it? The man was dead now.

Absently, Niall lifted the cup again to his lips, and once more his stomach did a violent turn. "I think I was poisoned," he said aloud.

Ruadhri and Cormac put down their ales in alarm.

"Not here," Niall said with a wave of his hand. "The night the English and Banan were killed." He traced circles on the table as he tried to stitch what happened. "Banan must have put something in the ale."

"That would explain how muddled you were," Cormac said.

"Then it was the drink," Ruadhri said. "I can believe that. You were never a man to drink himself to forgetfulness."

Niall frowned, trying to focus on a voice that drifted on the edge of his memory. He looked down at the circles he had traced on the wood. "There was a third cup. Another man had been drinking with us." But the harder he tried to wrestle the memory into submission, the easier it slipped out of his grasp.

The woman of the house returned with hot bowls of rabbit and more oatcakes.

"It'll come to you," Ruadhri said, taking an appreciative sniff of the rabbit stew.

"Before O'Dwyer catches up to us, I trust." Cormac took his first bite.

Niall shifted nervously. He was truly an outlaw, hunted by both sides. This ruse must work or he'd be doomed.

They stayed long enough to be marked by casual observers before slipping out, one by one, to the courtyard. From there, they found the stairs that led to the room above the stables and the door unlocked as the landlord had promised.

Over the rest of the day and into the night, the three men took turns keeping watch at the window. Cormac was yawning to split his jaw when Niall relieved him after the sun had risen.

"See anything yet?"

Cormac arched his back to stretch out the kinks. "Nothing except domestic troubles between a woman with a flock of angry geese and another with a herd of swine."

Niall stared down at the square, at the distinct but loose boundaries set by the households encamped below. How long were these people expected to remain here while the English slept in comfort within the castle? The arrogance of these English whoresons, to command where an Irishman was to sleep and eat.

"The landlord will be opening the doors by now." Cormac rose from his stool. "I'll run across to see what sustenance the woman of the house has on offer." Before he could step away from the window, something caught his eye.

"What is it?"

"I thought I saw a man riding a piebald garron." Cormac peered through the window closely. "Passed between that shop and the white building. Only for a moment. The animal reminded me of . . ."

Niall peered through the window to where Cormac pointed. He saw a man leading a donkey and another leading a cart, but no—

There! On an open stretch of road, the rider appeared again. Niall's jaw tightened. The rider's head may have been covered by the cowl of his mantle, but Niall knew that odd tawny piebald garron.

"McTiege? He's the traitor?" Cormac asked Niall, his eyes narrowing. "You aren't shocked."

"I'm not shocked, no. Disappointed and growing enraged by the moment, but not shocked. I didn't want to believe it." McTiege was the traitor. Saints above, how he wished otherwise.

"You suspected—when?"

"Ay, I wasn't certain of him. The day after the raid, he left camp with dispatches from O'Dwyer, but Áine later saw him in the forest travelling in the opposite direction to Ross Castle."

Cormac gave him a strange look. "McTiege wasn't going to Ross Castle. O'Dwyer used him as a messenger between himself and Colonel Sankey."

Niall sat down heavily on a stool. "The treaty?"

"Ay. O'Dwyer has been negotiating with Sankey for the last couple of months, and he used McTiege to communicate with the English," Cormac said. "I thought you knew when you found out about the treaty. Wasn't this why you didn't want McTiege to come with us when we flushed out Garret? I thought you were wroth with him over the treaty dispatches."

"It could still be McTiege," Niall said. "There's not a piebald beast like his in all of Tipperary." He didn't want to believe it, but he hadn't wanted to believe that anyone would have betrayed them either. Niall searched the square, but the rider had disappeared again.

"I will not believe it," Cormac said. "McTiege was as furious as you when he found out where he was being sent and why. He'd sooner betray his grandmam. Besides, McTiege is taller, I'd swear it. Someone must have stolen his garron."

"Of all the horses to take, you'd take a yellow piebald?"

"I would if I wanted people to think I was its owner."

"Listen to you both arguing like fishwives," Ruadhri interrupted. He sat up, sharp-eyed, as if he had been awake for some time. "That's all very interesting, but if it isn't McTiege, who's the bastard on the horse?"

"Wait—" Cormac held up his hand. Strange sounds filtered from below. There was an odd creaking, as though the house were shifting. Very much like heavy boots on stair treads.

"Trap!" Niall shouted as he sprang for the door. He hadn't yet reached the portal when it flung open and a swarm of English soldiers poured in with muskets and drawn swords.

Niall flew back and scrambled to unsheathe his sword, but the enemy was already upon him. He dodged the butt end of a musket and shoved the soldier, driving shoulder and elbow into the man's exposed side.

Near him, Cormac and Ruadhri fought like cornered beasts. With no time to grab their weapons, they seized anything they could. A chamber pot smashed against an English face, and splintered chairs became lethal daggers. Ruadhri's roar filled the air.

A shot fired. The room lit up in a blinding flash, followed by an earsplitting crack. Someone kicked Niall, and before he could recover, he found himself overpowered.

They drove him to the ground, pressing his face against the planks. Cormac crashed beside him, his enraged howls smothered as the soldiers held him down. Ruadhri was the last to be subdued. All the while, the English were shouting at them.

Niall's mind raced. *Where did they come from?* There was no doubt that they knew precisely where their quarry was to be found.

The soldiers pulled Niall to his feet and rushed him and the others down the stairs and out into the early morning air. A troop of dragoons were gathered in the courtyard, and held between two armed guards stood the landlord, shivering in his nightshirt.

They forced Niall to his knees beside Cormac and Ruadhri.

When he struggled to rise, he was smacked on the back of his head with the butt end of a carbine. Pain exploded, and it was all he could do not to succumb to the stars firing off in his head.

A captain approached them, his pot helmet tucked under his arm. Niall recognised this man as another one of the prisoners O'Dwyer had ransomed along with Garret last year.

"I remember you," the Englishman said, stopping before Niall.

Niall had been struggling to remember this one's name, but the moment the man spoke, it came to him. "Captain Davis. I regret the day we allowed you and Garret to go free."

Davis snorted. "And I regret the day you captured us. All the ridicule we faced over allowing ourselves to be captured by wild barbarians. After Colonel Sankey was forced to ransom us, we've got naught but the shite assignments." He studied Cormac and Ruadhri a moment before he snapped his fingers. "Bring the landlord closer."

"I've done . . . I've done nothing," the man blubbered. "I'm no threat to you—we're in the protected area."

"You forfeit our patience when you harbour enemies of the Commonwealth," Davis said as though by rote.

"He didn't know who we were," Ruadhri said, then got a harsh cuff to the head by one of the troopers.

"Shut up—I'm speaking to this miserable bootlicker," Davis said. His fingers drummed against his pot helmet. "Speak the truth, land-lord. Will we find any more Irish brigands under your roof?"

The landlord shook his head, wringing his hands. "There are no more, I swear it. These men came in together. The rest of my patrons are tradespeople."

The captain drew closer to the trembling man. "You can be certain that we'll be making a thorough search of the house, every nook and cupboard. If I find any Irish rebels, I'll string you up on the gibbet along with these men and make an example of you to all who pass through this town. Understood?"

The landlord's gaze darted to the house. He licked his lips and nodded. "I know of no others—I swear."

The stable door swung open. Davis barely glanced up. "Are these the men?"

Niall heard footsteps on stone, but when he saw who walked into the circle and took his place beside Davis, he doubted his own eyes.

Not McTiege. The man who stood there was Eamon.

The blow to Niall was sudden and as punishing as if a fist had been driven into his stomach. The man he had known for years—the man he had admired for years. Everything slotted into place, and the memory of that night became clear. It had been Eamon's voice urging Banan to pour Niall more ale. His had been the third cup.

Eamon's gaze rested briefly on Niall before he nodded. "These are the men I promised you."

"You *whoreson.*" Niall sprang to his feet and lunged for Eamon, but before he could get his hands on him, a couple of soldiers seized him. Niall struggled to break free, but his arms were jerked behind his back. With every movement, their hold tightened, twisting his arms until his shoulders threatened to pop. Gritting his teeth against the shooting pain, he was driven facedown into the rushes. "I will destroy you. Traitorous bastard."

"Traitor to what, a lost cause?" Eamon asked, his voice edged with scorn. "I'm a pragmatic man. Better to form strong alliances that will secure my interests than to fight against the wind." He turned to Davis. "This is the man who murdered Captain Garret and two of his officers."

"I did not kill Garret or his men, and well you know it," Niall ground out. "It was Eamon Grace who did the deed and blamed me for it, the coward."

"This is nonsense, Captain. A desperate man will seize upon anything to save him." Eamon laughed, and for the first time Niall heard the man's insincerity in that tone.

Davis did not immediately reply and tapped his helmet, deep in thought. Finally, he said, "I heard what Garret did, and I'm inclined to believe Grace on this score."

Niall roared his frustration, and one of the soldiers pressed his boot on his back.

"I've already given you the coordinates to O'Dwyer's camp and where your men can find the sentries," Eamon said.

No! Niall struggled against his captors, but he was trussed up too tight. His brothers-in-arms. The camp. *Áine*. She'd be taken . . . "The Almighty's curse upon you, Eamon." A boot kicked him in the side, and the sudden flare of pain made him suck in his breath.

"As I understand it, Grace, you did the same for Garret, and that wasn't enough to secure the camp."

"Not my fault," Eamon said. "Garret's men allowed one of the sentries to escape."

But there had been two sentries who escaped—the man who sounded the alarm and Banan, who nearly had his head bashed in. Niall wondered why Eamon didn't mention him. Because Banan must have been helping Eamon until he was no longer useful—or useful in other ways.

"What I need, Captain Davis," Eamon continued, "is to have Colonel Sankey's binding agreement that my lands are restored to me and will remain in my possession and under my control."

"We've already made our agreement," Davis replied, almost bored. "I'll put in a favourable word with Colonel Sankey."

"In writing. Garret took liberties with our original agreement and overstepped his bounds."

"Bounds?" Davis didn't bother to hide his scorn. "We will not be dictated to by Irish informants. I'll document your assistance once I've captured O'Dwyer and his brigade. You already agreed to this."

"Yes, before these men arrived and we all ended up here," Eamon said with a mirthless laugh. "Now that you have these men, you need nothing more from me. They are proof that my information is gold— proof that I haven't played you false."

"He plays everyone false," Niall called out and got another boot to the side.

"Not where my land is concerned," Eamon said flatly. "Captain, you have no cause to hold back your signed statement."

Davis's voice turned surly. "You are not in a position to negotiate, Grace. Only when we capture O'Dwyer. Be content with that."

"And what of these men?" Eamon asked.

"I don't have time to deal with them now," Davis said.

"Then hand them over to me, I'll deal with them."

"Like you dealt with Banan?" Niall said, his voice muffled by the reeds.

Eamon struck Niall below the ribs with enough force to send waves of pain through Niall.

"Well, Captain, will you grant me this boon at least?" Eamon said.

"No," Davis said firmly. "Since he took the lives of three English soldiers, he'll face English justice. And the others, as his accomplices." Turning his back in dismissal, he started issuing orders. "Corporal, ride to the castle and rouse the garrison. Meet us on the road directly to the south of the castle." Then lower, as though speaking to himself, "I will wipe off this stain once and for all."

"Sir, what of these men?"

"Lock these men up and post a guard. Landlord, hand over the keys to your storeroom, or you'll share their fate. The next time I return to this godforsaken public house, I will see their heads decorating spikes at the gates." Then to his men, "Saddle the horses and prepare to ride. We have Irish rebels to hunt."

The soldiers hauled Niall and the others across the courtyard and to a storehouse. A sturdy iron padlock secured the door, and the soldiers used the landlord's keys to gain entrance.

Niall, Cormac and Ruadhri were pushed inside. When Niall twisted around to face the guards, the door was locked behind them. He overturned a pile of crates and bellowed his frustration to the rafters.

ÁINE DREAMT OF A MAGPIE. SHE JOLTED AWAKE, HER SKIN drenched in sweat, her heart racing.

Drawing up her knees, she rubbed her forehead. She had had enough of sorrow and ill omens. Once, she'd thought she had nothing to lose. Even her own life was of no consequence. Now she had more than herself to lose, and that possibility was unbearable.

Áine reached for the water buckets. "Come along, my boy," she called to Fionn, who had become her shadow.

But the wolfhound was pacing back and forth, agitating the

cows. He then ran to the entrance of the enclosure and yelped at her. Áine wondered at his unsettled mood.

"Fionn?" she called out to him. He abandoned his pacing and ran up to her. Instead of being content with a scratch behind his ears, he kept nudging her out of the cattle pens.

"What's the matter with him?" Maeve asked. She wiped perspiration from her brow with her forearm. "He's making the cows nervous."

"I haven't any idea," she said. "Fionn, stop that." The hound darted again to the entrance, turned and barked at her. Áine set the pail of milk to the ground and approached the wolfhound. Fionn grew more excited, and when she reached him, he flew out like an arrow towards the meadow. She glanced around but didn't see anything.

Fionn returned at a run.

"I suppose you needed some exercise," Áine said to him, absently. But instead of Fionn slowing to a trot, he shot past her and went straight for one of the cows. He had gotten behind the beast and nipped at its flanks. The cow snorted and charged out of the enclosure, heading for the pasture.

"Fionn, stop!" she yelled, but he did not heed her. Instead, he routed a second cow and chased a few more. Soon the entire herd was charging across the meadowland.

"What has that hound done?" Maeve gasped, running after them. "He's gone mad."

Áine ran after Fionn in a panic, shouting his name. The others scattered, trying to head off the cows. One of the girls ran for a horse to reach the hound while Áine and Maeve ran as fast as they could to stop him.

All sorts of evil things could befall the herd. Breaking their forelegs in the ditches was what Áine feared the most. Eireen would never forgive her if something happened to any of them. She was to have minded the hound; he was her responsibility.

They were a short distance from the camp when they caught up with the first cow. Maeve and Áine waved their arms to head it off, and, exhausted, it slowed to a halt. Áine yelled at Fionn, to warn him away from the skittish herd, and then stopped. A cold shiver tripped down her spine. He was standing alert, his back to her, facing in the direction of the camp. His ruff was prominent, and he was standing alert, like a soldier.

Áine then heard it, rolling across the encampment. The rumble of thunder following by the sound of shrieking.

CHAPTER 24

NIALL HURLED himself against the door. "Eamon, you bastard. I'll carve out your innards when I get my hands on you!"

Cormac heaved his shoulder against the portal, but neither he nor Niall had any effect on three-inch-thick oak.

"The camp won't stand a chance against the English," Cormac said.

Niall slammed his fist against the door. *Áine won't stand a chance.* This was all his fault. He should never have left her there. An image of burning shelters and screaming women rose up to torment Niall. He could hear Áine's desperate voice crying out for help. Help that would never come—if he didn't find a way out of this place, and soon.

How could he have been fooled by Eamon? Niall had trusted him, even looked up to him. The Graces had been the Mulrianes' closest neighbours for generations.

What had Eamon told the captain—*Garret took liberties with our original agreement.*

Original agreement. A cold chill washed over him.

Diarmuid had been captured by the English after he had met McTiege and had been given the direction of O'Dwyer's camp. But he had not disclosed this to the enemy. He had died with that information. If Diarmuid had not utilised that knowledge to save his life, then how had the English known of the Mulrianes? His cousin would sooner have betrayed O'Dwyer than his family. He'd never have placed them in jeopardy. Never.

The English had gone to a great deal of trouble to carry Diarmuid's head back to his father, as though the camp meant nothing to them. O'Dwyer must never have been part of Eamon's original agreement.

The hair rose on the back of Niall's neck. The Mulrianes had been.

Garret took liberties . . . overstepped his bounds.

Eamon must have been the one who turned Diarmuid over to Garret, and in so doing, had revealed the shiny bauble that had been the Mulrianes' estate — and the treasure of his family.

Niall roared and threw himself again at the door, slamming his shoulder against it. The bastard! The bastard had destroyed his family. The English were the match, and Eamon had lit it.

"Quiet down in there," an English voice from the other side of the wall shouted.

Cormac pulled Niall back. "It's not working. The door was built to protect the landlord's livelihood. We have to work with what we have. Even if we can break through there, we won't get far." He looked around the storeroom at the inn's supplies: rounds of cheese, bins of onions and turnips, kegs of ale and smaller casks of spirits. There were no windows in the hut, but a diffused light still entered.

Niall paced the storeroom like an agitated wolf. There had to be a way to get through that door. They must escape and warn the camp.

He stopped his pacing. *The light.* Lifting his gaze, he stared at the ceiling above. Gaps between the layers of thatch and the wooden rafters provided enough space for the light to filter down to them.

Niall strode to the barrels in the corner of the storeroom. Passing over the smaller kegs, he went instead for the large hogsheads. "Help me with this," he whispered to Ruadhri. "Move it across the floor, a few feet away from the back wall." The roof was slightly pitched, and this would put them on the leeward slope.

"Why?" Ruadhri asked.

"Because we don't have a ladder." Niall pointed upwards to the ceiling.

Cormac's eyes widened before an understanding grin spread across his face. Ruadhri nodded approvingly.

"We'll stack a few of the smaller ones on top," Niall said quietly. "That'll give me enough height to reach the rafters and poke a hole through the thatch."

"Big enough for a man to get through," Cormac finished.

"Once we're clear of the storeroom, head for the stables. Pray they've left behind horses," Niall said. "I don't know how long it will take to muster the rest of their men. We must reach the camp before the English arrive."

"First, we need to leave this village without being seen," Ruadhri said.

Niall had to count on Davis removing most of his forces to deal with O'Dwyer. "We each take a different route—one of us is bound to clear the village."

Together, they tipped the hogshead on its rim and, with initial grunts and shuffles, eventually started to roll it across. They had managed to get the barrel halfway across when the guard started banging on the door. "What's going on in there?"

Niall exchanged a look with Ruadhri, but Cormac was already on his way to the door. In his sweetest voice, he said, "Come in and check, if you like. We won't mind."

"Good try," the guard said. "The door stays locked until you hang."

Niall knew they wouldn't fool the guards a second time. "Keep talking to the bastard," he hissed to Cormac. "Tell him a story."

Cormac grinned and threw himself into this task with vim. While he droned on in English to the guards, who couldn't walk away or open the door to shut him up, about all the annoying, wicked spirits that could play havoc with a man's life, Niall and Ruadhri rolled the hogshead barrel the remaining distance.

Niall clambered atop the barrel and gauged the distance between his reach and the rafters. Motioning to the smaller kegs, he indicated for Ruadhri to bring him three. The first two became a secondary platform, and the last one topped it off.

He climbed to the top and grabbed one of the crossbeams. Slowly, he pulled himself up, muscles straining, until he hoisted his upper body onto the beam. From there, he was able to reach the thatch.

It took longer than he'd expected to make an opening while working as silently as he could. Cormac's persistent storytelling covered up the sounds of Niall's labours. When he cut through a large enough hole, he hoisted himself up and out of the storeroom.

Niall climbed onto the thatch roof, careful to stay low so that he wouldn't be spotted by the guards below. Peering around, he found the lane that would take them to the rear of the stables and as far away from the gibbet as possible. He poked his head through the hole and motioned for Ruadhri.

The hulking man scrambled up onto the roof with the grace of a cat, then edged down the back slope of the storehouse.

Cormac's voice grew louder as he stepped away from the door and neared the barrels. He finished in Irish with, "Go to hell, you filthy whoresons."

Niall held down his hand to help him up through the roof. When Cormac was through and sitting safely on the thatch, he rubbed his nose. "They'll miss my voice when I'm gone."

"They'll get over it." Niall shimmied down the roof and, hanging on to the solid eaves, lowered himself slowly as far as he could before dropping to the soft ground. Cormac followed, and together they set off for the stables.

The first sign Niall saw that matters had turned in their favour was two sets of boots sticking out from under a bush. Ruadhri had subdued the guards posted at the stable.

"There's no time to find our weapons," Ruadhri said, "but these two were accommodating." He divided between them four carbines, powder and shot, two swords and one dagger.

Niall mounted his own horse. "Set loose the spare horses. Leave these bastards nothing to come after us with. There's an abbey north of the garrison. Head for there—we can pick up the trails and approach the camp from the northern side. It'll be rough going, but it's a shorter route to the encampment."

As agreed, they each took a different route. Niall set off, forcing himself to keep to a leisurely trot, even though inside he was screaming to fly. To rush through the narrow streets at a breakneck pace would have alerted any English troops that may have remained in the town. He wouldn't have made it to the foothills.

Niall slouched and covered his head as he rode through the village. A few English guards occupied the square. He selected a side lane to skirt around them, keeping a maddeningly sedate pace so as not to stir their curiosity. He wanted to jump out of his skin. As he headed down the lane, an old man crossed his path. He looked up and saw Niall, recognition dawning over his face.

The town's farrier.

The man's gaze darted down the length of the lane to the square where the English soldiers were. Niall lifted a finger to his mouth, praying that the man wouldn't give him away. A moment later, the farrier nodded and turned away from the square.

Niall cleared the town without being challenged. Castle Cahir loomed in the distance, flying an English banner. He struck north and caught up with Ruadhri and Cormac near the abbey as planned, but a glance south towards the garrison made his gut wrench.

Davis's men were already on the move and riding for Glengarra.

A WAVE OF MOUNTED SOLDIERS CHARGED THROUGH THE CAMP with a volley of musket fire. People dove for cover; many were knocked aside and trampled by the horses. Others dropped right where they were.

Cold fear washed over Áine, locking her limbs. Nightmares replayed, never forgotten. Fionn tugged at her mantle with his teeth, urging her in the opposite direction.

Maeve's screams of horror cleared Áine's fuddled mind. When her friend ran past her towards the camp, Áine caught her and held her back. "No, we have to hide."

"I can't—my mother—I have to help—" the girl sobbed.

Áine looked around to Fionn and suddenly understood what the hound had been trying to tell her. Run. Hide. Get as far away as she could before the killing started. "To the woods!" she cried and pulled Maeve towards the haven of the woods. "This way," she urged the remaining women. *"Hurry."*

Áine dashed across the fields. The ground suddenly plunged in a slope, and she struggled to keep her balance.

"Áine!"

She turned to see Maeve urgently pointing to the cattle enclosures. A dozen soldiers gathered, scouring the grounds. Even from this distance, Áine saw one motion in their direction. Four of the horsemen broke off to chase after them.

Áine and Maeve raced towards the woods. The trees—the trees would offer shelter, a place to hide—if they could reach them in time. She risked a glance over her shoulder. The riders were eating up the distance—hunters running their prey to the ground.

Shouts filled the air. "Look at them run—"

"The redhead's mine!"

Áine cried out in panic. She'd never reach the trees in time.

The pounding of hooves shook the ground beneath her feet. A fell host swept down upon them. A rider shot past her and headed for Maeve, but before Áine could scream a warning, an ironlike grip seized her and lifted her into the air, hoisting her up into the saddle.

Áine twisted and kicked, trying to throw the rider's balance and unsettle his horse. The horse veered sharply right. Áine bucked against the rider, but his hold tightened until his arm dug into her ribs.

Then Fionn flew across the field and launched himself at the horse, tearing at the rider's legs. The man screamed, and his hold on Áine slackened. She slid from his grasp and, with a great heave, pushed herself off and crashed to the ground.

The wind knocked out of her. Panic flooded her as she gasped for air and couldn't fill her lungs. A moment later, she regained her breath but Áine was still too stunned to move. Far away, somewhere in the distance, Fionn's incessant barking broke through her stupor. Then his growls and barks grew louder, and Áine realised he was standing right beside her. *Get up*, he was saying. *Get up.* Her limbs wouldn't obey.

She struggled upright just in time to see two horsemen riding straight for her. Fionn locked himself in front of her, crouched low and ready to lunge. The horses were nearly upon her. With a strangled shriek, she curled herself into a protective ball and covered her head. Both horses whizzed safely past, one on either side.

Áine rose to her feet, her strength returning. She looked around for Maeve but couldn't make out where she was.

Then she saw her—Maeve draped over the shoulder of an English trooper, and he running for his horse. She kicked and twisted. Her struggles threw the man's stride, and he stumbled forward, spilling her to the ground. Maeve pushed herself from her grasping captor and tried to run. He seized her ankle, and she crashed again to the ground. Maeve clawed the turf as the soldier yanked her towards him.

No! A surge of fury burst through Áine's lips, and she sprinted to help Maeve. Fionn, still at her side, coiled and sprang ahead. The English soldier looked up in time to see the wolfhound flying towards him. With a cry, he released Maeve and held up his hands for protection, but he couldn't stop the hound's momentum.

Maeve sobbed when Áine reached her, then her eyes widened and she froze. Following her gaze, Áine whipped around to find two new soldiers bearing down on them.

CHAPTER 25

NIALL LED THE WAY. His fear for Áine rode him hard. He knew he shouldn't have left her behind. How could he have allowed himself to be persuaded? She'd be caught up in another raid—he had to get her to safety. Niall fought against the panic of not reaching her time.

The English had a lead on them. Niall scoured his memory for the road ahead. This was a shorter route to the camp, through wilder, more unpredictable country.

They reached a river, swollen with rain. Niall pulled up to the muddy bank and studied the frothing water. Cormac reined in beside him.

"This is impossible," Cormac said, turning his mount around.

Niall didn't answer. He rode a short distance downriver to where the bank widened and the water churned less. "We cross here."

Before Cormac could try to dissuade him, Niall urged his horse into the river. The waters surged, but the horse ploughed his way through the strong current and continued across the river. By the time Niall reached the other side, Cormac and Ruadhri were already halfway across the ford.

After a moment to rest, they left the river and struck a trail that ran northwest, winding through bogland that gradually gave way to forest. The road narrowed and plunged into a crisscross of tangled woods. They were forced to ride single file, ducking to avoid the snatching branches that were eager to pluck them off their horses.

A mile from the camp, Niall caught the sharp, acrid scent of burning wood, and with it, the memory of the charred remains of a byre and a stone cairn.

Devil take them.

"With me!" Niall yelled to Cormac and Ruadhri. He urged his labouring horse to press on. As they drew closer, he heard the unmistakable sound of screaming and scattered musket shot.

They gained the first group of shelters and saw an unruly skirmish unfolding at the far end of the camp. O'Dwyer's cavalry was in the thick of the fray, supported by Donogh's infantry, while the English were attempting to smash through and drive a wedge between them. At a quick glance, Davis's numbers were fewer than their own, but O'Dwyer had clearly been caught unawares and now was scrambling to launch an organised defence.

Hurtling toward the skirmish, Niall roared his rage. Cormac and Ruadhri followed his lead, both releasing a bloodcurdling cry. As one, they swooped in to nip at the enemy's right flank. Although they were only a few new swords in the fray, their sudden appearance encouraged the men of the brigade around them. The energy in the air shifted where they fought.

Niall had already discharged his only carbine and was slashing a path through the enemy with Cormac and Ruadhri protecting his back. He ducked as shots whizzed past his head. The smell of spent charge clogged his throat. He kneed his horse to push forward just in time. A bullet sliced through the edge of his mantle, narrowly missing his shoulder.

O'Dwyer had managed to shore up their defences and now fought hard to drive the English back. The enemy began to lose ground, which gave new wind to the defenders.

Niall fell back to survey the field. The enemy troopers had broken through their defences and were now charging through the camp.

Áine!

Niall slashed his way through the melee to reach Eireen's shelter. Every small surge forward felt as though he were trying to swim upstream. At one point, he came across Donogh's infantry fighting like beasts to dismount the enemy horse. Niall, Ruadhri and Cormac ploughed into the English flank, cutting a swath for their own.

As Niall looked around for a clear path, he locked on to Donogh's angry gaze. A moment later, a dozen English soldiers swept between them.

Then an opening appeared. Niall darted between two flaming shelters and urged his horse along the scorched lane running behind them. Everywhere was pandemonium. People dashed to get clear of the destruction.

He finally reached Eireen's shelter and found the place abandoned. "Áine!" No response. He wheeled his horse around.

Where would she hide? As though her voice whispered in his ear, he knew the answer.

Niall reached the cattle pens to find no one there and the barriers destroyed.

"Áine!"

Where could she be? A desperate knot of fear twisted tighter in his gut. He headed towards the river but stopped when he heard the distant barking of a wolfhound.

Fionn. His wolfhound would not have abandoned Áine.

Niall followed the barking to an open meadow. There, across the other end of the pasture, he saw a troop of horsemen chasing two women, one with autumn-flame hair.

Áine.

She and Maeve were trying to escape while Fionn darted in to slow the enemy down. The women reached the trees and plunged into the woods.

Niall dug his heels against the horse's sides and charged down the field. He gave the animal his head and barrelled down upon the soldiers, intercepting them at the treeline. His horse crowded an enemy's mount, upsetting the trooper's balance. Niall seized the moment of confusion and drove his sword into the man's side.

Niall wheeled his horse around in time to avoid the second rider.

He lifted his sword to deflect a lethal blow. Fionn lunged at the soldier's stirrups, snapping at the horse's flanks. The mount rolled his eyes and gave a sharp whinny. The horseman fought his mount, but Fionn was relentless. The horse panicked and, seizing the bit, bolted back towards the pasture with the wolfhound charging behind him. Cormac and Ruadhri were close behind and swept past to bear down on the other troopers.

A trumpet blew, an urgent, plaintive sound that checked the enemy's advance. They abandoned their pursuit of the women and now fought to elude a fresh wave of Irish cavalry that had reached the field.

"They're retreating!" Niall shouted to Cormac.

"Take a chunk out of their arses," Ruadhri roared and gave fresh chase.

Niall leapt from his horse as Áine flew into his arms. She trembled and sobbed as she clung to him.

He gathered her close, holding her tight, afraid she'd be spirited away.

"Are you harmed?"

She shook her head, unable to speak.

Another trumpet blast, this time from their side. Niall lifted his head to see O'Dwyer's colours being waved in triumph. Against all odds, they had done it—they had beaten back another bold attack. But he wouldn't call it a victory until Eamon had been found.

Niall released Áine and looked around. McTiege was holding Maeve, a fierce expression on his rugged face. Purcell caught up to them, sweat dripping from his moustache.

"Purcell—over here," Niall called out to him. "Protect my girl for me until I return."

"Where are you going?" Áine asked.

"My task isn't done." With that, her eyes widened in growing panic, and he pressed a quick kiss on her lips. "Purcell will protect you with his life. I will return to you, even if I have to fight the entire English army."

"Be safe."

Niall mounted his horse and whistled for Fionn. He reached

down and gave her hand a reassuring squeeze and headed into the woods, following the trail of the retreating English soldiers.

Eamon had proven himself to be a coward—and a crafty one. He might flee with the bulk of the English army, but only so far. Davis would have to explain his losses to his superiors, and Eamon, with nothing more to leverage, would be as welcome as a leper. By now, Eamon would have worked that out.

Niall was willing to wager that Eamon would find a hole to hide in until men stopped looking for him. Eamon knew Glengarra Woods well, but not as well as Niall, and Niall intended to flush out the traitor and make an offering of him to O'Dwyer.

Let Eamon learn how it feels to be hunted by both armies.

Individual tracks were impossible to make out since the ground had been churned up by the fleeing English horses, so Niall expanded his search beyond the main road. He was wagering that Eamon preferred the safety of the woods in his flight.

A section of recently broken branches led him to a trail with fresh horse tracks. Niall bent down to examine them carefully—the back hooves were decidedly wider apart than the front hooves, suggesting the horse moved in an oddly disjointed gait. From the shape of the hoofprint, the shoe was clearly Irish made.

Eamon had ridden into Cahir on McTiege's tawny garron, and unless he had switched horses, he'd still be riding the odd beast. McTiege's piebald was known for its disjointed and shambling gait, and now Niall blessed McTiege's fondness for the beastie.

He followed the trail and saw signs of recent passage—more broken branches and the same shuffling horse tracks. They led to the place where Niall had woken up in a drunken stupor—it had to be Eamon.

The woods grew thicker, the canopy blocking the light. Fionn ranged just ahead, and when he halted, nose scenting the wind, Niall dismounted.

Eamon had to be close.

Niall left his horse tethered to a tree and continued on foot so as not to alert his quarry of his approach.

In the distance, Niall caught the sparkle of light on water and a figure leading a horse through the trees. Niall touched Fionn's shoulder, silently willing him to stay close. Together, they crept the last distance.

A flock of birds startled in the trees, flapped overhead and swooped onwards to the river. Niall froze and looked around. He sensed eyes upon him, but the only creature he could see was the steady gaze of a lone raven. Nothing else moved. Niall pushed aside the feeling and continued, parting the branches carefully.

He found Eamon watering McTiege's yellow garron near a stand of willows, very near the spot where Eamon's men had grabbed Niall and trussed him up like a murderer.

Niall stepped through the trees.

Eamon whirled around and drew his sword. "How did you find me?" He looked wildly around, as though expecting to see others accompanying Niall, and visibly relaxed when it was clear they were alone.

"I can track anything, even a cowardly worm."

"If you think you're going to shame me into pleading forgiveness, you're a fool, Niall O'Coneill."

"How could you have done it, Eamon? We fought with you, protected your back. We bloody well broke bread when it was the only meal to be had for days."

"The English have won," Eamon shouted. "You're an idiot if you don't accept that. Now is the time for a canny man to negotiate for his future."

"Or protect himself," Niall said, drawing closer. "Is this why you killed Garret—before he could change his mind and betray you to O'Dwyer?"

"What do you care about Garret? I did you a favour by slitting his throat."

"You robbed me of my vengeance," Niall barked. "Then framed me for it, you heartless bastard."

"O'Dwyer might not have gone through with the hanging."

"This is your defence, that I might not have been hanged? And your excuse for Banan—he didn't mind having his throat slashed?"

"Don't pretend you have any sympathy for him. I know you didn't care for each other."

"He was a nasty piece of shite," Niall said. "I never understood how you tolerated him. He deserved a beating, but not to be killed."

"And I never deserved to have my land taken from me," Eamon snarled. "Generations of my forefathers bled for that land. I will do anything to keep every square inch of forest and glen and meadowland. Damned if I allowed the English, or any man, to take it from me."

Square inch. Meadowland. The words rang a familiar bell. Eamon had coveted a strip of pastureland between the two estates. He had even wanted to offer for the eldest Mulriane daughter, anything to secure his interest over the land.

"Diarmuid must have been glad to have found a familiar face — when you met up with him on the way to O'Dwyer's camp." Niall watched Eamon freeze. "You handed him over to the English. That was how they knew to target the Mulrianes."

Niall rushed him with his sword. The sudden attack surprised Eamon, and the man provided a poor and hasty defence. In three quick strokes, Niall had smashed the sword from Eamon's hand and levelled his own sword so that the tip pressed against Eamon's quivering throat. He breathed deeply, fighting for control.

"The land you coveted — it didn't just end at your border," Niall gritted out. "What foul deal did you cut the *first* time with the English, Eamon?" Niall pressed his blade until it pierced Eamon's skin and a droplet of blood pooled at his throat. "Admit it — the deal you struck involved giving up Diarmuid in exchange for my uncle's land."

Eamon clenched his eyes shut. "Not all the land — only the pasture that should have been owned by the Graces. I admit it. Stop. Don't kill me."

"You betrayed my kin for the price of a pasture and a hectare of river land. You do not deserve to be called a man, only a bottom-scraping coward."

"Mercy."

Blood surged in Niall's temples. "Mercy?" he roared. "I will speak of one you betrayed so that you will die with her name hanging as a lodestone around your neck when you face the devil himself. Mairead O'Coneill, my sister, my father's only daughter, had more worth than that scrap of meadowland you betrayed her for. I watched over her — always —" Niall's throat constricted, remembering lean times when he'd scraped food from his plate to hers so she'd have enough. "My sister, who was blessed with music and who made the angels smile with her gift. This was who your treachery took from me. *Took from my family.* Was it mercy that she was captured and shipped to the English colonies?"

Eamon's mouth worked as he struggled to answer.

"Answer me!"

"Niall, my lad —"

"Don't call me that," Niall spat. "I admired you — I trusted you — unburdened myself to you. I bared my pain to you and cried for my kin in front of you. And all that time, you were the cause of my misery."

"My argument was with your uncle, never you —"

"No more excuses," Niall shouted. "For once, own it like a man." He sliced a larger cut, just short of the vein.

"Yes, I admit it. I betrayed them." He choked out that last part. "I didn't know Garret would seize the women, that he would sell them to a merchant."

Niall tasted the desperation in Eamon's tone — desperation, not remorse. This man was incapable of feeling anything that didn't affect himself. He deserved everlasting torment. "May your soul be cursed to the hottest and lowest regions of hell." Niall spat in his face before he drove his blade deep into Eamon's throat, then gave it a final twist for good measure.

Eamon's eyes widened in surprise, then clouded by a spasm of pain. He sputtered blood and gasped for air. Slowly, his body slid down the trunk and slumped over at the base of the tree. Blood soaked his mantle. He twitched one last time before going still.

Niall lowered his sword and closed his eyes. Instead of exultation, he felt tired and worn. He released the breath that he had been holding all this time. Though he still may be damned, he now had his vengeance.

Fionn gave a loud bark and bounded past him. Niall whirled around to find Donogh emerging from behind a large beech tree. Donogh took in Niall's bloody sword and Eamon lying in a pool of his own blood.

Niall knew how this looked and that his only defence now lay dead. He braced himself for the repercussions.

Donogh sheathed his sword. "I heard."

CHAPTER 26

Áine and Maeve returned to the camp with Purcell and McTiege just as O'Dwyer was quelling the last of the resistance and rounding up prisoners. Shelters had been trampled to the ground, as though a giant had staggered across the field. The sheep had been scattered, and she heard that a group had gone out to locate the cattle.

Even Eireen's shelter had been smashed.

Tears pricked Áine's eyes, but she willed them down. She hadn't cried when the Mulrianes' byre was set to flame, hadn't cried when she watched it burn from a place of safety in the woods. She'd had no tears when the soldiers had left and she picked through the charred, smoky remains. She would not cry now over a flimsy shelter.

So many safe havens torn from her—had it all been punishment for running away from her troubles instead of learning to endure? Such hubris on her part, clinging to the hope that a better life might be in store for her once upon a time?

She rubbed her stinging eyes, which only made them worse. "We need to find Eireen," she told Maeve. And the Triad. Dared she believe the young women had managed to escape?

Áine and Maeve wandered through the camp. The destruction overwhelmed Áine. Only that morning, the day had dawned like any other. People had been at their work, cooking their meals and planning to meet with each other at the end of the day. Near the skirmish site, several bodies were laid out. Irish or English, in death, they all looked the same.

They found Eireen staring grimly at the destroyed cattle pens, her back a stiff line. Her linen kerchief had unravelled and was left to loop around her neck, and it lifted in the wind like a banner. Near Eireen stood one of the Triad—Blanche had made it. Where were the others? A little distance away, Brigid was comforting a sobbing Barbara. They had survived!

Eireen whirled around, her eyes red-rimmed and tired, but when she saw Maeve, she clapped a hand over her mouth and started shaking. "Maeve, my own dear girl!" The mother crushed her daughter in her punishing embrace and sobbed with relief and joy.

Áine hung back, giving the two their privacy, but Eireen lifted her head and spied her. Still clutching Maeve, she held out her arm for Áine and gathered her into her embrace. Though the woman's smock smelled of blood and ash, Áine couldn't be more content had she smelled of honey and wildflowers.

"You're both alive—unharmed," Eireen cried, her voice cracking. "I feared the worst."

Maeve laughed and looked around. "Where is that blessed beast Fionn? I wanted to ring his neck earlier, worrying the herd as he was, but I suppose he was just trying to get them to safety."

Áine sobered. "I suppose we'll be moving again."

"I'm afraid so," Eireen said. "That is what we do."

A commotion rippled around them, and Áine heard, "He's back."

Niall rode into camp with Fionn on one side and Donogh riding alongside the other. Trailing behind on a tether was a tawny piebald garron with Eamon Grace's body draped over its back.

Áine hurried towards him, wending her way through the gathered men until she reached Cormac and Ruadhri.

Niall halted before O'Dwyer. The two men did not speak at first. Áine was reminded that the last time they had seen each other, one had sentenced the other to death. Niall dismounted and hoisted Eamon's body off the piebald garron. He half carried, half dragged the body and left it at O'Dwyer's feet.

"Here is your traitor." Niall spoke loud enough for his voice to carry, but his gaze was fixed on O'Dwyer. "He betrayed us all, including my kin."

Donogh dismounted and joined Niall. "It is as he says. I was there. Eamon confessed to his crimes."

"He promised you to the English in exchange for his lands," Niall said, "but not before he sought to expand his holdings by betraying my uncle."

O'Dwyer's mouth pressed in a grim line. Gunpowder and blood streaked his face, giving him a fierce look. He stared in disgust at the man lying in the dirt. His attention shifted to Niall. "I owe you an apology. You're innocent of the crimes levelled against you."

Niall nodded. "My thanks. Now I must take my leave." He gave O'Dwyer a short bow before he started to walk away. Áine saw that he was heading in her direction.

"Where are you going?" O'Dwyer called out to him.

Niall halted but did not turn around. He said over his shoulder, "Will you still sign the treaty?"

The word caused a wave of reactions—nods, shocked surprise. It seemed that everyone was whispering at once.

"Yes," O'Dwyer said. "Yes, I must."

Niall sighed and faced O'Dwyer. "Then I want none of it."

"It may seem so now," O'Dwyer said, approaching Niall. "But when the ink is dry, you will see the wisdom of it."

"I can't—I don't think so." Niall continued to walk away.

"If you leave now, you won't be included in the settlement," O'Dwyer called after him. "You'll be in no-man's land. Without rights. Outlawed. Is that what you want?"

Niall did not stop. When he reached Áine, he took her hand and led her away from everyone. He did not speak a word, not even about Eamon. When they reached the stream near the empty cattle pens, he pulled her into his arms and crushed her to him.

"I can't stay here," he said. "I have to go."

"When do we leave?"

"We?" Niall looked down at her, saddened. "Áine-my-Áine—"

She touched her fingers to his mouth. She could feel his pain and his confusion, but she was determined to have her say. "You're always trying to send me away, do you realise? I'm beginning to think you don't want me."

"Purge the thought—"

"I know, it's for my own good," she said. "But you forget, I belong to myself alone."

Niall smiled wanly. "I stand corrected."

"Have you given any thought to where you want to go, or were you going to follow wherever Fionn led?" When he didn't immediately answer, she said, "Don't worry. I know of a place."

ÁINE AND NIALL LEFT GLENGARRA AT FIRST LIGHT. NIALL HAD secured McTiege's tawny garron for her use, giving the man Eamon's horse in exchange. Niall hadn't wanted anything of Eamon's, no matter how fine the horseflesh.

She found it hard to part from Eireen, Maeve and the Triad, but while they said their emotional farewells, with a number of hugs, tears, and embraces, Niall met a final time with his own men. Áine did not know what was said. He offered very little, then or on their journey.

Áine hated to see Niall this way, see him gnawing himself from the inside. He did not speak of Eamon, but she knew what was going through his mind. Once being a trusted friend, Eamon's betrayal must have been a sword to the heart. It must have left Niall to question everything he had once accepted as truth. She worried that he had gone down the road of vengeance too far to gently lay down his sword, and she feared where this would lead him.

They returned to the abandoned shepherd's hut that stood betwixt and between the Mulriane and Grace lands. Áine wasn't sure how Niall would react to coming here, but she suspected he needed to. She did too.

They didn't dare light a fire, but Niall had managed to see to their comfort by cutting down fresh reeds to make a soft pallet. Together, they had hauled the last bundle inside when the heavens opened. Soon after, Áine curled up on her side and listened to Niall moving about and the soft patter of rain hitting the turf roof. Drops pooled in the rafters and dripped steadily on the dirt floor. Her eyes grew heavy.

Later, Áine awoke with a start. She looked around, disoriented for a moment as to where she was. The rain had stopped, and now clear moonlight spilled through the gaps in the roof. She rose on her elbows to find Fionn curled in sleep near the door.

Niall's back was to her, his shoulders slightly sloped forward and his hair a tousled mess. His linen shirt shone white where the moonlight touched it. He sat with his legs drawn up, one forearm resting on his knee, and he appeared to be staring at a moonlight trail that stretched across the ground.

Áine rose from the pallet. He turned his head when he heard her coming, and she slipped beside him. As she wrapped her arms around him, Niall closed his eyes and leaned into her.

"Couldn't sleep?" she asked.

"Too many things going around in my head." The silvery light showed the hard planes of his cheekbones and jaw line, the hollow of his cheek.

"Do you wish for solitude?"

He didn't answer at first, and she was about to ease from him, accepting his silence as his answer. But he shifted so that he was looking at her. His eyes were dark, unfathomable, but searching.

"No. Stay. With me. Please."

Áine lifted her hand to brush aside a lock of hair from his forehead. Her fingers followed the contours of his cheekbones to trace the cut along his chin. Her fingertips continued their exploration along his bottom lip, revelling in the change of landscape from wind-roughened stubble to firm softness.

Niall closed his eyes and turned his face into her left hand. His tongue touched the inside of her scarred wrist. Áine's breath hitched in her throat, but she did not pull away. His eyes fixed on hers with an intensity that made her pulse quicken. Making no move to draw her into his arms, he waited. It was as though he were saying, *You must choose.*

Áine gathered her courage. She was through hiding, running away — through denying who she was and what she needed. She rose and climbed onto his lap, her legs straddling his sturdy thighs. He was hard against her.

His gaze did not falter, and there was something in his expression that encouraged her to continue at her own pace. She leaned in and brushed a kiss on his lips before she moved to his jaw, then his chin. She dropped a kiss on the base of his throat, where she could feel the beat of his heart and the heat of his body. He swallowed, and Áine knew the moment when his breathing became more shallow.

Áine wanted to taste his mouth, explore it with her own. His eyes flicked down to her mouth, but he did not move in closer. She understood his meaning. Her choice again.

She leaned in, breasts pressed against his chest, and touched her parted lips to his. Her tongue flicked shyly into his mouth. Áine loved his mouth — wide, firm but sensitive. She loved how they fit together, how their breaths merged. With a groan, Niall canted his head and kissed her back with a slow, building passion.

Áine was the first to break their kiss. She felt exposed, flustered and flushed. Her skin raged both hot and cold. Niall's hazel eyes bored through her, stripping the last of her reservations.

"I need you, Áine-my-Áine."

The huskiness of his voice made shivers trail down her spine and the little hairs lift on her arms. Would this be the moment when her fears rose up and flooded her with panic? This too was her choice, she understood, and she would not let them consume her. "I need you too."

"I will never hurt you," he told her. "Do you trust me?"

She nodded.

The kiss he gave her spoke of longing, of pain and sorrow and a fierce need for intimacy. Large hands stroked the curve of her back and, cupping her buttocks, hitched her closer.

Áine ran her hands down his shoulders and along the corded muscles of his arms, revelling in the feel of him under her palms.

His hand stroked her breast through the linen of her smock. Gentle fingers circled her nipple, slowly teasing it to life. He slowly undid her front laces, exposing her breasts. Áine's breath hitched in her throat. He lowered his head and touched his mouth to her other nipple, repeating the same motion with his tongue.

Áine gasped, awash with pleasure.

Niall stopped and lifted his head. "Do you like that?"

"I do."

"You can tell me to stop if it doesn't feel right."

"I know. Don't—don't stop."

Niall continued kissing her through the rough linen, exploring gently between her breasts. Then he lowered her onto the pallet and explored the soft, sensitive area around her belly.

Áine thought she was coming undone, every thread of her unravelling. He rose up and claimed her mouth, exploring her tongue with painstaking patience.

She pressed herself against his hard manhood, and his groan shot through her. Every square inch of her quivered with life. It nearly drove her wild, and she felt herself chasing a building sensation that she had never experienced.

She rubbed herself against him, and that sensation intensified. Her mouth became dry, and her breathing felt ragged. His hand slipped under her skirt, caressed her skin before his fingers slipped inside her. Áine nearly bolted, not from fear but from mounting desire.

Niall slowly undressed her, removing each part of her clothes as one would peel away layers of secrets. Her hands slipped beneath his shirt, delighting in the smoothness and warmth of his skin.

"Your turn." His whisper tickled her ear and sent shivers through her body.

Áine needed no further encouragement. He had awakened a need in her to learn more about her own body and his. She lifted his shirt over his head, then he guided her as she stripped him of his breeches.

"Let me love you, Áine Callaghan."

"I will. I love you."

"And I'll love you until my dying breath," he said.

He did not hurt her when he entered her. He held himself back until she adjusted to his weight, until she moved beneath him and tilted her hips to welcome him fully.

It was love they made to each other, and that meant all the difference in the world.

NIALL PRESSED A LINGERING KISS ON ÁINE'S TEMPLE BEFORE HE eased from her side. She stirred but did not awaken. Her lips were parted slightly in sleep, and her lashes fanned lightly over her cheeks. When the cold touched her skin, her brows puckered and she burrowed deeper into the straw for warmth. Niall covered her bare shoulders with his woollen mantle, tucking its warmth under her chin. She snuggled deeper into its folds.

He watched while she slept, taking great pleasure from the way her shoulders rose and fell with every breath she took, and the soft curve of her mouth. He reached out and plucked a tendril of hair that curled at her throat, and his fingers marvelled at the silkiness of it. His gaze followed the ripple of her tresses as they spilled across their pallet like a river of molten copper. Even in the dimness of the hut, each strand hungered for the light and swallowed it whole.

She deserved more than darkness and despair.

They had lain in each other's arms for the remainder of the night. Their lovemaking had transformed from tender to passionate as the night wore on. She had been shy at first, and he had held himself back, careful to lead her only where she was willing to go. But she had left him gasping with the depths of her passion and his own fulfilment.

The first signs of dawn showed between the slats of the walls. Niall needed to get some fresh air, to clear his head. He needed to think. Sort out his thoughts. His whole world had shifted since the last sunrise, and not all because of Áine.

Fionn lifted his head when Niall unlatched the door. The

wolfhound rose and stretched his full length before following him outside.

The sky had turned a dove grey. Birdsong surrounded Niall, but otherwise there was a stillness in the woods that he had missed for so long. The horses were still hobbled safely in their makeshift shelter. Fionn darted off into the forest, and Niall followed after him.

After a quarter hour, Niall found a narrow creek with an old tree limb bridging one side of the bank to the other. Fionn crashed through the trees, disappearing into the woods, leaving the snap and rustle of leaves and branches in his wake.

Niall leaned against a tree and stared at the moss and rocks along the bank. Vengeance had been his relentless companion, leading him further away from himself. He had craved blood, had dreamt of it, had even thirsted for it. No matter how much he drank from that well, it had not filled him.

Garret was dead, though not by Niall's hand. Niall had been obsessed with grinding him to dust, crowing while Garret's blood soaked into the earth.

Then why did Niall feel hollow, as if Garret's death was not enough?

Eamon's death should have filled Niall with grim satisfaction. The man had betrayed them all at a primal level. He had rolled the first rock down the hill, causing an avalanche of carnage and destruction.

When Niall had driven his sword deep into Eamon's throat, the debt should have been paid.

But it wasn't.

The sun's rays cut through the trees and lit unfurling leaves tipped red and green. Niall thought of Áine, and the answer drifted on the edge of his awareness. He focused on its shape and tried to grasp it.

Áine had sprung a lock inside him that secured a compartment built by despair and reinforced by rage. It was a corner of himself where he had tried to seal off the pain and horror—the place where his grief had been allowed to fester. It had been locked tight since he had first seen the charred byre and the cairn and had learned that

Mairead had been taken prisoner. But if he was honest with himself, it had been constructed earlier, from the first time he'd had to cut down someone from a gibbet.

A movement across the water drew his eye. Expecting to see Fionn, Niall wasn't immediately alarmed. Then a grey wolf emerged from the trees. He was a ragged creature, half-starved, with matted fur. In two long strides, he could have bounded across the creek and attacked Niall, but he stayed still and stared. Something in the wolf's expression reminded Niall sharply of himself. Weary. Despondent. Hunted.

The English had been hunting wolves for sport, without even the excuse of protecting livestock. They were as keen to eradicate Irish wolves as they were the Irish people. Purge the wildness from their world. Conquer and trample to the ground. He had never felt a kinship with a wolf before this moment. The wolf dipped his head in silent acknowledgment, as though he shared the same thoughts.

A slight sound of crunching leaves underfoot alerted Niall. The wolf's ears pricked. Fionn appeared beside Niall but did not growl a warning. Both wolf and wolfhound measured the nature of the other. Finally, the wolf sniffed the air and disappeared into the forest.

Things started to grow clearer to Niall, and it was as though he had stepped through the mist and saw the distant shore more clearly. It wasn't enough to see those responsible for his family's loss rot in the earth. Death did not change anything, only life did. The living did not need vengeance, they needed closure. *He* needed closure.

Niall knew then he wasn't finished. He had to find out what had happened to his sister—if he could. He breathed deeply of the crisp air and knew.

He had to go to Cork.

THE CREAK OF HINGES AWAKENED ÁINE. SHE LIFTED HER HEAD and realised Niall had stepped out with Fionn. Without the warmth of his body, the air quickly cooled her skin. She lay on the pallet, staring up at the rafters in the ceiling as she thought of the night before. Her cheeks grew hot, and a flush spread down her throat.

Áine tested her feelings like a surgeon would test the progress of a wound and discovered, to her surprise, that she experienced no shame, only a languid contentment.

Niall had made her feel cherished, worthy of love. Last night, they'd shared each other openly, honestly. There were no takers, only givers.

Her eyes pricked with tears as she thought of what she had missed these years, locked away within herself. She never wanted to be that woman again.

Áine had dressed and tidied up by the time Niall returned. The grimness of his expression cooled her good mood, and she braced herself for unpleasant news. "What's the matter?"

Niall sighed and drew her into his arms. He gave her a slow, lingering kiss, as though he were memorising every taste and touch of her. When he stopped, he touched his forehead to hers.

"You're going away," she said.

"Ay, I need to go to Cork," he said in a low tone. "I need to learn what happened to my sister, if I can." He traced her jaw with his thumb. "I won't ask you to come with me—I know what it will cost you if you do."

"No, Niall, you can't go there." Áine's panic built in her chest. "The town is an English stronghold—you will be caught." And she couldn't bear it.

"I can take care of myself." He brushed his lips against hers. "I need to know what happened to my sister—where they sent her. How can I ever return to my da without telling him what happened to his daughter? I owe this to him—he's asked for nothing from me. And I owe it to myself as well."

Áine stepped away from him, consumed by her own fears. The English would discover him, that much was plain. Even a half-blind man could see that Niall was a hardened soldier and would seize him for a prize. He had no connections, no knowledge of the town. But she did.

"I'll leave Fionn with you," he continued gently. "He'll keep you safe until my return."

Áine barely listened to his reassurances. Niall needed to go to

Cork, she could not deny him this, but it suddenly struck her that she did too. She had been a condemned prisoner waiting for her sentence for far too long. She had been holding her breath for years, imprisoned by her inability to face her tormentor—always running, always hiding—hiding who she was.

I'll never be that woman again.

"I'll come with you," Áine told him. "We'll do this together."

CHAPTER 27

THE JOURNEY south brought back sharp memories to Áine of her flight from Cork City four years earlier, except this time she was unspooling her steps.

With the caution required to elude English patrols, they only managed a few miles a day. Áine and Niall hid in byres and stole away before dawn. When they could not risk discovery, they passed the night huddled together in the woods. The situation grew more difficult the closer they got to the city since it was a strategic port for the English. Enemy patrols and convoys were thick on the road travelling between Cork City and Clonmel.

Áine was struck by the strangeness of heading back to the place she had vowed never to return.

The county had not changed. Still the same marshland interspersed with green pastures. The same signposts. Woodland thinned out and running into open country.

They reached a stone cross that Áine remembered. The marker's carvings had softened over time and more lichen crept over the column, but it still told her that Cork City was close.

"If we take the first road that branches off, there's a cheese-monger who will give us shelter. If the family is still there."

"How do you know him, my Áine?" Niall rode with one hand on the pommel of his sword, a restless energy wrapped around him.

"The Duggans were old friends of my mam's," Áine said. She gave the tawny garron an affectionate pat. "They gave me shelter when I left the smithy and didn't betray me when Muiredach came searching. It was their idea that I seek out your aunt."

"I'll be pleased to make their acquaintance."

"The Duggans can help us get into the city."

"We can hope."

They turned down a well-travelled lane and continued along newly ploughed fields. The rain had stopped, but a fine mist coated Áine's mantle. The pungent scent of marsh and rich earth hung in the air and beckoned them forward. When they crested a hill, they discovered a small herd of dairy cows grazing in the pasture.

"This is a good sign," Niall said.

They crossed a narrow wooden bridge that spanned a stream, one of the tributaries that flowed towards Cork and into the River Lee. The horses' hooves rang hollow as they traversed the bridge. In the distance, Áine heard the rhythmic strike of axe to wood.

The Duggan cottage was built of fieldstone and topped with a turf roof. A lazy curl of blue smoke drifted from the hole in the roof. The scents of peat and cooking made Áine homesick, not for Cork, for that had been no home to her. If she closed her eyes, she could picture the warmth of the Mulriane byre, Cook's oatcakes, the round of cheeses in the cheese house, and the little nonsensical dramas that unfolded inside a country house.

A gaggle of white geese were the first to greet them, and the birds made such a fuss that a head appeared at one of the windows. At the same time, a boy, no more than seven, dashed out of the cottage trailing a length of string while a sleek grey cat chased after it. The moment the cat saw Fionn, she arched her back and flattened her ears. When Fionn continued his progress, she hissed at him before darting off.

The boy turned around to see what had chased the cat away. When he saw Fionn, his eyes widened, and he dashed forward, unmindful that the wolfhound was large enough to eat him, if he so desired.

"Fionn, sit," Niall commanded.

Farmer Duggan came out of the cottage, his wife hovering in the doorway. He carried a mallet but held it so it was partially hidden in the folds of his mantle. Duggan gave no indication that he recognised Áine, and he approached her and Niall cautiously. "Get into the cottage with your mam, my lad," he called out to his son.

"Farmer Duggan," Áine called out, quickly dismounting. "Do you remember me?"

Duggan drew closer and gave Áine a searching look. His wife, on the other hand, hurried right past him with a wide smile on her lean face.

"Is that you, Áine? It is!" She swung around to her husband, "Did you not recognise Áine Callaghan?"

Duggan gave a sheepish smile and tucked the mallet into his waistband. "I hadn't, but I am glad to say I do now."

Niall dismounted and led both horses to Duggan. "Do you have seats at your table for several nights? I'll be pleased to pay in kind."

"Of course we have a spot for you at our table, don't doubt it," Bridie said. "Duggan, get their horses settled." She cupped Áine's face and clucked her tongue in approval. "You've matured well, Áine girl. Did Fianna Mulriane remember your nan?"

Áine exchanged a look with Niall, unsure as to what to tell this woman. "She did, and she did well by me. Alas, she departed this world a few months ago."

Bridie crossed herself. "I'm very sorry to hear that."

"Thank you," Niall said. A sad smile touched his lips.

"Bridie, this is Niall O'Coneill, Mistress Mulriane's nephew."

"Are you now?" Bridie smoothed down the wisps of hair that curled from out of her cap and smiled, pleased. "There will be no talk of you working for your supper, will there, Duggan?"

"Any kin of the Mulrianes is welcome any day," her husband answered.

Bridie ushered them inside the cottage. "You must be famished—

when have you had something hot to fill your bellies? Too long, I'd say. Cheese? A cup of my ale?"

Áine and Niall found themselves seated before a crackling fire with the Duggans, young and old, clustered around and greedy for news. Áine remembered now that the lad with the cat had been a toddler when she last was here, and now the Duggans had a new girl-child the same age as he was then.

"When did you marry, Áine? Your nan would have been pleased to have seen you settled."

Áine flushed. It hadn't occurred to her how they should present themselves. Until a few nights ago, it hadn't mattered. "We aren't married, Bridie," she said simply. Áine did not want to misrepresent herself to this dear woman, no matter the embarrassment it caused her. She felt Niall's stare like a probing touch to the skin, but she didn't dare meet his gaze.

Bridie's eyebrows lifted, but she held her tongue.

"What brings you this way, O'Coneill?" Duggan's calm manner saved Áine from embarrassment.

"I have business in Cork City," Niall said. "I'm looking for word of my sister, Mairead O'Coneill. She was taken prisoner by the English. I fear she was forced into indentured service and transported to the colonies."

"Poor wee maid," Bridie said.

"You said her name is Mairead O'Coneill?" Duggan asked.

Niall leaned in eagerly. "Have you heard the name?"

"There's an oddly familiar ring to it, but there are O'Coneills in Cork," Bridie said, wiping her son's nose with her apron. "But I'm sure I don't know any O'Coneills personally. Pay me no mind."

"I'd not be going in to the city until market day, were I you," Duggan said. "Once a week these days, but it's the only time the English don't demand passes to flow in and out of the city."

Bridie prodded her husband's elbow. "They can come with us when we bring in the cheese next."

Duggan looked doubtful, but his wife nodded with conviction. "The lad can be your nephew just come in from Youghal. Learning a new trade. They'd not question that."

"We can try . . . "

"And while you're there," she said to Niall, "you must speak with Master O'Riordan, the wine merchant. He does brisk trade near Merchant's Quay. There's not a ship that passes out of Cork that does not carry his barrels. Áine, sweet, you remember O'Riordan, do you not? I'm sure your stepfather knew him."

"I do," she replied. This would have been in the early years before her stepfather favoured the local alehouse.

"An excellent suggestion, thank you," Niall said.

"Be sure to keep your wolfhound here, and the horse," Duggan said. "Both are remarkable and will be remembered. And Áine, you'll bide your time here too?"

Áine knew what he was really saying. *Don't venture into the city lest Muiredach finds you.* Nothing had changed. Good people still considered him a feral beast. She questioned her sanity for the hundredth time—what foolhardy purpose would be served by confronting Muiredach? Nothing would change. As though sensing her hesitation, Niall took her hand in his and gave it a reassuring squeeze. Nothing *could* change if she continued to hide. "I'll be going in as well," she said, taking courage from Niall. "I too have business, but mine is with Muiredach."

ON MARKET DAY, CARTS, WAGONS AND PEOPLE WITH GOODS strapped to their backs flooded the road leading to Cork. Niall walked alongside Duggan's eldest son, following alongside the wagon loaded with rounds of cheese. Áine rode in the back of the wagon with Bridie and her eldest daughter.

Niall kept a sharp eye for any sign of trouble. To the east of the walled city stood a red sandstone castle with two towers. Watchers could be seen on the battlements and at points around the entrenchment. At the slightest sign of trouble, the castle could spit out its soldiers to protect Cork. He wouldn't want to be trapped between the castle and the city walls.

It took every ounce of effort for Niall to walk as though this was a usual market day for him. His hand kept drifting over to the scabbard he wasn't wearing. He felt naked without his sword, even though he had a couple of daggers hidden under his tunic. Duggan noticed his habit and tossed him a long walking stick. "Hold that instead. The English are not blind."

As they neared the walled city, Niall could tell that Áine was growing more anxious. Her attention kept drifting away from Bridie, and she tugged often at her sleeve and rubbed the scar on her wrist. He wished he could gather her in his arms, reassure her that he would protect her. She was proving to have as much, if not more, courage than any war-hardened soldier he had known.

Cork's North Gate Bridge loomed ahead, a massive timbered structure. A drawbridge spanned a river that carried refuse away from the crowded city. Duggan was forced to slow his garron as the road became clogged with people trying to cross the bridge and make their way through the city gates. The air was heavy with the decaying scent of marshland. Flying overhead, seagulls called out to one another, as though tallying all the people coming in for market. This was feast day for the aggressive birds. Niall suddenly felt a stab of homesickness for Galway and the birds that patrolled the skies there too.

Áine worried her lower lip and had given up speaking altogether. Niall could read her dread. They needed to be as natural as the others heading for market, or they would attract the curiosity of the guards in the gatehouse.

Niall slowed his pace so that he walked alongside Áine. He leaned in so his voice would not carry. "Try not to show fear, my Áine." Every soldier could smell it.

She drew her mantle tightly around herself and nodded.

"We'll be fine, won't we, my girl?" Bridie said. "Let me tell you a story of your nan and the stolen heifer. The way she carried on, you'd think she was trying to re-enact the cattle raid for the great bull of Cúailnge."

It did Niall good to see Áine smile, even wanly.

They were nearing the gates. "I had better walk with Duggan." What he didn't want to mention was that if the worst happened and the guards pulled Niall aside, Áine had a good chance of getting away. He wanted to make sure there was as much distance between her and danger as he could muster.

Duggan slouched in his seat, the reins slack in his lap. They were fifty feet from North Gate Bridge. Niall felt eyes boring through him. The guards watched over the same merchants going into market, week over week. They'd be attuned to anything out of the ordinary.

This wasn't going to work. He stood out like a wolf amongst sheep. He studied the area to see where he could run if they stopped him. With the clog of people, he'd be mired down.

Niall cleared his mind. He focused on market days in Galway. Dashing around the stalls. The anticipation of finding something unique, being able to go home to his brothers and taunt them for not seeing this wonder. He smiled at the memory and forced himself to relax.

"Duggan, did I ever tell you about the chapbooks sold in Galway market?"

A pair of guards holding muskets stood on either side of the gates while another examined the wagons and carts passing through.

By Jesus, we'll be stopped. Niall gripped his walking stick so tightly that had it not been made of stout blackthorn, he would have snapped it in two.

"I bought a chapbook the other week for my boy," Duggan said in an unhurried tone. "A pleasing story of a highwayman who robbed for the poor."

"Everyone must have a cause," Niall said absently. A few carts were ahead of them. He noticed the guards were questioning larger parties—like theirs.

"There is a bookseller in the city that sells these sensational stories," Duggan said, this time louder.

The shadow of the gates fell upon them. It took all of Niall's self-control not to glance back and check on Áine. "There's no better diversion for a lad."

Duggan chortled. "My boy rushes through his chores just to hear another."

One of the guards started towards their party. Niall braced

himself, ready to wield his walking stick as a weapon, but the man walked right past them and stopped the next cart.

Niall held his breath as their wagon trundled through the gates without more than a passing glance from the watch.

Once within the walled city, the streets narrowed. Niall fell back to rejoin Áine. "Are you well, my Áine?"

"I thought I was about to faint."

He reached across and brushed his fingers against her cheek. "Not my girl. You're made of sterner stuff than that."

As they progressed deeper into Cork, a spider's web of streets and lanes ran into each other. They passed down narrow streets lined with three-storied timber-framed houses and shops. Over their rooftops, a church spire stretched to the sky. Farther along, the buildings and outhouses gave way to a generous churchyard, and the church itself came into view.

They reached the market cross and found a group of English soldiers clustered before it. Niall had to force himself to look meekly down, even though his innards roiled.

Duggan headed straight to the market square. Stalls and awnings covered every bit of it, with bales of treated wool, crates of fowls and stacked cheeses.

Niall's attention fixed on an instrument maker seated at a stall. He was busy stringing a small harp before an audience of two children, a brother and a sister, by the look of them. The girl drifted in closer only to be pulled back by the lad. A lump settled in Niall's throat over a memory that came back to him sharp and clear. A similar day in Galway, with his sister Mairead hovering before a stand of musicians and he being impatient to lead her away.

A lump formed in his throat, and he coughed to clear it. "Where is this wine merchant?" Niall said, his voice hoarse.

"At Merchant's Quay," Áine said. "It's not far."

"Good fortune," Duggan said. "I hope you'll find what you're looking for."

"We'll be here until after the noon hour," Bridie said, passing Duggan a crate of cheese from the wagon.

Áine took the lead and headed away from the market, towards

the quay. The stench of burning pitch and rotted fish grew stronger, and once again Niall thought of Galway. Presently, she stopped before a shop under the sign of a wine barrel.

They cracked open the door and found a young man checking the markings on the casks against a register. He carried out his task with the bored air of someone who had done this countless times.

Áine looked around and, seeing no one else, approached the employee. "Is the purveyor here? This is still Master O'Riordan's store? We'd like to speak with him."

The man made a final tally on the paper before answering, "It is, but my master is presently occupied and has left express instructions not to be disturbed. If you leave your name, I'll let him know you were here."

Niall leaned in and dropped a coin on one barrel. "Be a good lad and let him know now. We'll wait."

The young man pursed his lips and plucked the coin from the barrel. "I'll be but a moment." He lay his register down on the barrel and disappeared up the creaking stairs.

A muffled conversation drifted down from the upper floor. Then Niall heard lumbering footsteps descending the stairs. A rotund man arrived, politely exasperated at the interruption. Behind him trailed his employee.

"All my barrels are bespoke, good sir. If you leave your name with my assistant, Mister Prendergast, I'm sure—"

"Master O'Riordan?"

The man looked at Áine, and his brows furrowed. He greeted her with a vague smile, as though he were searching his memory for a name. "You look familiar to me."

"I believe you knew my late stepfather, Blacksmith O'Keefe."

Dawning spread across his face. "Yes, of course. You have the look of your mother. Where have you been, my girl? I heard you disappeared so completely."

"I—I found a situation farther north," she said.

"Strange that Muiredach O'Keefe knew nothing of it."

Master O'Riordan rested his hands over his round belly and waited for her answer, but Áine held her tongue. She clearly had no compulsion to fill in the gaps, no matter how eager the vintner was to solve the mystery.

"We were hoping you might be of service." Niall stepped forward to divert the man.

"Service?" The merchant's instincts surfaced. "You may count on it, as it is within my ability, Master—?"

"Niall O'Coneill of Galway," then he added, "Áine's intended." He sensed Áine's gaze swivel to him.

"Felicitations," O'Riordan said brightly. Then his brows knitted together. "O'Coneill of Galway, you say?"

"Have you heard the name recently?" Niall said, drawing closer. "I'm searching for my sister, Mairead O'Coneill. She was taken prisoner by the English a couple of months ago. I believe she would have passed this way."

"She is near my age," Áine offered, "and about my height, though her hair is a light brown."

O'Riordan blinked and shook his head. "Poor lamb, but alas, I'm sure I don't know."

"I do." Everyone turned to stare at the assistant, Mister Prendergast, who had remained quiet during their conversation.

"You've seen my sister?"

Prendergast nodded. "I believe so. A couple of months ago. It was during that week when we had problems with the shipment of new casks," he said to O'Riordan, who nodded sadly at the memory. "I was on my way to the harbourmaster, when I was forced to step aside and allow a train of prisoners to pass. They were mostly women, although there were a few men in the grouping." The man gave Niall a sympathetic look. "A more bedraggled lot I haven't seen."

"Please—continue," Niall said.

"The procession attracted a sizeable crowd, and, as it was on market day, the streets were congested with people. One of the prisoners, a young woman as you describe, called out to the people as she passed, telling them her name—Mairead O'Coneill—that she was from Galway, which struck me as odd for her to be this far south, and that her father was Liam O'Coneill. I recall that clearly, for Liam is my own da's name. She kept repeating the message, always pleading for someone to tell her father what happened to her."

Niall couldn't speak. His whole body went cold, and tears welled up in his eyes. *Oh, Mairead.* He rubbed his eyes, and when he spoke, his voice was barely above a whisper. "Do you recall anything more?"

"I'm afraid not."

"Thank you." Niall fought to control his emotions. "I heard she was transported by ship to the English colonies. Perhaps you know which one she might have been on? I need to know where they sent her."

"That I can't say."

Niall's heart sank. He took a deep breath and exhaled slowly. "Who would know?"

"Check the ledger," O'Riordan told his assistant. "Which ships did we supply that day? They would have sailed out within a day or two, no more."

Prendergast took a heavy ledger from a shelf and flipped through it until he found the page he was looking for. His fingers snaked down a column and stopped halfway down. "That week we supplied three merchants. The *Endeavour* was bound for Massachusetts, the *Ithaca* is a Dorset vessel and would have been heading home, and the *Jane Marie* was for Barbados."

Massachusetts or Barbados. Opposite ends of a vast ocean. "There must be some records that tell which ship she would have been on?"

"The harbourmaster keeps the port books," O'Riordan said. "I've had a need to review his records on occasion, and I can assure you that he does not include information on human cargo."

Niall's ire flared. "My sister is a bright young woman. She is a musician and the joy of my father's life. She is *not* human cargo."

"My apologies for my unfortunate turn of phrase." O'Riordan had the good grace to flush. "An unfortunate business. Quite unfortunate. I'll be praying for your sister, Master O'Coneill."

Niall sat down on an empty stool, entirely lost and facing a stone wall. "What am I to do now?"

Vengeance and fury had driven him over the past couple of months, but where had this led him? Neither Eamon's death nor Garret's could restore his sister. "I've come all this way to find her trail, and there's none to be found. Where do I go from here?"

Áine knelt on the ground at his feet and laid a hand on his arm. "There's nothing else to do, except honour your sister's wishes and carry the news home to your father."

Tell Liam O'Coneill what has happened to his daughter.

Mairead had not cried out for retribution. As she had walked down the streets of Cork a prisoner, her only thought had been for their father. Niall now realised he had not wanted to give his father the ill news, not without a sliver of hope to soften the blow. Áine was right. A father should not hear this news from a stranger. Somehow, Mairead must have known that her words would find the right ears.

There was nothing else to do than to face the stark fact that Mairead was under the Almighty's grace and keeping.

He had no other choice but to accept this.

CHAPTER 28

COUNTLESS TIMES in Áine's nightmares, she returned to her step-brother's smithy at midnight. The dreams would always start with her walking down a deserted road choked with mist, her shoes tapping against the slick cobbles. Áine could see very little beyond a few feet ahead, for the moon never showed its face. Rows of shops and town houses flanked either side of the lonely road, their second stories leaning in, listening. Four magpies darted ahead of her: one bird balanced on the sharp edge of an iron railing; a second flitted from one shut doorway to the next; a third pecked at stones on the ground, trying to crack them like a nut; and the last watched silently from its perch on a windowsill.

Áine was not dreaming now, but this was still her nightmare, and it had sharp teeth. Although sunlight flooded the streets and people filled every corner instead of magpies, her beating heart did not make the distinction.

Niall walked alongside her, offering a reassuring touch at the small of her back and a reminder that she was not alone. She would have abandoned this mad quest had he not been with her.

I can do this. She *had* to do this. She needed to brave the dragon's lair and prove to herself that Muiredach was no longer the beast in her story.

The O'Keefe smithy was situated across town near Sullivan's Quay. With the marshy smell of refuse and dank water rose old memories of suffocating dread and tender bruises slow to heal. She rounded the corner and saw the smithy for the first time in four years. A long courtyard stretched between the shop and the residence, an ill-kept cottage that wore its neglect without shame.

Had this ever been her home? Once, she had hoped it would be, when she and her mother had first pulled up in a wagon loaded with their remaining household goods—bedding, a set of copper pots, a dresser and a carved wooden box. Áine had been six, sitting prettily in her best dress made from soft green wool.

Her stepfather had waited to greet them in the courtyard with his ten-year-old-son straining beside him. How pleased Áine had been to have an older brother, to finally have a sibling. When she'd hurried eagerly to greet him, she'd tripped on a broken flag and fallen to the stone ground, tearing her dress.

"Is she always that clumsy?" her mother's husband had asked.

"Careful she doesn't pitch into the well." Muiredach had snickered, then he'd cast a seeking glance to his father.

The well still commanded the centre of the courtyard, topped by a half-rotted wooden roof. The sight of it caused a cold sweat to break over Áine's skin.

Even now.

In that first year, Muiredach had often threatened to drop her into the hole. Every night, he'd wish her good dreams and then whisper, "In the well you go tonight." He'd made no secret of the fact that he was determined to send her away, and everyone knew that wells were one of the gateways to the Otherworld. Áine had taken to sleeping in cupboards, in the loft above where the animals were kept, anywhere that he might not find her. The scoldings she'd received from her mother were nothing to the possibility of being pushed into the well. The O'Keefes' only servant girl was the first to call her strange and a changeling, which Muiredach had combined to "strangeling."

Niall's hand rested on the small of her back. "Are you all right, my Áine?"

Only then did she realise she had stopped; her feet had grown roots.

"You don't have to do this," he said.

"I do." If she wanted to be free, she must.

She urged herself to continue past the shabby house to the smithy. The clang of a hammer striking an anvil made Áine flinch. Through the open doorway, the red glow of the forge spilled out on the stone flags. Even from here, she could smell hot iron. Her stomach flipped, and she wanted to vomit.

Fear sank its talons into her—she was once more a young girl tormented by an unpredictable tyrant. What was wrong with her that she didn't deserve protection or kindness from a brother?

"Áine?" Niall's voice was low in her ear.

She took a step backwards.

"Áine?" He touched her wrist, his thumb rubbing across her old burn. He took her cold hands between his own and gave them a reassuring squeeze. "I believe in you."

His words coated her frayed nerves like honey. Niall O'Coneill cared for her. She wasn't worthless; she deserved to reclaim her life.

Áine exhaled slowly and took her first step into the smithy.

Muiredach was at his forge, as she had seen him many times. His shoulders had broadened, and his neck was as thick as a bull's. He had always been a strapping lad, but now he looked like he could break her in two with a snap of his fingers.

He turned slightly, then fully when he saw her. The glow of the flames framed his back, casting his face in shadow. He scratched his head and blinked as though doubting his own eyes. Then he smiled with a feral expression that made her blood run cold.

"Hello, kitten. Fancy seeing you again. You've come home, and 'bout bloody time."

"This is . . . this is not my home." When Áine spoke, her voice wavered. Her heart pounded so hard in her throat that she couldn't draw a deep enough breath for speech.

Muiredach grinned, relishing her distress, even feeding on it. He laid his hammer down on the anvil and, taking his time, wiped his hands using the dirty rag tucked in his belt. "Look at you," he drawled. "You've filled out pleasantly well."

Áine had a compulsion to scrub her skin clean. She wrapped her arms around herself for protection. What was she doing here? Coming had been an act of madness. She glanced back at the threshold, where Niall stood in the shadows. He stepped forward when he saw her distress.

"Mind your tongue," Niall said, drawing Muiredach's attention for the first time, "or I will break my word and deal with you as you deserve." He turned to Áine. "Speak your peace so we can leave this place."

Muiredach planted his meaty fists on his hips, legs braced apart. "I speak as I will in my own smithy, and no one tells me what I can or can't do. And who the hell are you?"

"None of your concern," Niall answered coldly.

"The hell it isn't. I want to know the fool she's bewitched *this* time." When Niall didn't answer, Muiredach drawled, "She's a slut, plain and simple. Best you know that."

Niall made a low growl and would have lunged at him, but Áine gripped his arm. The men's posturing focused her thoughts and allowed her time to summon her courage. This was her moment to shed herself of Muiredach's vile shadow, and only she could do it for herself.

Áine faced her stepbrother. "You're a bastard, Muiredach. I've come to tell you that."

"Did you now?" His laugh ended with a belittling sneer. "You've deigned to rise from your whore's couch to tell me I'm the devil himself? Such a worthless gesture from a worthless—"

"I am not worthless. Too long you tried to crush me. Cut me off from everyone. Starved me of anyone who might possibly care. Even called me strangeling so that people would be clear of me. Why, Muiredach? Did you hate me so?"

"You think too highly of yourself, that I'd waste a thought for an insignificant chit such as you."

"I am not insignificant. I do matter. Nothing you can say will change that." Áine's conviction grew with every single word. "You'll not silence me this time, Muiredach. I've survived far worse than you. When you face your Maker, you'll owe Him a reckoning for the evils you've inflicted on others. May He have mercy on your soul, but you'll get no forgiveness from me."

Muiredach gave an exaggerated yawn before wiping his nose on the back of his hand. "Sorry? Did you say something?" He burst out laughing. "You were always too soft, kitten, and someone needed to take a firm hand to you." His words, almost playful, caused a shiver of revulsion.

"A firm hand?" She yanked back her sleeve and thrust out her burned wrist for him to see. "Is that what you call this?"

"Fire purges all evil."

Behind him, surrounded by the tools of his trade, the forge burned hot. A thought crystallised. "You were always determined to mark me, to bind me to this place," she said.

Muiredach snorted. "I never wanted you here." His gaze slid to Niall, and he spoke to him directly. "She was always a clumsy chit, always tripping on her own two feet. I told her time and time again to watch her step around the forge, but she always had her head in those useless stories."

Always trying to reduce her, make her invisible, but this time she was having none of it. Áine stepped in front of Muiredach so he could not ignore her. "So now it's *my* fault? How can you speak such a lie? And all the bruises, the bones that were broken, all my fault, I suppose?"

"Come, Áine," Niall broke in. "You're wasting your time with this one."

"Not yet." She would not be silenced, not by the man who loved her and wished only to protect her, and especially not by the man who had nearly destroyed her. Before her courage could falter, she blurted, "And how do you explain how you violated me, Muiredach? Did I trip into that too?"

Silence filled the space between them for a heartbeat or two. The only sound was the crackle of the flames in the forge. His lips curled back in a snarl. "I did nothing more than what you begged for, and if you say otherwise, it's a lie."

He might as well have driven his fist into her stomach, for he knocked the wind out of her. She had thought nothing could be worse than what he had done to her, but this . . . this was craven. Did he actually believe the lies that seeped from his mouth? "You were my brother. The only one I had. You had a duty to see to my welfare, not betray me in the cruellest way imaginable."

"I fed you and suffered a roof over your head. Others would have thrown you out on the street."

"And for that I should be grateful? I should thank you for the abuse I received under your tender care?" Áine began to tremble, and she feared she'd be ill right in front of him. "Why, Muiredach? Why me? You were never short of loose women. *Why did it have to be me?*"

"You asked for it, every day you hid from me, every time you simpered, pretending to be innocent. You had the knowledge of Jezebel that you used to tempt me, then Banan." His expression darkened. "It was only a matter of time before he had you on your back and your skirts hiked to your waist. Just like your papist whore of a mother—"

"Don't call her that—"

"Always tempting my father with her wiles." The muscles in Muiredach's corded neck pulsed with anger. "Taking over his household—turning his head. I curse the day you both came. The old fool wanted the flattery of a young, pretty wife to warm his bed so he could crow to the lads down at the public house what a man he was. And for the privilege of spreading her legs, my da had to pay the debts your papist father left when he died." He spit on the ground. "Such a fool for not taking what he wanted."

Áine was past outrage. She looked at this wretched man before her and felt only disgust. Pure poison dripped out of Muiredach's mouth, and it now occurred to her that everything he had done to her had been to bind her to his misery. The fire that licked at him was fear, and the hammer that shaped him was selfishness. "You're a weak fool to have been threatened by a defenceless widow."

"Weak?" He took a menacing step forward, nostrils flaring. "No one dares call me weak. I can break you as I did before."

Áine forced herself to hold her ground. "You never will again, Muiredach. I have survived your misery and abuse. I've been tempered by the fire, and I'm stronger for it. You will never break me." Indignation swept away the last of her fears. "Pitiful worm of a man. While better men than you fight for their lives, fight for their families and for their nation, you remain the drunken lout of the alehouse. You're nothing more than a cowardly swine."

"I'm warning you—"

"Only a coward torments a defenceless woman and blames her for their misfortunes," Áine said scathingly. "Only a coward blackens a woman's name and turns her into a leper. Only a craven scoundrel inflicts pain on a woman so he can feel like a man."

"Shut up, bitch!"

"I will not now and never will again." She drew herself up to her full height.

Muiredach's face darkened to a mottled purple, and the veins in his neck throbbed with anger. A strangled snarl burst from his lips and he leapt towards her, meaty hands balled into fists.

Áine recoiled and raised her arms to protect herself. But Niall threw himself in front of her, shielding her from Muiredach.

"Step back," he growled. "You won't touch her—you will no longer even look at her."

"You're telling me again what I can and can't do in my smithy, and I don't like it." Muiredach's eyes narrowed to slits. "You're not from around here. You wouldn't be one of those Irish rebels who are destroying this country?"

Niall did not answer, but his glare spoke of his rage.

"As I thought," Muiredach said. "How long will your arrogance last when I fetch the Watch to get you?"

Áine went cold. She had never considered that Muiredach would pose a danger to Niall. "Come, Niall," she said, tugging at his sleeve. "There's nothing more to say."

"I'm not finished with you," Muiredach yelled. He took another step, but Niall blocked him again. "Out of my way, you rebel whoreson. She's my sister. She's staying here." Muiredach tried to shove him out of his way, but Niall shifted slightly and elbowed him in the throat.

Muiredach coughed and gasped for breath as he stumbled backwards, coming up against his workbench. He shook his head and glared at Niall.

"Head for the door, Áine," Niall called out to her.

She hesitated. Niall still faced Muiredach, and he gave no indication that he prepared to follow.

"Go now!"

Áine headed for the door when a bellow of rage made her whirl around. Muiredach grabbed a sharp-tipped chisel from the table and charged. Niall pulled out his own dagger in time to block the attack. The chisel caught on the dagger's cross guard, and Niall pushed the knife aside.

Twisting his body, Muiredach ploughed his shoulder into Niall's chest, driving him against a post. The dagger fell out of Niall's hand, and Muiredach seized the advantage. He raised his chisel and stabbed downward.

Áine screamed.

Niall grabbed the man's wrist and strained to divert the force of the thrust while Muiredach threw all his strength into driving the sharp tip home. Niall drove his knee into Muiredach's groin and managed to throw him off. But the reprieve was short-lived, for Muiredach regained his balance and rushed at him.

Horrified, Áine watched as the two men grappled with each other. Muiredach had the advantage of his bulk, but Niall was quicker on his feet and had sharper reflexes. Everything moved so fast—she couldn't tell who had the advantage.

Their fight brought them too close to the forge. Too close to the flames.

Niall threw Muiredach against the anvil, and the hammer crashed to the floor. Her stepbrother tumbled head over arse and landed in a heap on the ground. Niall launched himself on Muiredach, pinning him to the ground, and pounding him with his fists, blow after blow.

He is going to kill him.

Áine grabbed Niall's shoulder and tried to pull him off. "No! Stop! Don't kill him."

Blood spurted from Muiredach's nose and trickled from cuts to his face.

Niall pulled back his fist but did not release him. Instead, he grabbed him by the throat and applied pressure. "You can't possibly care a jot for his miserable hide."

Muiredach grew desperate to throw him off, but Niall hung on.

"I don't—I care for yours." She tried to break Niall's hold and grew frantic. "Let him go! They'll hang you for him—he's not worth it!"

Niall finally released Muiredach, leaving him sputtering and coughing on the ground. "You're a poor excuse for a man." He turned away in disgust.

Muiredach rose to a sitting position, his face twisted and ugly. Áine recognised his mounting rage, given that it had so often been directed towards her. He climbed to his feet and bent down to steady himself, but as he straightened, he picked up the hammer from the ground.

Áine screamed a warning.

Niall ducked as the hammer swept over his head. He lost his balance and crashed to the ground. Now the advantage shifted to Muiredach—and there was no soft side of his Áine could appeal to.

Muiredach drove his foot down to stomp Niall's head, but he rolled away in time. Niall scrambled to his feet and faced Muiredach, drawing the second dagger from inside his tunic.

The two men circled each other, a sleek wolf against a scaly dragon. Muiredach swung his hammer again with enough force to drive Niall's jaw into his head, but Niall darted aside and slashed him across the arm.

Muiredach bellowed his fury. Still gripping the hammer in his left hand, he seized a tong from the workbench and whipped it at Niall, hitting him square in the shoulder. Before Niall could recover, Muiredach grabbed a bucket of sand and threw the contents into Niall's face.

Niall clawed at his face and staggered backwards. Muiredach shoved him, sending him sprawling to the ground. Then Muiredach was upon him, knee pinned against Niall's chest.

"Too bad you'll be no more, pretty boy," Muiredach rasped.

Áine saw the rest in a haze. Muiredach lifted his hammer, his left arm poised to smash Niall's head, savouring his moment of victory—the unholy gleam of exultation. Fear flooded her.

Niall's stag-horn dagger lay on the ground a foot away from her. She snatched the blade and leapt for Muiredach. A strangled cry of desperation burst from her lips.

Muiredach turned at the sound just as she drove the dagger deep into the right side of his throat.

Blood squirted from his vein like a fountain. He groaned and pressed his hand to staunch the flow, but blood continued to seep between his fingers. He looked at her, first with surprise, then horror, before dropping the hammer. It landed with a dull thump on the ground. Niall heaved him off.

Muiredach sprawled on the ground, blood staining his tunic and pooling beside him. He tried to form words but only gurgled. Impotent rage flared in his eyes, and Áine knew that if he could speak, he'd curse her with his dying breath. Then his eyes turned glassy, and he moved no more.

Áine still gripped the blade, blood dripping from its tip. She stood over Muiredach's lifeless body and stared at the man who had abused and shamed her—the man whom she had feared for most of her life.

She should have been horrified, but all she could feel was relief. Even if the Watch rushed in to seize her now, it didn't matter. He'd never hurt her or anyone she loved ever again.

Áine had slain the dragon.

CHAPTER 29

NIALL LED Áine back to the Duggans' stall in the market square. He had helped her wipe the blood from her shaking hands and secured the main entrance. Once they had left the smithy, Áine retreated within herself, moving in a daze. She didn't speak a word.

Duggan's eyes widened when they appeared at his stall. "Áine, you're trembling."

"She's had a shock," Niall said curtly as he scanned the market for any sign of pursuit. "We need to leave immediately."

Duggan did not question them. Together, they loaded the unsold cheeses into the wagon and made their way to the gates.

As they walked through the town, Niall expected to be stopped, for someone to raise the alarm that the blacksmith had been discovered murdered. Áine kept looking over her shoulder. Her skin was so pale it appeared nearly translucent. Niall took her hand and gave it a reassuring squeeze.

They made it out of the gates without being challenged. Áine regained some of her colour when the city was behind them.

"What happened with Muiredach?" Duggan asked Niall.

"Dead," he replied flatly.

"You killed him?"

CRYSSA BAZOS

"Ay," Niall answered without hesitation. No one need ever know that Áine had driven the blade home. "He will never harm her again." He watched Duggan turn this over in his mind. To his relief, the man nodded.

"He was always a bad seed, and good folk will not mourn him," Duggan said. "At least you've freed our Áine. Bridie will give her a tonic, and she'll be right as rain."

Niall hoped so. She had taken a life—never easy, even if deserved. He worried how she'd react when the shock wore off. She deserved peace, and he only hoped the devil would not plague her soul over this day's actions. One thing he was sure of, he'd not allow her to be punished for the bastard's death. He glanced back at Áine, to where she curled up inside the wagon. If they came for anyone, it would be him.

During the return trip back to the farmstead, Niall kept glancing over his shoulder for signs of pursuit. Thankfully, the road behind them remained clear, and they reached the Duggans' safely.

Later that night, when the animals had been bedded down and the Duggans had taken to their pallets, Niall and Áine slipped out of the cottage under a starlit sky and took comfort in each other's arms.

Áine laid her cheek against his bare chest as he cradled her. Neither spoke of the events of the day. Niall didn't know what the morrow would bring, but for this moment, he would fill his lungs with her scent and draw strength from the warmth of her skin.

She cried a little before dawn, and he gently kissed away her tears. Healing would take time—for both of them.

For the next week, Niall kept himself busy helping Duggan around the fields and briefly traded his sword for a plough. Fionn struck up a friendship with the Duggans' sheepdogs and did a fair enough job at herding sheep—or scaring them. But Niall kept his eye on the road, expecting the garrison men to ride up to the farmstead and enquire about Muiredach.

Rows and rows of furrows sewn with oats were enough to keep the Duggans and their animals for another season. Niall gazed across the fields to where the sheep grazed, with their coarse fleeces cream against the green meadow. He watched as Duggan walked amongst his flock, holding his blackthorn walking stick and with his sheep-dogs alongside him. The pace here was different, marked by the progress of the sun and the steady rhythm of the earth. Niall had only known two seasons these past ten years—the fighting season and winter quarters.

As he stood there mulling, Niall thought back on the glade he had shown Áine, with the spring water burbling and the grasses soft. She had woven a spell around him with her story of that Greek hero who had eagerly taken the life of an ordinary man for his next life. Niall smiled at the thought and made his way towards his host. A life such as Duggan's had been what the warrior had craved. After years of fighting, that had been his reward.

What would Niall's reward be . . . if there was one to be had?

He caught up to Duggan and together they headed back to the farmhouse.

"How have you managed to keep your flock from being poached by the English?" Niall asked. "With how close you are to Cork, I imagine this has been a challenge."

"They've taken enough sheep and cows, I won't deny it." Duggan squinted at the horizon. "But I keep my head down, go about my way and give the English no excuse to take away what is mine. They still might, but it won't be for anything I've done or failed to do."

"How can you stand that, to sit idly by and allow them to take what isn't theirs?"

"There's no idleness on the land. My livestock keep me plenty busy. My family too." Duggan glanced at Niall and shook his head. "Áine tells us your father is a merchant in Galway?" At Niall's nod, Duggan continued, "I wager he runs the gamut of customers he has to deal with, some more difficult than others, and many, I suspect, he wouldn't greet in the street if his livelihood didn't depend upon it. Likely wishes he could vanquish *his* troubles at the end of a sword. Who wouldn't? But don't underestimate the cunning it takes to put food on the table and keep the family alive for another day. It takes more courage to endure than to fight."

With that Duggan whistled to his sheepdogs and hurried along, leaving Niall to follow at his own pace.

Several days later, on the next market day, Duggan took his cheeses to Cork and promised to find out anything he could about Muiredach and what people might be thinking about who had killed him.

He returned late afternoon with news, but not about Muiredach.

Duggan unfolded a news pamphlet and spread out the curling edges on the table. The ink was still fresh, and parts had been smudged. "News about your Colonel O'Dwyer." The headline stood out like a scar upon the cream paper.

Edmund O'Dwyer signed a treaty with the English.

> *Articles of agreement, made and concluded at Cahir Castle, the Twenty-Third of March 1652, between Colonel Jerome Sankey, Commander in Chief of the English forces in the county of Tipperary, for and on behalf of the Parliament of the Commonwealth of England, and Colonel Edmund O'Dwyer, Commander in Chief of the Irish brigades, in the county of Tipperary and Waterford.*
>
> *That all the forces of horse and foot under the command of Colonel Edmund O'Dwyer shall, by the tenth day of April next, deliver up their arms and horses at or near Cashel to Colonel Sankey.*

The news pamphlet outlined the terms of the treaty. In exchange for surrendering their horses and arms, for which they would be compensated, they should have protection for their lives and personal estates and liberty to live in such places thought fit by Sankey. At that, Niall shook his head.

"The English are giving us leave to live where they would have us," Niall said with rising irritation.

"What does this mean?" Áine asked.

"We live under their sufferance," Niall answered flatly.

"A technicality, surely," she said. "They must have more important things to manage than where someone lays their head."

"A practical answer, my Áine," Niall said, threading his fingers through hers and dropping a kiss on her knuckles. What he didn't add was that he had an uneasy feeling the condition meant far more.

"It also says that they give the brigade leave to fight overseas,"

Duggan said, stabbing a section farther below. "They'd like nothing better, I warrant, than to see Ireland's finest defenders elsewhere."

"No one accused the English of stupidity," Niall muttered. He reread that particular clause. *Leave to go overseas to fight for any foreign prince, provided they do not raise arms against England.*

And like that, his future spread out before him. He could either accept the treaty, submit to the English at Cashel on the day specified or remain an outlaw, without protection, until they hunted him down.

Niall knew O'Dwyer had plans for his brigade. He would hire himself and his men out as mercenaries, and they would be like wild geese, migrating across the water to fresh feeding grounds. When they would return, no one could say.

"What will you do?" Duggan asked.

Niall was a soldier. This was his life. He was a man of the sword, and by the sword he would one day find his end. Whether that would be as a rebel, refusing to bend the knee to the English, or as a mercenary soldier, he still couldn't say.

Niall realised that the discussion around the table had died. Everyone was staring at him expectantly, waiting for his reply. Everyone except Áine. She was clearing the dishes as she would any other evening. When she reached over to pick up an empty cup, her hand visibly shook.

ÁINE HAD KNOWN THIS DAY WOULD COME. SHE'D ONLY HOPED TO have a little more time with Niall. *I am a soldier,* he had told her once. *This is my life.*

But that would not be her life.

She loved him deeply, and would with her dying breath, but she could not follow him. Their time at the Duggans' had crystallised this for her. Áine needed peace, to awaken each morning without fear of violence or danger.

No matter which path Niall chose, it would lead away from her. She couldn't continue to live in hiding as an outlaw, fearful that the English would flush them out at any moment. Nor could she be a camp follower, living under the threat of cannon fire and grapeshot in a foreign land.

Niall had helped her find her footing, helped her unfurl, even if the process had been painful. She had emerged stronger, more confident that she could and would survive. She'd need that strength to safeguard herself.

But a part of her wished that she hadn't learned to care so deeply. Before, her heart had been encased in a cage of steel, protected against injury. Niall had taught her to use it again, to trust. Now it ached so much she wished that she hadn't unlocked it. Almost, but not quite.

She still remembered how it felt to be sealed off from others, and this painful, heart-wrenching feeling that tore herself apart was the payment for having loved. Payment for joy.

Someone had once told Áine that everyone had an allotment of tears in their lives; some used their allotment over a lifetime, while others spent theirs all at once. She liked to think the tears meant happiness, and if so, she had used up her allotment on Niall. For the life of her, she would not regret it. None of it.

Niall found her sitting atop a stone wall, head tipped up to the purple skies painted by the setting sun. He stood before her. Against the fading light, his dark hair had deepened to the colour of a raven. She brushed her fingers to part the thick lock that fell over his brow.

"I hoped he wouldn't have had to sign the treaty," he said. "I wish he had found another way."

"You knew he had no choice."

Niall looked down and said wryly, "A man on his deathbed knows the end is near, and still he is surprised by it."

Áine smiled. How true. Painfully so. "What will you do?"

Niall didn't answer. His hand rested on the curve between her neck and shoulder, the place where his lips often settled. "Surrendering is abhorrent to me. I don't know that I can do it."

"Would you join another brigade?"

He shook his head. "If O'Dwyer was pressed to the wall, the others won't be far behind. Mark my words." He wrapped his arms around her, and she fit snugly under his chin. Áine felt the comfort of his heartbeat beneath her cheek. "I don't see that I have a choice, my Áine. I'll have to submit to the treaty."

She closed her eyes. He could still die in a foreign land, but living the life of an outlaw here would endanger him more. Áine sighed and pulled away, knowing her next words would change things between them forever. "Niall, you should know. I've decided to remain with the Duggans."

Niall held her gaze. In the depths of his hazel eyes, she read sadness and regret. He leaned in and pressed his forehead to hers. "I don't want to lose you."

"Nor I you, but I cannot go where the road leads you."

Niall closed his eyes and kissed her forehead. "It's for the best."

Áine nodded mutely.

"You will always be with me, Áine-my-Áine."

"And you will always be my heart."

He kissed her, a poignant expression she wished to capture as a memory for the years to come. It ended far too soon.

"One favour I will ask of you." Niall gently stroked her arms. "Come with me to Cashel. I'll bring you back to the Duggans, but be there with me, this last time. I don't know that I can do it otherwise."

She smiled through her tears. "I'll be there as you were for me."

ON THE TENTH DAY OF APRIL, NIALL AND ÁINE RODE TOGETHER on the tawny garron to the Rock of Cashel to submit to the terms of O'Dwyer's treaty with the English. Fionn loped alongside them. The rolling hills that spread out like a lover before him, dappled in myriad shades of spring green, nearly broke his heart.

The Rock of Cashel was a medieval church fortress perched atop a promontory with commanding views of the valley that stretched for miles. Hawks circled above the tops of its towers, making Niall think of a crouching limestone giant crowned by a circle of thorns.

Here, the ancient kings of Munster had once been crowned and blessed St. Patrick had converted a pagan king. That the English had chosen Cashel as the place to ratify the treaty was too bitter to swallow.

A steep and winding road led to the fortress, and the tawny garron resolutely plodded along. Niall turned his attention to the English guards posted along the walls.

He had brought his sword and pistols, as required, to turn them into the enemy's keep. The other horse and his uncle's sword were safely tucked away a few miles from Cashel. The English didn't need to know about those. Although the treaty allowed commissioned officers to keep their horses and arms, Niall wasn't about to take the chance with his keepsake and lose his last connection to his uncle. As for the garron, the English were welcome to the poor beast.

They cleared the walls and entered a gravelled path, leading to an open green. Near the abbey entrance stood Cormac, Ruadhri and Purcell. Fionn rushed off to greet them.

Niall dismounted and helped Áine down from the garron.

"Will you not tie the horse up?" she asked.

"He'll belong to the English very shortly," he said. "Let them chase it down the hill."

"A miracle before my very eyes and here on St. Patrick's Rock," Cormac greeted them. "I didn't think you would come."

"Neither did I," Niall admitted.

"I can only assume the softening of your heart is owed to the fair maid Áine." Cormac's eyes were unnaturally bright. Niall knew him well enough to understand that his forced joviality masked his pain.

"She's guilty of that, ay," Niall replied.

Ruadhri was unmoved. His arms were crossed, and he gave Niall and Áine a curt nod. "It's a sad day we find ourselves in this place, submitting to the enemy." He hadn't even limed his hair.

"Ruadhri, you're more cheerful than I expected," Niall said. "Not that I wasn't feeling entirely like shite."

"O'Dwyer's inside," Purcell said. "He's holding Sankey's representatives to their word."

"Representatives? The English commander couldn't be here?" Niall's annoyance sharpened.

"He's busy drafting new treaties," Purcell replied. "Other brigades are making haste to get their terms in. Fitzpatrick submitted a fortnight ago."

"To be expected," Cormac said. "When one wall collapses, the rest of the building soon crumbles."

Áine's hand slipped into Niall's own, and she gave it a reassuring squeeze.

"Did you lads all sign?" he asked.

"Ay," Cormac said. He bent down to scratch behind the wolfhound's ears. "Fionn, do us a favour and take a piss on the English. Any of them will do."

Niall grimaced. "This is it, then."

"From here, ay, but we won't be staying," Ruadhri said. "O'D-wyer has leave to assemble a brigade to fight for the Spanish on the Continent. There's fighting to be done in Flanders."

"As mercenaries," Niall said.

"As long as they pay to sharpen my sword," Ruadhri replied.

"The both of you too?" Niall asked the others.

Purcell nodded, and Cormac said, "Ay." Then he winked at Áine. "The Spaniards haven't heard my stories. They'll be sure to be impressed."

"I have no doubt," she answered, the corners of her mouth twitching.

"We'll be shipping out in a few months. Best get your affairs in order, O'Coneill," Cormac said. "Only the Almighty knows when we'll return."

Áine turned her head to stare at the tawny garron grazing on the turf. Her expression gave little away, but the lift of her chin and slope of her shoulders spoke to Niall of her determination to be resolute. He needed a measure of that resolve too.

"Best get this over with." Niall led Áine aside. "Will you come in with me?"

"Of course."

Niall lifted their clasped hands and kissed her knuckles. For once, he was at ease with himself. He knew what he needed to do. Together, they crossed the churchyard and entered the Tower House.

The inside of the archbishop's hall was dim, lit by sputtering tallow candles. As they crossed the stone floor, their footsteps echoed in the room. A large table was set up near the fireplace with various officials clustered around it. O'Dwyer and Donogh were there, talking amongst themselves. When O'Dwyer saw Niall approach, he said a final word to Donogh and went to meet Niall.

Niall slowed his progress, dreading this moment. He had looked up to O'Dwyer ever since he had first offered his sword in service. For years, O'Dwyer's word had been akin to gospel, and Niall's admiration had known no bounds. But during the last few months of hardship and high emotions, something had shifted between them. It was never easy to lose a hero.

"Wait for me here?" he whispered to Áine.

"Always."

Niall and O'Dwyer met in the centre of the hall. It might have been a trick of the poor light, but Niall had never noticed how much O'Dwyer had aged. The silver threads in his dark hair had multiplied, and the lines around his eyes and forehead had deepened.

"You've come," O'Dwyer said. "I'm glad you saw reason."

"I nearly didn't." Niall studied the floor.

O'Dwyer cleared his throat. "I regret that business with Eamon. We were both lulled by his glib tongue."

Niall nodded. He found it difficult to talk about it, even now. Garret, who had wielded the sword, had died by it, and Eamon, who had whispered in Garret's ear, would be forgotten like yesterday's wind.

"If it's any consolation, and you can believe this or not," O'Dwyer said, "but I had no intention of hanging you."

"But you sentenced me to the gibbet, and the word of an O'Dwyer is law."

"I reserve the right to change my mind. Once I cooled down, I knew you weren't guilty."

"What convinced you?"

"You swore on your sister's life. The Niall O'Coneill I know would never have made such an oath lightly."

Niall grimaced and rubbed the back of his neck. "I wish you'd told me that earlier."

"I'm disappointed in you, Niall. You should have known," O'Dwyer said. "Why else did I not send men to fetch you from

Cahir? Purcell was hardly subtle when he spread the rumours of your whereabouts."

Niall smiled. "I wondered, but I was counting on your preoccupation with other matters." He cast a meaningful glance at the officials impatiently waiting for him.

"After you finish with them, come speak with me. I'm making plans for our removal to the Continent. Spain is offering a handsome sum for seasoned fighters."

"Flanders, I heard." Niall glanced at Áine, who stood with her hands tightly clasped in front of her. She was very nervous, but she didn't want to give herself away. He was a soldier, this was true. He had followed O'Dwyer for nearly ten years. It had been everything he had wanted from his life—the chance to do something worthy of a bard's tale. "I won't be coming." He was surprised how easily those words slid off his tongue.

"You're exhausted and can't fathom the long trip to Flanders. I understand. But we won't be setting sail for a few months. Your future lies with us, and there's a lieutenant-major commission for you," O'Dwyer countered.

"Still not tempted," Niall said, smiling. He had made the right decision. "Ireland is where I belong."

"The years ahead will not be friendly with the English occupying Ireland. The Spanish will pay handsomely, and you are certain to prove your mettle."

"I'm staying."

"Where will you go?"

Niall's smile deepened. "For now, there's a little shepherd's hut that's betwixt and between two worlds. After? When the English lift the siege, I hope to return home to Galway and settle matters at home. I have news to share with my father."

"Then go with my blessing, Niall O'Coneill." O'Dwyer pulled Niall into a long embrace. "Your absence will be felt."

"May the Almighty watch over you and yours, Colonel," Niall said thickly.

"Is all well?" Áine asked when he returned to her. "Did he

mention service abroad?" She bit her lip, and Niall wanted to kiss it madly.

"Ay. The men will be shipping out to the Continent in a few months. He offered me the commission of lieutenant-major."

"Oh." She looked away. "I'm very pleased for you, Niall. Lieutenant-major. You'll be certain to distinguish yourself in action. Before you know it, they'll be calling you colonel." When she laughed, it sounded strained to Niall's ears. "A few months? Will there be time enough to return to Galway?"

Niall glanced up to the ceiling, half expecting a thunderbolt to descend upon him from the Almighty for his wicked ways, but he couldn't help it. Then, reconsidering his soul, he leaned in. "I said no." He cupped her face and kissed her deeply.

"I don't understand." Áine's glorious grey eyes were wide and searching. "How can you say no? You're a soldier."

"Newly retired soldier," Niall said. "I can be more than a sword for hire."

"You can be my love." Her smile widened until it lit her entire face.

"I thought I already was," he said and snatched a kiss from her. "Come, my Áine, let's put this behind us."

At the table, he placed his sword, along with his pistols, shot and dagger. Another dagger was hidden in the waistband of his breeches. The English didn't need to know about that either. "And one horse in the churchyard. A noble beast in its prime."

"Description," the clerk asked, and Niall gave him one in as favourable terms as one could a yellow piebald garron. "Very well. You will receive competent satisfaction for the horse." The clerk opened up a leather-bound box and took out a few coins.

"That's hardly competent satisfaction," Niall said, weighing the coins in his palm.

"The value has been determined by four officers of both parties," the clerk said.

"Still not satisfied, but you leave me little choice." It wasn't his horse anyway, and he'd give the coins to Cormac to pass them on to McTiege. But it was the principle of the matter.

Niall was about to leave when the clerk stopped him.

"We're not through yet," the man said. "Place of residence?"

"Why do you need to know?"

"The terms of the treaty."

Niall would have liked to have shoved the register down the man's gullet, but he cooled his ire. He suspected he'd be tempted to do this a great deal in the years to come, and he'd better master the restraint now. Finally, he answered, "Galway."

"And the woman? Name. Residence."

Before Áine could answer, Niall said, "Áine O'Coneill, Galway."

He signed the register, then handed the quill to Áine. Uncertainly, she took it from him and scratched an X on the document.

"A good day to you," Niall said to the clerk and led Áine away.

"You lied about my name."

"No, I didn't."

"But we're not married."

"We will be."

"You never asked."

"Well, what was that back there, Áine Callaghan, if not a promise to wed? The little English clerk even wrote it down, so you can't change your mind now."

Áine looked away, and her shoulders shook with suppressed laughter, but she could not contain it for long. "You're a bold one, I'll give you that. At least you're not trying to leave me behind."

"Perish the thought, Áine-my-Áine." He scooped her up in his arms, giving her a scalding kiss. When he finished, he murmured against her lips, "We belong to ourselves alone."

EPILOGUE

Galway City, County Galway
May 1653

A stiff sea breeze blew off the harbour and scattered a spray of leaves outside the O'Coneill mercantile. One bright green leaf landed in the open doorway of the shop as Niall came out of the storeroom, carrying a crate on his shoulder. He placed it on the nearest worktable before he bent down to pick up the wind's offering. Áine would call it a gift from the Faerie Folk and weave another story, possibly transforming the leaf into a seaworthy currach. Niall smiled at the thought, then, hearing footsteps, turned to greet his wife and infant daughter, Margaret.

"For you," Niall said, twirling the green leaf by the stem and offering it to her. He leaned in to brush a kiss on her lips.

"Hmmm," Áine said. "Lovely." She tucked the green leaf into Margaret's swaddling blanket. His daughter's round baby face blinked up at him. The top of her head showed promise of her mother's auburn hair.

"The kiss or the leaf?"

Áine smiled her response.

Niall and Áine had been back in Galway since the town surrendered to the English last summer. This past year, he had been helping
his father expand the family's trade in raw wool—different grades,
from coarse to fine. He had been relieved to find his father and
brothers had survived the siege. What had prevented a tragedy was
that the town hadn't been entirely cut off from supplies. Even so,
Niall had found his father aged beyond his years, and several more
had been added to the toll when Niall had given him the news about
Mairead.

Áine became a balm for his father with the stories that she spun.
Every night after their supper, they gathered by the hearth with any
of his brothers who happened to stop by and listened to Áine's
fanciful tales of the Otherworld and ancient Ireland.

It had been Niall's idea to write down Áine's stories for her, and
through his father's connections, they'd found a publisher in Galway
to print them. *One for Sorrow*, about an ominous magpie, had been
printed two months ago and had sold quickly, forcing the delighted
publisher to do another printing.

"How is the day faring for you, Daughter?" Niall's father
returned from the storeroom with Fionn and eased himself onto a
stool. He had once been a tall man with hair as dark as Niall's, but
now the hair he had left was threaded with grey, and the years of
hardship had made him more frail.

"Very well, sir."

"What's in the crate, lad?" his father asked, trying to peer inside.

Niall reached into the box and pulled out a chapbook of Áine's
story. "The printer has a bookseller in London who will sell these at
St. Paul's churchyard. I've offered to run these down to the harbour
so the merchant will have them before he sets out on the evening
tide."

"The London bookseller's young son loved the story," Áine said.
"Imagine that."

Niall's father held up the chapbook. "A shame that it isn't being
printed in your own name, my girl."

Áine had decided that the author's name should be anonymous.

Niall had balked that she would not publicly take credit for the stories, all of which were retellings of cherished Irish stories. No one would read it if they knew the author to be a woman, Áine had insisted. "Your father, kindly soul that he is, does not deserve such notoriety while we remain under his roof." His father wouldn't have minded it, but she remained adamant.

Áine laid Margaret in her cradle and adjusted the blanket. "Will you watch her for me, Father, so I may go to the harbour and back?"

"Ay." His father scowled, attempting to look severe, but he made a poor show of it. The little one was a blessing to them all, but even she could not entirely smooth all the lines etched in his face.

Worry about the family, worry about his wool business kept him awake at night. Niall could hear him pacing in the wee hours of the night. For the first few months, his father had haunted the Galway port hoping for any word of Mairead from a returning merchant ship, but none came. Lately, his father had given up going to the port altogether, so Niall did it for him.

"Come, Fionn." Niall hoisted the crate once more over his shoulder and left the shop with Áine and the wolfhound. The narrow streets outside were a contrast to the quiet of the store. Matters in Ireland had become more dire than Niall had feared. The city was flooded daily by displaced people from Munster and Leinster — displaced by the English who confiscated land to reward their supporters. Honest, hardworking people were being turned into beggars.

Niall and Áine walked down the few streets to the port. Several ships were anchored by the Spanish Arch. Their prows rose and fell in the current, and their trimmed sails gleamed white against the dark blue water. From beyond the headland, a sleek craft sailed into the harbour as smooth as silk

"She's a barque," Niall said, shading his eyes. "A handsome craft."

"What flag is she flying?" Áine asked.

Out on the water, the wind was stronger and whipped the flag about its pole, making it hard to see. All he could tell were its colours

—blue and white. "It's the Saltire," he said finally. "Scottish." Few vessels came from Scotland these days.

They watched as the anchor was lowered and cables winched to trim the sales. A boat was lowered into the water, over the side of the barque. A woman and a man climbed down the rope ladder and stepped lightly into the craft, followed by a pair of sailors. One last man, possibly the captain, joined them before the sailors pushed off and began to row to the docks.

The sunlight sparkled off the water, and Niall narrowed his eyes against the glare. His attention was fixed entirely upon the tender. He watched, mesmerised by how it skimmed across the swell. The wind gave a hearty gust across the water, and the woman's hood dropped to her shoulders.

Niall inhaled sharply. It couldn't be. The sun's glare made him see things. He rubbed his eyes and looked again. "God confound me, body and soul."

"Niall?" Áine touched his arm. "What's the matt—"

Niall bolted towards the pier, shouting, "Mairead! Mairead!" He bumped into people and darted around others. He didn't care if they took him for a madman. "Mairead!"

A burly man wearing a cloak of hodden grey stepped out of the boat first. He reached down to help the woman when Niall's yells reached them.

"Mairead!"

His sister stood up and quickly scrambled onto the pier. Niall barrelled towards her, caught her in his arms and whirled her off her feet.

"Niall? Could this really be you?" She was laughing and crying all at once.

"By Jesus—Mairead." Niall didn't want to release her in the event she was a figment of his imagination. But no, his sister was here, in Galway. Niall stepped back to take a good look at her. Her skin had turned golden by the sun, and freckles sprinkled her face. Although thinner than she had ever been, she still glowed with vitality. "I heard what happened. I was in Cork and learned the rest."

Tears sparkled in her eyes, and she simply nodded.

"Where the blazes did they send you?" Niall asked.

"Barbados."

Niall shivered. He had heard rumours of hell-hot sun and gruelling labour. They were enough to make a grown man quiver with fear. It had been a small mercy, after all, that he hadn't known where she had been sent. "Thank the Almighty that you're free of that place."

"We managed to escape," Mairead said.

"We?" Niall glanced up and found the burly man hovering near Mairead. "Who are you?"

"Your brother-in-law," he answered in a thick Scottish accent. "Iain Johnstone." Niall noticed how the man scanned the port without trying to be obvious. A sign of a soldier.

"We all just call him Locharbaidh. Or sometimes Ogre." Mairead laughed and linked her arm with her husband's. Her smile became tender.

Niall felt a soft touch on his arm, and he found Áine standing behind him. "I'm sorry, love, I lost myself," he said, holding out his hand for her.

"I know you," Mairead said, taking a step towards Áine. Her eyes widened. "You always came to hear me play. It's Áine, isn't it?"

"Yes," she replied.

"You survived that attack?" Mairead said in wonder. "How?"

"My wife is a survivor," Niall said, bursting with pride. "Underestimate her at your peril."

"I look forward to hearing the story."

"But first," Niall said, "there's someone who will want to see you."

They found Niall's father, still hunched over the table with his sleeping granddaughter in her cradle. He leaned heavily on his arms, crossed before him.

Mairead stepped gingerly into the shop, as though she too worried that this was all an illusion. Their father looked up and stilled.

"Look who I found," Niall said.

Their father stood up, unsteady on his feet, and held out his arms for the daughter he thought he had lost forever.

While his father and sister wept in each other's arms, Niall's arm encircled Áine's waist. He leaned in and asked, "How many magpies for joy?"

"Two. But that's another story to tell."

HISTORICAL NOTES

I never intended to write *Rebel's Knot* as a novel. Originally, it was to be a long short story, then it quickly became apparent that there was enough story to extend it to a novella. When I completed the novella, it was pushing novel territory, and I was at a crossroads: Should I trim it back and leave it as a novella or explore it further? Part of me was eager to mark "The End" and move on to the next novel I fully intended to write, but I knew that a novella did not do this story justice. I credit Liz St. John, who nudged me past this fork in the road and urged me to fully realise the story I had wanted to write.

My hope is that I've done justice to the history of the Irish resistance during the Cromwellian conquest of Ireland because what unfolded after all the treaties were signed and in the years to come was particularly unjust and heartbreaking. Many were exiled or lost their land and were forced to relocate.

Ireland had suffered invasions before. Land had been previously confiscated and given away to English supporters during the Tudor and early Stuart reigns. The new Commonwealth of England, always keen to improve and improvise, took it up a notch.

This period of Irish history (1649-1652) was one of the chapters of the War of the Three Kingdoms, also known as the English Civil

War. The conflict between England's Parliament and King Charles I, and subsequently his heir, King Charles II, started in England and spilled over to Ireland and Scotland. After defeating and executing King Charles I in 1649, Parliament turned their attention to stamping out all Royalist support in Scotland and Ireland.

Parliament was particularly eager to defeat Ireland. There was a great deal of anti-Irish and anti-Catholic sentiment in England. As well, they were eager to retaliate against the rebellion that had broken out between the Irish Catholic Confederation and Colonial Protestant rule.

In 1641, a rebellion began in Ulster and spread to the rest of Ireland as a result of years of Catholic discrimination and the creation of plantations given to Protestant settlers. The country would be in varying states of war between the Irish Confederation and Protestant Colonial forces, supported by English troops, until 1649.

This was a dark time with massacres and reprisals on both sides. One can't underestimate how strongly the rebellion reverberated in the English consciousness, particularly with men like Oliver Cromwell. The ferocity of the English response to Ireland can be understood against this backdrop. He was not only driven by the need to keep Ireland from supporting Charles II, but also by a desire to punish those involved in the rebellion, particularly the massacres of 1641.

Another layer that further complicated this history were the investors. In an effort to end the rebellion of 1641, Parliament, with full support of the king, enacted the Adventurers' Act in 1642. To raise funds to outfit the troops needed to subdue the rebellion, land in Ireland was promised to English investors. When civil war broke out in England months later, Parliament leveraged the Adventurers' Act to help finance their own war against the king. By 1649, the debt was coming due, and the English were eager to conquer Ireland.

On August 15, 1649, Oliver Cromwell landed in Dublin with a flotilla of approximately one hundred ships. Cromwell very quickly gained a ruthless reputation by how he dealt with Irish resistance, particularly at Drogheda, where the defenders were put to death after rejecting terms for surrender. This served him well, as many towns opted to accept his terms for surrender rather than face the possibility of massacre.

Over the course of the next three years, a centralised Irish war effort disintegrated, to be replaced by localised fighting brigades employing guerrilla tactics. These brigades were called Tories, from the Irish Tóraidhe, or pursued men. Throughout the story, I've referred to them as a brigade, or occasionally Tóraidhe, instead of Tories. For those who live in a Commonwealth country, you'll understand that the term Tory refers to a conservative political party and is not to be confused by these Irish forces.

The Irish brigades employed strike-and-run tactics to wear down the English and were quite successful at evading the enemy. They knew the landscape and used it to their advantage, such as losing their pursuers by slipping into bogs. The local populace also supported these troops with shelter and valuable information. The English took a hardline approach to any civilians caught collaborating with the brigades, and in the final months of the conflict, they passed decrees designed to cut off support to the Irish brigades. On January 13, 1652, they forced all tradespeople who were useful to them (e.g., blacksmiths and farriers) to report to the English garrisons. On February 13, 1652, they extended that to the populace in the contested areas to relocate to occupied territories by the end of February or be treated as the enemy. Markets were only to be held within a fortified town or garrison.

But the biggest threat to the brigades was simply a dwindling of supplies and provisions. Letters were sent to the exiled Charles Stuart (future Charles II) for aid, but he was living under the largesse of his cousin, the French king, and France was not eager to make an enemy of the new Commonwealth. Irish leaders were communicating with the Duke of Lorraine, urging him for the twenty ships he promised, loaded with much-needed war supplies.

On January 28, 1652, only four ships arrived. One ship landed at the Aran Islands and three more arrived at Inisbofin. The total supplies included £20,000 (less £6000 for the cost of negotiation), a thousand muskets, thirty barrels of coarse powder, and a thousand barrels of rye, most of which had been spoiled by seawater.

It must have been very clear to the Irish leaders that they would not be in a position to continue their resistance beyond the spring.

The conflict came to an end in mid-1652, when the individual brigades negotiated treaties with the Parliamentary forces. After the treaties were signed, the English encouraged the disbanded Irish troops to go to the Continent to fight for Spain. Mercenaries were a valuable commodity, not just for Spain, and they furthered English interests, provided they did not fight against England. These troops also provided a source of income to those Irish commanders who could raise mercenary forces. Thousands of trained Irish soldiers, referred to in history as the Wild Geese, flowed across the sea to the Continent.

Following the conquest of Ireland, Parliament passed the Act for the Settlement of Ireland in 1652. The Act offered a general pardon for those who fought against the English but excluded the clergy and participants of the Rebellion of 1641 as well as any rebel fighters who acted outside the authority of the Irish army. These parties could be condemned and executed. The Act was also responsible for major land confiscations, even as much as two-thirds of the vanquished estates. What remained to them could be exchanged for land in Connacht and west of the Shannon.

It's important to address the practice of forced indentured servitude. There has been an ongoing discussion by academics correctly refuting the claims of white slavery in relation to the Irish. There is a significant difference between indentured servitude and slavery. Although indentured servants were considered "unfree," their legal rights and status were profoundly different than enslaved persons. The indentured were bound to serve their master for the duration of their indenture, usually seven years. They had protection under the law, even if in practice few ever challenged their master in court. Any children born to them were also free of servitude.

On the other hand, enslaved people were slaves for life, and they had no protection under the law, in theory or in practice. Any children born to them were automatically enslaved.

When I referenced Niall's sister being sold, this did not mean that she was enslaved. There was a financial transaction involved with indentures that can't be separated from the indentured person. In exchange for the indenture, funds changed hands. When people voluntarily indentured themselves, they did so as a way to pay off their debts, but as colonial demand grew for labour, unscrupulous agents would kidnap and forcibly indenture people, obtaining a fee for everyone transported to the colonies. During the War of the Three Kingdoms, Parliament solved the problem of having to deal with prisoners of war, both Irish and Scottish, by transporting them as indentured servants to colonies such as Massachusetts and Barbados. Most everyone profited except for the prisoner of war, who was forced to work off a forced bond. Some managed to build a new life after their indenture, while many succumbed to disease and back-breaking labour. This is explored in my second novel, *Severed Knot*.

In *Rebel's Knot*, the majority of characters came from my overactive imagination; however, there were a couple of notable exceptions.

Edmund O'Dwyer was appointed Commander in Chief of the Irish forces of Tipperary and Waterford by the Irish Confederate Council. At the time of his signing the treaty with the English, he had approximately 2,700 men under his command.

The O'Dwyer lineage stretches back from before the Norman invasion, and they were mentioned even in the days of Brian Boru. Edmund O'Dwyer was not the chief of the O'Dwyers, but he was noted as being a close cousin. The actual chief had passed away a few years earlier, and the next clan chief was never settled.

What do we know about Edmund O'Dwyer? Not a great deal, which causes consternation for a historian but makes the historical fiction writer rub their hands in glee. According to Sir Michael O'Dwyer, in his history *The O'Dwyers of Kilnamanagh*, Edmund O'Dwyer appears only in sporadic references. We know he was an experienced solider and was listed amongst the troop of horse that the Marquess of Ormonde raised to support King Charles I against the Scots (before the English Civil War). He also appears in a letter dated 1648 about being held a prisoner in Dublin Castle after the Battle of Duggan Hill.

Well-liked and respected by his people, O'Dwyer was also highly considered by the enemy. Colonel Jerome Sankey, the English Commander in Chief of the forces in Tipperary, praised O'Dwyer for the "punctuall [sic] performance of his word" and "honest and friendly demeanour."

We don't know exactly where O'Dwyer and his brigade were quartered. I chose Glengarra Woods, not only due to the varied landscape and proximity to the Galtee Mountains, but in September 1651, prior to the fall of Limerick, the Viscount Muskerry was reported to have met with O'Dwyer near Glengarra Woods. It also made sense to me since the area was situated in the Barony of Clanwilliam, the ancestral lands of the O'Dwyers.

On March 23, 1652, O'Dwyer came to terms with Colonel Sankey at Cahir Castle. The treaty prescribed that O'Dwyer's men, excepting the commissioned officers, deliver their arms and horses on April 10, 1652 at Cashel. In exchange, they would be given protection for their lives, the liberty to live where Sankey allowed them, compensation for their equipment, up to a month's pay and the leave to go overseas to fight for any foreign country provided they didn't fight against England. Over the course of the next year, O'Dwyer gathered troops to ship to Flanders in support of Condé. In August 1654, he was killed in the field during the storming of Arras against the French.

Another historical figure who piqued my interest was Donogh O'Dwyer, cousin to Edmund O'Dwyer and brother to the late clan chief Philip O'Dwyer. Very little is known of Donogh. He was given a commission to lead a regiment of infantry and served under Edmund O'Dwyer. Donogh was the late chief's brother, but he did not succeed him, possibly because his own life was cut short.

There was a clause in the treaty exempting from protection those who participated in the 1641 rebellion. Donogh was captured by the English and tried for his part during the rebellion in 1641 when he was involved in seizing Cashel. He was hanged November 1652. He denied the accusations to his death.

I've tried to envision the size of these encampments and the supplies they must have had. When Colonel Sankey routed Irish brigade commander Fitzpatrick's camp near the Great Bog of Monley (likely located in northern Tipperary near the Silvermine mountains) in December 1651, Sankey noted that "we have taken many hundreds of their cows and garrons, and 300 and odde troop horses, and a very great number of saddles, pistols, pikes, muskets and other armes." Given that Fitzpatrick had a similar force under his command as O'Dwyer had, I used that as the basis for the size of the herd in my story.

It's not often that we have the opportunity to hear about how the common people lived, so I was very pleased to come across a first-hand account by John Dunton called *Teague Land or A Merry Ramble to the Wild Irish* (1698) about his travels through Ireland. Dunton was a London bookseller who travelled to Dublin to sell his wares, and he took the opportunity to explore other parts of Ireland, including Connacht. His account may have been biased, but the information he gave about how people lived, and their diet, was particularly revealing.

Dairy was the main staple in the Irish diet in the seventeenth century with a number of dishes made using new milk, buttermilk and curds. Bonny clabber was described by Dunton as being made by scalding fresh milk mixed with buttermilk. The resulting curds were topped by fresh butter and eaten for breakfast.

Another dish that Dunton referenced were oatcakes. In fact, Dunton was particularly mesmerised by the "immodesty" of the woman of the house who ground the oats using a quern right in front of him. As I understand it, today oatcakes are more common in Northern Ireland, but they appear to have been common farther south in the seventeenth century.

Cottages would be built of mud and hazel wattles, and a cook fire would be set in the centre part of the room with a hole overhead in the ceiling to draw the smoke. Livestock would be typically housed in the cottage at night to protect them against wolves. In the latter part of the seventeenth century, a well-off family would have about half a dozen horses and cows to provide labour for the fields and food for the family.

In the seventeenth century, the Irish wolfhound was referred to as a greyhound and was used to hunt red deer. In my story, I preferred to use the term wolfhound so that the reader wouldn't picture a modern greyhound.

A note on wolves in Ireland: during the Cromwellian conquest and the subsequent years, the English actively hunted wolves and, combined with areas of deforestation, eliminated the wolf population in Ireland.

Some of my first literary loves are myths and folklore, and it seemed natural and necessary to incorporate both in *Rebel's Knot*. Myths reflect the culture that created them. They are aspirational and inspiring, and two in particular reflected elements of my story.

The first was the *Táin Bó Cúailnge*. The *Táin* is the epic story of the King and Queen of Connacht trying to invade Ulster to steal the Great Brown Bull of Cúailnge while one man, Cúchulainn, stood in their way. Against all odds, Cúchulainn saved Ulster from the conquering force. The invaders often resorted to trickery, but in the end the hero prevailed.

The second myth was the story of Fionn mac Cumhaill and his outlaw warriors, the Fianna. This hero was exiled from his birthright, hunted down by a rival clan and forced to be an outlaw. He was a great hunter who had two enchanted wolfhounds and a bride who had once been transformed into a deer by a jealous druid. In a charmingly romantic twist, Fionn's bride found her true form when she met Fionn, and he brought her home with him.

Folklore also inspired me. When I was researching *Rebel's Knot*, I found a site that documented Irish folklore compiled from Irish school children in the 1930s called the *Schools' Collection*. Although compiled centuries after my story was to be set, the collection fired my imagination, particularly the notes about magpies. Superstition has been part of the magpie myth for centuries. You may be familiar with this old rhyme:

> *One magpie for sorrow.*
> *Two for joy.*
> *Three for a marriage.*
> *Four to die.*

Five for money.
Six for gold.
Seven for a story that can never be told.

Long after the magpies came to roost in my story, I learned that magpies were not always thought to be in Ireland. The earliest reference to magpies was recorded in 1676, when someone noted a dozen of them flying in from the Irish Sea. I will argue that it's highly unlikely that this incident coincided with the actual timing of a magpie migration, so this is one historical liberty I felt justified in making.

If you're interested in learning more about the history of this time, visit my website at cryssabazos.com.

I want to thank you for reading *Rebel's Knot*. I hope you've enjoyed the story!

ACKNOWLEDGMENTS

Without the encouragement of friends and family, none of this would be possible. First and foremost, I'd like to thank my husband, Angelo, for his unwavering support and for keeping everything moving forward when I was hunkered down in the seventeenth century. I'm truly blessed.

I would like to shine a spotlight on my writing tribe, who understands the acts of borderline madness that go into creating characters and stories. Thank you to my critique group: Gwen Tuinman, Tom Taylor and Andrew Varga, who push me to dig deeper and keep me from killing off more characters than are on the page; to the Amigas, Elizabeth St. John and Amy Maroney, who keep cheering me along and have become as invested in my characters as I am. Thank you to Elaine Powell, who was generous enough to read the manuscript and offer brilliant feedback. A warm thank you to Annie Whitehead, Char Newcomb and Anna Belfrage for your continued support and friendship from the beginning when I was first discovering my tribe.

I would also like to thank Ken Cameron for naming Fionn the wolfhound. There were many conversations around the work pod to come up with just the right name.

Thank you to my sister-in-law, Mignonne Dalmaridis, who has

never failed to answer frantic calls for various and sundry graphic design requests.

And to my dear friends, Denice Morris, who knows how long I've wanted to write an Irish novel, Lora Avgeris, Sharon Overend and Pat Ward.

A huge thank-you to Jenny Quinlan, my editor and cover designer and best person to brainstorm ideas with. You have guided me down this path and kept me moving forward.

I'd like to thank my aunt, Helen Voudouris, who inspired me to write through her example, and to my uncle, Nikos Marinakis, who instilled in me a love for myth and history.

I dedicated *Rebel's Knot* to my mother-in-law, Demetra Bazos, who left this world a couple of years ago. She lived a full and long life, having survived the German occupation in WWII, civil war in Greece and famine. She immigrated to Canada, where she did not know the language or the customs. Yet still, she raised a family and called her adopted country home. Demetra Bazos was a true survivor. We still miss her zingers, apple pie stories and unwavering pragmatism. She will live in our hearts always.

And finally, I would like to thank all the readers who have engaged with me over my novels, recommended me to their friends and who have asked when the next book is coming. You are the reason why I write.

ABOUT THE AUTHOR

Cryssa Bazos is an award-winning historical fiction author and a seventeenth century enthusiast. Her debut novel, *Traitor's Knot* is the Medalist winner of the 2017 New Apple Award for Historical Fiction, a finalist for the 2018 EPIC eBook Awards for Historical Romance. Her second novel, *Severed Knot*, is a B.R.A.G Medallion Honoree and a finalist for the 2019 Chaucer Award. Rebel's Knot is the third book in the standalone series, Quest for the Three Kingdoms.

Visit cryssabazos.com for articles on history and storytelling. Sign up for her Newsletter to keep up with writerly news and upcoming releases.

facebook.com/cbazos

twitter.com/CryssaBazos

instagram.com/cryssabazos

goodreads.com/cryssa

Printed in Great Britain
by Amazon

49626511R00209